"E.E. Burke understands the heart of romance and delivers it! The undeniable pull between Amy and Buck, two people who have every reason to hate each other, the sizzle of a passion that can't be denied, those moments that put a knot in your chest...*This* is romance, my friends."

~*New York Times* bestselling author **Maggie Shayne**

Steen On!

E E Burke

Her
BODYGUARD

E.E. Burke

DEDICATION

Writing is a solitary endeavor, but creating a novel and putting it out into the world isn't a journey one makes alone. I'm fortunate to have companions who bless me every step of the way. I couldn't have made it this far without critique partners Heather Snow, Katy Madison, Keri Smith and Julie Mulhern, or the faithful support from my friends and fellow writers at MRW and MARA.

Special thanks to my husband who gives me the gift of time to write, to my daughters for their unflagging encouragement, and to my mother for raising me to be a woman who believes she can do anything she sets her mind to.

This book is dedicated to my dearest friend and sister, Miriam, who repeatedly told me, "You really ought to write a book." I finally took your advice.

OTHER BOOKS BY AUTHOR

In the *Steam! Romance and Rails Series*
Passion's Prize by E.E. Burke,
Jennifer Jakes and Jacqui Nelson
Kate's Outlaw by E.E. Burke

CONTACT THE AUTHOR

www.eeburke.com
www.facebook.com/AuthorEEBurke
www.twitter.com/author_eeburke
www.amazon.com/author/eeburke
www.goodreads.com/EEBurke

Reviews are greatly appreciated.

AUTHOR'S NOTES

Welcome to *Steam! Romance and Rails*, a series that features stories from America's Golden Age of Steam. In the second half of the nineteenth century, the United States entered a time of explosive expansion. The country had just emerged from a devastating war and people needed to have faith in something. That something turned out to be what railroads represented: unlimited opportunity and hope for the future.

The great construction race between the Missouri, Fort Scott & Gulf Railroad Company (nicknamed The Border Tier) and the line that became the Missouri, Kansas and Texas Railway (more commonly known as "The Katy") is a story that encapsulates the spirit of these times, along with its challenges and rewards. The race took place primarily in 1870, when both lines were laying track as fast as they could to get to the border of Indian Territory (modern day Oklahoma). The government promised the line that reached the border first would win free land grants and exclusive rights through the corridor into cattle-rich Texas.

When I first started researching, I found surprisingly little written about this fascinating event. Then I uncovered a gem: a 1967 thesis paper written by then-graduate student, H. Craig Miner. Within these typed papers, I found a story as fascinating as any fiction I'd ever read, only it was factual. Dr. Miner's meticulous research and marvelous way with words made the people in this drama come alive. To name a few: James Joy, the real estate tycoon turned railroad baron; Octave Chanute, a brilliant French-born engineer who built

Joy's railroad and went on to help the Wright Brothers learn to fly; Amos Sanford, the fiery editor and leader of the Anti-Joy Land League. The story itself had all the makings of great epics: crooked politics, underhanded landlords, angry mobs, liars, cheats and killers. It wasn't difficult to craft a tale around these colorful characters. My challenge was developing primary characters as compelling as the supporting cast. Once again, I dove into the history books. The fiercely independent Kansas women who championed suffrage and equal rights served as models for Amy, and the tough-as-nails but troubled survivors of Missouri's guerrilla war gave me inspiration for Buck.

I'm grateful for Dr. Miner's research and wish I'd had a chance to thank him personally, but he passed away a year before this book was written. From what I've learned of him, I think he would've been pleased his research was helpful to another author.

Two other gentlemen who provided assistance with research were Don Miller and Fred Campbell with the Fort Scott Historic Preservation Association. Thank you for introducing me to historic Fort Scott and delightful pioneers like Charlie Goodlander and Heiro Wilson. Special thanks to Miss Pat at Lyon's Twin Mansions, the lovely inn that inspired me to write a story set in Fort Scott.

I hope readers enjoy this glimpse into an exciting era in America's history. Although that time is far behind us, it left an indelible mark that helped shape our country into who and what we are today

E.E. Burke

CHAPTER 1

March 1, 1870
Former Cherokee Neutral Lands, Southeast Kansas

Hell must be like this. Not lit with blazing fires, but cold and gray, barren as the dead prairie. Even the wind howled like a deranged demon, flinging bits of ice into Buck's face. He drew the blanket and oilskin tighter, although nothing warmed the persistent chill in his bones that'd gotten worse as he'd ridden north through Indian Territory. He was a walking dead man here in Kansas, so it seemed somehow fitting he'd entered the abode of the damned.

He patted Goliath's neck, glad for the company of his horse. He had few acquaintances, even fewer friends, and none who would risk their necks for another man's cause. Buck wouldn't have risked getting his neck stretched had the plea not come from his only remaining kinsman. Although at this point, freezing to death seemed more likely than being lynched.

The saddle creaked as he straightened. All around, he could see nothing but mounds of switch grass and stunted trees. No houses or barns, not even smoke from a chimney. He swore, his breath sending out a white cloud. The wind snatched it away. His plan had been to reach Girard before dark, buy a hot meal and a warm bed before meeting with his cousin to get details on the job he'd come to do. But he couldn't risk going on. He had to find shelter.

The fading daylight and worsening sleet made it difficult to see, but was that something just ahead? Buck touched his heels to his stallion's sides, moving closer to the mass taking shape. A buggy, slumped to one side. In front of it stood a single horse with its head down and a woman huddled in a cloak, removing the traces. What the hell was she doing out here all by herself?

Buck sat back in the saddle, uneasy. He'd made it a habit to avoid damsels in distress after being betrayed by one. However, he couldn't very well leave a woman out here on a lonely road in the middle of an ice storm. With a muttered curse, he kicked Goliath into a fast trot.

On his way to her, he passed the buggy's rear wheel, lying on its side in the brush like a wounded animal. Odd, he'd never seen a wheel fly off like that. Generally, the metal rim popped or a spoke snapped. Had the axle nut been loose when she started out? She was damn lucky the buggy hadn't rolled on top of her. He had seen *that* and it wasn't pretty.

His stallion whinnied, excited by the scent of the woman's horse. The mare threw its head and answered.

The lady hadn't noticed him because she was so focused on unhitching the fidgety bay. But now she whirled around. Her hood, drawn low over her face, shadowed her expression but it was clear by her startled response she hadn't expected anyone to come up on her. Rather than calling out for help, as he anticipated, she dashed toward the buggy's compartment.

The mare shied away from the sudden movement, then reared up, squealing. The buggy started to rock.

"Look out," Buck hollered.

The woman didn't move away from the danger. Instead, she dove into the compartment.

"Goddamn it!" The curse was lost in the wind. He came out of the saddle, dropped the reins on the ground. In a few long strides he'd reached her. "Get out of there."

What the hell was she doing? Trying to crawl beneath the buggy's seat?

The contraption tipped dangerously to one side. Buck snaked an arm around her middle and hauled her out of the death trap.

She twisted around, yowling like an enraged cat. "Get your hands off me."

Her horse squealed and tried to run. The lame buggy hopped.

"Stop screechin.' You're scaring the hors—" Something blistered Buck's cheekbone. "Ouch! What the devil?"

"Let me go!" She went for his face again with her claws.

"Stop that." He swatted her hands away, but managed to keep hold of her while he backed away from the buggy. "I'm just tryin' to—"

Her sharp teeth sank through the leather glove into his finger.

"Blazes!" He yanked his hand away and then grabbed a flailing arm, pinning her against him. Splaying his fingers over the side of her head, he smashed her cheek against his chest to prevent her from biting him again.

Furious screams became muffled growls. Her booted feet, dangling above the ground, lashed out to kick him. Thank God her skirts got in the way or she would've hammered his shins.

"Stop fighting, you loony woman." He sucked in a breath and checked his temper. Large as he was, and with her no bigger than a minute, he could easily break her.

As he adjusted his hold on her, the hood of her cloak fell back. His fingers slid through a silken mass of hair. In an instant, he became aware of the woman he held—her soft breasts and flaring hips, a delicate fragrance like wildflowers. Something hot and primitive coursed through him. His body responded before his brain could catch up.

She must've sensed his reaction because she started swinging her legs again.

He held her tighter. "Will you *listen?* I'm tryin' to help."

"Not…helping." She gasped the words. "You're…choking me."

Buck eased his hold. His physical reaction couldn't be helped, but he could sure as hell control his strength and keep from hurting her. "All right. I'm setting you down." He hesitated a moment before releasing her. "Don't fly at me with those nails."

She raised her eyes. The black centers swallowed the golden irises like an eclipse of the sun.

His gut clenched. He'd seen that look in the eyes of men he'd faced down, but not women he aided. He hadn't meant to frighten her. He frowned, more comfortable with being annoyed. "That horse about pulled the buggy over on top of you. That's why I grabbed you."

Her dark brows winged up. "You...you were *helping* me?"

"That was the plan."

She seemed further confused when he snatched his blanket off the ground where it had fallen during their tussle and flung it around her. Then he set off to retrieve her horse. That buggy wasn't going anywhere.

He approached the nervous mare with soft, shushing sounds and laid his hands on its quivering withers. The frightened creature stilled and let him remove the traces.

Sleet peppered the brim of his hat, although the worst of the storm seemed to have passed. He took a look around the bleak surroundings. They were still were in danger of freezing if he didn't find shelter soon.

After unhitching the harness, he brought the horse around. Thankfully, the woman hadn't run off. She'd inched over to the buggy compartment and was rummaging around again, maybe looking for something.

"Unless you've got an axle nut in there, we can't fix this buggy. Can you ride?

She whirled around with a tiny pistol clutched in her hands. "I'm not g-going anywhere with you."

Buck's pulse kicked up a notch. Her hands shook so hard he worried she might actually fire the damn thing before he could talk some sense into her. "You plan on staying here?"

Her chin came up. "I plan on taking *my* horse."

He bit back a curse. Did she think he was *stealing* the nag? Why was he even bothering to help her? He might as well head off down that road, leave her to her own devices. No one could blame him. Only...he'd never abandon a woman. Not even one that was stark raving mad.

"Christ, I don't have time for this foolishness," he muttered.

He offered her the reins, but when she reached out to take them, he locked his fingers around her wrist and nabbed the gun. Then he hauled the reluctant damsel to where he'd left Goliath.

The stallion had remained, as trained, right where they'd stopped. He didn't dare put the woman on her horse. Frightened as she was, she'd probably race off and end up breaking her neck. He looped her mare's reins around his saddle horn.

"Wait!" she burst out. "I have m-money. I can p-pay you more."

"What are you clatterin' about? I don't want your money." Buck nearly added if he'd wanted to rob her, he'd have done it and been gone by now. "We got to find shelter before we freeze to death. You live nearby?"

The woman stared up at him, her eyes rounding. Was she so addled she couldn't understand what he was asking? Maybe the cold had gotten to her. He'd take her and head down that road, which he assumed led into Girard.

He lifted the woman onto Goliath and mounted behind her. There wasn't enough room in the saddle for two, especially with all those skirts, but somehow he managed to get her situated across his lap. Thank the saints she didn't go into conniptions.

The ends of her cloak snapped in the wind. She shuddered so hard it made *his* teeth rattle. He opened his greatcoat then wrapped them both in the blanket and oilskin.

She burrowed into his chest like a baby rabbit. Her vulnerability tugged at his heart. Wouldn't kill him to offer her comfort.

He curled his arm around her. "Warmer now?"

She nodded her head.

"Where do you live?"

"I...*we* have a farm...I'll see to it you're well compensated if you take me there."

So, she was married. No surprise. With so few women out here, even a crazy one would be snatched up, especially one smelling this sweet and with soft curves in all the right places.

"How far is it?"

"Up the road, just a little ways."

"A little ways? As in few minutes?"

"I...I'm not sure exactly."

Buck snorted in disbelief. She didn't know where she lived? "We can't wander around. It's getting dark."

"We could make Girard. It's maybe a half hour's ride."

Maybe? He turned the stallion and peered in the direction she'd indicated, gave a grumbling assent. He was going to Girard anyway. Although he wasn't sure they'd make it before night set in and the temperatures dropped even lower. "Anything else nearby?"

"Our farm..."

"That you can't find."

Shit.

Grudgingly, Buck nudged Goliath onto the road. According to his cousin's letter, thousands of settlers had poured into these former Indian lands. If so, where were they? Did they all live in town? Or was this strip of land reserved for the railroad's use? The exorbitant price they'd put on a godforsaken wilderness seemed ludicrous. Of course, why anyone would want to farm it was also a mystery. Didn't matter though. Sean had settled here, had worked the land, and now the railroad's owner—rich bastard—was trying to cheat him out of it.

Buck tilted his head down to keep the wind from snatching his hat. The woman turned her face into his vest like she was trying to warm her nose. He cradled her closer, felt her relax in his arms. Warmth spread through him, and not just from the heat of their bodies, it came from someplace deep inside, a part of him he'd thought was long dead.

He squelched a flare of alarm. Concern for another living creature, that's all it was. Nothing more. He didn't give a tinker's damn about anybody, save his family—what was left of it.

They'd gone only a few miles when something caught his eye. He straightened and peered at a shadow. Whatever it was, it was big. Then he sighed with relief. "There's a barn over there."

She peeked out from beneath her hood. "It's abandoned, and the house was burned down. We can't stop there."

The hell they couldn't. "So long as there's a roof, we're stopping."

Kun Kun Kun

The stranger wrestled the barn door open and then dragged Amy off his horse. Before she could protest, her feet left the ground and he carried her into the dark interior. He dumped her on a pile of hay before vanishing back into the night, taking his warmth with him.

The wind shrieked in a wild tantrum and the barn creaked and moaned, as the stranger rustled about getting the horses settled somewhere on the other side. Amy stared blindly into the darkness, hugging the blanket, shivering, both from cold and lingering fear.

Seemed her rescuer wasn't the mysterious assailant who'd been skulking around after her. When the towering stranger had come up on her out of nowhere, she'd feared the worst and had gone for her gun in the buggy. The first time, he'd pulled her away before she could find it. Then, once she'd retrieved her pistol, he'd disarmed her. That he'd done it so easily was beyond humiliating. The cold must've slowed her mind and her reflexes. Even after he assured her he meant no harm, she'd worried he might only be telling her that so he could take her somewhere and abuse her before killing her. But he hadn't done more than cuddle her close, as if he wished to comfort her. For some inexplicable reason, she'd let him.

She chewed her lip, her thoughts whirling. If the Land League hadn't sent this frighteningly large fellow after her, where had he come from? He didn't look like a farmer, not with that Henry repeater holstered by his saddle and those revolvers strapped to his hips. Not to mention the knife as long as her forearm, which she'd discovered while huddled close to him. On the other hand, he might've armed himself in light of the increased violence in these parts.

Was that why her typically protective suitor hadn't made it back to town to escort her? Had Fletcher been waylaid by thugs working for the Land League? Or had he, too, been caught unawares by the change in the weather? If she'd known a late winter storm was imminent, she would've found someplace to stay in town, despite the risk.

Her nerves jumped at the scrape of a match. Light flared. Amy blinked as the stranger approached with a lit taper. Not just well armed, but well prepared.

Her gaze traveled from his scuffed, square-toed boots up long legs encased in checkered gray trousers of the California style cowboys favored. A heavy greatcoat hung past his knees. Around his neck, he wore a faded bandana, its color indistinguishable. His hat looked older than his shoes and its brim shadowed his expression. Was he one of the countless drifters passing through, looking for work?

"At least we'll have some light." His spoke in a low drawl, raspy as gravel in a dry creek bed. Strangely enough, she found the sound soothing. After securing the candle to the underside of a bucket, he set it nearby. "Careful not to knock this over. I'd build a fire, but with all the hay this place would go up like a torch."

Why did he feel the need to explain as one would to a child or a very old person?

"My mental faculties aren't so deficient I'd set the barn on fire." She tried to adjust the blanket more securely, but her numb fingers wouldn't obey and it kept slipping off.

The stranger knelt, removing his hat. Flaxen hair fell in tangled waves past his collar, and the light revealed a ruggedly handsome face—in sore need of a shave. Brown whiskers bristled on lean cheeks and a tawny mustache nearly hid his mouth. But it was his eyes that captured her, their color, so unusual—somewhere between blue and gray, but pale as a washed-out sky.

"Give me your hands." He stripped off his gloves as he issued the command. Rather than waiting to see whether she'd obey, he began to chafe them between his calloused palms. "How come you're not wearing gloves?"

She bristled at the disapproving tone. He'd made it clear he believed she was a simpleton.

"I had need of my fingernails." She didn't explain the problem with the frozen harness strap, which had necessitated the removal of her gloves to pick away the ice. No doubt she'd dropped them during their struggle, and she'd been too flustered to retrieve her muff. Not that he would've let her go back to the buggy after she'd pulled a gun on him.

His wintery eyes narrowed. Along his cheekbone, a crusted line of dried blood marked a scratch she'd put there. Her insides coiled tighter. She shouldn't have made it sound as if she'd intended to hurt him. She didn't even remember doing it. All she recalled was the sheer terror that had overcome her when he grabbed her.

He released her hands and began to unbutton his vest and shirt.

Her heart fluttered with renewed fear. "What...what are you doing?"

"Ravishing your frozen fingers."

Capturing her hands, he threaded them through the opening in his shirt, then sandwiched her palms against his chest. His body radiated heat like a furnace, and soon her fingers began to burn. With a moan, she tried to pull away, but he held fast.

"It's good if you feel pain. That means you won't lose your fingers."

Lose her fingers? *God forbid.* She burrowed through crisp hair on his chest, seeking the warm skin beneath.

His eyes widened a split second before his features turned to stone.

The heat she'd taken from him went straight to her face. What was she *thinking* to touch him like that? She stilled her hands.

The muscles beneath her fingers flexed. Her skin tingled in response. The startling sensation spread up her arms and curled around the tips of her breasts. With a gasp, she yanked her hands away and tucked them under her arms.

Almighty. Was she *attracted* to him? She'd never been drawn to rough men like this one. It had to have something to do with the strangeness of the situation. She hugged the blanket as her teeth started chattering. He hadn't molested her, but that didn't mean he wouldn't if she kept touching him. Cold or not, she wasn't taking the chance.

He reached over and snatched away the blanket.

She squeaked in protest. "What are you doing?"

"We need to get you warmed up."

"If you t-take my blanket, how do you suggest I get warm?"

He grasped a handful of her damp cloak. "You won't, if you stay in those wet clothes."

He was right. Amy cursed another lapse in reason. Her fears had rendered her senseless. "I should've retrieved my valise. There is a dry outfit in there—"

"Fair to say it ain't dry any longer." He snagged his saddlebag. Thrusting his hand inside, he withdrew several items of clothing. "Here, put these on."

She wrinkled her nose. He didn't really believe she'd don his undergarments, did he?

He frowned at her and shook them. *Yes, he did.* And she'd be a fool to refuse dry clothes. Perhaps his shirt over her underclothes, just until her other things dried out.

Before she could act, he plopped down, yanked her foot into his lap and began to undo the laces on her boot. His touch set off another bout of shivers that had nothing to do with the temperature of the air.

"What are you doing?" She jerked her foot out of his hands.

"Taking off your wet clothes, since you seem too addled to take care of it."

"I am *not* addled." She scooted back. "I can tend to myself, if you would be so kind as to give me some privacy."

He stood, seemingly tall as a mountain, his eyes gleaming like polished silver. "Good to see you recall how to get undressed. I wasn't looking forward to doing it for you."

Buck strode to where he'd stabled his horse, anxious to get away from the all-too-appealing woman he'd rescued. He'd held her close enough to feel those sweet curves. Come to find out, her face was just as nice. Still, he hadn't been prepared for the surge of lust when she'd splayed her fingers over his chest.

She'd felt something, too. He'd seen it in her eyes. And for a half second, he'd considered taking her right there on the hay. Only, she was frightened...and *crazy*. Couldn't forget that.

Inside the stall, he scooped up a handful of straw and began to dry the remaining dampness from the stallion's smoky coat. Goliath pawed and snorted, preening for the mare in the adjacent stall.

"You better behave," Buck whispered. "If she's like her owner, she'll kick you into next Sunday for messing with her."

The stallion whinnied.

"You're right. Might be worth it. Still, better not take the chance. Besides, that woman's none of my business." Buck's hand stilled. He'd made her his business when he brought her in out of the cold.

He sighed, shaking his head. They were stuck here for the night, so he had to make the best of it. But once he got her safely to wherever it was she was going, he'd find his cousin and focus on the only business he cared about—getting justice for his family.

From the other side of the stall came the unmistakable shush of garments being shed.

Buck wrestled his conscience, but the temptation was too strong. Taking advantage of his height, he peeked over the wall, curious as a crow with a shiny object in sight.

She had her back to him and he couldn't see a thing below her neck because she'd pushed up a pile of hay and was hiding behind it. *Smart gal*...and not as crazy as he first thought.

Her green dress went over a rail, along with countless petticoats, each fancier than its neighbor. Lastly, she set aside a bedraggled headpiece too small to call a hat, but with plumes he was sure were peacock feathers.

He shook his head, more intrigued than ever. With those fancy clothes, she could've walked right off a fashion plate in one of those ladies' magazines he'd seen in his stepfather's mercantile. Who was she, and what was she doing out here, smack dab in the middle of former Indian land? This place was still wild, and based on what Sean had reported, it was getting a lot wilder since the settlers' dispute with the railroad had exploded into an all-out war. Was her husband involved? That might explain why she'd reacted with fear.

Buck's heart raced as he watched her lift her arms to shake out a glorious length of chestnut hair. The candle's light reflected off golden strands. He swallowed hard, his hands fisting. God, he would kill to run his fingers through those tresses.

His mind conjured an image of the voluptuous beauty stark naked, beckoning him to join her on his blanket. Sizzling heat shot straight to his groin. Biting back a tortured groan, he turned away before she caught him peeking at her.

He rested his arms on Goliath's withers. "Just my luck. I had to rescue a *Venus*," he muttered. "Why couldn't she be ugly and buck-toothed?"

"Sir?" Her voice drifted over, breathy and uncertain. "If you want to come back, I'm decent."

Decent? Sure she was. But those curves weren't, and no shirt of his was going to help. He'd lied through his teeth when he told her he wasn't looking forward to unwrapping her. Except, she'd claw his eyes out before he could see anything.

He touched the scratch across his cheekbone and winced. Should've announced his intentions before grabbing her, but he'd been so shocked to see a woman out alone in this weather, then when that buggy started rocking, well, he'd just leapt off his horse and raced to the rescue. A wry smile twisted his lips. That gal sure hadn't seen a white knight. Not that he was interested in being one.

Against his better judgment, he ventured back to where he'd left her, sitting on the hay next to the bucket that held the candle. She had her legs tucked up beneath her and that scratchy blanket wrapped clear to her neck and was clutching at it like she was afraid he might take it away. His conscience tweaked him. He'd all but threatened to strip her if she didn't undress. It'd been too long since he'd been in the company of decent women. This would be an uncomfortable night for both of them if he didn't at least try to ease her fears.

He unbuckled his gun belt, wrapped it around the guns and went down on one knee, carefully laying the revolvers within her reach. The Bowie knife went beside the holsters. Her eyes followed his every move. At last, her shoulders lowered and the tense expression softened. More than that, he could actually *feel* her distress draining.

Buck rocked back on his heels, bemused. Over the years, he'd honed his instincts, relying on gut-level intuition to stay alive. But this strange connection seemed to extend to an ability to pick up on the ebb and flow of her emotions, which tugged at his own like the current in a river.

She offered a slight smile. "Thank you for saving me, Mr.—?"

"O'Connor," he blurted, absurdly pleased by the gratitude shining in her eyes. On second thought, he should've given her an alias. Still, it was unlikely she'd ever heard of him. He wasn't as well known as his friend Cole Younger. "Couldn't let you turn into an icicle."

His breath clouded the air. Come to think of it, this ramshackle barn was damn frigid. It offered shelter from the sleet, but did little to keep the cold out. "Here, let me pile up some hay. It'll block the drafts and keep you warm."

"What about you? Are you warm enough?" She hugged the blanket, shivering.

"You want my coat?" His hands went to the buttons. Should've thought to offer it earlier.

Her eyes widened. "No, I wasn't implying that. I just thought *you* might be cold. We can share the hay."

For a moment, he was speechless. It'd been so long since anyone cared about his comfort, he hadn't expected it and didn't know how to respond. He shrugged to hide how much her concern touched him.

"Ah, don't worry about me. You hungry?" He rummaged through the saddlebag, finding the last piece of jerky. "It's not much, but it'll take the edge off."

"Thank you." She gifted him with a smile that snatched his breath.

He leaned back on one arm, trying his damnedest not to look like an infatuated schoolboy. Instead of sitting here mooning over her, he ought to find out what he could about the local situation. Whatever she knew might come in handy when he started searching for that railroad promoter.

"So, you live out here, Mrs., uh…"

"Langford," she finished.

He tried the name in his head. *Mrs. Langford.* Nope, he preferred Venus.

She bit off a small piece of jerky with perfect white teeth, chewed slowly and swallowed before continuing. "Yes, I live…" Her voice trailed off and her lashes lowered.

He leaned forward, worried. "Something wrong?"

She shook her head. "I'm sorry, Mr. O'Connor. I wasn't honest before. I don't live around here. I was headed for a friend's house before starting back to Fort Scott."

That she'd fibbed about where she lived didn't surprise him. She'd done it so he'd think her husband was nearby. But where she was going astonished him. "Fort Scott? That's another two days' ride."

"By rail it's only a couple hours. But the line hasn't reached Girard yet, so we have to go a few miles north to meet the workers' train."

"We?"

"I was traveling with an escort. He attended a meeting earlier today in Baxter Springs and didn't make it back. We'd arranged to stay overnight at a friend's farm, so I thought I'd meet him there."

"Your husband *abandoned* you in Girard?"

Irritation flickered across her face. "He's not my husband, and he didn't abandon me."

It was on the tip of Buck's tongue to ask why she was traveling with a man who wasn't her husband. But then, what did he care who she traveled with? He opted for a safer question. "Why were you there? From what I hear, it's not exactly a safe place for a woman."

She finished chewing the last bite before responding. "I had business in town."

"Business?"

Her lips sealed. Apparently, she didn't wish to elaborate.

Buck smoothed his mustache with his thumb and forefinger, mulling over her hesitation. Just what kind of business would a wealthy lady have with a bunch of rowdy settlers? When he'd come up on her, she'd been terrified, even after he told her he was trying to help. Had even offered him money. *More* money...

His scalp began to tingle, a sure sign something wasn't right. He leaned forward, draping an arm over his knee to appear casual. "I didn't mean to frighten you when I rode up. You must've been expecting trouble."

"Trouble is one way to put it...." She toyed with a curl at her cheek, not meeting his eyes. "You see, I thought you were going to kill me."

CHAPTER 2

"Kill you?" Buck released a weak laugh and scooted back to give her more room. Or maybe he was the one who needed the extra space. *Jesus, Joseph and Mary.* She couldn't possibly know why he was here. And even if she did, she couldn't think he was after *her*. "How'd I give you that idea?"

"The axle nut." Her fingers, white as bone, clutched the edges of the blanket. "I believe it was tampered with and that's why the wheel came off. I assumed whoever sabotaged my buggy had followed me."

Sabotaged? Worry stabbed through him. "You sure it wasn't just an accident?"

Her expression grew pinched. "I've had two other mishaps within the last two weeks, both under suspicious circumstances. The authorities attributed it to bad luck. But now this wheel falling off...well, that's one mishap too many to be considered ill fortune."

Her brow furrowed. "Right after the second incident, I thought I saw a man running away, but I didn't get a good look at him."

The wind whistled through cracks in the boards, a sound that made Buck's skin crawl. Or maybe it was her story, or the thought he kept trying to dismiss. That she might have something to do with the reason he was here.

He picked up a piece of straw and toyed with it, uncomfortable with meeting her eyes. Why would the men who'd hired him want to hurt Venus? She looked about as dangerous as a six-week-old kitten. Might be it wasn't her they were after, but someone close to her.

"What about your husband? Does he have any enemies?"

"My husband?" Her eyes slid off to one side. "Ah, well, that's something else I failed to mention. I'm a widow."

Buck's gaze swept over the blanketed beauty in front of him. *Not a wife, but a widow*, which meant.... He pinched out a flare of interest. That didn't mean she was available, only that she wasn't married to the railroad promoter he was after, which was a relief. Maybe she'd heard rumors and had jumped to conclusions about what was going on.

"Why would someone want to hurt you?"

"Because of my work, I presume." She rubbed at her fingers as if she were trying to warm them. After a moment, she pulled them inside the blanket, giving the image of being tucked inside a tepee with just her head sticking out.

"Your work?" he prodded.

"Among other things, I've been organizing efforts to support the immigration of young ladies out west—"

"Somebody wants to kill you for *importing wives?*" Buck struggled to keep a straight face. Talk about jumping to conclusions. She'd leapt off a damn cliff.

Her expression flattened as if she realized he was no longer taking her seriously. "No, Mr. O'Connor. They want to kill me for daring to *dream*…like my father. They fear I'll make a difference by offering men who truly want to settle this land the kinds of things they long for. Homes and families."

The remaining tension drained from Buck's shoulders. This had *nothing* to do with why he was here. Delivering brides, for God's sake. Who'd want to kill her for that? "Pardon me for saying, but shipping in wives seems like an odd dream."

"Shipping in wives?" She drew back, looking offended. "You make it sound so crass. And what's odd about wanting to make peoples' lives better? Lonely men need wives. Young women with no other prospects need hope, and the chance to have a family."

"All right." He held up his hand, stopping her. He wasn't interested in hearing about her dreams. He'd given his up long ago. "But I still don't see how it could get you killed."

"You must not be from around here."

He shook his head, answering her question without offering more information.

"Some of the men who've moved into the area aren't interested in settling down. They're greedy, out for their own gain. They want to speculate on land and grow rich from the railroad."

"The railroad?" Buck frowned. How had she gone from murder to wives to the railroad? She jumped around more than a damn grasshopper. "Let me get this straight. You're bringing in wives for the settlers who want them, but those who don't are trying to stop you."

"That's right."

Thank the saints. He liked simple explanations. It made sense, now. She was a do-gooder, like the temperance crusaders who went from town to town to pray in front of the saloons. They'd been attacked, drenched, some of them even assaulted. He actually admired those stalwart women. And he admired Venus, too, for wanting to put a stop to the violence. However, shipping in women wasn't going to answer the settlers' concerns about the railroad cheating them out of their land. Sean's letter was sparse with details, but he'd been clear enough about that.

"Look, it's not my place to tell you what to do, but you might reconsider getting involved if these bas—," he caught himself. "If these bad men are trying to hurt you."

"They're not just trying to hurt me. They want to stop me. But I won't let them. I *vowed* not to let men like these win. They care nothing about this land, or the future of our state." Her voice wavered with emotion. She firmed her jaw as if to reinforce her resolve.

Softhearted and hardheaded—the lady was most definitely a crusader. Buck could sympathize. Before the war, he'd been like that, full of fine ideals, but too stubborn to see his cause might be the death of him. Unfortunately, it'd done worse than kill him.

A protective urge welled up. He quashed it. *Hell no*, he was not getting involved with pure trouble in a pretty package, no matter how tempting. He was here for one reason—to stop a railroad from ruining his cousin Venus and her problems weren't his concern.

"I didn't say stop. I just said you ought to reconsider getting involved with these rowdy settlers. Maybe you can find someone to help you with your, uh, program."

She released a sigh that clouded the air. "That's why I'm here. To meet with one of the farmers who'd volunteered to head up the Immigration Society. He didn't show."

Once more, she adjusted the blanket, this time tucking the ends beneath her legs. The hay might've helped a little, but there was nothing he could do about the drafts. Damn, her lips were getting blue and she was shivering again.

"You're cold." He stood and stripped off his overcoat.

She gave an emphatic shake of her head. "I'm not taking your coat."

"This here is thick wool. It'll warm you." He draped the greatcoat over her shoulders and tucked it around her. "And I can pile up more hay."

"All right. So long as *you* don't get cold." Her lips curved in a wan smile. "It is very warm. Thank you."

She rubbed her finger over a dark area near the shoulder seam where captain's bars had been stripped off. "This is an officer's overcoat, but you've removed the markings. Is it yours?"

Venus was a tad too perceptive. This wasn't the first time he'd donned a Federal uniform to fool potential enemies. He sat and leaned back on his arms, putting on like he wasn't particularly concerned about her astute observation. "I didn't steal it, if that's what you're asking."

"I wasn't accusing you. Just wondering." She tipped her head to one side and a crease marred her brow. "If you're not from around here, where are you from, Mr. O'Connor?"

"Came up from Texas."

"That doesn't sound like a Texas drawl."

Again, she surprised him with her perceptiveness. "Didn't say I was born there. Just worked there. Herding cattle."

"You do seem like a man used to taking charge, but I wouldn't have guessed cows."

Buck lifted a shoulder in a nonchalant gesture even though he was anything but. "Oh, I've done all kinds of things to keep food in my stomach, like most men."

"I see." She nodded. He wondered just how much she did see. "If you're looking for work, I could find you a position. Tell me what you know how to do."

"What I know how to do?" he echoed. If he offered to give her a demonstration, she'd probably slap him. On the other hand, flirting with her might deflect further questions. A smile tugged at his lips. "That's an awful long list. Not sure where to start."

"Why don't you start with the truth?"

Surprise splashed him like a face-full of cold water. How had he missed the sharpness in those caramel eyes? She'd ambushed him by looking so delicious. He scrambled for cover behind a suggestive smirk. "Don't fret, Venus. I won't exaggerate my skills."

She drew back, frowning. "You forget yourself, sir."

No, he'd only forgotten to be careful.

"You said to be honest."

Still frowning, she cocked her head and took to studying him. As her gaze moved from his face down his body, his skin quivered as if she'd stroked it.

He struggled to maintain the cocky smile. It'd been a long time since he'd been with a woman this beautiful and he was far too susceptible. "So, what do you see?"

The muscles in her face stiffened. "I see a clever man who ought to know better than to try to fool an intelligent woman."

The heat on his face melted his arrogant smile. *Hell's bells.* He hadn't blushed since he was twelve. "You see more than I thought."

"Just because you've told me very little doesn't mean I can't deduce something of your character."

"My character?" He shook his head. She'd thrown him again. "You sure I have one?"

"Every man has character, good or bad. I think you mean, what do I make of yours?" Her eyes softened, pulling him in. "You haven't taken advantage in a situation where you clearly have the upper hand. So I assume under your rough exterior beats the heart of a gentleman."

Buck wanted to laugh, but he couldn't. She wouldn't call him a gentleman if she knew half of what he imagined doing with her. Yet, she'd picked up enough to know he wouldn't act on his fantasies. She'd also put her finger on the very thing he'd taken pride in before war and privation had turned him into an animal. His honor.

"Am I right, Mr. O'Connor?" The openness on her face made her look so young and vulnerable he couldn't hold back the answer she sought.

"Close enough."

Her lips trembled. Apparently, his answer hadn't relieved her. He came to his feet before he could think about resisting the urge to go to her, but at the last second pinned his arms to his sides. If he wrapped them around her, it would shatter her delusions about his honor.

"You still cold? I can pile up more hay."

"It's not that." Her expression grew strained as she looked up at him. "Someone out there wants me dead. But the authorities don't believe me. *Nobody* believes me."

The anguish in her voice wrenched his heart. He sank down and put his arms around her. "Here, now. *I* believe you. But you can't wait around 'til the scoundrel succeeds in hurting you. Won't your family help?"

"I don't have any family left."

Neither did he, except for a cousin he hadn't seen in ten years. An ache started in the center of his chest. He knew the pain of loneliness and isolation, but he had no hope to offer. With her youth and beauty, she'd have a flock of swains at her feet. One of them would champion her cause. "You got to know *somebody* who can help."

She drew back, her eyes widening. He could see the moment she seized upon the solution—and it scared the hell out of him. "You're looking for work. I could use a man like

you. Would you consider a job as a bodyguard? *My*
bodyguard?"

"Your *bodyguard?*" Alarm flashed in her rescuer's
crystalline eyes, startling her out of the warm cocoon he'd
created when he wrapped her in his arms.

Amy shrugged off his embrace. Thank goodness he took
the cue and moved back to where he'd been sitting. But his
departure opened the space between them and cold air
swirled in.

She clamped her teeth together to keep them from
chattering. He might try to hold her again. Why had she let
him in the first place? Because something about him made
her feel secure, and she hadn't felt that way in a very long
time. Still, she'd given him the wrong idea, so no more
hugging. "I'm speaking of a *business* arrangement."

"A business arrangement." His sandy brows pulled into a
frown. Possibly, he was considering it, or he wasn't taking
her seriously.

Yet, she *was* serious. Although she wanted to believe she
could take care of herself, this spate of mishaps had shaken
her confidence. Being a single woman out alone much of the
time, she was vulnerable. Why, just today her escort had
failed to show up and she'd faced a choice to leave alone or
spend the night in a rough boomtown.

"Rest assured, I am in earnest. I need protection and you
appear capable of providing that service." She glanced at the
weapons he'd put within her reach. Actually, he seemed a
good bit more than capable.

He leaned back on his arms with one knee drawn up. The
frown disappeared, replaced by a speculative gaze that
traveled from her face downward.

The air crackled like the split-second before a lightning
strike.

Her fingers tightened on the lapels of the overcoat he'd
tucked around her. Perhaps she should ask for references,

though it was doubtful he'd provide any. His reluctance to answer questions implied he had a checkered past.

On the other hand, he didn't wear the fearful look of a man fleeing justice, nor did he strike her as an outlaw. She'd recognized his accent. Missourians from across the border had the same drawl. Many men from that divided state had left after the war to escape reprisal from unhappy neighbors. Perhaps he was one of them. Did it really matter? He'd saved her life, fed her and kept her warm, all without demanding anything in return. Beyond that, she sensed she could trust him. Her father had instructed her that there were times one must rely on intuition in making a judgment. This would be one of those times.

"What do you say, Mr. O'Connor? Are you interested in the job?"

"First, tell me something. Why is this immigration program so important to you?"

She nodded, willing to supply the details. He would need to know what he was up against. "I believe it's the last chance we have of resolving this land dispute before it turns into a war."

His gaze sharpened. "A war?"

"The settlers in Crawford County have been organizing against the railroad. The last few weeks, they've crossed the line from protesting to violence. The government sent troops, but more guns won't solve anything. If we can offer the more reasonable men an incentive to settle the conflict peacefully, we can avert disaster.

"With women?"

"Not just women, Mr. O'Connor, decent young ladies who want a better life with more opportunity. We bring them out here to meet men who want the same things they do: homes, families, the kind of prosperity that only comes with peace."

He nodded solemnly. "See your point, but I don't get how that's going to resolve a land dispute."

"The Border Tier is offering meaningful incentives to men who participate in the program."

"Border Tier." He said it so softly it seemed he might be talking to himself.

"The Missouri River, Fort Scott and Gulf Railroad. That's a mouthful, thus, the nickname."

He nodded, but the way his brow furrowed indicated his mind was racing ahead. "You got the railroad to support your program for delivering wives? You must know the management pretty well."

"Know them?" She breathed a laugh. *What an understatement.* "I'm on the board."

Surprise flashed across his face. Most men thought it odd she was involved with railroad business, or any business for that matter. Unlike other men, Mr. O'Connor didn't appear compelled to comment on it, which was another mark in his favor.

He shifted forward, twisting a piece of straw in his fingers. The man rarely stopped moving, even when he seemed at ease. Some might call it restlessness, but she sensed this was more along the lines of readiness. His body remained taut, every muscle coiled, ready to spring into action. This was good, because a bodyguard would need sharp instincts and quick reflexes.

She pulled the coat and blanket tighter, but the layers didn't warm her like before. Pity nothing stayed the cold except his arms. She wasn't about to ask him to hold her again. As employer and employee, they needed clear boundaries. "Will you accept my offer?"

"Give me some time to ponder it."

She nodded. Her gaze roved his shaggy hair and weathered face, the mustache that needed trimming, the strong line of his jaw and chin.

He returned the study with equal intensity. The image of a pale-eyed wolf flashed through her mind. Managing a man like this one would be no easy task, yet wasn't he exactly the kind she needed?

She released a sigh and a white puff of breath hung in the air. Her chills started up again, rattling her teeth like a set of dice.

He straightened. "You're cold."

"Perhaps I will try your suggestion about using the hay."

"That only works if you've got heat left. You're pale and shivering. You need warming up." He stood and plucked his coat from around her, then the blanket. "Body heat's the only thing that works when you're bone cold."

He scooped the hay and threw the oilcloth down like he was forming a bed. Awareness jolted through her. Did he expect her to join him there?

"No." She shook her head to emphasize the point. Given her body's undisciplined response to his nearness there was no way she was lying down in this man's arms. "I'll just wrap up and pull the hay on top of me."

Ignoring her protest, he dragged her down beside him, tucking his coat and the blanket around them. His heat seeped through their clothes, warming her more than the thickest wool. Despite her reservations, she huddled against him. She'd always claimed she didn't need a man. But right now, she needed this one.

With his arm, he cradled her head, the movement bringing his face close to hers. For a heart-stopping moment she thought he might kiss her. Her lips tingled in anticipation. His gaze caressed her mouth. Bringing his hand to her face, he brushed the hair out of her eyes.

Infernal tears welled up again. She turned her face away, embarrassed by her weakness, but more disturbed by her trembling response to his nearness. "We shouldn't be doing this."

"Nobody has to know." He wiped the dampness from her cheek with the edge of his thumb. "Besides, if you stay cold, you'll get sick. Can't let that happen. Not if I'm gonna keep you safe."

Buck knew the instant Venus fell asleep when her body relaxed in his arms. That she trusted him enough to be vulnerable stirred up soft feelings. He quashed them. If he accepted her offer, it'd be because it suited his purpose.

Her revelation had surprised the hell out of him. Imagine, Venus on the board of the railroad. Must be an honorary position because of her late husband, but that didn't make it any less advantageous. Playing the part of her bodyguard, he could find out what she knew and get close to the promoter he had to remove. Along the way, he could flush out the rascal who was after her. How hard could it be? He'd taken on entire regiments with fewer than a hundred men. Surely he could handle one woman, no matter how pretty.

Pretty?

He studied her face relaxed in sleep. Her dark lashes lay like fans against creamy skin without a single blemish. She wasn't just pretty. She was downright beautiful, like those famous paintings of the legendary goddess he'd named her after. Even her hair was magnificent, all thick and wavy and just begging to be touched.

He fondled a silken strand. The fragrance he'd smelled before, sweet as a summer field, took him back to a gentler time, to another place where he'd been a different man.

Alarmed, he shook off the curl clinging to his finger. What the hell? He shouldn't be thinking about how good she smelled or how right she felt in his arms. His purpose in holding her was to share his warmth. At least her lips weren't blue anymore. They'd turned an irresistible shade of pink.

Unable to resist, he brushed his thumb over her mouth. Her lips parted on a sigh.

Arousal—sharp and immediate—forced a groan up the back of his throat. His eyes fell to the open collar of the shirt he'd given her. Did the fabric touch her bare skin? Maybe he could open these few buttons and see…

He snapped his eyes shut. *No.* He wouldn't take advantage of a lady who'd put her faith in him. Curiosity provoked another look. Why on earth had she chosen *him*? Certainly, he'd saved her from the weather, but that alone wouldn't account for the level of trust it would take to bring a man— and a stranger at that—so intimately into her life. She must have no idea what a bodyguard did, or how disruptive he'd be to her daily routine. But she was about to find out.

Buck moved his arm to make her more comfortable.

Her lashes fluttered, and she blinked up at him in sleepy confusion.

Saints. If she noticed his erection, which was damn near pressing against her thigh, she'd flee the barn.

She gazed at him, not with fear but with the kind of look a woman might give the man she adored.

His heart kicked in his chest a mere second before his brain woke up. She'd offered him a job, not undying devotion. Besides, he wasn't some damn Galahad. His intentions were far from pure. She shouldn't look at him like he was her hero.

"Go back to sleep, Venus."

The admiration in her eyes wavered. "Stop calling me that. My name is Amy."

"Amy." What a simple name, especially for a woman who was getting more complicated by the hour. "You can call me Buck."

Her brow creased. "You may call me Mrs. Langford."

Buck bristled at the command given by the tiny general in his arms. He didn't take orders from men, much less women. Still, he'd humor her—for now. "Sure thing, *Mrs. Langford.*

The frown smoothed into solemn regard. "So you'll take the job?"

"I said I would, didn't I?"

Her eyebrows shot up in surprise. "No, you did not."

He took a deep breath and let it out on a slow count of ten. With the way she affected him, he'd need all the control he could muster. At least it was only for a few days, the time he anticipated it would take to get rid of that pesky promoter causing trouble for Sean and the settlers. "Yeah, I'll take the job.

The last of the candle sputtered and they were cast into darkness. Buck's senses heightened, and he became painfully aware of her closeness.

"I'm feeling better. You can let me go." She wiggled, God help him.

He clenched his teeth. "It's freezing."

"Do you want the blanket?" Her hip bumped his erection.

He jerked back, his breath rushing out in a harsh pant. "Damn it woman, stop moving."

She froze. "I…I don't mean to be a bother, but…could you light another candle?"

"You're not a bother," he grumbled. She wasn't tempting him on purpose, but his body didn't know the difference. He got up and complied with her request.

When he returned with a lit taper, she was sitting up and had his coat buttoned to her chin. Didn't look like she was still cold. Her cheeks were rosy and her eyes glowed like warm honey. That body heat had worked wonders. Maybe they ought to try it again, this time without clothes between them.

Buck speared his fingers through his hair to keep from dragging her to him. He had to stop fantasizing and focus on finding out what she knew about the railroad. After fixing the candle to the upturned bucket, he sat in front of her, rested his arm on one knee. "So, you ship in wives for horn— I mean, lonely settlers."

His new employer politely ignored the near faux pas. "Actually, the Young Ladies Immigration Society pays their way, with help from the railroad."

"And you work for this ladies' whatever-it-is organization?"

Her lips tipped up. "No, I get the organizations started, but I'm not employed by them." She drew the blanket over as if she were going to wrap it around her, and then seemed to change her mind and held it out to him. "Here, I'm sure you're cold. This coat is enough."

Oh, he was plenty warm, thank you. "Wrap up so you don't get sick."

The smile she bestowed on him made him want to give her a dozen blankets. "You asked what I do. I have different interests, but right now I'm working for James Joy."

Buck's scalp tingled. His cousin's letter had mentioned some big bug with the railroad. Had a funny name, like Joy. What could Amy be doing for a railroad magnate? "You're on the board with him?"

She nodded. "And I'm responsible for selling the railroad to communities along the line."

"Selling the railroad...?" The tingling sensation spread, racing across Buck's skin, prickling the hair on his arms. He shook his head in disbelief. No, she *couldn't* be the one he was after. Not Venus. Not the woman he'd just sworn to protect. "You mean like, hosting parties?" he asked, hopefully.

Her gold-flecked eyes rebuked him. "No, Mr. O'Connor. I'm not a social secretary. My job is much bigger than that. I'm the Border's Tier's chief promoter."

CHAPTER 3

The sun had already started warming things up when Buck headed into town. That's where Amy wanted to go, and he was eager to find his cousin and the newspaper editor who'd hired him under false pretenses. He looked forward to giving those two an earful.

They'd sicced him on a *woman*, for chrissake. The same woman who'd hired him to be her damn bodyguard. What kind of men sent hired guns after women? Only bullies and brutes, and he hadn't sunk so low he'd work for people like that. No sir, his cousin would have to clear things up before he went one peg further.

A wagon piled high with building supplies rolled past, slinging filth onto boards forming a rickety sidewalk. Despite the knee-deep muck, the town was packed with men. Those thousands of settlers Sean had written about, were they all here? Which ones wanted Amy dead?

She leaned over to take a gander at the mare, traipsing along on a lead.

Buck bit back a lustful groan. He'd suffered through an hour of having her snuggled on his lap with her derriere rubbing against him. If the air weren't so cold, the heat she'd generated would've incinerated him by now.

"There," She pointed to a freshly painted sign above a building that looked as though it had been thrown together with wood scraps. "Our temporary depot. The *Weekly Press* is next door. I hope to catch up with the editor before we leave."

Her meeting was at the *newspaper* office?

Alarmed, Buck hauled back on the reins. Hopefully, his cousin had smartened up and wouldn't give him away, but just in case, he'd distract Amy until he could get Sean alone.

He peered over her head, surveying the town square. Unpainted frame buildings dotted the perimeter, interspersed with white canvas tents standing in for permanent structures. Was one a grocery? His stomach growled. It'd been days since he'd had decent food. "Doesn't look like much."

She twisted on his lap, causing him to jerk. Was she purposely torturing him? "Oh, it's not finished yet. Once the tracks reach town, we'll bring in brick and build a proper depot."

"I'm not talking about the depot."

Amy held his gaze for what seemed like a full minute. His temperature rose to an uncomfortable level before she seemed to realize they were staring at each other. Her cheeks colored and she swiveled her head. "Oh, you mean the town. It hasn't been here long, but they've already got a hotel and a mercantile—and two newspapers."

"Two?" Buck arched his eyebrows, more surprised than she knew. "This place doesn't look big enough for two dogs, much less two newspapers."

"Well they wouldn't have two, if Amos Sanford hadn't taken over the first newspaper and turned it into a recruiting tool for the Land League." Disdain dripped from her lips.

Ah, he'd found the *right* editor.

"My meeting is with Dr. Warner," she finished. "He publishes the *Weekly Press.*

Relieved, Buck headed for the depot. He tied Goliath to the rail and helped Amy down, taking care to set her on the boardwalk rather than the muddy ground. "I'll take your horse to the livery and find somebody to fetch that buggy. Don't go anywhere 'til I get back."

A frown flashed across her face, but she said nothing, only reached beneath her cloak and withdrew a pocket watch, snapping it open to take a look. "That shouldn't take you too long. I'll be ready to leave at half-past ten."

"Got it." He watched as she went inside, still trying to get over the shock. She was the railroad promoter he was supposed to get rid of, and he'd signed on to be her damn bodyguard. Had to be divine justice because he was certain God was laughing his ass off right about now.

Just as Amy predicted, it took Buck no time at all to do his errands. Afterwards, he strode off in the direction of the other newspaper, which he discovered was conveniently located across from a saloon.

He opened the door and a bell jingled as he stepped inside.

A grizzled codger sitting behind a desk piled high with newspapers glanced up. Was he the editor? Another man sitting in front of the desk twisted in his chair, then bolted to his feet, his eyebrows arching to a sweep of black hair.

Buck met a pair of pale eyes similar to his own, but untainted with the icy gray of the cold-hearted bastard who'd sired him. He took an uncertain step forward, waiting a heartbeat for the familiar grin. "Sean?"

Relief flickered across his cousin's matured face, but Sean didn't embrace him, as in years past. Instead, he offered a handshake. "We wondered whether you'd show up."

Buck squelched his disappointment and gripped Sean's outstretched hand. He hadn't really expected to be greeted with open arms. After all, they hadn't seen each other for years and had served on opposite sides of a bitter war. Still, he'd hoped for a warmer welcome.

"You asked me to come. Here I am." His gaze flickered over his cousin's shoulder to the older man who'd stood, waiting to be introduced.

Sean did his duty. "Buck, this is Amos Sanford. He's the editor of the *Workingman's Journal.* I wrote to you about him. He heads up the Land League that's helping us settlers organize against the railroad."

Sanford inclined his head but didn't come out from behind the desk to shake his visitor's hand. "Mr. O'Connor, good to see you could make it here to help us out."

Buck held a neutral expression. "What kind of help would that be?"

"What kind?" Sean looked startled. "Well, the kind I wrote to you about." He sent a worried glance in the editor's direction.

"We need your help with removing an obstacle." Sanford's smooth reply made Buck's skin crawl.

"An obstacle? Is that what you call her?"

When neither man answered, he strolled over to the desk and picked up a newspaper. The headline urged settlers to rise up and defend their rights. Where'd he heard that before? These Union boys were starting to sound like Rebels. Simmering, he rolled the paper like a club and tapped it against his palm. He had a good mind to beat these two over the head with it. "You got the wrong man for the job. I don't kill women."

Sanford sat and leaned back in his chair, stroking a gray beard that reached to the top button of his vest. Canyon deep lines rearranged themselves into a paternalistic frown. "You must've misunderstood, Mr. O'Connor. We haven't asked you to kill anybody, much less a woman."

Buck tossed the newspaper aside and snatched Sean's letter out of his pocket. He slapped it on the desk. "States here you want me to get rid of a railroad promoter. That don't mean sending a body away on a pleasure excursion."

The chair creaked as Sanford reached for the letter. He peered through round spectacles perched at the end of his nose, perusing the lines like he'd never seen them. The old fox had probably helped Sean craft the damn missive. After a minute, he folded the letter and crossed his arms over his chest. "There are many ways to remove obstacles, Mr. O'Connor. I suspect you're bright enough to figure it out. Sean told me you led a company of irregulars during the war. The fact that you're alive proves you've still got a few tricks up your sleeve."

An alarm tripped in Buck's head. So *that's* why the Land League wanted to hire him. They thought he was still in the ambushing business. He looked at Sean, who wouldn't meet his eyes. He'd risked getting his neck stretched by returning to Kansas, but honor demanded he at least try to right the wrong done to his kinsman. Now it appeared he was a fool who'd walked into a trap.

His cousin stood at rigid attention, his tanned face drawn tight as the hide on a drum, not meeting Buck's eyes. An ache started in the center of his chest. Despite their past, they were the only family each other had left. How could Sean have betrayed him like this?

Pulling back his coat, he rested his hands on the twin Colts at his side before pinning the editor with a cold stare. He hadn't killed anyone since the war had ended, but he would reinforce the perception he was a dangerous man to cross so they'd think twice about hiring him to do their dirty work, then trying to collect a reward. "My wartime sentiments don't have a damn thing to do with this."

Sanford huffed. "We don't care about your sentiments. It's your skills we need."

"So, you admit it. You want to hire a big gun to take care of one little lady."

"Don't be fooled by that pretty face," Sanford blustered. "Amy Langford will do anything to advance that cursed railroad. With this Young Ladies Immigration Society, she's using the age-old strategy for dividing men—Women."

Buck snorted a derisive laugh. "What's so dangerous about importing wives for a bunch of horny settlers?"

The editor swelled up like a toad. "She's dangling petticoats as an enticement to get us to pay those exorbitant prices her boss is charging for land. These boys were soldiers and most of them are unmarried. I suppose you've noticed how few decent women there are out here. It's a devilishly brilliant scheme concocted by a woman who'd sell her soul for thirty pieces of silver."

It was a brilliant idea, but Buck had already figured out Amy was smart. Her motives, however, weren't so clear. Was she really that greedy? "I met her already, so I know what she's up to, but she thinks somebody's trying to kill her."

He narrowed his eyes in a way that put most men in a fearful sweat. "*If* I decide to help, I need to know whether you've hired somebody else—and don't even think about lying to me."

"We don't have enough money to hire somebody else," Sean grumbled. "If somebody's trying to kill her, it's probably 'cause she robbed him blind."

Sanford grunted an agreement. "Maybe she's making that up so you'll feel sorry for her. Where did you say you met her?"

Buck didn't say, nor was he interested in providing the details. "I happened across her. She was waiting on some fellow who was supposed to help with that immigration society you mentioned."

Sanford's eyes sharpened with interest. "We had a talk with him. I don't think he's interested in volunteering anymore. Did she happen to mention her next move? We can't afford to lose any more leverage against the devil who's behind this fraud."

James Joy. The force behind the Border Tier and Satan incarnate, if the settlers were to be believed. He was Amy's boss, so what did that make her? Last night, she'd looked downright angelic, even wringing wet.

If Sanford hadn't hired another gun, then her attacker was likely a renegade. Was he an irate settler, an unhappy farmer, one of the men who'd signed up for her program and gotten an ugly wife? The list could be endless.

"She didn't mention her plans." Buck lifted his hat and threaded his fingers through his hair, his unease getting worse. She hadn't told him much, but she'd played him masterfully to gain his promise of protection, something he'd offered to no woman since being betrayed by another smart, pretty one.

Still, he'd given his word and he wouldn't go back on it. He adjusted his coat, covering the guns at his sides. "Just so we're clear, I'm not using violence against a woman, so I don't know what it is you want me to do."

Sanford jerked to his feet. "Distract her. Deceive her. Discredit her. We don't care, so long as you prevent her from succeeding in her schemes."

The frown dissolved as the editor came out from behind the desk and clapped a hand on Buck's shoulder. "Why don't you boys go over to the saloon and get reacquainted? Tell them I'll pay for your drinks. I'm sure after you hear Sean's side of things, it will clear up any misgivings you might have about ridding us of that troublesome woman."

Buck shrugged off the unwanted familiarity. He hadn't signed on for this kind of work, but he couldn't walk away without at least hearing what his cousin had to say.

Sanford rested his fingers on a dog-eared Bible at the corner of his desk. "You recall the story of Samson and Delilah? Makes a man think twice about falling for a pretty woman."

Ten in the morning and already the saloon was crowded, or maybe these men hadn't left from the night before. Buck stalked past Sean, who'd strolled up to the bar and snagged a bottle, and found an empty corner table. He scraped his chair around, turning his back on the noisy clamor, and sat facing Sean so it would be easy to see if his cousin was lying.

"What the hell's going on? Why are you licking that Sanford fellow's boots? I don't trust him." Buck wasn't sure he trusted his cousin, either, but he would give Sean the benefit of the doubt—for now.

Sean tossed back the contents of a glass and blew out a satisfied breath. "Ah, that's fine brew Mr. Sanford purchased for us." He poured a second glass and pushed it across the table. "Have a drink, coz."

Buck's temper boiled up. The very last thing he needed right now was a drink. "Tell me why you brought me here to get rid of a woman."

Before Sean could reach the bottle, Buck set it out of reach.

His cousin's face darkened and his eyes narrowed.

Don't touch me whiskey, Bucko. The whispered words rasped like a file on metal.

Buck's skin went clammy. Had Sean said that, or was he hearing things? An image flashed in his mind of another lean face, one flushed with liquor and malicious intent.

Next time ye pour me whiskey into the fire, I'll stick yer hand in the embers.

Buck sucked in a sharp breath, throwing off the wretched memory. He flexed his fist, feeling the slight pull of old scars, and his stomach tightened. Bastard still managed to torment him, even from the grave.

Sean's puzzled expression came into view. "You alright?"

"Slow down," Buck ordered.

"Ah, now you're sounding like me Ma. It'll take more than a tippling to make me drunk." Sean dragged the bottle over and poured another glass. "Here, let's toast to old times."

Buck leaned back and crossed his arms. There was nothing in his past warranting celebration. "Tell me straight. What have you got yourself into?"

Uncertainty flickered in Sean's eyes. "You don't seem too interested in helping me out."

Buck smoothed his features, sensing his cousin's doubts. He had a few of his own, but he'd set them aside for the moment. "You're family. Far as I'm concerned, that's all that matters."

The hard set of Sean's jaw relaxed. With a heavy sigh, he rested his arms on the table. "Like I told you in that letter, I'm broke. All I got is the land I staked out. If that lady promoter convinces more men to give up the fight, I'll lose that, too." He raised his eyes, pleading. "I'm not asking you to hurt her. Just get her out of our way."

Buck kept his face fixed. He wasn't committing to anything until he knew the full story. "Start at the beginning. The letter you sent didn't give much detail."

Sean rested his elbow on the table, gripping the bottle like a lifeline. "Me and some boys from my company moved out here 'bout three years ago. Staked claims on land the Indians gave up after the war. We figured the government would sell it for a dollar and a quarter an acre, like they did that other Indian land."

Pausing to refill his glass, he frowned. "But them politicians in Washington hornswoggled us. They told us to go settle the land. Then they let that railroad bigwig buy it for next to nothing. Now he wants six dollars an acre for land we've lived on and improved." Sean drained the glass, and slammed it on the table. "T'ain't right."

"Since when did politicians care about doing what's right?" The knots in Buck's shoulders eased a bit. Crooked congressmen and rich tycoons were enemies he could understand. "I hear there were troops sent in against you."

His cousin nodded. "We started with peaceable demonstrations. That got us nowhere. So we burned ties and tore up track to show 'em we meant business. Then they sent the army to help King Joy guard his railroad. These troops, they're men we fought alongside. We don't aim to kill them for something they got no control over. But we won't sit still and let this bastard steal us blind." Anger flashed in Sean's eyes. "A man gets respect only if he's got land—or a gun."

Buck rested his arms on the table. His guns had certainly earned him respect, but not the kind that ensured a long life. He turned his glass with his thumb and forefinger, as he worked the problem in his mind.

Getting justice for these settlers would be no easy task, and Amy represented his only ace at this point. How should he play that card? There was a powerful attraction between them. He'd felt it and knew she did, too. His stomach turned at the thought of using her that way. But if the widow was as black-hearted as her reputation, he could justify the means to achieve his goal. After all, he'd only known her a few hours. Sean was his kinsman. "If I get this promoter out of the way, what makes you think Mr. Joy will deal with you?"

Sean leaned closer, his expression intense. "He's in a race, Buck—a race to the border. There's a second railroad, the Katy. They're building a central line through Kansas. Only one railroad gets to lay track through Indian Territory into Texas—"

"So only one of them gets all that cattle business," Buck pushed his glass aside.

His cousin smiled. "You get my meaning. If we can slow down construction, I'm sure it'll put Mr. Joy in a more negotiating state of mind."

"Sounds reasonable. But there's too many contingencies." Buck hated contingencies. That's what got men killed. "That railroad promoter, she knows somebody's after her. She hired me to be her bodyguard."

His cousin's eyes grew wide as silver dollars. His low chuckle erupted into a chortle. "Ah, Buck, but that's brilliant! However did you manage it?"

"Wasn't difficult." No need to share the details. The fact that he was sitting here plotting against her was bad enough. "If I can keep her busy, what are your plans for slowing down the railroad?"

Sean's voice lowered to an excited whisper. "There's a new load of ties, thousands of them, laid out alongside the graded bed south of Girard. We'll have us a bonfire if we can get close."

"You won't with those troops guarding the tracks."

"We'll figure out a way to get rid of them."

"Not good enough." Buck straightened, squelching his unease. Four years as a partisan captain had taught him how to wage guerilla warfare, and that's exactly what this was shaping up to be. He'd rather burn ties than deceive women, but he'd landed in a perfect position to benefit Sean's cause. Wasn't that why he was here, to gain justice for at least one member of his family?

"You'll need a distraction. I'll think of something and send instructions." He shoved the chair back and stood up. "You can keep your land, cousin. I'll see to it."

Amy shifted, seeking a more comfortable position on the bench where she'd kept vigil, awaiting her friend, Dr. Warner. The new building housing the *Girard Weekly Press* had been deserted when she'd arrived, although the smell of newsprint and ink still hung in the air. She'd hoped the editor would be here so she could check on the article he was supposed to have written in support of the immigration program.

She dug into a pocket pinned to her jacket, consulting her watch again. Gracious, she'd been waiting nearly two hours. With an impatient huff, she crossed to the large window facing the street. There was no sign of her bodyguard, either.

Buck. Was that his given name, or a nickname? What did it matter? They weren't on a first name basis. Perhaps Mr. O'Connor had changed his mind about accepting her offer. Drifters weren't the most reliable of men. Still, she'd been so sure he was different and her instincts had never failed her.

A man wearing a beaver hat and fur-collared greatcoat strode past the window. *Fletcher.*

Amy gasped in surprise. She raced to the door and jerked it open, calling his name.

He turned and his eyebrows shot up. "Amy! Great Jupiter, where have you been?"

"I was going to ask you the same question."

In two strides, he reached the door and as soon as it closed behind him, dragged her into a tight embrace. "Thank God you're all right."

Her nostrils flared at the spicy fragrance of his cologne, which warred with the scent of leather and wool that still clung to her from being wrapped in another man's arms. Feeling guilty, she pulled away. "I'm fine, Fletcher. Quite well, thank you."

"Are you sure? You look tired." He eyed her with concern before turning to hang his hat on a brass rack. He smoothed straight dark hair back from a broad, intelligent forehead. "I hope you'll forgive my tardiness. Our meeting didn't conclude on time and I couldn't leave Baxter Springs much before dark."

"I did worry."

He smiled apologetically. "Did you go out to the Warner's? I couldn't get there after that freak storm blew in. That was an unwelcome surprise." With a frown, he plucked something out of her hair. "What's this? Hay?"

Her cheeks heated with embarrassment. Heavens, she must look like she'd slept in a barn—and she had. Feeling self-conscious, she took a step back. "I was on my way to the farm when it started to sleet, and then a rear wheel fell off the buggy and I was stranded—"

"Good God." Fletcher's usually composed features twisted in a look of horror. "You might've frozen to death."

"I was fortunate. A Good Samarian on his way into town came to my rescue." Her hand drifted to her jacket collar. She'd leave out the part about undressing and letting Buck hold her. No need to go into that detail. "We found shelter in a nearby barn."

Surprise flared in Fletcher's brown eyes, but his expression held no hint of censure. "That is fortunate."

"I knew you'd think so." Amy smiled, relieved. Thank goodness he wasn't the type to hold something like this against her. He was much more progressive than most men, which was why they got along so well.

He rubbed his fingers over a neatly trimmed beard, looking thoughtful. "I wonder if that wheel was loose when the livery rented it out? I should've checked before I left."

She shook her head in dismay. "Oh, I didn't mean to imply this was your fault. In fact, there's something you need to be aware of because you might be in danger. I believe someone tampered with the axle nut."

"Tampered with...? Your buggy?" He looked shaken. "Those wretched settlers. They horsewhipped one of our agents just last week, but I never dreamed they'd be so low as to go after a woman." He gathered her bare hands in his gloved ones, his eyes appealing. "Forgive me, Amy. I never should have allowed you to remain here unescorted."

Allowed? Her chin came up. "You didn't *allow* me to do anything. As a member of the railroad board, I chose to come down here. If anyone bears the blame, it is I."

His brow relaxed as if he were relieved she'd let him off the hook so easily.

"But now I'm certain those accidents weren't by chance. Whoever sent that cart of bricks my way, and let that horse charge me must've followed me down here."

Fletcher looked down at where her hands were clutched in front of her, and frowned. "Where are your gloves?"

She smiled ruefully. "I lost them."

"Good grief. Your hands must be freezing." He stripped off his gloves and tucked them underneath his arm, then took her hands and sandwiched them between his. It was a gesture reminiscent of what Buck had done. Only, Fletcher's palms were smooth and cool, not calloused and warm, and she doubted his chest felt solid as a tree trunk.

She lowered her lashes, blushing at the inappropriate thought.

"Darling…" Fletcher's voice dropped to a deep baritone. Amy closed her eyes, refusing to compare it with her bodyguard's gravely drawl. "If we were married you wouldn't be such an easy target. Bullies are far less inclined to bother a woman who's under the protection of a man, especially one with money and powerful connections."

A rock-sized lump formed in her throat. Should she tell him she didn't have to marry for protection because she'd hired a protector? Gads, she'd look like a fool if Buck didn't show up.

"Oh, you know how resourceful I can be. Should help not have arrived, I would've unhitched the horse and ridden to safety."

There was a moment of awkward silence before he spoke. "I must keep reminding myself how independent you are."

Her eyes flashed up, meeting a frustrated gaze. "You've always said independence is a quality you admire."

"I do, but I hope you don't wish to remain entirely independent." His sable brows gathered in a frown. "Amy, you know I long to make you my wife."

Her cheeks grew hot under his intense regard. The handsome banker was a perfect choice for a lifetime partner—intelligent, educated, enterprising and ambitious. Precisely the type her father would have approved of, and exactly the kind of man she'd imagined by her side. Only…she wasn't *certain* she was in love with him.

"I know, and I *am* giving your offer serious consideration." Uncomfortable, she pulled her hands away and went over to gaze out the window. "Please, just…just give me just a little more time."

There was no sign of Buck or his big gray roan. Perhaps it was for the better. Being attracted to someone so obviously wrong for her wasn't going to help matters.

She turned with a look that begged understanding. "So, tell me, how did you fare at your meeting in Baxter Springs?"

Fletcher smoothed the hurt from his features. "We had a fruitful discussion."

"I'm sure it was with you leading it." She bestowed a proud smile. He'd worked tirelessly on behalf of the railroad ever since being named to the board, at her recommendation. "Did you find more investors there? That's a miracle, considering we're bypassing their city."

"Actually, they increased the incentive for us to adjust our route." He drew on his gloves, not noticing her stunned surprise.

"We *can't* change the route. Baxter Springs is miles away from the approved crossing point into Indian Territory. If we don't comply with the treaty we risk losing the race—and those land grants." Her heart thudded in apprehension. "You didn't agree, of course."

Fletcher arched an eyebrow. "I did, with Mr. Joy's blessing. He expressed an interest in this arrangement and personally requested that I pursue it. I thought you knew."

Amy swallowed her shock. Why hadn't the railroad's chairman seen fit to fill her in on his plans? If her board position didn't warrant respect, then her large investment in his railroad certainly did.

She twined the silken cord of her reticule around her fingers. "We don't have permission to pass through the lands of other tribes. It will take months to gain the necessary approvals through Congress, not to mention the courts. Surely, you agree this is a mistake."

Fletcher approached her with a stiff expression. "I don't agree. Mr. Joy can handle the politicians and the lawyers. He expects us to seize opportunities when they come along. There are good reasons to shift the route. Water, for one."

"This isn't about water. It's about money."

"Yes, it is, and you, of all people, should appreciate how much we've lost to vandalism."

She stiffened at his rebuke. "The vandalism would cease if the board would get behind my immigration plan."

"Your immigration plan?" He held her gaze for an uncomfortable moment, and then shook his head. "Is that why you're so angry, because the board doesn't like your plan?"

Amy flushed to the roots of her hair. "You make it sound like I'm being childish. I am appropriately upset because the risks we take by changing the route far outweigh the potential rewards. Mr. Joy is letting his greed get the better of his common sense."

Fletcher took her arm. "I understand how this news might upset you. You've had a fright after rushing out into that storm."

"Don't patronize me." She wrenched out of his grip. "I did *not* rush out into a storm. It wasn't even raining when I left."

Behind her, a door creaked.

Amy whirled, and then tried to mask her disappointment as the white-haired editor stepped inside. She forced her lips into a smile. "Dr. Warner. How good to see you."

He hesitated, as if he realized he'd caught them in a private discussion, and then sketched an antiquated bow. "Mrs. Langford, Mr. Bain. What a surprise to find you here."

"Dr. Warner," Fletcher smiled pleasantly, not looking at all like a man who'd just had his head bitten off.

Amy winced at a twinge of guilt. His refusal to consider her concerns and his placating tone had annoyed her, but she should have held her temper. She extended her hand as the editor approached. "I hope you will pardon me for not making it to your home last night. Please give my regards to Mrs. Warner."

The elderly doctor took her fingers and bent over them. His fitted coat and standing collar were a decade out of fashion, but he still managed an air of sophistication. "She is in town today. Perhaps we could arrange to meet for luncheon?"

"Thank you, but we must decline." Fletcher captured her released hand and tucked it into the crook of his arm. "Mrs. Langford has been through a trying ordeal. I'm taking her home."

Amy frowned up at him. Did he think he had the right to dictate her comings and goings? This was something she could not allow, not if she wished to be taken seriously as a woman of business. She withdrew from his grasp and turned her most glowing smile on the editor. "No need to rush off. Do you have a moment to show me that article on the immigration program?"

The newspaper editor darted an uncertain look at the rigid figure standing next to her. "Why, yes. Of course." He crossed the room to a roll-top desk and shuffled through a pile of papers. "I've long espoused the immigration of young women into Kansas. Their calming influence will tame this frontier faster than troops or guns."

"I'm so glad you agree with me." She perused the draft, then turned to Fletcher, holding out an olive branch. "You should take a look at this article. It makes a compelling case for the men to take wives instead of picking up guns."

Fletcher kept his hands at his sides. "I'll take your word for it."

She withdrew the paper, restraining the urge to smack it against his chest. He was simply behaving like a man—giving orders and expecting all of creation to follow. They would have their differences, like every couple, but in every way that mattered, the darkly handsome financier was the exact type of husband she needed at her side.

Unbidden, another image rose in her mind, one with flaxen hair falling in careless waves and a shaggy mustache quirked in a sardonic smile. The door flew open and papers blew off the desk as the man who'd captured her thoughts stepped inside.

Their eyes met and a shameful thrill fanned out. "Mr. O'Connor. We've been expecting you." Actually, she had been the only one looking for him, as she'd not gotten around to telling Fletcher about her decision to hire a bodyguard.

"Allow me to present Dr. Warner, editor of the *Girard Weekly Press.*"

The doctor inclined his head politely, but didn't step forward. Instead, he eyed the big man as if he were a dangerous species.

Indeed, Buck did appear dangerous. It wasn't just the twin revolvers visible beneath his coat, nor was it as tangible as the sheathed blade strapped to his belt. Danger shimmered in the air around him. It glinted in his silvery eyes and radiated from a deceptively relaxed body taut with animalistic readiness.

Her gaze dropped to his gloved hands and the memory of his calloused fingers stroking her face set loose the butterflies trapped in her stomach. She swallowed to keep them inside. Why couldn't she have this fluttery reaction to the man who wanted to marry her?

She snapped her gaze upward and gestured to her left. "This is Mr. Bain. He owns a bank in Fort Scott and serves with me on the railroad board."

"Pleased to meet you." Buck gripped Fletcher's hand, but his eyes were on Amy. "Sorry I'm late. Got derailed by a fellow who needed my help. I did get that buggy taken care of."

"Ah," Fletcher declared, as if he'd suddenly become enlightened. "You must be the kind gentleman who aided Mrs. Langford." He pulled a roll of greenbacks from his pocket. "Allow me to give you something for your trouble before we leave."

Amy's patience unraveled. Fletcher might be well intended, but she was not about to let him, or any man, direct her life. It would erode what little she had gained by holding firm in her insistence she be treated as an equal. "I've hired Mr. O'Connor as a bodyguard. I'll be giving him an advance, so you can put your money away."

Fletcher's mouth dropped in a slack expression, as though he couldn't quite wrap his mind around what she'd just announced. Dr. Warner's forehead wrinkled with a worried frown. Buck's gaze shifted to hers and a tawny eyebrow notched up in a silent salute.

The butterflies turned into bats, frantically beating their wings on the inside of her chest. On second thought, perhaps she should have let Fletcher pay him off. Now she had committed to hiring a man she couldn't be around without feeling the inexorable pull of passion.

"There's no need for you to hire a bodyguard," Fletcher sputtered. He stared at her as if she'd suddenly transformed into a drooling idiot.

Amy wanted to stomp her foot—directly on his instep. "I didn't ask your permission."

His brows slashed down in a thunderous frown. She winced as he grabbed her arm. "I understand you're frightened, but you've got no reason to hire some thug."

Buck's fingers clamped around Fletcher's wrist, and Amy watched in horrified fascination as he twisted, forcing the banker to release his grip. "Appears to me she's got a good reason, and you'd do well to back off. If you want to keep your hand."

Fletcher flushed brick red. "You misunderstood, sir. Mrs. Langford is under my protection. She is my intended."

Buck threw Amy a questioning look and sent her pulse galloping. Her close relationship with Fletcher was a detail she'd neglected to share, although she couldn't say why.

Flustered, she dragged her attention to her *intended*. He glared down at her, daring her to contradict him. She wasn't about to cause a scene. However, she refused to renege on her decision to hire Buck. That would make her appear feeble-minded.

She clutched her reticule in both hands to keep them from trembling. "There have been threats on my life and Mr. O'Connor has experience that leads me to believe he will be able to discover the source whilst ensuring my safety."

Actually, she knew very little about Buck's experience. Only her intuition told her she could trust him, but she wasn't going to admit as much to a man who relied on numbers and hard facts.

An inexpressive mask fell over Fletcher's features. He would challenge her no more at this time, but she would hear about it later…hopefully, much later.

Amy wanted to kick herself for handling this so poorly. She should have told Fletcher about her decision to hire a bodyguard, but she hadn't been sure Buck would show up.

Her bodyguard cleared his throat, breaking the tense silence. "The livery will take care of collecting the buggy." He handed her a wad of bills. "They refunded your money after I told them about the wheel being loose and suggested they ought to be more careful."

"Thank you." She stuffed the money into her reticule.

Fletcher retrieved her hand and tucked it into his elbow, holding it there. "I'll alert the sheriff and have Major Roy assign a special detail. We'll find whoever's responsible."

Was he still hoping to convince her she didn't need a bodyguard? "We can talk to the authorities, but they have their hands full, and pulling troops away from the railroad is playing into the hands of this brute. I suspect that's exactly what he wants us to do."

Fletcher's brow furrowed, communicating without a doubt he wasn't happy with her answer. "Very well. But I don't want you out alone anymore. It's not safe."

"That's why she hired me," Buck interjected, his eyes gleaming with what looked astonishingly like amusement. "And I plan on sticking closer than a tick on a hound. Starting right now."

CHAPTER 4

March 2, 1870, Bourbon County, Kansas

The skeletal outlines of trees sped by as the worker's train chugged northward toward Fort Scott. Amy slid a furtive gaze at Fletcher, who was sitting next to her staring out the window. Thankfully, he wasn't harassing her about her decision to hire Buck, but she was certain she hadn't heard the end of it.

The self-proclaimed *tick* had taken the seat directly across from them. He also seemed preoccupied with observing the scenery, which was fine with her. The last thing she needed was another tense scene like the one in the newspaper office. She had other things to worry about.

Shifting restlessly on the wooden seat, she calculated the remaining days required for their workers to lay track from Girard to the state's southern border. If the weather cooperated for the remainder of the spring, they could make up for lost time and win the race against their only serious competitor. That is, unless this blasted detour ruined everything.

Almighty. This couldn't be happening. Years of work wasted, all because of an unnecessary change in direction. If the Border Tier didn't win this race, the fortune she'd invested would be lost. Worse, her father's vision would go no further than that map mounted on the wall of her study. She couldn't let that happen. His life's work must be completed. She'd sworn, as he lay dying, that his dreams wouldn't die with him.

Her head throbbed and she pressed her fingers to her temples. She had to do *something*. Only, challenging Mr. Joy directly wasn't an option. Once he made a decision, he didn't change his mind. Unless...

Amy trained her attention on the man sitting in front of the walnut-trimmed rail car. What if Mr. Joy's most trusted associate advised against it? The brilliant French-born engineer had been brought in to design and build the railroad, and Mr. Joy was so confident in the man he'd made him his primary business contact. If James Joy could be swayed, Octave Chanute would be just the man to do it.

Encouraged by the idea, she stepped into the aisle and started forward, the train's wheels rumbling beneath her feet. As the car swayed, she steadied herself and her bustled skirts brushed the sides of the benches. Thankfully, she didn't have on the hoops she'd worn until recently.

The railroad's chief engineer bent over a book balanced on his lap, jotting notes on a scrap of blue paper. He carried those bits of paper around in his pockets to record the progress of construction in meticulous detail, which he would then report to his boss. He took his job with the utmost seriousness and she felt certain he would agree with her about the risks of this detour.

"I beg your pardon, sir. May I trouble you for a moment?"

Mr. Chanute set the book aside and stood. "Yes, Mrs. Langford?"

She smiled congenially. "I hope you don't mind that we caught a ride back on the workers' train. I know you had this car reserved for your personal use."

"You are employed by Mr. Joy and a board member, therefore you have a right to ride this train without my express permission."

His unsentimental remark pleased her. At least he acknowledged the truth of her relationship with James Joy. Others refused to accept her role as his chief promoter and took pleasure in spreading ugly rumors—as if she could carry on an affair with a man a thousand miles away.

Mr. Chanute removed his reading spectacles and peered at her with a slight frown. "Is there something you wish to discuss?"

"Yes, I..."

"Please, have a seat." He moved over, making room for her on the bench.

Amy folded her hands in her lap and straightened her shoulders. Maintaining proper posture and taking regular, deep breaths would help her mind stay sharp. "I understand an agreement has been made with Baxter Springs to route the line through that town instead of Chetopa."

He regarded her with characteristic solemnity. "It is what Mr. Joy wants."

The message couldn't have been clearer. What Mr. Joy wanted, Mr. Joy got.

Amy took another deep breath, refusing to be intimidated. Her success depended on her ability to influence the opinions of powerful men, something she'd learned under the tutelage of a powerful man—her father. "Yes, but do you agree we should change the route?"

"There are advantages. We don't have to cross the Neosho River—an expensive proposition—and there are natural springs close by, which will provide an easy and affordable source of water."

"But Baxter Springs is miles east of the legal crossing point."

"Seventeen miles, to be precise."

Amy rubbed her thumb with her forefinger, growing uneasy. It sounded as if Mr. Chanute favored the detour. Perhaps she needed to remind him of the risks. "If we don't adhere to the treaty, we might not get certified by the state."

Annoyance flickered across his face. "Governor Harvey will certify this as a first-class railroad, because it is."

"Of course," she replied quickly. Heavens, she hadn't been questioning the quality of construction. "I only meant the existing treaties don't allow us to cross into Quapaw land. If we pass through Baxter Springs, that's where we'll end up."

"Mr. Joy is certain we'll be accommodated. I believe he has assurances from the Secretary of the Interior." Chanute gathered up his notes and hooked his spectacles over his ears. "If that's all…"

Amy stayed seated. He might desire to end their conversation, but she wasn't going to let this railroad plunge off a cliff without trying to stop it. "Mr. Cox can't push through a new treaty without congressional approval, and who knows how long that might take. While we wait around, the Katy will have time to catch up and they will win the land grants."

"Only if they're certified as a first-class railroad and if they cross before we do, neither of which will happen if we continue at our current pace without interruption. That depends, of course, on you. How are you faring at winning the settlers' support for your program?"

She drew back, not expecting him to go on the offensive. Thus far, her plan for *importing wives*—as Buck had so aptly put it—hadn't gained the groundswell of support she'd anticipated. Worse, local leadership had dissolved like mist on a spring morning. "Some have responded to our offer, and Dr. Warner has agreed to run a front page article promoting it."

"What about these threats on your life? Mr. Bain tells me you've hired a bodyguard."

"There have been…" How did she put this without raising alarm? "Unfortunate incidents. I thought it prudent to hire additional security."

He regarded her over the top of his lenses. "Your position is highly visible. It may be the settlers perceive you as bait for bigger quarry. You should put your talents to work on a less hazardous venture, like that seed work you're doing with the schools. Mr. Joy wouldn't want you risking your life, much as he appreciates your support."

Amy's heart raced. He'd put her into checkmate. However, she wasn't giving in or giving up. She'd made a hardscrabble climb up an impossible mountain. Her dreams were hitched to this railroad and everything it represented.

She shook her head. "Sir, I am at no greater risk than if I were running the woolen mill or involved in my mining interests. There will always be men who oppose my participation in business, and if I let them stop me—"

A male throat cleared loudly behind them. "This train sure does move fast."

She jerked her head around, and her surprise turned quickly to aggravation. What on earth was her bodyguard doing? She'd made introductions earlier, but not so he could attach himself to her and join her private conversations. She twisted in her seat. "Mr. O'Connor. I'm sure you'll excuse us."

The chief engineer turned to the interloper. "You've never ridden a train before?"

"Oh, maybe one or two," the tick replied. "Don't recollect them moving this fast or this smooth. You must've greased the rails."

"Mr. O'Connor," Amy said between clenched teeth. "We are having a business discussion."

"Don't mind me." He removed his hat and took the seat behind them.

She stared, incredulous, as the dratted man continued to sit there, grinning at her.

Mr. Chanute draped his arm over the back of the bench. "The difference isn't what we put on the track, it's how we're building it—with fifty-eight pound rails, and twenty-seven hundred ties per mile, ties made from white oak, not pine."

Amy twisted back around, her hands curling into fists in her lap. The chief engineer had jumped on the distraction, no doubt looking for a way to end their prickly debate.

"We're grading properly and building stone culverts over creeks instead of filling them in like Mr. Parsons' crews are so fond of doing. He'll be washed out come spring." The derisive remark revealed Chanute's disdain for their rival.

Amy, on the other hand, had a healthy respect for the wealthy entrepreneur who drove the hurried construction of the competing line. Seizing the opportunity, she jumped in. "The Katy may not be laying track that will last, but what will it matter if they make it to the border before we do? I hear their line is nearing Iola."

"Iola?" Now she had Chanute's attention. "That's not so close as to cause concern. We'll be pulling into Baxter Springs no later than May, and we'll cross the border less than a week after that. Well ahead of the Katy."

"But they're building faster than we are, and their investors are throwing everything they have into winning this race."

The chief engineer's dark eyes flashed a warning and her stomach clenched. She'd crossed the line, but it was too late to retreat.

"I noticed your men were moving fast this morning," Buck interjected. "One of them told me they'd been laying half a mile of track every day."

Amy shot him a dark look. The last thing she needed was another voice arguing against her, even if he didn't intend it that way. "Sir, you need to find another seat."

"This one suits me fine." He leaned back and stretched his long arms across the back of the oak bench. His mouth lifted in a lazy smile as he fixed his attention on the man in front of him. "Even if the Katy matches your pace, sounds like they're still more than a hundred miles behind. You got nothing to worry about."

That did it. She leapt to her feet, begging pardon as she stepped back to where her bodyguard sat. He gazed up at her with wide-eyed innocence. "A word with you, please."

Amy started back down the aisle without looking to see if he'd followed. She'd fire him on the spot if he ignored her again. The train lurched and her hip struck a seat. The draped overskirt snagged the back of a bench, throwing her off balance. She flailed her arms to break her fall, then a large pair of hands slipped around her waist.

"Careful," Buck murmured, steadying her against his solid form.

The intimate contact released a battalion of butterflies in her stomach. Horrified, she jerked away and hurried to the middle of the near-empty car. She pointed a shaking finger at a mahogany seat. "Sit."

"Woof." Buck plopped down with a grin.

Ignoring his feeble humor, she positioned herself sideways on the seat in front of him, close enough so she could talk without being overhead but not so close she'd be distracted by his nearness. She pitched her voice low, but firm. "Mr. O'Connor—"

"Buck."

Oh no, she would not be on familiar terms with her employee. "*Mr. O'Connor*, let me make one thing perfectly clear. You are employed to keep a madman from killing me. You are not a business associate, personal assistant, or a friend. Therefore, I would appreciate it if you would keep your uninformed opinions to yourself."

His amused smile faded. Leaning forward, he froze her with an icy stare. "Let me make something clear, *Mrs. Langford*. I'll succeed in protecting you only if I figure out who's trying to kill you. And the best way I can do that is by inserting my ignorant self into every closeted corner of your orderly little life."

Amy drew back, her face burning from the verbal slap. "Mr. Chanute isn't a suspect."

"*Everyone* is a suspect, until we know for certain who's behind these attacks."

Her fingers tightened on the back of the bench. In her heart she knew he was right, although it galled her to admit it. "Understood, but you don't need to add your sentiments to the mix."

"I was trying to help you."

"*Help* me? By interrupting an important conversation?"

"By smoothing his ruffled feathers." The chill left Buck's eyes and his mouth quirked in a wry smile. "I figured you wouldn't get what you wanted if he stayed annoyed with you."

Amy's throat tightened with dismay. How had this uneducated cowboy so easily read the situation, and how had she lost control of it? She'd let her emotions get the best of her. Hadn't she learned anything? Emotions, particularly strong ones, were her enemy, just as they'd been her mother's downfall. She had to be on her guard against them.

"Is there a problem?" Fletcher's voice cut through the silence. He rested a hand on her shoulder, hovering protectively.

Amy glanced up, and gave him a warm smile. He was just looking out for her, but there was no need to drag him into this. "We were just discussing the terms of Mr. O'Connor's employment."

Her bodyguard resumed his sprawled position, exuding disregard. "You got a problem with that, Mr. Bain?"

Fletcher's expression turned openly hostile. "As a matter of fact, I do. You don't seem to be taking these threats on Mrs. Langford's life very seriously."

Buck's eyes narrowed. "From what I saw, your interest in her well-being didn't start until she hired a bodyguard. Makes me wonder what's really got you all worked up."

"You want to know what's got me worked up?" Fletcher fisted his hands at his sides. "A *leech* attaching itself to a wealthy widow, banking on a free lunch."

Alarmed, Amy jerked to her feet. "Stop it, both of you."

With a stiff expression, Fletcher took her arm. Not wanting to make things worse, she allowed him to lead her to a seat closer to the front. Thankfully, Buck held silent.

Mr. Chanute hadn't turned around, but he couldn't have missed the heated exchange. He bowed his head and her stomach turned over. He was probably writing one of those little notes, reporting on her lack of progress, telling her boss she couldn't even manage two difficult men, much less a town full of irate settlers.

Buck nudged Goliath into a trot to keep up with the landau, which had arrived for Amy shortly after the train pulled into the station at Fort Scott. The stallion seemed in good spirits despite the two-hour ride in a cramped stall. Amy, however, wasn't near as agreeable.

She hadn't said a word or spared him a glance since that unfortunate scene on the train with her *intended*. He'd wanted to do her a favor and throw the arrogant ass out the window, but she would have fired him for sure.

At least the trip hadn't been a total waste. That detour she was so worked up about might actually work to his advantage, if he could prevent her from getting things back on track. Saints, she was a tenacious little thing, going nose-to-nose with that railroad man, who looked like he'd rather be put in a den of lions than face off with Mrs. Langford.

Buck released a low laugh. Venus sure as hell fired his anger—and his lust. Even when she'd insulted both his intelligence and his conduct, all he could think about was dragging her over that bench and into his arms. Seducing her as a form of distraction held more appeal with each passing hour.

"And it'd serve that uppity banker right," he grumbled under his breath. Amy's snooty betrothed was no better than a toothless watchdog. He'd left her to fend for herself, and then had the nerve to tell her she didn't need protection.

The carriage turned down a crowded thoroughfare. Buck hauled back on the reins to avoid colliding with a cart filled with bricks. The smell of paint and sawdust mingled with mud and manure. Pounding hammers echoed from inside an unfinished hotel looming several stories above brick buildings on either side.

Fort Scott was booming, thanks to the railroad. Was Amy's home along this busy street, or in a quieter neighborhood?

Buck kept the carriage in sight as they left the noise behind and the street began to narrow. Soon, there were fewer houses in between fields of Indian grass.

A moment later, a three-story mansion rose out of the prairie like a mirage. As with the other homes, it was mostly brick, but that was where the similarity ended. The wide front porch featured colossal white columns supporting a flat roof. Above that, more columns soared to a pitched gable. Light-colored stone formed decorative arches above the windows, and the eaves were painted with bright geometric designs. At the top, a square cupola with close-set windows gave the impression of eyes looking eastward, a watchman on alert.

Buck's mouth dropped open when the landau pulled through the gate and headed toward a carriage porch on the side of the grand manor. He'd guessed Amy had money, but he hadn't reckoned she was *that* rich. He patted the stallion's neck and huffed a laugh to ease the tightness in his chest. "What do you know, Goliath? We got ourselves hired by royalty."

Hired was right, and he'd best not forget it. Amy wouldn't have given him the time of day had he not rescued her from that storm. At his best, all he'd ever been was a merchant's apprentice with no opportunity to inherit the business from his stepfather, who already had two sons. Now, he was nothing more than a drifter with pocket change.

The driver, a nattily dressed Negro man, helped Amy down. He eyed Buck with suspicion as she paused to give instructions. She gestured with a queenly wave. "Mr. O'Connor, this is Jacob. He'll show you to your room above the carriage house. I'll see you at dinner. Seven sharp."

Buck snapped a mock salute. What did it matter if she was rich or beautiful? He wasn't here to win the hand of a prairie princess. He had to stop her from expanding her kingdom.

An hour later, he fingered damp hair into place as he strode out of the building that served as both carriage house and stables. Why the hell was he so jittery? Dinner with Amy was an unexpected boon, a perfect opportunity to discover what she was up to and map out a strategy for helping Sean.

Trailing behind the manservant, he passed through the back entrance into the house, the servant's entrance. He frowned, vexed at the snub, and more than a little disappointed by his boss's obvious intention. So, she meant to rub his nose in his own insignificance? He thought she had more class than that.

Trying to ignore the twinge in his chest, he followed his guide through a roomy kitchen. His mouth watered at the savory smells. Another servant labored over a big cast-iron stove fancier than any Buck's stepfather had carried in their store.

The woman looked up as they stopped.

"Sophie, this is Miz Amy's new...bodyguard." Jacob stumbled over the word as if it were unfamiliar—or maybe just undesirable. The strapping groomsman seemed to have taken an instant dislike to his lady's new hire.

The cook eyed him with equal disapproval. "I'll see if she's wantin' company."

Enough.

"I'll find my own way." Buck rumbled. He stormed through the pantry and banged out a door—then stopped abruptly. He'd entered what appeared to be a large dining room. Hanging from the middle of the ceiling, a huge chandelier cast a luminous circle of light that didn't quite reach the dark corners. Amy sat at the end of a table big enough to seat an army.

"Mr. O'Connor." She rose from her chair and glided towards him, her skirts swishing with a sound only silk could make. Her gown, which matched the golden lights in her eyes, showed off every luscious curve. "Why were you in the kitchen?"

Buck's heart hammered as his eyes fastened on twin mounds of creamy flesh above the fitted bodice. Mercy. He would expire if he couldn't set his lips on that smooth skin. "I, uh, came in through the back."

"The back? But I sent Jacob after you."

"That's who showed me in."

Her brows knitted. "I suppose he considered that the most direct route."

Sure he did—the most direct route for the hired hand.

Buck flushed with embarrassment. He'd scrubbed himself near raw with a cake of soap he'd found by the pump and put on a fresh shirt. But in his buckskin coat and patched trousers he looked like a bum next to this glittering beauty. "You really ought to see about getting yourself a bigger house," he quipped, throwing his arm in wide arc to deflect her attention from his wardrobe. "It's awful cramped in here."

Her lips twitched. "Yes, it is a lot of space."

She didn't elaborate on why a single lady would live in such a grand house. Of course, she wouldn't be single for long. *What a shame.*

Buck followed, strangely uncertain. He hadn't felt this awkward with a woman since he was fifteen. At the end of the table, he yanked out her chair, but resisted the urge to drop a kiss on the back of her neck. That would be moving far too fast.

He took the adjacent seat where the only other place had been set. Were just two of them eating in this palatial hall? "Where's your watchdog?"

Amy didn't crack a smile. "Fletcher had a business meeting tonight."

She lifted a tented napkin off a china plate. "On the way back, you mentioned the need to gather more information. We both need to eat, so I thought we could share a meal while we discuss your plans."

Plans? What plans? He couldn't drag his eyes away from her bare shoulders long enough to formulate his next step.

A plate clattered in front of him.

He nearly bolted from his chair before seeing it was only the servant from the kitchen. He hadn't even heard the door open because he was too focused on the treat in front of him. Hell, he'd better be more careful. He hadn't lived this long by letting himself get distracted.

"You'll like the pork shank." Amy indicated with her fork. "It's one of Sophie's best dishes."

Sophie glared at Buck before she turned to leave. *Another watchdog.* Amy seemed to have a few, but none had been able to make her feel safe. She'd turned to him for that. The thought pleased him more than it should have.

He picked up a fork and knife. "You must have quite a few servants."

Her eyes flashed with some emotion he couldn't read. "Sophie and Jacob live here. They help me with whatever needs to be done. But I wouldn't call them...servants."

What else would she call them? Buck shook his head, perplexed.

Amy's lashes lowered. She took a dainty bite of meat, leaving a spot of gravy glistening on her lip. Buck longed to lick it off. Forcing his eyes to his plate, he picked up the fork and knife and focused his attention on separating a piece of pork from the bone.

Hell, it'd been too long since he'd dined with a gently reared lady. If she noticed he was leering at her, she'd have him thrown out before he got any useful information.

"Have you lived here all your life?"

"No." She dabbed her mouth with the napkin. "When I took this job, Mr. Joy asked if I would move to where the railroad has a primary office."

Buck looked around the opulent room with its flocked walls and carved moldings. "Your boss told you to build a palace?"

The smile curving her lips somehow managed to look both seductive and shy. "This home was built right after the war by a man who moved from New York. He hoped it would convince his wife to join him, but she never came out here. He died before it was completed."

"From a broken heart, or boredom?"

This time she laughed. Just a little. "How could anyone be bored here? Our city is growing. We already have one railroad, and soon we'll have more." Her face lit with excitement as she leaned forward, affording him a better view of her ample bosom. "We'll entertain all manner of people passing through, including important dignitaries."

"So, you plan on being the city's grand dame." He drew the word out like a Frenchman, amused by her grandiose vision for the frontier cow town.

She drew back like he'd offended her. Again.

Damn, he had to stop being such an ass. He tried to smile past his discomfort. "Meant no offense."

"None taken." She took a sip of wine from the stemmed goblet beside her plate. "Perhaps I sounded ridiculous."

"Not at all. An important lady ought to have a big, impressive house."

She regarded him with arched brows as if she didn't buy his sincerity. She gestured to his full glass. "You haven't touched your wine. It's from Missouri. I think you'll be surprised by how good it is."

He curled his fingers around the stem and smiled at her unintended insult. "Surprised something good could come out of Missouri?"

She regarded him intently for a moment before answering. "I imagine you already know whether anything good can come from that state."

His face warmed. She'd flushed him out like a covey of quail. Lifted his glass, he pretending interest in the wine. Admitting he hailed from across the border would open the door to topics he didn't want to discuss. He'd just have to continue this flirtatious game and hope for the best. Taking a sip, he held her gaze. "It is good. Like most things from Missouri."

Her cheeks reddened. She took another hasty sip of wine, catching a ruby drop as it spilled down her chin.

Buck fastened his attention on his plate and fought a triumphant smile. That'd done the trick. Now she wouldn't be eager to ask questions. He stabbed a tender piece of meat, chewing slowly to allow her time to regain her composure.

"What kind of information do you need?" Her tone had returned to brisk and unemotional. She was attempting to regain control of the conversation, but he wasn't going to let her.

"Tell me a little more about your life. Your background."

"My background?" Her brow furrowed. "I'm not sure my personal history is pertinent."

"'Course it is. Your past can turn up all kinds of interesting things."

Her eyes narrowed. "Such as?"

A piece of potato lodged in his throat—he forced it down. Why had he made that idiotic remark? He cleared the remaining obstruction with a covered cough. "Oh, you know, folks with a grudge. Mistakes. Things like that."

She studied him with a keen look. "Is that why you were in Texas? Someone had a grudge against you?"

His scalp started tingling—a sure sign he was in trouble. She'd turned the tables on him, and not for the first time. If he was going to come up with a plan to stop Amy Langford, he'd better cease flirting and start paying attention. He schooled his expression into neutrality. "When you fight a war you can't help but make enemies."

"Were those enemies trying to kill you? I know of men who lost their lives to vigilantes after the war." Her eyes softened, driving a nail into his heart. That look of concern didn't mean a thing. She was just trying to get information.

"Nobody's on my tail." That much was true enough. Those who wanted him dead had probably stopped looking. For the most part, they were faces he wouldn't recognize, families he'd never met. He crossed his arms. "I thought we were going to talk about your problem, not dig up bones out of my graveyard."

She set her napkin on the table, averting her eyes. "What do you want to know?"

He exhaled a relieved breath. Finally, they could move on to a more comfortable topic. So, what did he want to know? Everything. Every damn thing about this woman fascinated him. "Why don't you start with your family?"

Amy folded her fingers around the stem of her glass, tapping lightly in a way that conveyed her restlessness. "My father was a successful lawyer...and a visionary. He wanted to see this country grow into a place where anyone could succeed based on hard work, not the color of their skin or circumstances of their birth. That's why he moved from Boston out to Kansas when I was a baby. My mother..." She paused and a look of pain flashed across her face. "My mother passed away when I was ten."

So, her father had been an abolitionist, but why would someone target Amy and why now, after the war? It didn't make sense. Buck waited for her to continue, but she seemed hesitant. Perhaps if he offered up a tidbit, something they shared in common, she would open up.

"I was ten when my father died." The words slipped out with numb indifference. That was the only feeling he'd ever been able to dredge up for his Da's violent end. It was his mother's death seven years later that left him grief-stricken and without the only anchor in his life. Even now, the loss would hit him at the oddest times.

Amy's sympathetic smile tweaked something in his chest, a tender feeling he'd forgotten. "Do you have any brothers or sisters?"

Oh, she was a sly one, trying to turn the conversation around again. If he went into all the details surrounding his stepfather's family they would never get back to her. "I was their only child. How about you?"

"The same. My father took it upon himself to educate me and bring me up like a son."

"He couldn't have been confused. You don't look anything like a son."

That garnered a flicker of amusement. "What I mean is, he gave me a great deal of freedom. When I was older, he allowed me to work alongside him on some of his ventures. He was a great leader and a wonderful mentor. Everyone loved my father, all the people who worked for him, his business associates, everyone who knew him..."

All hesitancy vanished and her face glowed as she spoke of a father figure Buck couldn't begin to imagine. Suddenly, he didn't want to hear any more about her illustrious sire. "How did you get involved with the railroad?"

"Through my father. He believed the railroad would bring prosperity for all. He called it the great equalizer. When the opportunity presented itself, he got behind the LL&G, along with Senator Lane."

Senator Lane? Bitterness burned up the back of Buck's throat. Her father's business partner was the leader of those Jayhawkers who'd burned out his family and ruined his life? He swirled the wine in the glass and kept his eyes fastened on the liquid to avoid giving away his reaction. "How did your father get tangled up with—" No, he wasn't going there. "How did you meet Mr. Joy?"

"He bought out the LL&G after Senator Lane's death. I'd been instrumental in raising funds and gaining community support, so he asked if I would promote another line that had a better chance for success."

Buck leaned back in his chair, impressed. Despite her father's bad taste in business associates, Amy had flourished.

"You got yourself hired by one of the most powerful men in the country. That's no small feat, Mrs. Langford."

Her smile staggered him like the beauty of an unexpected sunset. "Mr. Joy is a progressive thinker. Like my father."

Buck fought against a current threatening to pull him under. He couldn't afford to let himself get drawn in by a woman, no matter how beautiful. He lifted his glass. "Here's to Mr. Joy's good judgment."

She raised her goblet and finished the last of her wine. Then her expression slid into sadness. "He may not think so highly of me once he gets Mr. Chanute's latest report. We're no closer to an agreement with the settlers than we were a year ago. In fact, things have gotten worse."

That was good news as far as Buck was concerned. Still, her faltering mood threw a pall over the conversation. He stared at his still-full glass, mulling over how to return to more comfortable territory—her seduction.

He'd read the signs correctly. His ability to understand *that* kind of interest didn't trip him up. No, his worst defeats stemmed from trying to decipher more complex relationships, particularly the ones involving his heart.

He released a long breath to relieve pent-up tension. He wasn't here to get involved with anybody. He was here to help his cousin. If that included a pleasant interlude with a pretty widow as a way to distract her from her job...well, he would enjoy it while it lasted and then walk away. "So, you were telling me about yourself."

She sighed and scooted back her chair. "There's nothing more to say. If you're finished eating, we can go to the study. I've drawn up a list of suspects."

The study? Why it couldn't be more perfect. They'd be alone, out of sight of the servants. Elated, he stood and took her hand to help her stand.

Amy swayed the tiniest bit towards him, triggering a fierce hunger. He reined it in. This genteel lady wasn't trail chow. She was a fine meal to be savored. He needed to reach back—way back—to find the finesse he'd need to woo her.

Her eyes flickered with an uncertainty that belied her earlier bravado. "You mentioned people with grudges. My father was murdered before he could realize his dreams. Now, I'm afraid someone wants me dead…"

Concern rushed in, along with something else Buck refused to name. He cupped her cheek in his palm and stroked petal-soft skin with the side of his thumb. "Nobody's going to hurt you, Amy. Not on my watch."

Her eyes became dark pools of anguish. "I can't fail."

Buck wrestled with guilt. He couldn't promise she wouldn't fail. In fact, he had to make sure she would. Before he left, however, he'd find the filthy bastard who was trying to hurt her and eliminate the danger. It was the least he could do. "You said someone killed your father. Was it because they opposed the railroad?"

She blinked and a tear slid down her cheek, wetting his hand. "No, it happened during the war when we were living in Lawrence. My father was murdered by William Quantrill and those hell-spawned fiends who followed him."

CHAPTER 5

The ground shook beneath Buck's feet as his past rose up in a ghostly specter that had dogged his heels for seven years. The image wavered, and then took shape in the form of a cold-eyed raider who was dead but not forgotten. William C. Quantrill had made damn certain he'd *never* be forgotten.

Captain O'Connor, we gained justice, didn't we? Paid back the grief those Jayhawkin' abolitionists visited on our families.

Buck's gut knotted. There'd been no justice in that slaughter. It hadn't brought anyone back, hadn't righted any wrongs. In fact, it'd accomplished nothing, save turning them all into wretched outcasts whose souls were damned to hell.

He drew his hand away from Amy's cheek. She wouldn't want him touching her. On the contrary, she'd want to plunge a knife into his heart if she ever found out he had ridden into Lawrence with the Devil.

She took a step back, clearly shaken but not seeming to notice his distress. Perhaps she was too focused on her own. The vulnerable woman disappeared behind a businesslike mask. "Let's go upstairs. I'll give you my list of suspects."

Her skirts swayed as she exited through an arched doorway that led out of the dining room into a dim hall.

Buck shook off the stunned paralysis and followed her. He passed by a set of tall mirrors that caught the light from gasoliers mounted on the wall. Shadows reflected in the glass writhed like dark apparitions. He shuddered, and locked his eyes on her back as she mounted the stairs. Never had he imagined his past would come back to haunt him in the form of an irresistible woman.

Amy led him down a hall to a darkened room. She turned a knob on the wall and gas hissed, fueling a domed lamp hanging from the ceiling. Light bathed the interior and the paneled walls gleamed golden brown.

Buck hesitated at the doorway. His flesh prickled as it seemed cold fingers closed around his arms. He shook off the sensation. What the hell was wrong with him? He didn't believe in ghosts. Those were tales told by old grannies to keep children in line. Besides, her father had never lived here.

As he entered, he took a careful look around. Her study was as fancy as the other rooms he'd seen. Was that pink quartz around the fireplace? He'd only seen it once before—in a mansion. And the paneling was red oak, not pine.

On one wall, ceiling high shelves were lined with books and neatly dated business journals. Behind the desk, suspended from a picture rail, hung a large map showing a broad swath of America's midsection.

While she dug through a drawer, Buck went to take a closer look at the map, eager to focus on something other than Amy's earth-shaking revelation. He couldn't even think about that without his palms getting sweaty.

The map showed states and territories marked in capitals. From a circle labeled Fort Scott, a dozen black lines stretched out like the legs of a spider. The map's legend indicated those thick, dotted lines represented railroads. "I didn't think this town had so many connections."

Amy turned around. "Only the Border Tier is in operation. Those are proposed railroads, the ones Fort Scott plans to have running over the next five years."

Awful big ambitions for a town that was nothing more than an army outpost a few years back. But with Amy at the helm, Buck didn't doubt it could happen. A smile tugged at the corner of his mouth. "A railroad kingdom. Who's gonna rule it?"

Her lips twisted in a wry smile. "It's not a monarchy. There's opportunity for everyone."

"Even the settlers?"

"Everyone." Her mirth vanished as she closed the drawer. "We're not here to debate the validity of each side's claims. I hired you to stop whoever is trying to kill me."

Her lashes lowered and she trailed her fingers along the edge of the desk at the same time releasing a soft sigh.

A sizzle shot down Buck's spine as he imagined her fingers stroking his skin. "That's a fine piece of furniture."

"It belonged to my father."

Her words had the effect of a bucket of cold water being poured on his head. What the hell did he do now? Seducing the daughter of a man killed in a raid he'd taken part in seemed vile, even for a former bushwhacker.

But wait, he hadn't killed her father. This much he knew. Still, he'd shed plenty of blood. His soul was damned, so what was one more sin added the multitude?

"Here's the list I drew up." She extended a sheet of paper.

Their fingers brushed. At her sharp intake of breath, he met her eyes. She couldn't deny this attraction even if she wanted to.

Her hand drifted to her chest and her fingers spread like a fan over her bounty. Was he making her nervous? Or did she want him to look? She must, considering she'd picked out that dress.

"Well?" She gazed at him with an expectant look.

Well what? Oh yeah, the suspects. Buck jerked his attention to the list. "Who are these men you've named?"

"The first dozen are those I've had disagreements with, mostly business related. I listed only the ones I believe to be of an unscrupulous nature. The rest are from letters to the newspaper protesting my involvement in the railroad. I only considered ones with a threatening tone. If I wrote down the name of everyone who disapproved of me, the list would be too long to investigate."

The hurt in her eyes tugged at his heart. He masked his weakness with a mocking smile. "Not too popular with the men folk around here, are you?"

Once again, her vulnerability vanished, replaced by a professional veneer. "Let's just say I haven't been well accepted. However, wealth and connections do open a few doors. I'm part owner of a flouring mill and a coalmine, and I've invested in other ventures besides the railroad. However, I don't suspect my partners, if that's where you're going. They need my continued support too much to do away with me."

He held his face still to contain his astonishment. Beautiful, smart, rich *and* successful—the list kept growing. He'd better tread carefully so he didn't end up being the one deceived. "Could it be somebody inside? Do any of your railroad pals want your job?"

She sighed and shook her head. "I don't know of anyone who wants my job, especially now. The only insiders who'd care have always been supportive, if for no other reason than their boss hired me. They're loyal to Mr. Joy."

Buck ticked through a list in his mind. "What about those two downstairs?"

She barked a laugh. "Sophie and Jacob? Never."

It wasn't so far-fetched. "Do you plan to leave them money?"

"I do, but—"

"I knew of a slave once who was going be granted freedom after his master's death. He just hurried it along."

"Let me finish," she snapped. "Sophie was freed during one of Mr. Lane's raids into Missouri. My father took her in, gave her a job, taught her how to read and write. She raised me after my mother's death. Sophie wouldn't hurt me for all the money in the world. And Jacob was shot trying to defend me during Quantrill's raid. They don't just work for me, they're the only family I have left, and I won't stand here and let you insult them—"

"Whoa. Slow down." Buck cupped her shoulders in his hands. "I'm not insulting anybody, but you got to look everywhere, not just in the obvious places."

She shrugged off his touch, but not before he'd felt a shiver. "What you said might make sense in some cases, but I refuse to believe two of the dearest people in the world would ever wish me harm, much less cause it. Especially after the atrocities we suffered."

Buck's jaw tightened. She wasn't the only one who'd suffered *atrocities*. "Your friend Senator Lane did more than just free slaves when he rode into Missouri."

Amy frowned up at him, seeming confused by the abrupt change of subject. Then, understanding dawned in her eyes. "Was your family one of those who...?"

She didn't finish the thought, but rested her fingers lightly on his arm. Her touch drained his anger like she'd opened a festering sore.

He blinked down at her, thrown off balance. Why the hell had he opened that closet? He couldn't manage any more skeletons—his or hers. "Never mind. We're here to talk about who's trying to kill you."

"Did you lose someone dear to you in those raids?" The sadness in her eyes drew him in, but he resisted the temptation to spill his guts. If she knew the truth of who he was, sympathy would be the last thing she'd feel.

Steeling himself, he held up the list. "Have you shown this to anyone else?"

She searched his face. God help him if she could read anything in his expression. To his relief, her gaze shifted to the upheld paper. "No. I did seek out the sheriff earlier when I became convinced someone meant me harm, but he treated me like an overwrought child seeing a bogeyman around every corner."

How could anyone spend five minutes with Amy and think she was given to imagining things? "What about Fletch?"

"Fletch? Oh, you mean Mr. Bain? He suggested we get married. The way he sees it, if we're properly wed and I'm under his protection, it will silence a great many of my critics."

Buck clenched his jaw, fighting an unnerving surge of jealousy. "He ought to be out there making sure you're safe, whether or not you've said your vows."

Gratitude shone in her eyes.

He nearly dropped to one knee to pledge his undying devotion, but warnings clanged in his head. He'd tried that hero thing before. Bad idea.

"Fletcher isn't ignoring these threats, but until today, I think he believed the accidents were only pranks meant to frighten me."

Why was she defending that arrogant asshole?

"Someone tampering with your buggy isn't frightening. It's deadly."

"As I said, he's revised his theory." She gave a long sigh. "He is correct, though. Marriage will make me more...acceptable."

Hell, Amy was far superior to that pompous airbag. Any man fortunate enough to win her hand would be respected and admired. Buck stuffed the list into an inside pocket. "Mind if I keep this?"

"Not at all. I can always retrieve it if I decide to bring in the cavalry."

"They're not billeted in the stables?"

The beginning of an amused smile faltered. "Honestly, I haven't raised the alarm because I was worried Mr. Joy might decide he wasn't willing to put up with bad publicity. There's too much ill will already."

The worry in her eyes rankled him. Did no one care what happened to her?

"No, I reckon you wouldn't want to bother the great Mr. Joy with some little problem like threats on your life."

Her fretful expression relaxed in a smile, letting her soft, sultry beauty shine through. "But I've got you now to take care of it."

"That's right. You got me now." His blood heated. Was it so wrong to ignite this passion between them? Amy was a widow, not some untried virgin. She had enough experience to know where this was leading, and she needn't ever find out about his past. Buck stuffed his guilt back into the lockbox that held his conscience and drew closer.

Amy's pulse raced as her bodyguard loomed over her. Lord, he was tall, though that didn't begin to describe him.

There was something about him that made him seem larger than life, like one of those heroes in Beadle's dime novels. His presence filled a room when he entered it. He commanded attention, and he certainly had hers now.

She'd hoped a cozy dinner would loosen his tongue and she could get more information about his background, thus satisfying Fletcher's concerns and some of her own misgivings. Instead, her wily bodyguard had deflected the conversation away from himself and back to her. He was a puzzle, and she'd always loved puzzles. Perhaps that's why he fascinated her.

Recovering her voice, she asked, "What more do you need?"

A predatory gleam lit his eyes, along with a smoldering sensuality that stole what little air remained in her lungs. "Seeing as I'm your bodyguard, I'll need to stick close."

Her heart rapped a distress signal. What had possessed her to invite this hunter into her lair? She squared her shoulders and met his eyes in an attempt to remain in charge. "You may go with me tomorrow, so long as you remain in the background. After breakfast I have a meeting, and then I'll need to stop by a dress shop...." Her words trailed off as he leaned over.

She caught his scent and nearly swooned. Did leather and lye soap contain some sort of aphrodisiac?

He paused, just a heartbeat, before his hand cupped the back of her head and he brushed his lips against hers in a titillating invitation.

A debate ricocheted through her head. This wasn't right. But it felt good. She was nearly engaged. Not yet. Buck was the wrong man. But Fletcher couldn't hold a candle to the bonfire stoked by this rough Missourian.

His soft mustache tickled and teased, sending shivers dancing across her skin. A moan slipped out of some needy place deep inside. He slanted his mouth and molded his lips to hers.

At the lush pressure, her head grew light. Had he not been holding her, she would have sworn she'd stepped off a cliff.

His large hands, which had warmed her when she was frozen, now caught her up, lifting her until her toes barely touched the floor.

Admonitions echoed, a distant thunder. She ignored them, circling his neck with her arms, threading her fingers through the thickness of his hair, combing through it as she'd imagined doing in a wicked fantasy.

Rumbles rolled up from his chest and he lifted her higher. One arm wrapped like a steel band around her middle, while his other hand gripped her hair. The overpowering hold would've frightened her if his kiss hadn't gentled.

He nibbled at her lips, tasting them, probing the seam. With a delicious shiver, she gave him entry. The sensuous slide of his tongue against hers made every nerve spring to life. She gripped his hair as her body hummed with restless energy. He seemed to sense her need and began to meet it with bold, confident strokes.

Other men, other kisses, all faded into a bland memory. Nothing had prepared her for this…this taking. It should have terrified her. Instead a thrill shot through her at his domination, as she sensed it was her power that fed it.

"So sweet," he murmured as he trailed kisses across her cheek. With the tip of his tongue, he traced the curve of her ear. Then he nipped the soft lobe, making her gasp with pleasure. He burned a path down the column of her throat. With both hands, he lifted her higher, nuzzling the cleft between her breasts. Her nipples tightened into rigid knots that ached for his touch.

She trembled, waiting…wanting. "Please."

He raised his head. In his eyes, passion burned like blue flames. "Please what?"

No, she couldn't say it, couldn't admit to wanting him because it would mean she was no better than her mother.

When she didn't answer, he went back to kissing her quivering flesh.

The passionate storm grew stronger, becoming frightening in its intensity. Savage winds tore at her moorings, threatening to rip away the last of her resistance. Desire gripped her. Her body ached, and her need became the only thing that mattered.

From a dark corner of her mind, a memory taunted: her father's grief-stricken cries, her mother's face, twisted in agony, pale as a wraith, both of them victims of the indiscriminate ravages of unfettered passion.

Amy stiffened with alarm. What was she doing in this man's arms? She put her hands against his shoulders but it was like pushing at a boulder. Panic bubbled up, bursting out in senseless noises. She struggled, unable to break free. Oh God, she had to escape.

"No! Let go. You...you *beast.*"

Buck froze in an instant. He blinked furiously, fighting to regain control of his body in spite of the mind-numbing lust. *Beast?* Had he heard right? The insistent throbbing in his groin made it impossible to think clearly. He lowered her to the floor, carefully setting her on her feet.

Her chest heaved as she panted. She backed away, and humiliation shone through the tears welling in her eyes.

Confusion swamped him, along with a more uncomfortable feeling. He couldn't have misread the looks she'd given him earlier. She wanted him—at least for a time she had. Perhaps he'd scared her when he lifted her off her feet so he could more easily reach her treasures. He hadn't realized she was struggling to get away, had thought those noises she was making were sounds of pleasure. If he'd known she had doubts, he wouldn't have taken advantage.

His conscience mocked him. Who was he kidding? If she hadn't cried out, he would have taken her. Probably right there on that desk. Would've tossed up her skirts and buried himself to the hilt. The crude thought teased his weakened mind a second before guilt ballooned in his chest. Stricken, he reached out. "I'm sor—"

What could he say? That he was sorry? True enough, he was a sorry son-of-a-bitch, having had plenty of practice over the years. But he hadn't meant to...hadn't thought...would never.... "I would never hurt you."

"Go away." She hunched over like she was trying to curl into a ball. "Just go away."

Her agonized plea cut into him, slicing open what was left of his shriveled heart.

He fled the house, debating whether he ought to go back to his room over the carriage house, or saddle his horse and ride like hell.

Amy stumbled into her bedroom. She slammed the door on the firestorm of passion she'd ignited through her own foolishness. Trembling, she listened for the sounds of Buck's footsteps, which had fallen heavy on the stairs moments after she'd rebuffed him.

There was only silence. He must have let himself out.

Relieved, she pressed a hand to her heaving chest. Thank the Lord he hadn't pressed her. For a moment, she thought he might.

An inner voice chided. Nothing in his actions had indicated he would've forced himself on her. So why had she called him a beast? It was *her* fault this had happened in the first place. She could've stopped him when he'd hesitated in that brief moment before he kissed her. But she hadn't. Instead, she'd fallen prey to passion's lure and had nearly thrown away her future to taste forbidden fruit.

Just like her mother.

With a groan of self-loathing, she threw herself across the bed, letting the tears flow. With any luck, they would douse the fire that still licked at her body. God help her. She couldn't be like her mother—controlled by a wild, ardent nature that had wrecked a marriage and devastated a family. But passion was like that. It devoured the body and destroyed the soul. She was better off without it, and most definitely better off without a rough character like Buck, no matter how competent he appeared.

Her conscience pricked. That wasn't a fair assessment. Buck hadn't been rough. *Oh, no.* He'd treated her with tenderness, even as his touch set her ablaze. His evasiveness still bothered her, but like many men, he probably just wanted to put the war behind him. More than likely, he was exactly what he appeared to be—a drifter without a dime to his name, but caring enough to brave a storm to rescue her. Unfortunately, he was also, very clearly, a libertine, and not at all the kind of man she needed in her life.

A sharp rap on the door brought her up on her arms.

"Miz Amy? You need help gettin' undressed?"

Sophie.

Amy swiped at her face with the back of her hands. She swallowed to staunch tears that seemed to be gushing up from some endless spring. This wouldn't have happened if she hadn't hired Buck. She would release him first thing in the morning and be rid of a temptation that would lead her down the road to ruin.

"Just a minute," she called, wiping her nose with a handkerchief. She turned the gas tap to extinguish the lamp until the only light came from the fireplace, hidden behind an embroidered screen. The darker the room, the less likely Sophie would notice her reddened eyes and nose and begin to fret.

When she opened the door, the housekeeper swept in with a tray containing a mug of warm milk sweetened with honey, Sophie's secret for a restful sleep. Tonight, not even a bath in warm milk would help.

Sophie set the tray on the bedside table. "That bodyguard of your'n took out like a pack o' hounds was at his heels."

"We'd concluded our business." Amy turned, letting Sophie undo the buttons down the back of her gown. "I'm sure he was ready to seek the bed."

Her remark was met with silence. Amy's face warmed when she realized what she'd said. He'd been ready to seek a bed, all right. Hers.

Sophie unlaced the corset and Amy breathed deeply for the first time that day. She wouldn't wear the tortuous device if it weren't for the dictates of fashion. She'd already defied convention about as much she dared and didn't want to risk alienating her colleagues.

The remaining layers were peeled off and she slipped into her nightgown.

"Did that man hurt you?" The gentle touch on her shoulder nearly undid her.

She couldn't bear to share her humiliation, but it would be wrong to allow Sophie to think Buck had molested her. She'd all but invited his attentions, starting with that ill-conceived notion of dining alone with him. What had she been thinking?

She turned with a forced smile. "I'm fine. No need to worry."

Sophie's black brows drew down with concern. "Child, don' you let him—or any man—take advantage of your sweet nature."

Sweet? That wasn't a term Amy typically heard used to describe her. Hardheaded, driven, ambitious, perhaps, but not sweet.

"You needn't worry about Mr. O'Connor. I'll be sending him on his way tomorrow." She crawled into bed and pulled the covers up to her chin.

The mattress sank as Sophie sat beside her. "Hmm. And that evil man what's been following you, what you gonna do 'bout him?"

Amy's stomach twisted. For a brief time, she'd felt safe knowing Buck would be protecting her. Now what should she do? She scooted up against the headboard and draped her arms over her drawn-up knees. "I could go to Major Roy and ask for military protection, except the army has its hands full. I suppose I could seek out the sheriff, although he's not going to be convinced I'm in danger until someone pulls a gun on me in the middle of Main Street."

Her throat tightened. The options were slim. "Fletcher suggests we get married."

"That's gonna stop whoever's after you?" The incredulity in Sophie's voice made Amy wince. She didn't buy the argument, either.

It wasn't her marital status that had men up in arms. It was her insistence on being part of their world, and that wasn't going to change just because she married. "It might help, but that's not why I've decided to marry him. It's time I married, for respectability if nothing else."

Sophie arched her eyebrows.

"Don't look at me like that. I have good reasons for choosing Fletcher." Amy raised her chin, defying Sophie to disagree. "He's educated, erudite, a man of business, exactly the kind of husband I need."

Wasn't her friendship with Fletcher over the past three years evidence enough they would have a companionable marriage? It might not be a passionate love match, but that fiasco with Buck proved passion was the last thing she needed.

"I hear what you say, but I's thinking your Mr. Bain ain't gonna know how to keep you safe. That other one, though…" Sophie shook her head. "He just plain scares me."

She wasn't the only one scared.

Amy sank beneath the covers. Tomorrow, her bodyguard had to go.

CHAPTER 6

March 3, 1870, Fort Scott, Kansas

The plank floor creaked as Buck strode to the washstand in the corner of his room above the stables. He'd cleaned up this morning, but he still wasn't sure he was ready to face his new employer, the woman he'd tried to seduce—and failed.

He bent his knees to bring his head level with a small mirror hanging on the wall. Dipping his fingers into the basin, he used water to tame his hair into some semblance of order. If she paid him that advance she'd promised, he'd be able to get a haircut and a shave. Maybe then he wouldn't look so scary.

What had gone wrong? He'd asked himself that question at least a dozen times. Amy had wanted that kiss. All the signs were there. But then, she'd called him— *Beast.* His chest tightened with familiar dread. He turned away from his scowling reflection and began to pace. Ironic, and more than a little disturbing, that Georgia had used the same epitaph, right before she'd walked out of his life for good.

Damn it, he wasn't a brute like his father. He'd tried to make up for the wrongs he'd done. He'd released Georgia from her vow, helped her free the man she loved, sent himself into exile and even laid down his guns—until his family called for help.

Buck went to the window, staring out at the empty yard below. He had to remember why he was here, to distract Amy and slow down her railroad. Only, he wasn't feeling so good about carrying through with his planned seduction. He'd just have to find another way to give his cousin a shot at justice.

Justice, not revenge. Not like Lawrence. Stopping a railroad wasn't murdering innocents, and even if he had to deceive Amy, he could still protect her from whoever was trying to kill her.

He grabbed his coat from the peg by the door and dug out the list she'd given him, scanning the names and locking them in his mind. With a deep breath, he released the last of his misgivings. Keeping her safe might not erase his sins, but it had to count for something.

She'd be leaving soon for that meeting and he needed to tag along so he could keep an eye on her. Not only that, he needed information in order to come up with a plan for distracting the troops who guarded the railroad, so Sean's men could burn up track.

A few minutes later, he stood in the yard holding Goliath's reins and waiting for his employer to finish tugging on her gloves—a task that was taking far too long in his estimation. For some reason, she'd come out back, rather than being picked up at the side entrance. Her ensemble this morning included a buttoned-to-the-chin dark blue jacket that covered up far too much of her creamy skin. Disappointing, but probably for the best.

"Good morning, Mr. O'Connor." She tilted her head, bobbing the feather attached to the side of a little hat that didn't appear to serve much purpose—except to remind him to remove his.

"Mrs. Langford." He kept his tone respectful.

As she approached, he spied shadows under her eyes. Had she been so upset with him she couldn't sleep? That wasn't an encouraging thought.

He rubbed his thumb across his hatband, encountering a silver brooch that had belonged to his mother. The reminder touched off memories of her admonitions about gentlemanly behavior. He jerked his thumb away and replaced his hat to shield his eyes.

Amy had to lift her chin to look up at him. "Mr. O'Connor, I've decided to release you from your duties. I shall pay you for your trouble, of course."

Buck blinked in surprise. She was firing him over one little kiss? She'd all but asked for it, even if she had changed her mind after the fact. He clenched his teeth to keep from bellowing an objection. This was *his* fault, not hers.

She fumbled with her bag and drew out a roll of bills.

Unbelievable. Did she think to pay him off so she could rid herself of the embarrassment of having to deal with her attraction to him? Not in a million years would he take that money. His pride demanded he call her bluff, but a sensible voice urged a calmer approach.

He arranged his features in an appropriately apologetic expression. "Mrs. Langford, I understand why you'd want to fire me. But I haven't upheld my end of the bargain. And I don't break my vows."

"Yes, well, I appreciate your desire to keep your word, however you must realize this...arrangement won't work." Her eyes dropped level with his chest, her distress telegraphed over some invisible wire stretched between them.

He refused to analyze the strange connection. The only thing he cared about was keeping this job. Otherwise, he'd have to start over and there wasn't time. If that railroad reached the border without resolving its issues with the settlers, Sean could kiss his land goodbye.

"Amy..." No, not so familiar, or she'd harden in her resolve. "Mrs. Langford. I won't take advantage again. Let me stay. Just until I'm sure you're safe."

She lifted her gaze. Uncertainty flickered in the amber depths. Buck could see she wanted to believe him, wanted to trust him. His heart hammered against the breastworks he'd erected around it. What she thought about him after all this was over didn't matter. Right now, he had to coerce her, hold what little ground he'd captured by remaining in her inner circle.

"Please, give me a chance to find this man who's threatening you." Did it sound like he was begging? He wasn't. He never begged. Not since the day his hand had been thrust into a fire.

Tears glistened in her eyes.

Something tore at him. *Regret?* But he was doing the right thing, keeping her safe while getting justice for Sean. He didn't have to choose. He could do both.

She ventured closer and stuffed the roll of greenbacks into his coat pocket.

He gripped her wrist. "I don't want to fail any more than you do."

Her eyes grew wide. It struck him it wasn't fear he was seeing, so much as cautious yearning. A barrage of emotions exploded in his chest. He released her like a hot coal.

"Why?" she whispered. "Why do you care?"

He dared not mine his heart too deeply for that answer. Keeping her safe represented a kind of absolution, but how could he explain without revealing himself and facing consequences he was desperate to avoid?

"I owe a debt. This is the only way I know how to repay it."

A blinding sun warmed the chilly air. Peering up at a cloudless sky, Amy wondered if she'd dreamt the ice storm. But no, Buck stood by the carriage, as solid and real as the bustling city coming to life around them.

She held out her hand so he could assist her down. He ignored it and instead gripped her waist, lifting her up and over the foul-smelling mud to set her on the walkway in front of the railroad offices.

Her body tingled even after he'd let go. Was she a fool to give him a second chance? She rarely backed down from a decision, but her resolve crumbled the moment she'd looked into his eyes and seen some desperate need.

What debt did he owe, and how did helping her relieve him of it? She didn't understand, but what was done was done. At least she'd gained his agreement to keep an appropriate distance. If he broke his word, she would fire him without a second thought.

"I'll pull the carriage around and pay someone to watch it, then meet you inside." Buck hopped back onto the seat.

With an absent wave, she hurried toward the double doors, her mind focused on the problem awaiting her inside. The railroad directors were voting on whether to continue supporting the Young Ladies' Immigration Society. She had to ensure they would keep funding it so the program would have a chance to succeed.

Not nearly enough settlers had signed up, but a picnic would take care of that. The idea had come to her just this morning. What better way to welcome the new arrivals? And the young women could prepare picnic baskets that the men could bid on, which would generate interest and excitement. Churches did this all the time and it worked like magic. There would be weddings in no time, and the settlers' riots would be a thing of the past.

Her nerves jumped as her bodyguard strode up beside her. My, he moved fast.

Buck removed his hat, threading his fingers through thick blond hair. Amy tightened her grip on her reticule as she recalled the surprising softness of those wavy tresses. Gracious, she'd loved touching them. But she wouldn't be touching any part of him again.

She eyed him as they walked in silence up the stairs. His hair looked clean but untidy, always falling in his face if he wasn't wearing his hat. From the look of it, he'd put on last night's shirt. And that buckskin coat, with its ragged fringes and numerous repairs, had seen better days. On the gun belt slung low on his hips, twin revolvers hung out of holsters shiny with wear. His knife wasn't in plain view, but she suspected it wasn't far from reach. Great days, he looked like an outlaw. She couldn't let him accompany her into the boardroom.

"Why don't you wait here in the hallway?" She gestured to a bench shoved up against the wall. "It might make the directors nervous to know I've hired a bodyguard."

He arched an eyebrow. "You think they don't know? That kind of news tends to get around fast."

This would be a short reprieve if he thought to gain an explanation for every directive.

"I don't want them to feel threatened. I need their support."

"It wouldn't hurt to show you won't be intimidated." Buck eyed the door. "Any of those fellows on your list?"

"One, but I only included him because he so adamantly objected to my appointment by Mr. Joy. I don't really believe he'd resort to violence in a public meeting."

"Better to be safe."

She pinned him with her most authoritative glare. "This is a very important meeting and I cannot afford to alienate these men. Now, wait out here. We'll be done in an hour."

As she reached for the decorative brass knob, he grabbed it first and threw open the heavy door. She drew a deep breath to calm an anxious flutter in her chest and stepped inside.

The railroad directors, including several of Fort Scott's most influential businessmen, were seated strategically around an oval table, with the president anchoring one end and the chief engineer positioned at the other. They all rose as she entered the room.

She nodded a greeting, and held her head high. Any sign of weakness and her latest program would fall victim to the axe they wielded with frustrating regularity. Her smile faltered as every eye fixed on something behind her.

Ice water pooled in her stomach. She knew what she'd see even before she cast a glance over her shoulder. Her bodyguard. He'd planted himself in front of the closed door, feet braced with his hands folded behind him.

She twisted the cords of her bag around her fingers. By heaven, she wanted to wrap them around Buck's neck. Why couldn't this gun-toting rowdy do as he was told?

He met her eyes with an impassive expression. If she ordered him out now, it would draw more attention. He could stay—she narrowed her eyes in warning—but he'd better keep his mouth shut. At least he had the good sense to pull his coat over those Colts.

She whipped her head around, forcing a pleasant expression. "Good morning."

One man moved to pull out a chair. As she adjusted her skirts to sit, a horrid gurgling sounded. Her face fired up like a furnace. Why did her stomach have to announce her jitters?

"Morning, Mrs. Langford." Charlie Goodlander accompanied his greeting with a friendly nod. His lips were barely visible beneath the walrus mustache, but his blue eyes twinkled with undisguised mirth. "Would you like to introduce us to your, uh, escort?"

No, she would not. "This is Mr. O'Connor. I brought him along for...additional security."

"Are you feeling threatened by someone in this room?" The president's bushy brows gathered in a stormy frown and her insides quivered. The last thing she needed was to offend Kersey Coates. The man was far too influential.

She paused to compose a proper response. "Of course not, I..."

"Mrs. Langford wants to put your minds at ease after those attempts on her life."

Her head swiveled around. What did Buck think he was doing answering for her?

"She asked me along so you gentlemen won't feel obliged to withhold your support because you fear she might come to harm." He crossed his arms, his flinty gaze moving from man to man, as if daring them to object.

Dread trickled down her spine. With that attitude, he was going to get her booted from the meeting. She smoothed her features, not wanting the board to think she wasn't in complete control, and addressed the president. "This is only a precaution on my part. A statement, if you will, that I'll not be intimidated by bullies."

"Well, I, for one, am glad you've taken steps to ensure your safety. We were concerned when we heard about your troubles." Her friend Charlie, who owned the local lumberyard amongst other businesses, leaned back in his chair and pressed his lips tight. Was it to keep from laughing? Only he would find something like this funny.

The other men nodded, all except for Mr. Chanute. His face remained an inscrutable mask. Had the chief engineer written to Mr. Joy about her *troubles*? She hadn't alerted her boss because she hoped to have the issue resolved before his planned visit in May.

The president cleared his throat, breaking the awkward silence. He braced his arms on the table. "All right, then. Let's get down to business."

An hour later, Amy longed for a cold rag to put on her aching head. The board had been arguing nonstop about the best way to compel settlers to pay the price set by the railroad for land they were squatting on. Land rightfully owned by James Joy, but claimed by the settlers under the old pre-emption rights. Some of the board members wanted to ask the government for more soldiers to protect the railroad against further vandalism and disruption. The presence of troops had already caused numerous clashes and bloodshed. Couldn't they see strong-arm tactics weren't working?

She tapped her fingers on the table to gain their attention. "More troops won't compel these former soldiers to cooperate. The lure of home and family will convert them faster than guns. We need to bring more eligible young ladies out west."

Around the table, heads nodded. Most of the directors appeared to be in agreement, or at least willing to give her the benefit of the doubt. She'd invested significant time and resources gaining the support of these local businessmen. Might as well strike while the iron was hot.

"Why don't we vote on the motion to increase funding for the immigration society?"

"Proper protocol should be observed. Does the president wish to ask for a motion?" Mr. Chanute had finally spoken up—to call her down. "Personally, I don't believe another trainload of women will buy us an ounce of cooperation. Didn't you tell me just the other day that only a handful of settlers have shown any interest? More troops are needed."

"I disagree. This immigration effort *will* work. We just need to draw more attention to the program." She drew herself up, projecting as much authority as possible for a woman in a room filled with men. "I've personally sponsored twelve young ladies who will arrive next week. What better way to generate excitement than a picnic? We'll hold a rally beforehand and the men can bid on the baskets of the women they want to get to know better. Marriages will follow and agreements can be made. The settlers pay the asking price for the land they want and the railroad covers the cost of bringing them wives. It's good for all concerned."

"Pardon me, Mrs. Langford, but that sounds like pure balderdash." The president leaned back in his chair with an air of disdain. "These settlers are up in arms, and you think a *picnic* is going to appease them? I think we've given this little diversion of yours all the attention it deserves."

Amy seethed. Why did Mr. Coates never express an opinion until he was certain of where Mr. Chanute was headed?

"You fellows just spent the better part of an hour backing and filling and you still can't agree on how to dot your i's. Might as well give Mrs. Langford's idea a chance."

Her eyes widened at the familiar voice from behind, and all heads turned—including hers. Buck met their incredulous stares with a challenging gaze. Did the man never back down?

Deep inside, respect flickered and gratitude lit like fire on dry kindling. She should be furious with him for interrupting again. But instead, his defense warmed her to her toes.

Charlie Goodlander was the first to recover. Was that a wink, or had she imagined it? "I agree with Mrs. Langford's assistant. There's no reason we shouldn't have that picnic rally."

The other men turned to Mr. Chanute. They all knew Kersey Coates was little more than a figurehead. It would be Mr. Joy's trusted advisor who made the final call.

Octave Chanute gave a dignified nod. "Mr. Joy would certainly have no objection to a picnic, so long as it doesn't dissolve into a brawl, which is how most gatherings in the

Neutral Lands have tended to go. Should that happen—" His dark eyes met hers. "I can assure you he will look most unkindly on the person responsible."

CHAPTER 7

Buck slowed his strides to match the pace of Amy's shorter steps. He could hardly hear her over the rumbling coming from a long line of covered wagons thundering down Market Street. Probably a good thing he couldn't make out what she was saying. His ears would be burning for sure.

He'd known full well Amy would be choleric when he followed her into that meeting. But he had to make up his own mind about whether any of those men represented a threat. He'd also hoped to learn how to slow down the relentless advance of her railroad. Her picnic basket plan had given him an idea. First, however, she had to be convinced she was taking those women into a lion's den.

The noise of traffic faded for a moment and her voice cut through. "While I appreciate your desire to help, I can't afford to be seen as weak." She bit off the last word like it offended her. "Not if I am to hold my own against these men in business dealings."

He rolled his lips between his teeth to keep from smiling. Her tirade made him want to kiss her again, if for no other reason than to shut her up. Amy's anger might be directed at him, but its source stemmed from what had happened in that room. She'd won over every man except the one that mattered most, the chief engineer she'd called Mr. Joy's right hand. Was it possible Octave Chunute had hired someone to scare her away?

Buck's gaze swept across open windows, up to an uneven line of flat and pitched roofs, and then down to the busy street and crowded walkway. There were so many people swarming around he would have to keep a sharp lookout for potential threats.

A bearded man in paisley trousers stopped and lifted his hat as Amy passed by. The fellow leered at her backside, until he looked up and met Buck's warning glare. Then he wisely hurried away.

She lifted her skirts to step off the boardwalk.

Buck leapt into the street and scooped her up before her feet could sink into the mud. The wide, gooey ruts, created by a combination of last night's rain and heavy wagon wheels, would swallow this petite morsel in one gulp.

Amy shoved at his chest. "Stop toting me like a package!"

For a moment, he was tempted to drop her, but he tightened his hold instead. He dodged a flatbed piled with hay, sidestepped pungent piles of manure, and finally set her on the opposite sidewalk. "No sense messing up that dress, unless you're wanting it in a different color."

Her eyes flashed. "I am fed up with you thinking you know better in every situation. You are not my keeper. You're my bodyguard. *If* I allow you to continue in that role. But you are dearly taxing my patience. That meeting could have gone disastrously because of your interference."

Interference? Hell, he'd rescued her twice when those men would've sent her packing. He planted his fists on his hips. "I know you think I don't have half a brain but—"

"I'll concede three-quarters."

His anger dissolved. Damn, if she didn't provoke and amuse the hell out of him, all at the same time. "Stop chewing on me for a minute and let me explain. I followed you in there because I needed to get a feel for whether any of those men mean you harm. I can't do that by looking at a list. I got to rely on my instincts. You'll have to trust me."

Her brow smoothed, but he could see aggravation simmering beneath the surface. "All right. However, you can't go around inserting your opinion into every discussion."

"No matter the merit?"

With a roll of her eyes, she turned sharply and started up the sidewalk, her heels tapping a rapid beat. He trailed a half step behind, passing beneath signboards announcing drugs, shoes, and every conceivable service one might need.

He gave her a few minutes to cool down before casting his lure. "Have you thought about how to protect those women you're taking down to Girard?"

Her steps slowed. "What do you mean?"

"There's bound to be a lot of settlers coming in for that rally once word gets out. Men lose their good sense when they haven't been around women for a long time." Buck came up alongside her and tucked her hand protectively into the crook of his arm. "Having twelve pretty ladies up there while those fellows bid for their baskets... Well, things could get out of hand."

She furrowed her brow, looking worried. "What do you suggest?"

Buck pursed his lips like he hadn't fully considered the problem even though he had the answer worked out long before he posed the question. "Maybe you should ask that major if his troops would keep the peace. Can't imagine he wouldn't oblige."

"I'm not sure it's a good idea to take the soldiers away from their duties so they can stand guard at a picnic. They're here to protect the railroad."

Buck tossed out the bait. "Mr. Chanute seemed concerned those settlers might get rowdy. That's not going to make you look good to Mr. Joy."

Amy nibbled her lip and he could almost see her mind circling the suggestion. "Let me think about it."

He straightened, smiling. The hook was set. Now he'd bring her in, nice and slow, so she wouldn't slip away. This picnic rally would make a perfect distraction for the soldiers, so Sean's men could get to those ties. Once they burned them up, construction would halt and the railroad would be pressured to sweeten the deal they were offering. How simple could it be?

A cold wind whirled down the street. Amy drew a paisley shawl tighter around her shoulders. Why had she brought that fancy little napkin instead of a heavy cape?

Buck shrugged out of his coat and wrapped it around her.

"Thank you," she murmured.

They walked along in companionable silence, her head bobbing by his shoulder. She was a little thing, but her personality made up for what she lacked in height. He'd always appreciated petite women. Only, Amy wasn't fragile like some of them. She had a curvy fullness he could explore without worrying he might break her.

He studied her face, now scrunched in thought. "Is something wrong?"

"Do you think this rally is a good idea? Most of the directors seemed convinced, but not Mr. Chanute."

"I reckon it's fine." Fine enough to be a distraction. He had no idea whether any of the settlers would be desperate enough to pay her price, no matter that a woman might be attached.

She sighed. "Perhaps my argument wasn't effective. What might I have said differently?"

Buck arched his brows in surprise. She was asking *his* opinion? Wonders never ceased. His heart warmed at the small show of trust. There was no reason he couldn't help her in her dealings with these businessmen. "It wasn't what you were saying, so much as how you were acting. You were challenging them. Men don't like that in a woman. You need to use your advantage."

She regarded him doubtfully. "Flirting doesn't work. Men won't take you seriously."

"That's not what I meant." He pulled her aside to let the traffic pass, then put his hands on her shoulders and looked pointedly at her uninspiring outfit. "Take that jacket, for instance. It's nice and obviously expensive, but it's boring. If you'd worn something a little bolder and sashayed into that room like you owned it, you would've had every one of those men eating out of your hands."

Glancing around, she lowered her voice. "I think I understand what you're saying, but that kind of dress is inappropriate for day wear."

"No, I'm not talking about a dress like that one you wore last night."

Her eyes flashed up. "What are you insinuating?"

"Nothing." He threw his hands up. "That's a fine dress, nothing wrong with it, a real pretty dress." But she'd better not wear it to a business meeting. He'd end up having to kill somebody. "What I'm saying is, don't work so hard at fitting in with the men. Don't fight on their terms. Exploit their weaknesses. If they're thinking how pretty you look, they won't be paying attention to how smart you are."

Her brows drew down. "I don't know. I've never been comfortable with my.... I mean, I don't like using those sorts of tricks."

"I'm not suggesting you do anything unladylike. But you're at a disadvantage in a man's world. Use the weapons you've got."

She looked at him through her lashes. "You make it sound like war."

His mouth went dry. Who was it that said something about beauty launching ships? Amy's lovely face and voluptuous form could sink a fleet. If she learned how to harness her power, she would be unstoppable. Uneasy, he shook his head. "Those are the only terms I can think of for how to explain it. But what do I know about business?"

He held his breath as she regarded him a moment longer. Finally, she nodded, allowing him to tuck her hand over his arm as they set off. God help him if she figured out how to use his own advice against him. He was far too susceptible already.

She stopped in front of a large window embellished with a flourishing script that announced it as the best store to find the latest fashions—probably not a dangerous place. "I need to pick up a dress I ordered."

Her eyes drifted over him and she knitted her brow. "There's a barber next door. Why don't you go visit him? I don't want my business associates to think I've hired a border ruffian."

Buck stiffened. She'd sure put him in his place. He didn't need to worry about her susceptibility.

Amy turned the page of a well-used copy of Godey's Ladies Handbook and feasted her eyes on the latest designs by Charles Worth. With her fingertip, she traced a picture of the lemon and cream gown she'd ordered. The scooping neckline and fitted bodice would be something Buck would appreciate. Not that she cared. Fletcher's likes and dislikes were more important, considering he would soon be her husband. She would focus her thoughts on him and tame this unruly passion for the wrong man.

Maggie swept out of the back room and set a box on the counter. "Your dress, all wrapped up and ready to go. I have no doubts you'll send all the ladies rushing out to order one just like it when you wear this to the Wilson's dinner party."

Perhaps. However, Maggie could start a stampede. That lavender day dress perfectly complemented her raven hair and lithesome figure. She certainly had the form for fashion setting, just not the fortune.

Amy's conscience chided. What right did she have to be envious? Maggie was a dear, and didn't have a malicious bone in her body. She was as beautiful inside as out, which wasn't something Amy could say about herself at the moment. "It's Mr. Worth who should get the credit. I'm simply bearing witness to his talents."

"I think you do more than that, and I'm certain Fletcher would agree." Maggie's green eyes twinkled, as though the relationship between the banker and the wealthy widow was a well-kept secret rather than the talk of the town. "Are you decided on him, then?"

"I always planned on accepting his proposal, at the right time. He's exactly the kind of a husband I need, and I selected very carefully, as you know."

Maggie breathed a soft laugh. "You make it sound like you're picking out upholstery."

Amy forced a smile. Her friend knew Fletcher was an excellent choice. So what if his kisses—the few she'd let him steal—failed to make her heart pound and her knees go weak. Pulse-racing passion wasn't what she wanted anyway. That led down a road to ruin. "It's past time I married. Maybe that will stop whoever is harassing me."

Maggie's teasing smile fell into a look of concern. "Tell me about this bodyguard you mentioned. Do you think he'll be able to stop these attacks? I've been so worried."

Amy glanced back at the magazine as she considered what to say. She shared nearly everything with her friend, yet she didn't want to mention her troublesome attraction to Buck. It was too embarrassing. "Mr. O'Connor seems capable, but he insists on accompanying me everywhere. He's rather rough around the edges so I'm hesitant to bring him along to meetings and important social gatherings."

"Sounds dreadful." Maggie cocked her head. "Where did you find him?"

That wasn't something Amy wanted to go into either. "Near Girard. Fletcher isn't too pleased with my choice, but he understands the need to ensure my safety."

She sighed, flipping the pages of the magazine, letting her eyes wander over drawings of well-dressed men. *Gentlemen.* The kind she needed to marry if she wanted to assure her position in a town that was becoming increasingly sophisticated.

In some ways, she felt like a circus performer walking a tightrope, balancing her desire for more independence with her need to be accepted as an influential member of society. The right man could help her keep that balance. Fletcher was the right man.

The bell tinkled and she looked to the door, then jerked her head around in a double take when she recognized who had entered.

Buck stopped a few steps inside the store. He held his hat fisted in his hand, the only indication he might be nervous. His flaxen hair had been shortened and smoothed, although willful strands curled behind his ears and above his collar. A neatly trimmed mustache framed his mouth, drawing her eyes to those firm lips that had melded with hers in a hot kiss.

"Mr. O'Connor." Oh no, not breathless, she needed to sound firm, in charge. "Come in, and meet my good friend, Mrs. Timmons, the owner of this shop."

Buck tipped his head, not quite getting to a bow. "Mrs. Timmons. My pleasure."

Amy turned to her silent friend.

Maggie's lips were parted and she stared like she'd been struck dumb. Blinking out of whatever trance she'd been in, she dipped a quick curtsy and a coquettish smile appeared. "The pleasure is mine. I've been looking forward to meeting you."

Looking forward to... What?

Searing jealousy boiled over before Amy slammed the lid. Why should she care if her friend found this exasperating man attractive? He wasn't her personal property.

Buck ventured closer, his gaze flickering over dresses draped on steel frames shaped to look like women's figures. He acknowledged Amy with a nod, and then proceeded to engage Maggie in small talk, smiling in that mockingly flirty way of his.

Her friend didn't look so odd standing next to Buck. In fact, Maggie made a perfect match, with her classic dark beauty next to his fair, rugged handsomeness.

Amy bit back an agonized groan. She felt like a plump brown hen compared to her beautiful, willowy friend. She couldn't care, wouldn't care, but she sure hadn't come here to play matchmaker. She stepped away from the counter, anxious to be gone. "If Mr. O'Connor plans to accompany me all over town, we need to go to Baumbergers to purchase proper clothes for him."

Maggie's eyes lit up, her pleased smile shining on Buck. "That means you'll be at the Wilson's dinner party. I've been invited as well, and I know Mr. Bain will be escorting Mrs. Langford, so..."

Amy wanted to strangle her friend. She'd all but asked Buck to escort her. "There's no need for Mr. O'Connor to attend. I'll be with Mr. Bain and he can see to my safety."

Buck turned, his pleasant expression shifting to a disapproving frown. "Maybe your Mr. Bain can keep you safe, maybe not. But it's important I meet everyone you know. I thought I'd explained that earlier."

Her aggravation blossomed into anger. How dare he continue to challenge her? She reached for the package on the counter. "We can discuss this later. Now that I think about it, I doubt Mr. Baumberger has anything readymade that's large enough to fit you."

"Oh," Maggie cried. "I think I may have a solution. My best client lost her husband recently, and I've been holding on to some things she ordered for him. He was a big man, like you. Let me fetch them and you can try them on." She breezed into a back room.

Amy swung around, feeling alarmingly out of control. She glared up at Buck. "You cannot continue to countermand my orders, especially not in public."

His tawny brows shot up. "Your orders? Is that what's got you so heated up, that I don't follow orders? I thought maybe my *ruffian* appearance was rubbing you the wrong way."

"Rubbing me…?" Her breath rushed out in a short burst. "I could care less what you look like, except for the fact that you're trailing after me and it's important I maintain a certain image."

He moved in, but instead of looming over her, he propped his hand on the counter and leaned down, bringing them eye-to-eye. "You're right about one thing, darlin'," he rasped in a low voice. "You didn't give a damn about my appearance last night when you kissed me like there was no tomorrow."

"Why you…." She drew back her hand to slap him, but he caught her wrist in an iron grip. "You are no gentleman."

His eyes narrowed. "And you're not behaving much like a lady."

As footsteps sounded behind her, he released her arm and stood abruptly, putting on a bland expression.

"Here you are." Maggie handed Buck an armful of clothes. "Why don't go to the back and try these on?"

Amy's face burned. Had her friend witnessed that dreadful scene?

Buck's footsteps receded and the room fell silent...crushingly silent.

After a moment, Maggie's hand came to rest on Amy's shoulder. "What was that about?"

She screwed her eyes shut to hold back hot tears of humiliation. What kind of explanation could be made for her abominable behavior? Buck had acted in his normal manner, with complete disregard for convention. But she knew better. What was it about him that sent her emotions spinning like a top? He could seduce her one minute and infuriate her the next. "Nothing. It's been a trying day."

Maggie's concerned expression swam into view. "You can talk to me, you know."

Amy longed to throw herself into her friend's arms and weep. Instead, she drew in a steadying breath and straightened her shoulders. "I'm glad no one else was in the store to witness that unpardonable display. I promise I won't embarrass you again."

Her friend gave a gentle laugh and embraced her with a quick hug. "You? Embarrass me? I can't imagine you ever would, but it wouldn't matter if you did. You stood by me when I first moved here and everyone treated me like a pariah. I never could have bought this shop or gained acceptance without your friendship and support. Everyone respects you, Amy. Not because of what you wear, or the man you choose to marry. They respect you because of who you are."

Unease quivered through her and she gave her friend a wan smile. "Respect is a tenuous thing. All it takes is one misstep. And I have to maintain my standing in this community if I'm to have enough influence to complete my father's work."

"How much more do you have to do before you're satisfied?" Maggie asked softly.

Amy's throat tightened with dismay. There wasn't an answer to that question, because she wasn't the one who needed to be satisfied. It was her father and he was no longer here. "When my investment in this railroad pays off, then I will be in a better position to use my wealth as a tool to influence progress."

Buck's footsteps sounded behind her. She tensed. Then he stopped in front of her, and she gasped. He clutched the lapels of an evening coat, which was cut away to reveal a crimson vest accentuating the snowy shirt and black satin tie. Light gray trousers hung perfectly over his long legs, breaking at the tops of his boots. Had she thought him handsome before? Dressed like a gentleman, he was devastating.

"Will this be appropriate?" His polite tone belied a glint in his eyes that was anything but deferential.

Her hand drifted up over the rebellious organ in her chest and she nodded, not trusting speech.

"It looks like it was made for you," Maggie enthused. She walked around him, her fingers to her chin and a speculative gleam in her eyes. "All you need now is a hat and gloves." She snatched one of the remaining items off the counter. "Here's the hat. Those gloves were ordered with the suit, but I'm not certain they'll fit."

Amy eyed Buck's large hands—the same hands that had held her suspended off the ground while he'd ravished the tops of her breasts. Her flesh quivered at the memory. She raised her eyes, blushing as she met a heated stare.

He settled the black hat on his head, and one side of his mouth curled in a dangerous smile. He'd shown he knew enough of manners, when he chose to use them, but she had focused on his rough edges, unwilling to even consider he could be polished to a shine.

A bolt of panic shot through her. *No.* Buck might make her feel safer in some ways, but he was far too dangerous in others. Her fingers shook as she lifted the gloves off the counter. These would never fit Buck's powerful hands. She wasn't sure there were fine gloves made to fit hands like that. Mr. O'Connor might be salvageable, made presentable, but he wasn't the gentleman he was pretending to be. He was far too unpredictable. Uncontrollable. He personified passion, and that devilish look in his eyes told her he would use this advantage. She would unmask the impostor for Maggie's sake, as well as her own.

She raised her eyes, meeting Buck's challenging gaze. "You can always tell a gentleman by how he draws on his gloves. Does he pull them on with an air of sophistication? Or does he jerk and tug like an uncouth workman?"

Without a word, he snatched the gloves from her hands and plunged his fingers into the soft leather. Her heart constricted the moment she saw him realize his mistake. Disbelief flickered in his eyes, then embarrassment and something else that sank hooks into her heart.

He frowned and flexed his fingers, trying to loosen the skin-tight gloves enough to peel them off. She winced as the leather ripped across his knuckles. His breath whooshed out in a sound somewhere between aggravation and disgust. "Let me get changed and I'll pay for these clothes."

He strode off without sparing her a glance.

She whirled away from Maggie's wide-eyed astonishment. Guilt gnawed at her insides along with the miserable jealousy that had spurred her to taunt him. "Put the clothes on my tab," she choked out. "The gloves, as well."

Maggie wrapped the item in sticky silence.

When Buck returned, he cradled their package in one arm. Without a word, he flung open the door and waited while she passed.

She glanced up, and trembled. His gaze was cold as a frozen pond. She dropped her lashes, her face burning with shame, and directed her feet toward the carriage. How could she explain? She couldn't. All she could do was apologize.

"I'm sor—" She gasped as she was pitched forward, driven by the force of Buck's hands. A splintering crash sounded behind her a second before she was drenched in a shower of icy water.

CHAPTER 8

Buck groaned. His shoulder was on fire, he was soaked to the skin, and his face was pressed into a damp, frilly bustle. What the hell just happened? He'd heard something scrape above them a second before he pushed—

His gut clenched with fear.

"Amy?" He dragged himself to his knees, grunting at a sharp pain radiating down his arm. Felt like someone had yanked it out of the socket.

Amy twisted around and stared at him with wide eyes. Her hair clung to her neck in damp clumps. She looked like a drowned cat balled up in pile of wet silk.

"Are you all right?"

"I think so." She pushed at the sodden hat, hanging off to one side.

Buck jerked to his feet, gritted his teeth to keep from groaning. What the hell had struck his shoulder?

Behind him, jagged pieces of wood and twisted metal rims were all that was left of a large rain barrel. Had it fallen off the roof? He looked up.

A bearded man peeked over the edge, then disappeared.

"Blazes!" Buck trotted backwards into the street. He whipped his revolver out of its holster and fired a shot.

The attacker leapt onto the roof of a neighboring building.

Buck swore more vehemently. By God, he was going to get that sneaky bastard.

Keeping his eyes trained on the fleeing man, he trotted down the street, but the mud was like molasses, it sucked at his boots, slowing him down. He tried to hold his dangling arm against his chest, but the damn thing wouldn't follow his command. Dislocated, no doubt.

The wiry man hurled himself at the next rooftop.

Buck halted and blinked to clear his vision, then fired. Nearby, a woman screamed, but he kept his eyes fixed on the top of the building where the man had vanished.

A crowd formed, buzzing like confused bees in a hive. He broke through the press of bodies to keep his prey in sight.

Atop a brick façade, the fleeing man appeared. Like a damn monkey, he hurled himself onto the next building.

Buck shook his head, disbelieving, and forced his feet to keep running. His target could be hiding behind that parapet, or he could've slipped into that door on top of the hardware store. No one in his right mind would come out the front, which meant he'd likely go out the back.

With a curse, Buck scrambled over a picket fence and stumbled into the narrow space between two buildings. He stopped, gaping in disbelief at the rear of the hardware store. There was no *back*. This store bumped up against a building facing the next street.

Ignoring the excruciating agony in his shoulder, he jogged to the other side and into an open square. The agile bastard had probably jumped over on top of that general store. Buck ran inside, shielding his gun with his coat so as not to panic the customers.

An old man and a boy were chatting with a clerk behind the counter.

"You see a skinny fellow with a beard and dark coat come through here?"

The trio looked perplexed.

Buck huffed with frustration. His description fit more than half the men in town, but he couldn't give a better one. "Are there stairs leading to the roof?" He ran toward the back, not waiting for an answer.

As soon as he passed through the doorway, he raised his gun and flattened himself against the wall of the storeroom. Forcing his breathing to slow, he scanned piles of boxes and stocked shelves. Familiar smells—wool, flour and tobacco—

called to mind an image of his stepfather's store, another ghost from his past. He still wore the key around his neck to serve as a reminder of a man who'd trusted him, a man he had failed. He wouldn't fail this time. He would save his cousin's land, but keep Amy safe while he was at it.

With the back of his sleeve, he wiped the sweat from of his eyes and peered down a dark hallway. There was no movement, not a sound, not even the scurry of rats. His perusal stopped at a closed door halfway down the corridor. Cocking the gun, he slipped over and tried the knob.

It was locked.

"Blazes!" His anger soared as he rushed back outside. Amy's attacker could have gone into another building. Any building. By now, the wily bastard had probably run into the street and disappeared in the crowd. Buck turned in a slow circle, looking around the town's square, wanting to kill somebody, but not having an appropriate target.

He peered at a buckboard parked by the city scales. A bearded man in a sack coat hopped onto the seat of the loaded wagon. Was that the attacker, posing as a farmer? Buck stumbled in that direction, his arm numb and his whole side throbbing. He lifted his revolver, intending to order the impostor to step down.

A soldier on horseback appeared in his line of vision. "Put away the gun, mister."

He scowled. Where the hell were these Federals when that bastard nearly dashed Amy's brains out? They always did have lousy timing. Buck kept the revolver trained on the farmer's back and wet his lips so he could speak. "That man," he gasped, "tried to—"

Something cracked on the back of his skull and he dropped like a stone.

Buck groaned as he sat up on the edge of a narrow cot. He couldn't lie on that moldy blanket another minute. Stunk like it'd been used to carpet a stable.

With careful motions, he rotated his injured shoulder, better now that a doctor had come along and jerked it back into place. That was more than he could say for his aching head. He touched the egg-sized knot on the back of his skull and winced.

Those damned soldiers had knocked him out, tossed him in a cart and hauled him to jail like *he* was the criminal. On top of that, he'd been eluded by a suit-wearing monkey and duped into ruining a perfectly good pair of gloves. How much more humiliation could one day bring?

He surveyed his temporary quarters with disgust. He'd been locked in one of the limestone-block cells that'd served the fort and the city for the better part of the last two decades. During the war, this jail had been where the Federals kept prisoners stacked twenty deep in lockups designed for one man. Buck knew this only from second-hand accounts, having never been captured. He wouldn't have seen the inside of a cell, at any rate. He would've been hung from a convenient tree, or shot and his body rolled into a gully to be picked clean by scavengers. The Union army had given no quarter to partisan soldiers, and thus hadn't received any.

Lurching to his feet, he paced the room, his body thrumming with pent-up tension. Damn, he had to get out of here before somebody got suspicious and started checking around. He wasn't well known like William Quantrill, who'd masterminded the attack on Lawrence, or Bloody Bill Anderson, who'd carried out the kill order with merciless glee. But even after seven years, the lust for revenge still burned in the hearts and minds of people who would never forget. People like Amy.

Buck dropped down onto the cot and slipped his throbbing arm into a makeshift sling. The source of his anguish wasn't purely physical. His regrets could fill an ocean, but they wouldn't turn back the clock or change a decision made in hot-blooded rage. This time, things would be different. He could gain justice for his cousin without harming innocents.

Footsteps sounded in the narrow hallway. Buck lifted his head as Amy's voice drifted in. "I still don't understand why you had to arrest my bodyguard."

"He was running through the streets shooting off a gun. We thought it best to detain him until we figured out what was going on." A diplomatic answer from the officer who'd brought the doctor. He'd introduced himself as Major Roy.

"Don't you think your time would be better spent tracking down a *real* criminal?"

Buck's lips twitched at Amy's chilly response. His boss had come after him and she was tearing into that major like a terrier. Not an ideal strategy for getting on the man's good side. Had she decided against asking the commanding officer to assign troops for her rally? This was something that would need to be corrected. Having soldiers there would serve Sean's purpose, but they would also provide her with added protection.

A key rattled in the lock and the door creaked open. Buck stood as the contingent swarmed in: Amy, her dress and bonnet still damp but restored to order; Fletcher, looking every inch the rich banker; the sandy-haired major and a baggy-eyed man with a star pinned to his vest.

Buck tamed his nervousness. That would be like scent to a hound for the lawman and a seasoned army officer.

Amy halted in the middle of the cell, clasping her gloved hands together. Her nostrils flared and a look of consternation crossed her face. Buck sympathized. If the rancid odors offended him, he could only imagine what they were doing to her sensibilities. Her gaze locked on the sling holding his arm and a crease appeared between her brows. "You're hurt."

The soft concern wrapped around those two words melted away the last of his annoyance with her for that clever little trick with the gloves. "The barrel hit me. Must've thrown my shoulder out." He shrugged. "Old injury. Acts up sometimes."

As she started to move closer, Fletcher snagged her arm and pulled her back. "Can you give us a description of Mrs. Langford's attacker?"

Buck reined in his irritation at the possessive gesture. "Didn't get a real good look. I'd say wiry, dark hair, bushy beard…like a monkey."

The banker scowled. "This is no time for jests."

"I'm not jesting." *Asshole.* "That fellow was jumping from building to building like it was nothing. I lost him somewhere around that mercantile out on the square."

Fletcher's eyes narrowed like he was working out the next move in a game of chess. He slid a glance at the sheriff, who seemed to take it as his cue to comment.

The lawman gripped his gun belt. "That's not much to go on."

"Well, it's more than we had before," Amy shot back.

The sheriff gestured with his chin. "This fellow here, he's your bodyguard?"

"That's right." She looked confused at the abrupt turn in the conversation.

Buck held the lawman's calculated stare. Did the sheriff know something or just have a hunch?

"Where'd you find him?"

Amy lifted her chin defiantly. "He came recommended. From Texas."

Buck could have kissed her, but instead he kept a straight face. Amy knew he wasn't from Texas, but for some reason she stayed true to his story.

The sheriff furrowed his brow. "Why did you hire a man out of Texas?"

Amy drew up straight as a ramrod and leveled a look that would freeze hot iron. "I have been attacked and nearly killed, yet you are interrogating me as if *I* am the criminal."

Buck wanted to applaud. He flicked a disgusted glance at Fletcher, who suddenly seemed to wake up to the fact that he hadn't come to his lady's defense.

"Sheriff Lawson, I believe you owe Mrs. Langford an apology."

Nice recovery, Fletch, but too late.

Lawson's face darkened. "Pardon if I offended, ma'am. I want to get to the bottom of this much as anyone. That's why I ask so many questions. Got to turn over every rock. You never know where you might find a scorpion."

Amy's cheeks glowed pink. "Mr. O'Connor saved my life today. I hardly think that constitutes the actions of a scorpion, as you so colorfully put it."

Buck couldn't restrain a proud smile. By the saints, Amy was beautiful when she got riled up. If he had a woman like her by his side, he'd—

Hold on there, Bucko.

He released the dangerous desire with a slow breath. That kind of thinking would earn him nothing but pain. He was here to help his cousin. Sure, he could protect Amy while he was at it, but he wasn't risking his heart again. She'd just rip it out anyway, once she learned the truth.

The major, who'd been quietly observing the proceedings, turned to him. "That man you were holding a gun on, was he the one you saw on the roof?"

Buck rubbed his forehead, trying to recall. "I'm not sure."

Amy's shoulders slumped. The disappointment on her face made him long to take her in his arms and haul her off somewhere safe—somewhere far away from here. "I'm sorry he got away, Mrs. Langford. I'll be ready for him next time."

"Let's hope there isn't a next time." The officer's remark opened the opportunity Buck had been looking for.

He fought a twinge of conscience. It was for Amy's good, even if she wouldn't see it that way. "We need to make sure you and those other women have adequate protection for that rally."

Her eyes widened.

Buck anticipated the checkmate.

Major Roy shot her a puzzled look. "Rally? What rally?"

CHAPTER 9

March 15, 1870, Girard, Kansas

Amy turned her back on a stiff wind to address the group of women standing behind her on the railroad platform. "Come to the front, ladies."

The girls stayed huddled like a gaggle of geese, albeit well dressed fowl. Amy had seen to that before she left Fort Scott. In fact, she'd planned everything down to the last detail to ensure this rally would be successful. Soon, these hopeful young women, most of whom had fled poverty and deprivation, would have husbands and homes. Giving them this opportunity to find better lives wasn't just beneficial for the railroad. It was good for everyone.

She gestured to a battered table, gripping her notes tighter as they fluttered in her hand. "Stand in front of your picnic basket, but hold onto it or this breeze will whisk it away."

"Breeze?" The incredulous question was posed by one of the more outspoken girls.

Amy smiled. Even though she was only a few years older, she had a hard time thinking of these young women as anything other than girls, given their fresh-faced ignorance of the life they'd stepped into. The flyers sent east had proclaimed the plains to be a veritable Eden, but it wouldn't hurt to enlighten them as to the reality of paradise.

"You've not yet experienced a true Kansas wind, but you'll know it when you do. That's why I had you sew lead shot into the hems of your skirts."

Amy eagerly scanned the crowd. There had to be at least a hundred men. They'd appeared minutes after a bell-clanging, steam-puffing Manchester engine had announced the arrival of the train. The brand-new engine still hissed as it sat resting on the track behind her.

Six more engines would soon chug down these tracks when the Border Tier linked Kansas to the lucrative cattle country in Texas. With trade would come prosperity, and not just for the rich, but for all who took part in this new era of commerce. Her father's dream was so close she could smell it in the oil and smoke.

Smiling, Amy stepped up to the podium. Based on current projections, they would cross into Indian Territory within the month, handily beating their rival. That is, if she could prevent the Land League from getting in the way. "Good afternoon, gentlemen."

The crowd roared their welcome.

She pitched her voice to project over the clamor. "We're delighted to see so many of you here. We'll have a prayer, and then we'll get started on bidding for these picnic baskets. What better way to welcome the newest members of our community?"

"Forget the prayin' and get to them picnic baskets!" The shout came from a man who'd leapt onto the back of a wagon, presumably to get a better view.

Two soldiers at the perimeter of the crowd nudged their horses toward the buckboard. At the same time, Buck stepped up onto the platform, but not before Fletcher had reached her side.

Amy rested her hand across her stomach, willing her nerves to settle. Major Roy had been good to his word, bringing his troops into town to provide additional security. In fact, he'd insisted on it, after Buck had blurted out that comment about seeing to the safety of the women.

Why couldn't her bodyguard keep his mouth shut? She hadn't wanted troops present because it would be interpreted as more heavy-handed tactics. But she had allowed it out of fear of something happening to these girls. The chance wasn't worth taking.

"Let me remind you before we get started." She raised her voice to draw attention away from the scuffling at the wagon. "The Young Ladies Immigration Society is sponsoring a dance this evening out at the Jansen place. Keep in mind, the Society is bringing more young women to our fair state. So if you don't win the hand of one of these lovely ladies, you'll have another opportunity in the near future." Amy smiled as applause erupted.

For the first time in weeks, she breathed easy. This rally would be a turning point. She felt it clear to her bones. She gestured to the reverend standing beside her on the platform. The diminutive preacher secured his stovetop hat and stepped up to the podium, smoothing down what appeared to be several sheets of notes.

Oh dear. Hopefully, he wouldn't go on too long. She had purposely forgone speeches to avoid losing the crowd.

"Let us pray." His booming bass droned on for what seemed like hours. He blessed the generosity of Mr. Joy; then he gave thanks for the railroad, making some convoluted comparison between the miracle of steam and the magical genie released from Aladdin's lamp.

Good grief, wasn't he overdoing it a bit?

Amy tilted her head and peeked up at the man on her right.

Buck spied at her through half-closed lids. He put his lips near her ear. "Next thing you know, he'll be turning wine into steam."

His warm breath sent a shiver racing across her skin. She nudged him and whispered. "That's disrespectful."

"I agree. A waste of good wine is downright sacrilegious."

Amy curled her lips around her teeth to keep from laughing. She darted a glance at Fletcher, who stood at her other side with his head dutifully bowed.

A frown creased his brow as he watched her through his lashes. Was he upset with her for whispering, or was his antipathy for her bodyguard? Hopefully, the attacker would be caught soon and she could send Buck on his way and her life would get back to normal.

She tried to ignore the trickle of disappointment. Wasn't normal what she wanted?

"Amen." The reverend stepped back.

Scattered applause rippled through the crowd. Perhaps they were clapping out of relief, but she couldn't fault the good man's intentions. He was the only preacher within fifty miles who supported the railroad.

Her jitters started up again. Which of these men were members of the secretive Land League? They'd no doubt infiltrated this crowd. No matter. She would preempt their troublemaking by focusing on why these men were here—to meet decent young women.

Amy stepped up to the podium. "Let's get started."

Out of the corner of her eye, she saw Buck leave the platform. He'd told her he would be milling about, looking for anyone who resembled the man who'd fled across the rooftops.

She turned, gesturing to a golden-haired girl in spring-green calico. "Why don't we begin with your basket, Martha?"

"Hold on there!"

Amy's head whipped around at the angry shout.

A robust man clad in farmer's denims moved closer to platform. "If I marry one of these gals and sign your agreement, does it give me rights to any piece of land I staked out?" He waved a tattered piece of paper. "This letter King Joy posted all over creation puts a whole host of limits on our claims. Are you saying he's changed his mind?"

Amy moistened her lips. The angry settler must be referring to town site claims, one of the most hotly contested issues. "Right-of-way can't be claimed, nor can town sites. The railroad reserves the right to hold back these acres so we can ensure a fair means of selling the land to those who'll actually reside there. We don't want speculators to abuse good people by taking prime real estate and then selling it back to them at exorbitant prices."

"Well, hell, little lady, ain't that exactly what King Joy is doin'?"

She gasped as the man leapt onto the platform. His feet had barely touched the wood when he flew backwards and then landed flat in the dirt with a startled expression.

Buck glared down at the prone man. "You're not allowed on the platform with the women."

The red-haired farmer stood slowly. He picked up his hat and slapped it on his thigh. His narrowed eyes locked on her bodyguard.

Vicious insults and profane encouragements peppered the air. The crowd spread out, opening a circle around the two men.

Amy's stomach clenched. God forbid this gathering disintegrate into a brawl.

"You men move back!" Major Roy's directive rang out. His troops urged their mounts forward through the tightly massed bodies, their guns at the ready.

"No!" Amy cried. She would not allow this to turn into a bloodbath. She shook off Fletcher's constraining hand and moved to the edge of the platform. "Mr. Joy wants nothing more than to see those who'd settle and improve this land be given the opportunity to do so."

She yelled over the shouting men. "He's acting in good faith by offering incentives, like providing the means for eligible young ladies to come west, so you can marry and have families. Let's get back to the reason we're here, to bid on these baskets and meet some of these ladies."

Finally, the soldiers broke through. One of them escorted the grumbling farmer away at gunpoint. The crowd shifted like a human sea, their discontented voices rising in waves.

Desperate to avoid a riot, Amy hauled the reticent young woman up beside her. "I'm pleased to introduce Martha Lennox."

The girl trembled, clutching her basket as if it were a lifeline. Had it been a mistake to bring these girls down here?

"Martha is an excellent cook. I can smell the fried chicken she's packed in this basket, and a delicious apple pie."

The rumbling subsided. Amy anxiously searched the faces in the crowd. Some glowered, others appeared disgruntled, but most looked interested. For the most part, these were decent, God-fearing men who were looking for a better life, men who needed wives and wanted families. But the troublemakers were stirring things up.

Buck remained in front of the platform with his arms crossed and his feet planted in a wide stance. Her rational mind told her one man couldn't stop a mob, yet there he stood like a knight before his lady, willing to defy the dragons who would devour her.

"I'll take that basket!" The shout had gone up from the middle of the crowd. A pleasant faced young man elbowed his way forward. But before he could approach the platform, a black-haired settler stepped in front of him.

"Before we get started, I want to know for certain our titles will be secure. We won't sign off on cutthroat trust deeds and be at the mercy of some Boston capitalist."

Murmurs of discontent swept through the crowd.

Amy met the man's sky blue eyes. A vague familiarity flickered. Had she met him before? "The investors have no interest in taking away your land."

"S'at so?" His lips curved in a mocking smile. Ah, now she knew. His cocky attitude reminded her of Buck. "As it stands now, the railroad can foreclose without us even knowing."

Amy moistened her dry lips. He'd touched on a prickly issue: the right of the railroad to revoke the settlers' titles by posting publication of foreclosure in eastern newspapers. It was a move designed to protect investors in case struggling farmers didn't make their payments, but it appeared to be an attempt to swindle these men out of their land. "No one is going to take away your land if you pay for it."

"*You* say. But why should we believe it? You work for King Joy."

The grumbles grew louder.

Fletcher touched her arm, his eyes asking permission. Amy stepped back and let him have the podium. Lord knows she didn't have a good answer for that volatile question. He gripped his lapels and faced the crowd as if he could calm the storm with a single word.

"The reason you men are gathered here today is to pursue what we all want—homes and families. Those of you who truly desire this have nothing to fear. No one will take your land if you are honest and hardworking. The richest soil is yours to till, and this railroad will open the door to markets eager
for the fruits of your labor. The possibilities are boundless." Fletcher's rich baritone projected over the crowd, conveying firm conviction and deep empathy.

"But there are those among you who would spoil your hope for happiness." He paused and seemed to search the upturned faces. "Yes, that's right. These men want you to suspect Mr. Joy and the railroad because it takes the attention off their own misdeeds. They don't want to till the land. They want to get *rich* quick at your expense. They want to twist the truth and disrupt the peace until you've missed the opportunity to benefit from the wealth that will come to you on this track." He gestured behind him, his expression pleading. "*If* it can be completed. Don't let these wolves fool you. They are your true enemies."

The soft hiss of the engine seemed to punctuate his fervent appeal.

Amy held her breath. The men were listening. Fletcher exuded confidence and empathy and his brief speech had been downright poetic. He had the makings of congressman, even a senator. Working together, they could accomplish great things. The future shone like a beacon, luring her to its light.

Thundering hooves shattered her reverie.

"They're burning the ties!" The shout came from a soldier on horseback, tearing down the middle of the street. He waved his arm. "Major, the settlers, they're burning the ties laid out by the railroad bed. You can see the fires for miles."

Chaos erupted. Men shouted, some running away while others cheered. Even the wind kicked up its heels, flinging dirt into the air. Amy blinked, her eyes and nose stinging.

In what seemed like mere minutes, Major Roy had rounded up his men and galloped out of town, leaving a dusty brown cloud in their wake. What was left of the crowd dissipated until only a handful of men, looking vaguely disappointed, wandered down the street.

"Come along, ladies." Dr. Warner shooed the colorful flock towards his office.

Behind them, the train stood silent.

Fletcher swore softly.

Numb with shock, Amy sank to the edge of the platform. The bright future she'd glimpsed flickered and vanished, as she tumbled back down to the foot of the mountain she'd worked so diligently to climb.

She'd been so certain the answer to their problems was bringing wives to these men who longed for families. The loneliness and yearning in their faces was proof enough it was something they wanted, something that would be good for everyone. Now, the Land League had taken even this away. There was no chance she'd be able to convince the directors to continue supporting her program. She would be fortunate if she kept her job.

She clenched her fists until her nails bit into her palms. By heaven, she hadn't come

this far to be defeated. Her father hadn't struggled and died in vain. He had started this state on a path to prosperity, and she would see his work completed even if she had to drag every man, woman and child kicking and screaming down that railroad track.

"Mrs. Langford?" Buck's shadow blocked the bright sun.

She raised her eyes. He only used that deferential tone when he wanted something.

His brow furrowed. "Are you all right?"

"Are you an *imbecile?*" Fletcher hovered over her. "Of course she's not *all right*. This rally was a disaster."

Buck snorted. "You're just sayin' that to make her feel better."

Amy shot to her feet, furious with herself, the situation and these two exasperating men. "If you want to fight like mongrel dogs, go do it somewhere else and stop wasting my time. I have to figure out how to get things back on track. This railroad *will* strike the border by May. Even if I have to spend every penny I have to ensure it."

Buck tied the reins of his horse to a spindly sapling, the only tree in front of a sod cabin that blended in with the brown landscape.

Nearby, a stable had been constructed from what looked like a mixture of clay and sticks. Three cows plodded past fence posts awaiting rails. Based on Sean's hurried directions, this had to be his place, but it sure didn't look like much.

Approaching the open door, Buck eased his revolver out of the holster, a habit he couldn't seem to break. He'd learned too well the lessons of war, where an ambush could wait at what seemed a welcoming home. He peered inside.

Sean sat at a small table, hunched over and scribbling on a piece of paper. Glancing up, he smiled. "Come in, cousin."

Buck holstered his gun. Still uneasy, he crossed the dirt-packed floor, inspecting the cluttered room. Dried herbs dangled from rough-hewn ceiling beams, along with a blackened venison haunch. Clothes and blankets were piled on a narrow bed. Farm implements poked out of a loft overhead, but none appeared to have been used much.

He pulled a chair up to the table, positioning it near the fireplace where glowing embers would warm his back. Setting his hat on the table, he met Sean's gleeful gaze. "Thought I might find you here. We need to talk about our next move."

"I think we can afford to celebrate a little first." Sean lifted a jug off the floor and poured clear liquid into a tin cup. "Made it myself. Call it Stone Fence, 'cause you'll feel like you smacked into one if you drink too much." He chuckled and poured into a second cup he'd scooped off the floor. "Let's toast the bonfires burning between here and Baxter Springs."

Buck crossed his arms. The image of Amy's face and the stricken disbelief in her eyes had tormented him all the way out here. He wasn't used to crushing dreams and was finding he didn't much care for it.

Sean tossed back the liquor, scrunched his face, and then released a harsh breath. "Ah, that'll cure what ails you." He leaned forward on his arms, his face alight with excitement. "So, how's the job going? Have you crawled into her bed yet? I betcha she's hotter than—"

"Shut your foul mouth." Buck lunged out of the chair, grabbing Sean by his shirt and dragged him halfway across the table. "That's a *lady* you're talking about, not a strumpet."

Regret struck the moment Buck met his cousin's stunned expression. He released his cousin's shirt and forced himself to sit down, sucking in a deep breath to calm the unexpected rush of rage.

"What the hell's wrong with you?" Sean straightened his shirt with an angry scowl. "Are you fallin' for that Jezebel?"

"She's not a Jezebel, and I won't listen to that kind of talk about a lady." Buck jerked to his feet and paced the small room like a caged animal. God, he'd wanted to smash his fist into Sean's face when he'd insulted Amy.

Sean eyed him warily. "She's a pretty little colleen, I just thought—"

"I'm not here to talk about Mrs. Langford." Buck's anger reignited, but he pinched out the fuse. This was his cousin, his blood kin. He had to keep reminding himself. "I agreed to help you keep this land. This place you said you've been improving. Doesn't look to me like you've done much more than get by."

Sean's complexion darkened. "What're you sayin'?"

Buck sank into the seat again, unsettled by the emotions bouncing around in his chest. He had to be on guard against caring more for Amy than he already did, or the conflicting loyalties would tear him in two.

He stared out the open door until his anger subsided. "Just tell me what you're up to, besides farming. I don't care what it is, but I need to know the truth. We got to have trust between us if we're to do this thing together."

Sean folded the piece of paper he'd been writing on and pushed it aside. "I'm not speculating on town sites like that farmer at the rally, if that's what you're asking. I staked me out a good piece o' land, aim to sell some and farm the rest. But I stopped making improvements when I thought I might lose it."

Buck leaned back and stretched his legs out. "Makes sense."

Sean gestured to Buck's untouched drink. "Have a nip. It won't kill you,"

"Don't need it."

"Why are you so dead set against drinking my whiskey?" Sean shoved the cup over, splashing some of the contents on the table.

Buck leveled a hard look at his cousin. "You'll recall my old man was stabbed to death in a brawl. A drunken brawl."

Da's death wasn't the only reason he avoided strong drink. It was his own weakness for the foul brew, but he wasn't going to admit that.

Sean's expression sobered. "I recall Uncle Seamus had a fierce temper."

Buck hunched over the table as a familiar pall cast its shadow over the room. An evil spirit of rage and violence had cursed his father and wanted to destroy him as well. During the war, the beast had ruled him until that fiasco in Lawrence had forced him to face what he'd become.

Since then, he'd vowed not to lose control, not to release that vicious creature ever again. He curled his hand around the tin cup but made no move to drink. "I was surprised to see you at the rally. Thought you'd be out burning ties."

"There was plenty of boys willing to burn things," Sean said with a dark smile. "I wanted to find out whether that railroad promoter would have any luck selling her picnic baskets. Did you notice how nervous she got when we started asking questions?"

"She didn't look nervous to me." Buck crossed his arms, perturbed. "She stood up to that crowd and showed more grit than those cowardly blowhards. Regardless of whether you agree with her position, she defended it well enough."

And without deceit, which was more than he could say for himself.

Sean poured another splash into his own cup and took a swig. He wiped his mouth with the back of his hand. "You've gone sweet on her haven't you? She's fooled you just like Amos said. If you've been listening to her, you haven't got the real story."

His cousin's face grew stiff with resentment. Buck recognized the look, considering he'd seen it in the mirror for most of his life. Only, these last few years it had hardened into bitter hopelessness, which he covered up with mocking humor and feigned indifference. "So what's the *real* story?"

"They're a pack of thieves, nothing more. Even if I took out a loan to pay King Joy's ridiculous price, he can foreclose without me even knowing. Not only that, but if I want to sell, I can't. The title isn't assignable until full payment is made, or unless the railroad pleases to grant me the privilege, which they won't." Despair flashed across Sean's face. "We can't trust them, but we have to do business with them if we want to stay here."

Buck stabbed his fingers through his hair. God, he wished he'd never heard about this damned railroad. "You still think slowing them down gives us the best bargaining chip?"

"What else have we got? The only way that bastard will deal with us is if we're negotiating from a position of power. If we can't squeeze him, we can't get him to budge on price or terms."

Buck rubbed his temples. His head ached just thinking about this snarled-up mess. "Burning more ties isn't the answer. That's just going to bring the army down on your head in bigger numbers and with bigger guns. You can't win that war. Believe me, I know."

Discouragement crept in. He'd vowed to get Sean a fair deal, but how the hell could he ensure that and protect Amy in the process? Some devil had provoked him, made him crazy enough to think he could do both. Now, he couldn't walk away from either commitment. His honor, tattered as it was, wouldn't let him.

The ache in his head spread to his heart. Annoying how it decided to start feeling again about the time he met Amy. Sitting up, he took a deep breath. "We'll figure this out together. But I need your help. I got to find out who's responsible for these attacks on Mrs. Langford and stop him. Killing her, scaring her, or whatever the hell he's trying to do, isn't going to accomplish anything."

Sean opened his mouth like he was about to object.

Buck held up his hand. "Trust me on this. Making war on women will only hurt your cause. I'll work from the inside. Help you slow things down. Find ways to influence whoever has the power to make changes to these terms."

"That's not enough. We got to strike now." Sean slammed his fist against his palm. "While they're reeling from this blow."

His cousin had a point.

Buck rested his arms on his knees, staring at the floor as he sifted through what he knew. "The railroad is being routed through Baxter Springs. Amy—I mean, Mrs. Langford— thinks that's a bad idea because the legal crossing point into Indian Territory is west of there, near Chetopa. Her boss doesn't agree with her, but if he can't bribe enough politicians and Indians to get the agreement changed then the railroad will have to lay an extra seventeen miles of track."

He straightened up, looking at his cousin to see if Sean caught his drift.

Sean's brows shot up. "I'll be damned. That'll slow 'em down. But we got to be sure the other line has a chance to catch up, so the pressure is on to act quickly." He rubbed a finger across his upper lip. "The railroads have been fighting over qualified workers."

Siphoning workers wouldn't require hurting Amy or shaming her. She wouldn't even have to be involved. Buck warmed to the idea. "Any idea how to do that?"

"We can put out word the Border Tier is having a slow down because of vandalism. Men don't get paid if they don't work. Those track layers will go right to the Katy's offices."

That would put the focus back on the burned ties, which would make Amy's misstep look all the worse. Buck shook his head. "It doesn't take much to correct a rumor like that. I'll come up with something else and let you know."

Sean's brow wrinkled in a look of concern. "Be careful about cozying up to that woman. If Amos suspects you might turn on us, he knows enough to make trouble for you."

So, Sanford thought to blackmail him into doing their will. Buck stood and glared down at his cousin. "You tell Amos the last man who crossed me didn't get the chance to do it again."

Something flickered in Sean's eyes that hadn't been there before. *Fear.*

Buck's stomach turned. He had no desire to inspire that feeling and he sure as hell didn't want his cousin looking at him that way. But he hadn't stayed alive by showing weakness. "You got nothing to worry about, so long as you keep your mouth shut."

CHAPTER 10

Fletcher threaded Amy's arm through his, starting up the red-carpeted stairs to the second floor of the hotel. She gritted her teeth when he patted her hand for what seemed like the hundredth time. "No doubt, Mr. Joy will respond quickly to your telegram."

"No doubt," she echoed, her voice heavy with resignation.

She'd telegraphed the dreadful news to her boss so he wouldn't hear it from someone else, but now she needed to come up with a plan for replacing those burned ties without an outlay of additional money—an impossible task.

She took shallow breaths to calm her churning insides. The railroad was already in financial distress, having far exceeded construction estimates, thanks to Mr. Chanute's *first class* materials. Not only that, but the disaster today would cost precious time and that was a commodity no one could replace.

"The Sedalia paper predicts the MK&T will make the border by mid-May." Her voice wavered. "I don't see how that's possible if they're as far behind as we think."

Fletcher patted again. "Don't worry. We'll be in Baxter Springs long before the Katy comes anywhere close to striking the border, even with this slow down. And once we've crossed out of Kansas and into Indian Territory, all will be forgiven."

If only. James Joy hadn't earned a reputation for mercy. How many board members and assistants had he gone through over the past few years? She'd lost count, largely because she'd never imagined she would be in their position.

She pulled a handkerchief from her sleeve and dabbed away the excess moisture in the corners of her eyes. "This hotel smells of paint and new carpet. The odors are bothersome."

"They are noxious."

Amy released an aggravated breath. Fletcher's agreeable mood was wearing thin, especially after he'd flared up at Buck and then made that disparaging remark. He hadn't meant to hurt her and had only spoken the truth. The rally *had* been a disaster. Still, he needn't have pointed out the obvious. Belatedly, he seemed to pick up on the hurt he'd caused and had spent the past six hours trying to make up for it. But she didn't need his head nodding and handholding. She needed ideas for how to fix this mess.

"There is a possibility... no, a very high probability that Mr. Joy will release me from my duties with the railroad." Amy raised her chin, refusing to let it quiver.

Her father wouldn't have put up with tears and an attitude of defeat. His confidence in her abilities and his insistence on nothing less than her best effort had gotten her this far. He would be ashamed of her if she gave up now. She'd find some way to help this railroad win, even if she couldn't do it from the front lines.

They reached the door to her room and Fletcher took her arms. "Amy, look at me." His eyes were warm as morning chocolate. "*You* didn't burn those ties. Mr. Joy is astute enough to realize that, and also to know how foolish it would be to shut you out. You've gained tremendous support in Fort Scott for his railroad. This trouble with the settlers isn't your fault."

She wanted desperately to believe Mr. Joy would be so benevolent. "Nevertheless, he'll certainly withdraw support for my immigration program. I should never have allowed Major Roy to divert his troops. That was bad judgment on my part, and I shall have to shoulder the blame."

"The blame?" Fletcher's eyebrows rose. "I recall it was the major who insisted on assigning troops for this rally. He should've arranged to have enough men in both places. I hope you included that little fact in your report."

Amy shook her head, emphatic. "The Army's troops are already spread too thin trying to protect all the lines that are building west and south. I refuse to lay the blame on Major Roy. *I* should've found some other way to arrange security. Honestly, I wouldn't have given a thought to using those troops if Mr. O'Connor hadn't—"

"You aren't giving credence to anything that ignorant gorilla suggests, are you?" Fletcher looked appalled.

She gripped the doorknob, intending to ignore his caustic remark and retire on peaceful terms, but irritation crawled under her skin. She'd never get a moment's rest if she didn't put a stop to this. "Mr. O'Connor is not ignorant, nor is he a gorilla. He prevented that man from accosting me today and his quick actions saved me from having my brains dashed out by a rain barrel. He is doing his job. I will do mine. Please try to get along with him. For my sake."

Fletcher's face clouded over. She waited to see whether he would start arguing with her again. Instead, he put his hand on the door and pushed it open. Before she realized his intentions, he hauled her inside, shutting the door behind them.

"What are you doing?" she cried.

"I need to talk to you in private. Just for a few minutes."

Being alone in her room with him for a *single* minute was a bad idea. "What if someone saw you come in here? This is not appropriate."

He placed a finger on her lips. "Don't scold, darling. I have something for you to consider that might help your standing with Mr. Joy."

She tilted her head, regarding him suspiciously. "What might that be?"

He gripped her arms with an easy familiarity that made warnings clang in her head. "Because of my excellent work in Baxter Springs, Mr. Joy is giving me a special role with the railroad. I'll be leading negotiations with the Indian tribes whose land we'll pass through on the way to Texas. If I'm successful—and I know I shall be—I believe he will select me to replace Mr. Coates as President. He has said as much."

Amy's chest tightened. Fletcher's good fortune should make her heart sing. So why was it playing a funeral dirge? She would never become president of a railroad. Investing as a silent partner and using her wealth to influence men's decisions was all she could expect. It should be enough. "That's wonderful, but I'm not certain how this pertains to my situation."

Of course, she knew what was coming, but she hoped there was something else. Something he had thought of that would keep her from being relegated to the background.

"Marry me, Amy. Be my life partner. Work beside me. I need your support, your
intelligence, your good business sense." The words tumbled from his lips in a hurried stream. Slipping his arms around her waist, he drew her close, pressed his lips to hers.

Despite her misgivings, she allowed the kiss because she was curious about her reaction to the man she planned to marry. His lips were smooth, but without the firm warmth that sent pleasure coursing like honey through her veins. The hair on his face wasn't as soft as... *Good heavens.* Was she really analyzing his kiss and comparing it to Buck's? And what was she doing letting Fletcher kiss her in the first place?

Flustered, she pulled back. "We can't. You need to leave."

He held tight. "My darling, I can't help myself. You are so lovely." His mouth moved across her cheek and down her neck, leaving a damp trail.

She closed her eyes, waiting a moment longer. Fletcher was the man she had chosen, so shouldn't she feel at least a twinge of interest? Perhaps it was better if she didn't. What she felt in Buck's arms threatened the tight control she maintained. If she allowed passion free rein, what would happen?

Her mother's guilt-stricken face flashed in her mind.

No, this wasn't passion. Sadly, she felt very little of anything. Perhaps she was too numb with shock. With a sigh, she put her hands on Fletcher's silk vest and gave a determined push. "It's time for you to go."

Capturing her hands, he dropped to one knee. "Marry me, Amy. Give me a day to look forward to…this week, or next."

"We can't get married in a week. It will take at least six months, maybe more, to plan a proper wedding."

He stood, but didn't release her hands. "It's best if we marry sooner. That way, we can draw attention away from this unfortunate incident. We can always have a reception later, a party to celebrate."

Heavens, he'd been begging her for her hand, and the more she resisted the more adamant he became. Was it because she represented a challenge? He was fiercely competitive. Once they were married, would his ardor cool? "I can't imagine a few months will make much difference. I want to invite our associates and friends, and they can't make plans on such short notice."

"But—"

"We can talk about this later." She pulled her hands from his and started for the door. "You need to leave. Now."

A knock sounded.

She whirled around in time to see Fletcher dart behind the door. He gestured for her to answer. Dismayed, she shook her head. Was he crazy? Anyone could see him standing there. It was best not to answer.

The knocking became insistent. Was it Dr. Warner, or one of the girls? Not likely, as they had retired to the boarding house. Pasting on a smile, she cracked opened the door.

Buck glowered down at her. "You didn't ask who I was before you opened that door."

"Why are you up here knocking in the first place?" she demanded.

He held his hat fisted in his hand and his hair was pushed back as though he'd run his fingers through it. The scents she'd come to associate with him—leather, wind, horses— teased her senses. Her heart thumped harder. Could he smell the sweetish odor of Fletcher's pomatum?

"I'm about to retire for the night. What do you want?"

The fine lines beside his eyes crinkled in a speculative look. "Aren't you interested in what I found out?"

For a moment her mind went blank. Had she sent him on some errand? She couldn't recall what he'd said when he left after Fletcher had escorted her away from the platform.

"Do you have a minute?" His gaze shifted over her head. "I need to talk to you."

Good Lord, he couldn't come in here. "Let me get my shawl and I'll join you downstairs." She slammed the door before he could reply.

"Why did you agree to meet him?" Fletcher growled.

"Because it gives you an opportunity to get out of my room." Amy balled her hands, wanting to smack him. "If you hadn't forced your way inside, we wouldn't be in this predicament."

"Will you at least give me your pledge you'll marry me before the railroad strikes the border?"

"I have to go. We'll discuss it later."

He followed her to the door. "What about Mr. Joy? If you tell him we're engaged, he may reconsider how he handles this situation. I'm sure he'll allow you to keep your position until after we wed. Then you can resign and say you're focusing on a broader agenda. That way, you preserve your reputation. You can always find a new project."

Amy's throat closed up. There was no project as important as this one. However, Mr. Joy would certainly release her from her duties after this fiasco. She thrust aside self-pity. If she married Fletcher and he was named to the coveted position of president, she could work alongside him and still see to her interests in the railroad's success, albeit behind the scenes. And hadn't she already made the decision to accept his suit? Love was something that could grow between them, given time.

She turned, resolved. "All right. I'll marry you the week after the railroad strikes the border. I can't possibly arrange things in advance of that."

The corners of Fletcher's eyes lifted in a pleased expression. He raised her gloved hand to his lips. "Darling, you have made me the happiest man alive."

ぺ♡ ぺ♡ ぺ♡

Amy hugged her shawl as she stepped out into the cool night. After she'd checked to be certain no one was lurking in the halls, Fletcher had slipped out of her room. *No harm done.* Now, she could see what Buck wanted and have a talk with him about the necessity of getting along with her husband-to-be until it was time for him to leave.

"I didn't mean to disturb you."

She nearly shed her skin as Buck stepped out of the shadows beside the door. "It's no bother. Where have you been?"

"I checked out the damage. Talked to some settlers. The Land League isn't claiming responsibility, but everybody knows they organized it." Buck gazed down at her, but in the darkness she couldn't make out the subtleties always present in his expression. "The foreman said it's a total loss, he guessed about twenty thousand ties."

"Twenty-four thousand, to be exact. The major already told me. He apologized profusely." Amy dipped her head to hide the tears that sprang to her eyes. She could've refused the major's help, insisted he keep the troops guarding the tracks, but she hadn't. She had no one but herself to blame.

Buck tucked her hand in his elbow. The simple touch eased her anxiety, something Fletcher hadn't been able to accomplish with hours of nearly constant hand patting.

Moonlight silvered the forms of men wandering across the square in the direction of the saloon. Sounds of celebration poured out into the street. Amy's heart constricted. Why were these men being so shortsighted and ignorant? They were only hurting themselves.

The noise faded as Buck led her in the opposite direction. He stopped in front of the land agent's office and nodded towards a bench in front of the darkened window. "How about here?"

Here was better than in front of that saloon. She hitched her bustle so she could sit and then arranged her skirts.

Buck relaxed into his usual sprawl with his thigh resting against her leg. Her body tingled at the slight touch. Irritated, she pulled the shawl tighter. Why? Why did it have to be Buck who elicited these responses?

"Are you cold?" He shifted forward, removed his coat and draped it over her shoulders.

Some perverse voice urged her to snuggle up next to him. Instead, she gripped the lapels and huddled in the substitute for his arms. Just sitting here wrapped in a coat that carried his scent made her feel safer, more secure. "Were you able to learn the names of those involved?"

"Everybody knows I work for you so they won't give me names. They just confirmed the involvement of the Land League."

So, he'd discovered nothing she didn't already know. Disappointing, but not surprising.

He stretched his arm over the back of the bench. Her heart pulsed like a steam engine.

She bit her lip, wishing she could feel ashamed instead of eager for his embrace. What kind of woman longed for another man moments after becoming engaged?

"How much will this set you back?"

"We'll lose at least four weeks if we have to wait for new ties to be shipped."

"Any ideas how to make up for lost time?" His fingers brushed her shoulder.

She stiffened her spine, shifting her body forward, out of his reach. Whatever was inside her that responded to him, she had to constrain it. Bind it. Crush it. "I considered hiring more men and letting them cut down trees and make ties, only there's a shortage of workers as it is."

"How's that?" He invaded her space, almost as if he were testing her reaction.

Refusing to look at him, she stared at the lighted saloon. "The Katy is starting work on another line running east through Fort Scott, as well as the line we're racing south. I fear Mr. Parsons railroad will increase wages when qualified workers become scarce. But we can't afford to pay more. Our resources are fully tapped.

"You might suggest your boss has lost enough money and should negotiate with the settlers." Buck's rough voice caressed her like fingers gently scratching her back.

What would happen if she gave in to this itch? Dread trickled through her. She'd end up as soiled and dirty as her mother. She fisted her hands in her lap. She wasn't weak. She could resist this unwelcome attraction. "If we give in to blackmail, the demands will never end."

"But your boss is unbending. It's only escalating the conflict."

"I know." She shook her head miserably. "Both sides are so entrenched a compromise is all but impossible. I'd hoped to find something that would benefit everyone. That's why I proposed bringing young women out here, so the men here could marry. Have families. Build communities that would attract more people, produce more opportunities. I thought they'd see the value and be willing to put down their arms."

Buck cupped her shoulder. His confident touch conveyed familiarity. Ownership.

She shrugged off his hand. Now was the time to tell him she was engaged and demand he act appropriately. Her mouth opened, but the words wouldn't come out.

"Amy, the settlers see those women as a bribe. Just another trick. They don't trust the railroad to deal honorably with them. They've put considerable energy into improving the land and they want something back for their efforts. Your ladies-for-sale program didn't address their complaints, which are price and terms for ownership. You're trying to buy goodwill. That's something you won't be able to do."

She drew back, disbelieving. Where had this come from? "You sound like you're quoting from an article in The Workingman's Journal. Who have you been talking to? Amos Sanford?"

He hesitated before answering. "Some of the settlers. I'm just trying to help."

"Help?" She glared at him. "I think you've *helped* enough, Mr. O'Connor. Using troops for protection during the rally was a costly misjudgment, although I blame myself entirely for allowing it. I suggest you put your efforts toward discovering the identity of my assailant, rather than attempting to solve a problem you don't fully understand."

He brought his face even with hers, and even in the dim light she could see his thunderous expression. "Listen here, I'm sick and tired of your insults. I may not have all the facts, but I'm not so ignorant I can't comprehend the complexity of this mess. And I sure don't see you, or anybody else, doing a very good job figuring it out. So stop packing your failures in my saddlebag."

Amy's face burned, but more than that, her heart bled. Unlike Fletcher, her bodyguard didn't offer sympathy or try to smooth over her weaknesses. Instead, he cut through her pretense and, like a mirror, reflected back the imperfections she didn't want to see. But she wouldn't sit here and let him humiliate her. "Let's return to the hotel. I don't think you have any additional information I need tonight."

"Wait." He grabbed her arm. "I didn't mean it like that."

She tensed when he took her shoulders in a firm but gentle grasp.

His eyes pleaded, although he hadn't asked for pardon. "Look, you're making progress. Those men, they were excited about the women being here. I could see it in their faces. You mentioned a dance. That's a good way to smooth things over. It'll give you a chance to make a new offer. Not tied to a purchase contract, but something that gives everybody a boon."

Amy shook her head, near tears and torn by doubt. She was juggling misguided greed on both sides and all the while tripping over her own missteps. Only this time, her father wasn't here to rescue her.

"I can't...please everyone." She forced the words out of a clogged throat.

He gathered her against his chest and brought his mouth close to her ear. "Why would you even try? Most folks don't appreciate the effort and the rest misunderstand. Don't do things to please other people. Do it because of what's inside you."

Distraught, she clung to him. Why did it seem he was her only anchor in the storm?

He rubbed circles on her back and eventually she relaxed, until her inner governess chided. Reluctantly, she pulled back. "How do you know if what you're doing is right?"

A crease formed between his brows, and he looked surprisingly uncertain before the sardonic mask fell over his face. "Who said anything about being right? I just follow my instincts."

That was a disappointing answer. It made her angry because he took the easy way out while challenging her to step up. "Why would you let instincts guide you if you don't have a noble cause? You might find you're deluded, acting out of gross self-interest or self-protection."

"What if one man's noble cause destroys another man's dreams?"

His question stopped her cold. That couldn't be what she was doing. Her intentions were good ones and her path honorable. "My father told me people don't always know what's best for them. It takes someone with vision to lead them and take them to a better place."

"I guess if he talked to burning bushes he might have got the directions right, but even Moses couldn't get folks to follow him into the Promised Land."

A smile tugged her mouth. So now he was quoting the Bible. Her bodyguard continued to surprise her. He had more facets than a diamond. "Maybe Moses couldn't, but Joshua did."

Buck leaned back with an appreciative gleam in his eyes. He stretched his arms over the back of the bench and shrugged with his hands. "You got me there, Josh."

Pleasure curled inside her, more so for the fact that his concession wasn't easily given. Buck was like iron sharpening her steel. He forced her to rethink her actions and defend her stance, much like her father had done.

Buck? Like her father? The thought stunned her. Why, the two men couldn't be more different. Buck was earthy, at times even coarse, eminently practical and scathingly direct. Her father had been polished, intellectual and tactful. Yet, both men had a sharp intelligence, along with an ability to bring people around to their way of thinking.

She winced at a twinge of guilt. "I apologize for my remark earlier. It was uncalled for. I.... Well, I think you're very intelligent, although you like to keep it to yourself."

His mustache lifted on one side. "Don't fill my balloon with too much hot air."

A soft laugh slipped out before she could stop it, but then the light moment gave way to melancholy. Once she was married, she would not be able to enjoy this kind of intimacy with another man—particularly *this* man. She clasped her hands together and focused on the gauzy fog hovering above the ground. "I'll be marrying Fletcher as soon as the railroad makes the border. I would appreciate it if you'd make an effort to get along."

Buck's silence drew her eyes to his face. Was that sadness in his silvery eyes, or just a reflection of what she was feeling? He shifted forward and for a moment she thought he would take her hand to help her rise. Instead, he cupped her cheek in his palm and lightly brushed his thumb across her lower lip.

Her mind halted like a mechanism that had wound down. Passion sizzled beneath her skin, sparking a fire that licked at her body. He drew closer, his gaze fastening on her mouth. *Oh, yes.* That was what she wanted, too. She closed her eyes, waiting, anticipating the kiss.

His warm lips skimmed hers, barely touching. "It's not your instincts deluding you, Venus. It's your noble cause."

CHAPTER 11

March 16, 1870, Girard, Kansas

The music swelled as couples whirled, their faces flushed and smiling, around the clean-swept floor of the barn. Amy stood beside a makeshift stage, tapping her toe in time to the lively tune.

The young ladies in their pastel gowns looked like a scattering of wildflowers in a field of dark suits and blue uniforms. There were at least a dozen men for every woman, which boded well for her latest plan.

She jerked back as Buck swung past, guiding his partner in an exuberant waltz. The golden-haired girl he was partnering had been flirting with him all evening, as had just about every other young lady in attendance. He seemed to take wicked pleasure in flaunting his success at pairing up with the prettiest immigrants.

Disgusting. Amy forced an indifferent expression and looked past him.

The music shifted into the chords of an energetic polka and a trio of fiddlers sawed away at their instruments with enough steam to fuel a locomotive.

She sipped the refreshing cider while shifting her weight from side to side to relieve her aching feet. Her dance partners had included farmers and soldiers, as well as her betrothed.

The only man who hadn't asked her to dance was Buck. No surprise, considering the set down she'd given him when they'd parted the night before. She had burned his ears for almost kissing her, even as she'd cringed with shame for wanting it so much. Releasing a breath, she tried to purge the confusing emotions that swirled in her chest with every glimpse of him.

Beside her, Fletcher conversed with the local leaders. He'd been working the crowd like a politician on polling day. Perhaps he did have notions of running for office. If so, she wouldn't object. He turned as the small group dispersed. "The mayor is grateful you rescheduled this dance for tonight. I think they were afraid you'd pack up these girls and go home."

"That wouldn't have served any useful purpose." She brushed a bit of lint from the lapel of his evening coat and shifted her gaze to his eyes. Being slightly above average height, he didn't tower over her. He didn't make her feel tiny as a kitten, although she had no desire to curl up in his lap.

He bent closer and lowered his voice. "When will you extend your new offer?"

She smiled, confident in her inspiration no matter the source. Buck's comment about finding a way to help both sides had given her an idea for a way to get the settlers to replace ties burned by the Land League. The women had voiced their excited approval when she'd shared her thoughts earlier. "I'm letting the ladies make the announcement a little later this evening. The men will respond to them better than they will me."

Fletcher's eyes sparkled with amusement. "You're brilliant. But you know that, don't you?"

His effusive praise sent pleasure coursing through her. "If my idea works, it should smooth things over with Mr. Joy and get us back on schedule. I truly believe most of these settlers are ready to put differences aside and get on with their lives. "

Her conversation with Buck had stayed with her through the night, troubling her sleep. She wasn't crushing men's dreams just because she was behind the railroad. Her intentions were good even if her original plans hadn't worked out quite like she'd imagined. This new approach would be better. She would show Buck how a noble cause was far superior to letting instinct rule. That was what animals did, not people.

"Speaking of timely opportunities, I wanted to tell you about one." Fletcher's face grew animated, as it did whenever he had some new idea to share. "I've purchased blocks of land around Girard and Baxter Springs. Property that will be quite valuable as the towns grow."

She blinked up at him, not sure she'd understood. There wasn't a square foot of land around those towns that hadn't been staked out. "Isn't that land already claimed?"

Glancing around, he lowered his voice. "The men squatting on the tracts I purchased moved onto the land *after* Mr. Joy bought it, not before. They can't claim the same preemption rights as those who were on the land before he purchased it. I spoke to the land agent about this and he confirmed it. The law is on my side."

Using a legal loophole to buy land out from under the squatters didn't make it right. She was surprised he wasn't troubled by it. "Even if those settlers are there illegally, someone will have to force them to leave. We have problems enough as it is."

"There's no need to remove the squatters until after we've crossed the border and resolved our issues with those who have valid claims. We'll just sit tight until things settle down, and then move these men off one at a time." Fletcher eyes glowed with pride. "This land could be worth millions over the next few years. These squatters know this as well as I do, but they're trying to use this dispute to get it for nothing. I've paid for it, free and clear."

"How much? I know Mr. Joy is asking top dollar for properties close to town."

His face tightened. "You might exhibit a little more faith in my business acumen."

Like most men, Fletcher was easily offended, particularly when it came to matters of business. She knew him to be financially astute from her dealings with him as her banker over the past three years. Lately, though, he seemed drawn to riskier ventures, perhaps spurred on by the enormous wealth being made through land speculation.

In fact, the man he most admired, Mr. Joy, wasn't interested in operating a railroad. He was a real estate tycoon who saw an opportunity to increase his wealth by owning the land his railroad would pass through. Amy wanted to run the railroad.

"I suppose I have a more conservative bent and prefer to put my money into businesses rather than speculate on land." She placed her hand on Fletcher's arm in a placating gesture. "I trust your investment will return a good profit."

"I assure you, it will."

His curt tone made her bristle, but she swallowed her ire. Once they were married, she would insist they make decisions together. However, chiding him now would accomplish nothing. The better course would be to model what a marital partnership should be like.

"I'd like to get your opinion on a number of new investments I'm considering. Why don't we discuss it when we meet to review the annual audit of my accounts?"

His eyes widened, and then a smile appeared. "Of course. I'd be delighted."

Clapping broke out as the music came to a temporary end.

She turned her attention back to the crowd, smiling with satisfaction. This dance was just the thing to get the settlers in the right frame of mind.

Buck passed through her line of vision as he escorted his giggling partner to the punch bowl. After pouring them drinks, he turned her over to an eager settler and walked away without a backward glance.

Amy released a pent-up breath. Apparently, his interest in these girls was as fleeting as each dance. Her eyes followed him as he moved with a long-limbed grace that reminded her of the big cats she'd seen lurking on the bluffs above the river. They were wildly beautiful, but too dangerous to approach.

Buck wove through the crowd, combing his fingers through hair that was dark with dampness from his exertions. An illicit thought formed of running the tip of her tongue along his neck, tasting the tanginess and texture of his skin. Her breath hitched as the fantasy provoked the same pleasurable ache she felt whenever he touched her.

"Amy. I asked if you wanted to dance."

She jerked her gaze back to Fletcher. He shot a scowling glance in Buck's direction, but the other man had disappeared out the open doors of the barn. Her face flamed. "I, uh, my feet. They hurt. I think I'll sit down until it's time for the announcement."

Buck fanned his face with his hat as he strode out of the hot barn and into the cool night. He drew a deep breath, letting rain-washed air calm an agitation that had him heated up from more than dancing. He was behaving like an ass, parading those women under Amy's nose. But every time he saw her in the arms of another man it made his gut twist up and something mean inside urged him to strike out.

He glanced up at a full moon, wanting to howl with frustration. He'd danced with every woman in there except the one he wanted. Amy was a fever in his blood. Every time she came near he used any excuse to touch her. He craved their every contact and ached for her caress. The idea of bedding her held more appeal than ever, but it would be like putting a match to gunpowder. He'd never survive the explosion.

Sean clapped him on the shoulder. "You planning on giving anybody else a chance? I swear you danced with every gal in there."

Buck wiped the sweat off his forehead. "Just getting some exercise."

He had caught Sean's eye when he'd headed outside to cool off, which was just as well. It was time to stop pining after a woman and focus on the job he'd come to do. He needed to fill his cousin in on their next move.

The wet grass dampened his boots and trouser legs as he headed toward an open field some distance away from where the other men were clustered, talking and smoking. "I got an idea for keeping that railroad slowed down a bit longer."

"Ah, I knew you'd come up with something."

"It's nothing I came up with, just something I heard." Something deep in his chest began to throb. He hated betraying Amy's confidence, but he had no choice. He stopped and faced his cousin, determined to get this over with. "That other railroad is starting a new branch line and there's a shortage of workers to build it. The Border Tier can't afford to increase wages."

Understanding dawned on Sean's face. "So if the Katy paid more to lure away workers..."

"The Border Tier can't afford to get them back." Buck paused, having not yet worked out exactly how they'd make use of this information. "Of course, this all hinges on whether that other railroad will increase wages, and who knows if they will."

Sean gave a confident nod. "Oh I'm certain they will."

Certain? Suspicion crawled up the back of Buck's scalp. "How can you be so sure?"

Sean's eyes rounded with a look of innocence. "Why wouldn't they? There's been a history of these lines outbidding each other."

Buck clenched his jaw, but he held back his anger. "Why are you doing this?"

"What, the railroad slow down? You know why."

Damn him for a liar. "What's your land worth if the Border Tier loses the race?"

His cousin shrugged. "We're just making 'em sweat. They're too far ahead to lose."

"If more workers jump lines and they have to build another seventeen miles of track they could lose the race. And if the Katy wins, it'll be the only railroad allowed to expand into Texas. The only one to pick up all that cattle trade."

Sean's expression turned wary. "What are you saying?"

"You know damn well what I'm saying." He stiffened his arms to keep from slamming his fist into Sean's face. "Your land won't be worth squat if they lose the race. So either you're a stupid, stiff-necked son-of-a-bitch to risk everything, or you're tucking something in your other pocket. What the hell, cousin? I gave you not one, but *two* chances to tell me the truth."

Sean's face twisted in a resentful scowl. "I *did* tell you the truth. I can't afford to pay King Joy's price for that land, and I'll see the bastard in hell before I let him succeed in his schemes."

God, this was too much. Did Sean think he was dealing with an idiot? "What's that other railroad paying you? Whatever it is, it better be enough to get you far away from here once your friends figure out you're double-crossing them to line your own pockets."

With a curse, Sean surged forward throwing a punch.

Buck jerked back and at the same time grabbed the other man's arm and flung him over an outstretched leg. His cousin tumbled face first into the grass. Buck dropped his knee onto Sean's back and grabbed his hair. With icy calm, he whipped out a knife and held the blade to the man's exposed throat.

"You lied to me." He spoke through clenched teeth because if he let up the pain would surge through him. Why had he trusted again when those closest to him were always the ones who broke faith? "I thought family meant something to you, but you're just using me in some game you're playing."

The hand clenching the knife trembled. Christ, was he ready to slit his cousin's throat? Revolted, he jerked away, thrusting Sean's face to the ground before rising to his feet. "I'm finished with you."

Sean stood slowly, wiping away bits of grass and dirt that clung to his face.

Buck sheathed his knife. He wouldn't kill Sean, but he would beat the shit out of him if he chose to continue this fight. Their eyes held for a long moment. Finally, Sean broke the stare, dropping his head to stare at the ground.

"I didn't lie about needing your help." The roughness in his voice grated on Buck's nerves. "I am near broke. I was counting on getting that land cheap and then selling enough so I could improve my farm. But...I wasn't certain things would work out. So, I took an offer from the Katy. Their foreman said they'd pay me for information, and doing what we're already doing."

Music drifted out of the barn. The joyous sound seemed to drive the nails deeper into Buck's heart.

"That letter you were writing the other day when I came to your place. Were you reporting to this foreman? About the ties?"

Sean raised his eyes, they begged for understanding. "I wasn't working for the Katy until a week ago. I was out checking their progress and met some of the boys working that line. They're *micks*, like us. They introduced me to their foreman and he made me an offer. I figured if we didn't win this war with Joy, At least I'd have something for my trouble."

Tension tightened Buck's shoulders. He started to pace, wanting to hit something. "For chrissake, Sean. I told you I didn't care what you were doing. I asked you to shoot straight with me, but you didn't."

"I thought you might want part of what they were paying me."

Buck turned, incredulous. "You *lied* to me because you didn't want to share?"

His cousin's dark brows gathered in a defensive frown. "I told you, I didn't lie. I just omitted the fact that I was working with the Katy. I didn't think it was all that important. You don't care if the Border Tier wins or not. And I figured you were getting paid by that railroad lady, so you don't need the extra."

The excuses piled up, but Sean didn't get—or refused to acknowledge—the real issue. If he could lie about this, he could lie about anything.

"I don't want your damned pocket change." Buck started back toward the barn.

"Wait. You can't back out now. I still need your help. " Sean trailed alongside. "I swear that's the only thing I didn't tell you. I was wrong to hide it, but that's all I was hiding."

Buck lengthened his strides to put more distance between them. How could he trust his cousin again? Sean had deceived him. No matter that he claimed it was a small thing. Betrayal always started with the small things. He'd seen it before, in his own men, in a woman he'd given his protection to and offered his name. Resentment burned in his gut. Georgia's betrayal had been the worst. He'd offered her his love, his vow—and she'd left him to go after another man.

She left you because you're no good, Bucko.

"Buck, stop." Sean grabbed his arm.

His anger surged—at his cousin, at the situation he found himself in. With condemnation still echoing in his head. Buck whirled, raising his fist, ready to pound the other man's face. If nothing else, fighting would release the savagery inside him and let him focus on something other than his own pain.

Sean took a step back. His arms dropped to his sides. "I won't fight you."

Buck's breath came hard and fast. He blinked to clear a red haze that nearly blinded him. *Damn it*, not again. If he released his rage, the beast would rule him, and he'd do something he would sorely regret. He let his hand fall. The movement released a tide of weariness. God he was tired, mostly tired of being a fool. But it seemed he never learned from his mistakes.

He heaved a heavy sigh. "What do you want from me?"

"What I told you before. I want your help getting a fair deal. You were right when you said my land is worth more if the Border Tier wins the race. But it won't be my land if I can't afford to buy it." Sean came closer, pleading. "You've gotten close to that lady promoter. Maybe she'd listen to you, or you can use her to influence her boss."

"Use her?" Buck's stomach turned. Hadn't he done that already? Even if he hadn't bedded Amy, he'd still used her. He had manipulated her, won her faith, and then betrayed her. She'd entrusted him with her life, had opened her home, maybe even her heart. Yet, he'd been willing to betray her.

For a good cause.

He swore under his breath. He'd come back to Kansas to serve justice, but whose justice? It wasn't so clear to him, and he was having a hard time ignoring a conscience that was speaking up with increasing regularity. "I won't use her. Not anymore."

Sean held his gaze. "I talked to Amos and the other members of the Land League, like you asked. Nobody admits to trying to kill Mrs. Langford and I think they'd tell me if they were."

So, his cousin would play the only card he had left, information about Amy's attacker.

Buck crossed his arms over his chest. "How do I know you're not lying to me?"

"You'll have to trust me."

Buck shook his head. Saints, his cousin had some nerve. "I won't feed you information, or trick Amy into doing anything that'll hurt her."

"You'll figure something out. You always do." Sean held out his hand, but when Buck didn't take it he slipped it into his pocket. "I know you don't think you can trust me, but you can. If I'd wanted, I could've turned you in and taken the reward." One corner of his mouth lifted in a slight smile. "Though they're only offering a couple hundred dollars. They must not think you're worth much."

The band around Buck's chest grew tighter. "You holding that over my head to gain my cooperation?"

Sean drew back, seemingly offended. "I'm not a complete bastard."

"Keep working at it, you'll get there." Buck's anger drained, replaced by a painful loneliness. He had imagined— no, he'd foolishly hoped—things would work out differently and he could reestablish ties with at least one person who cared about him. But why should his cousin care any more than his father, or his stepbrothers, or Georgia, or anyone else in his godforsaken world?

"I won't betray you, cousin," Sean declared. "Even if you decide you can't help me. I'll try to keep Amos from sniffing around. I've not told him everything about you, and I don't intend to. You're family, and I am loyal." He shrugged sheepishly. "Just a wee bit selfish."

Buck released a resigned sigh. His cousin had played the ace. Family loyalty. He couldn't turn his back on his only living kinsman, much as he wanted to. He'd try to influence Amy, but he wouldn't seduce her, trick her or cause her shame. He would, however, continue this charade. If he revealed the depth of his deception she'd throw him out—or more likely turn him in.

"Hey fellows, you missed the big announcement!" The shout came from a lanky farmer, who loped toward them. It was the same fellow who'd tried to bid on a basket at the rally. "Mrs. Langford says we can wed the ladies without having to pay their expenses, regardless of whether or not we sign our contracts."

Buck frowned. Amy wouldn't play her hand without advancing her game. So what's she up to? "She didn't put any requirements on it?"

The farmer shook his head, a big grin stretching his face. "Nope. But them gals said the men who cut the most ties will get the first shot at marrying them."

CHAPTER 12

March 26, 1870, Fort Scott, Kansas

Buck peered into the small mirror, fumbling with a black silk tie. How hard could it be to knot the damn thing into a bow? He finished up and turned down the points of his shirt collar. Stepping back, he bent his knees to bring his head down. He'd forgotten to purchase a tonic and his hair wasn't cooperative on the best of days. Licking his fingers, he smoothed the mutinous strands.

Why the hell was he so jittery about going to a party? It wasn't as if Amy would be paying him much mind, not with that trained hound at her side.

"You're a damn fool," he muttered to his image. "Why do you care what she thinks?"

The train ride home from Girard had been more excruciating than the dance. Amy and Fletcher had sat in front of him, their heads close together, absorbed in deep discussion over something he didn't catch. She was marrying the pompous ass, and that was all there was to it. They would announce their formal engagement tonight at the Wilson's party, and Buck got to go along to make sure she didn't get killed.

He huffed in disgust. Why did he care who she married? What he ought to be focused on was how to change her mind about helping the settlers, not to mention catching her assailant. Some of the top businessmen in Fort Scott would be at tonight's party. None of them were on Amy's list, but

Buck wanted to determine on his own what these men thought of her. She might not have correctly guessed. Betrayers were often those closest and most trusted, as he knew from experience.

Picking up his new coat from where he'd tossed it over a chair, he pulled it on. Then he looked at his bare hands and swore under his breath. What should he do about gloves? All gentlemen wore them. He couldn't wear the ones he'd torn, but the new ones he'd ordered hadn't come in yet.

A light rap on the door drew his attention. Might be Jacob, who liked to talk horses. Amy's groomsman had warmed up to him once they'd discovered common ground. Their tentative friendship was probably the only thing that kept Sophie from poisoning him after Amy had decided against extending any more dinner invitations.

Buck opened the door—and his heart slammed against his chest.

Amy stood at the threshold, a mouth-watering confection in a frothy yellow gown that showed off every lovely curve. Dainty lace sleeves were drawn off her shoulders, baring a lovely expanse of chest, and her waist looked so small he could easily span it with his hands.

All he could do was stare and wonder. What was she doing out here in the carriage house?

"May I?" She gazed up at him, her fine brows drawn together as though she was uncertain of her welcome.

He swallowed hard. "Come in."

She rustled into the room. The ends of a black velvet ribbon adorning her neck trailed down the back of the gown, drawing his gaze to her backside hidden somewhere beneath a cascade of flounces and frills. His fingers itched to peel away the layers of silk and lace and expose the creamy flesh beneath.

The heavy ache of an arousal drew him up short. Better lasso his imagination before it dragged him into dangerous territory.

Amy turned around and with both hands held something out in front of her.

Buck took the offering, a pair of light gray gloves. Looked large enough to fit him, and made of the softest leather he'd ever felt. He looked at her, afraid to ask.

"I had them made special." Her eyes beseeched. "I'm sorry…about the other ones."

A strange lightheadedness stole over him, an odd, giddy feeling unlike anything he'd ever experienced. She'd bought him gloves. Didn't matter it was because she felt guilty. Amy had ordered something made just for him. His throat tightened. No one, save his mother, had ever done anything so thoughtful.

"Thank you." His voice sounded funny. He cleared his throat, blinked away the burning in his eyes. Hell, it was just a pair of gloves.

Amy gestured. "Try them on."

He slid his fingers into the supple leather and flexed his hand. "They fit perfectly."

Like we would. God, he was such a fool.

Taking his hand, she turned it over and examined the glove. With her fingertips, she stroked across his palm.

Desire jolted through him. He clamped his teeth together, holding back a moan. God in heaven, she might as well be touching his naked body, and he was going to lose the battle for control if he didn't do something fast.

He stepped back and drew on the other glove. "Did I do that right?" he asked, raising an eyebrow. "Like a gentlemen?"

Her face paled as his barb found its target.

Ah Bucko, you're such a mean bastard.

"Just teasing." He backed into an apology. "I don't recall anybody ever doing something so nice for me."

She clutched her bag in front of her like a shield. "I probably deserved that, so you don't have to go so far as to suggest I've done anything special."

Oh, but you have. When he was an old man, he would still wear these gloves and her kindness would still touch him.

He cleared his throat again. "Your dress, is it the one you picked up at your friend's store?"

Her hand brushed the low neckline in a nervous gesture. "It's one of Charles Worth's new designs. I've been dying to wear it, though now I'm not sure...."

"It fits..." He couldn't think of what else to say. She looked so damned luscious, but he wanted to compliment her, not offend her. "Like a glove."

Her eyes widened a split second before she gasped. "Oh, you almost had me there. That was subtle." She eyed him with a saucy tilt of her head. "I shall take care not to split any seams."

Did she think he was still poking fun about that prank with the gloves? She had to be aware he lusted after her. But did she know her smile took his breath away? And when she gazed up at him, those golden brown eyes snapping with intelligence, his heart took off like a runaway horse. "Mr. Worth must've had you in mind when he designed that gown. I can't think of any gal who'd look prettier wearing it."

Her lips parted slightly, and her eyes took on a soft, bemused expression.

It was poor flattery, considering what he really wanted to say. But he had no right to say those things a man would only tell a woman he loved.

Loved? Dread twisted Buck's insides into a painful knot. *God, no.* He couldn't be in love with Amy. Not twice a fool—and this time an even bigger one for knowing all along *this* woman wasn't meant for him. What the hell did he know about love anyway, except how to fail miserably at it?

Flustered, he turned away to retrieve his hat. "You shouldn't have come all the way out here just to give me those gloves. You'll get that dress dirty. I'll see you back to the house."

The rustling started up again, this time closer. "Jacob brought the landau around. He's waiting downstairs. We need to stop and pick up Fletcher on our way into town."

It was beyond rude to keep his back to her, but that startling realization had thrown him and he couldn't risk the chance she'd see how he felt. He'd never let himself be that vulnerable again. He cast about for a subject that would deflect her attention away from his awkwardness.

"Have any more settlers taken you up on that offer to cut ties?" He schooled his features into an indifferent mask as he turned around. "I never told you, but that was a neat trick."

She cocked her head, seeming confused by his abrupt shift in direction. "It wasn't meant as a trick. I simply found something that would benefit both sides. You told me to come up with a fair deal."

A fair deal. Ah yes, the reason he'd come here in the first place. Not to fall in love, but to get justice. Justice required fairness. If he could get Amy to see the settlers weren't being treated fairly, it would change her perspective and she would be more willing to influence her boss. But how could he make the case? And when? Over the past week, it'd been impossible to pry her away from Fletcher, who wouldn't take his side in any matter.

"Why don't you ask the settlers what they'd consider a fair deal?"

Her brow furrowed. "They've made their demands eminently clear."

"I didn't say demands. A fair deal is generally something you negotiate."

"They've been unwilling to negotiate."

"So has your boss. Why don't you take the initiative and talk to them?"

She chewed her lower lip, then twisted her wrist to grasp the dangling reticule. Whenever Amy was troubled, she worried the strings on her bag. "I'm not in a position to carry through. Only the board of directors, or Mr. Joy, can extend an offer."

Buck ventured closer. He gently pried her fingers open and took her hand. With his thumb, he stroked the back of her glove. Her eyes widened, then she yanked her hand away, but not fast enough to hide a tremble. It was
small consolation to know that at least in this way, she wanted him. "Don't promise anything, other than to take the deal you negotiate back to the board."

She stared up at him. "There have been countless attempts to forge a compromise. I don't know that I'll be any more successful."

He couldn't restrain a smile. Few men could refuse the appeal of a beautiful woman who was on their side. "That's because everybody only considered their own interests. You go talk to the settlers, really put yourself in their shoes. I bet you gain some sort of compromise your board will listen to, especially now. You're short on workers, short on time and short on money. Remember what I told you once? About using the right weapons?"

A delightful flush pinked her cheeks. He held her gaze. He wanted to travel a little lower, but that would be counterproductive to this conversation. After a moment, she narrowed her eyes. "I'm not sure I trust your advice, considering how things turned out last time."

The rally. He wouldn't point out she hadn't taken his advice, so he'd been forced to trick Major Roy into offering protection. If she realized that, she might begin to suspect him. "What do you mean? You took my advice and offered those settlers a fair deal when it came to those women, and that's worked out to your benefit."

She rolled her eyes, but the thoughtful frown that followed suggested she was at least considering his suggestion. "If I decide to do this, I'll need to go to the board first, to gain their support in advance."

"As a general rule, it's a bad idea to reveal your strategy to your opponents."

"They aren't my opponents, but I take your meaning. I'm just not sure I want to risk it, given how badly things turned out at that rally."

"If you're able to forge a compromise, one that both sides can agree to, that would more than make up for whatever went wrong before."

He waited, seeing the silent struggle in her eyes as caution warred with ambition. Her lips tightened, and then her breath left in a rush. "All right, I'll consider it." She stepped back, smoothing her dress with a nervous gesture. "Let's get going. Fletcher will be waiting."

Buck clamped down on a surge of jealousy. She'd made her choice. Not that he was ever in the running. At least he'd gained her agreement to meet with the settlers, which could lead to a breakthrough if they came prepared to engage in true negotiation. He'd get word to Sean to ensure they acted in good faith.

He secured his hat, then offered her his arm. "I'm ready."

Her gaze traveled over him. "You look very nice. Handsome."

Pleasure coiled in his belly. Lower, the fire started burning.

Her lips curved in a smile that didn't light her face. "Maggie will be pleased to see you."

Maggie? He didn't give a damn whether Maggie would be pleased to see him. He bit back a sharp retort. He could kick himself for flirting with Amy's friend. He'd only done it to tweak her. Hell, he'd danced with every woman in Girard just to get a rise out of her, but she had only glared at him as if she believed he was nothing more than a womanizer.

Resigned, he led her out the door. Perhaps it was just as well she thought the worst. He couldn't tell her the truth—about anything.

The hostess clapped her hands together and a mischievous glint lit in her eyes. "It's time for an announcement, and after that, we shall retire to the parlor for games."

Amy nodded agreeably to the woman who sat at the head of the table presiding over dinner. As matriarch of Fort Scott's first family, Elizabeth Wilson could order her parties any way she chose…but Amy dreaded the games. It seemed the Wilson's primary reason for playing were the forfeits afterwards, which often involved embarrassing activities, the more outrageous the better. There could be no getting out of the games, but she would not be paying a forfeit. Which meant she had to win.

She laid down her fork, staring with dismay at the mound of potatoes still on her plate, along with most of the roasted turkey. Even taking shallow breaths, she still felt like she was suffocating. Mercy, her corset was tight. Thank heavens no one seemed to have noticed her discomfort. Not even Fletcher, who was seated to her right.

Heiro Wilson, at the far end of the table opposite his wife, lifted his stout form out of the chair. He regarded his guests with uncharacteristic solemnity. When he had everyone's attention, he motioned for Fletcher to rise. "We have a very important piece of news tonight. Mr. Bain, as most of you know, has been courting Mrs. Langford for some time. It seems his fondest hopes have finally been realized."

Gasps went up from the ladies.

Fletcher stood, taking hold of the lapels of his evening coat. The light from a sparkling chandelier reflected off his snowy shirt and white tie. He made a measured survey of those seated, not missing the opportunity for a bit of dramatic flair. "You all know Mrs. Langford. She has become in three short years our most benevolent benefactress, through her untiring work for our railroad, her generous support of our businesses, and in the countless hours she spends on educational and cultural endeavors. She is admired by many, but adored by one."

Titters rippled through the air. Fletcher smiled more broadly.

His effusive praise brought a blush to Amy's cheeks. She'd worked hard to establish herself in Fort Scott, and had fallen in love with her adopted city. Was that love returned? The smiling faces around the table seemed to confirm this, but she was astute enough to realize that affection often grew in proportion to the wealth of its object.

"As we are eager to be off to our games, let me be brief." Fletcher was never brief. "I see a day when our fair city will be a Mecca of commerce; a gateway for those traveling west. Our state, the youngest in the Union, is a shining star of progress. Kansas has more than eight hundred miles of railroad track, most of which has been laid over the last three years. Opportunity is unfolding for the farmer, the businessman and laborer alike. All of us gathered around this table are leading the way to a bright future, but none more so than Mrs. Langford. This fine woman, whom I have long admired and pursued with diligence, has done me the honor of agreeing to become my wife. She and I will be wed one week after the Border Tier crosses the boundary into Indian Territory. May that day come soon."

Polite clapping broke out. Congratulations were given. Toasts were offered. Amy waited for the thrill, but her body hummed with anxiety. Perhaps she was experiencing a bout of cold feet.

Across the table, Maggie's eyes shone with warmth. She looked lovely in an emerald gown that set off her dark hair. Buck lounged next to her, affecting his usual countenance of wry amusement. Amy clutched her hands in her lap, silently willing him to look her way. Why hadn't he acknowledged her during the whole of dinner?

After that odd moment in the carriage house, he seemed almost intent on ignoring her. Had she embarrassed him with her gift? He'd been surprised, but more than that, the look on his face had nearly broken her heart. She would've sworn he was about to cry, until he'd fired off that snide remark. Inexplicably, he'd given her a compliment that made her body quiver and her spirit soar. Then, he had turned his back on her.

Irritated, she tore her gaze away. Why was she spending a single minute fretting over his mercurial moods? She ought to be concentrating on her betrothed.

"My dear, I am *so* happy for you." Mrs. Wilson laid a hand on Amy's shoulder. "We've all been wondering when you two would finally get around to tying the knot."

Was that why they called it the bonds of matrimony? Somehow, the thought of marriage didn't elicit the joy she imagined she would feel. Nevertheless, everyone appeared quite pleased. That spoke well of her choice, didn't it? At least marriage to Fletcher would be calm, with no surprises, unlike the union of her unpredictable mother and unfortunate father.

Fletcher reached for her hand and she stood, basking in the attention given to newly engaged couples.

A half-hour later, Amy shifted nervously on the flocked divan she'd sought out as soon as they'd entered the parlor. Hopefully, the plan she hatched with Fletcher would relieve them both of any embarrassing moments as a result of the much-anticipated game of "Marriage."

Suspecting they would have to play the Wilson's favorite game, she and Fletcher had pre-selected their characters and agreed to work around the order so they would face off. He would present his suit, in character, and she would accept him as her perfect mate. That way, she wouldn't end up paired with someone outrageous like Charlie Goodlander or, God forbid, Buck. Just thinking about having to kiss him in front of the whole company made her shudder. Her attraction would be apparent to all and she'd be made a laughingstock.

Lizzie Goodlander, the Wilson's eldest daughter, sank onto the couch and took Amy's hands. Her hazel eyes flashed with pleasure. "You and Fletcher will have to come by and pay us a visit soon. Charlie recently returned from a buffalo hunt and has a whole new repertoire with which to entertain."

Wealthy and outlandish, Lizzie's husband was quite likable, but his practical jokes ran a bit too crude for Amy's tastes. However, he was one of the most successful businessmen in town and served on the railroad board. She couldn't afford to slight Charlie Goodlander, and liked Lizzie too well to even consider it.

Lizzie's sisters gathered round, waving to the other women to come join them. "Mother has changed the rules on us," Jennie whispered, seemingly delighted by what Amy viewed as terrible news. "We don't get to choose our own characters. The men are writing down female characters for us to select from, and we must write down male characters for them." She giggled like a schoolgirl. "I say, the more romantic the better."

Her sister Fannie handed out pencil stubs with bits of blue paper like those Mr. Chanute favored. Dear heavens, was this an omen—or God's idea of a practical joke?

Amy chewed her lip. How could she be sure of winning the game now? There was nothing to do but forge ahead and hope for the best.

"I've got mine," she muttered, jotting down Romeo and folding her paper. She sent up a silent prayer before tossing it into the hat.

Sitting beside her, Maggie offered a sympathetic look. "I'm sure you won't have to get down on all fours and bray like last time, Amy dear. You're bound to find a suitable match."

Oh good heavens, was her distress *that* obvious?

Jennie exchanged hats with Charlie and scurried back to the group. "Why don't you pick first, Amy?"

Amy closed her eyes and reached into the hat.

Lord, make it Juliet.

Her fingers closed on a folded bit of paper. A shivering sensation danced across her skin. This had to be the one. Excited, she unfolded it, and then stared in horror at what was written.

Venus.

There was no question where this had come from. *The scoundrel.*

Amy closed her eyes, listening to gasps and laughter as the other women made their selections. Romeo could make a good case for marriage to Venus—if Fletcher had drawn that character.

"Line up ladies, the gentlemen have already arranged themselves."

Lizzie pushed Amy to the front. "As our honored guest, you must be first."

Relief swept through her when she saw Fletcher move to the front.

Grinning beneath a walrus mustache, Charlie Goodlander caught his arm. "Let's not make this game too predictable. It takes all the fun out of it."

"True enough," Lizzie retorted, with a sharp look at her husband as he took first place in line. "Amy, why don't you come back here behind me?"

As everyone rearranged, Amy heaved a sigh. This was going to be a long night. If a woman turned down a man, she went to the next and the next until she had selected the most appropriate mate for her character. The remaining men were shuffled back through.

The game wore on, women and men pairing off until only four remained. Amy curled her fingers into fists to contain her nervousness. Maggie faced Fletcher. Her friend would turn him down, of course, and move on to Buck. Dear Maggie would take Buck even if he were Hades. This would leave Fletcher the last man standing, and Amy could easily accept his suit and not forfeit the game. It couldn't be more perfect.

Maggie clasped her hands together and spoke in a voice so soft Amy had to strain to hear. "I am Juliet. Who comes to ask for my hand in marriage?"

Fletcher stepped forward, the muscles in his face tightening. "I am Romeo."

Giggles went up from the women who were seated around the room with their respective *mates*. Amy bit her lip to hold back a groan. Dear Lord, how had this happened? Could Juliet refuse Romeo? She had to, because the alternative was unthinkable.

"What do you have to offer, sir?" Maggie asked softly.

"My heart and my life." Fletcher intoned.

Romeo didn't sound convinced. Perhaps Juliet would turn him down solely on the basis
of his being so obviously disinterested.

"Come on, Romeo, you're not putting forth much effort for the hand of the fair Juliet." Charlie chided. Other guests around the room chimed in, insisting Fletcher play his part.

Fletcher's face reddened. "I would *die* for you, my sweet Juliet," he blurted.

Amy held her breath, staring at her friend's stiff back. What was she waiting for?

"I can't think of any man who would do so much," Maggie whispered. "I accept."

"What?" Amy clapped her hand over her mouth a second too late.

All eyes shifted in her direction. Some glinted with amusement, others with surprise, a few reflected sympathy. Her skin felt hot and dry, as if she'd suddenly come down with a fever.

Maggie stepped forward to share a chaste kiss with Fletcher, whose face looked like Amy's felt. His mouth froze into a tight smile as the happy couple took their seats.

She blinked in hurt disbelief. How could her friend have done such a thing? Maggie must've been flustered by Charlie's goading. That was the only explanation.

Amy steeled her nerves. Best to have this over with as quickly as possible. "I'm Venus," she snapped. "Who seeks to marry me?"

With a sly smile, Buck took her hand. He brushed the back of her gloveless fingers with his lips. Desire crackled through her, as if he were lightening and she the rod. Still holding her hand, he raised his eyes. Within the silvery depths flickered wry amusement.

Damn him. He was enjoying her discomfiture.

"Casanova, the world's greatest lover, seeks the hand of Venus, goddess of love." His gravelly drawl caressed the name.

Heat suffused her face. *The cad.* She was not a love deity and he was no Casanova, however he might fancy himself to be. By jingo, she would strip away that civilized veneer he'd put on with those clothes and reveal him as a fraud. "What can a mere mortal offer?" she replied in her most arrogant goddess voice.

Buck's amused smile didn't waver, but surprise flared in his eyes. What had he thought? That she would turn tail and run?

"Pleasure," he murmured. He swept his thumb across the backs of her fingers, triggering another sizzling bolt.

She yanked her hand away. If she were to defeat him, she couldn't let him touch her. The uncontrollable reactions were too distracting. "I already have pleasures aplenty."

He arched a sandy brow. "Not the sort you'll find with me. I've spent a lifetime cultivating knowledge of a sensual nature, learning all there is to know about pleasing a woman. With me, every day will bring new delights you can open, like a present."

Gasps went up from the ladies, along with the low chuckles of men.

She blushed to her toes. Where had Buck learned about Casanova? For that matter, where had he picked up that educated elocution? He'd surprised her—again.

Against her will, her gaze moved from his broad shoulders and chest, down to narrow hips and long legs, taking a return trip north to linger on his lips. Temptation whispered sordid suggestions in her ear. What would it be like to throw propriety to the wind and lay with a man like this? To explore things she'd thought of in the dark, but wouldn't admit to in the light. Shivering, she shook off the sensual reverie. She had no desire to do *that* with Buck.

Liar.

With a shaky breath, she put a hand to her stomach to still the fluttering army of insects that had taken up residence inside. "Perhaps you've learned a few pleasures I might find interesting, but you see, I'm already married. I can't have two husbands."

Buck crossed his arms over his chest, holding her gaze prisoner. "You gods don't live by the same rules as we *mere mortals*. At least, the legends reveal you're not too particular. But if you prefer, we can have a marriage of the heart without all those messy vows of faithfulness."

Amy's head jerked around at a loud guffaw. Lizzie smacked her husband's arm. This conversation wasn't going in the right direction. If Buck won, he earned a kiss. If he lost, he had to pay a forfeit. And she dearly wanted to see him pay.

"I have an eternal lover, Mars, God of war. He can satisfy my needs more than a feeble man like you."

Buck's lips twitched. "I may be feeble compared to your war god, but I would treat you more tenderly than that nasty-tempered fellow."

He dropped to one knee. This brought him even with her chest. At the smoldering heat in his eyes, she feared her breasts had tumbled out of the low-cut gown.

She struggled to breathe.

He captured her hand once again. "Only a man who is expert at making love—not war—can truly appreciate your gifts and the essence of who you are."

"Heavens, he would have had me at Casanova," Lizzie quipped. "I think you've met your perfect mate, Venus."

Shaken, Amy stepped back, taking her hand with her. She shook her head. None of this had the slightest basis in truth, no matter the seductive promise in his eyes. Buck was toying with her. Playing his part to the hilt.

"You're a rogue, a lover of women who can't be satisfied with just one. I'm a jealous goddess and I won't abide your unfaithfulness, even if I'm not held to the same standard."

He remained on one knee, but held out his hands like a supplicant. "That might've been true in the past, that I couldn't be satisfied with just one woman, but you are not one woman. You are the epitome of every man's fantasy, all women rolled into one. You would satisfy even the largest appetite."

His tongue swept his lips, and she nearly came out of her skin. "Accept my proposal. Take me, for as long as you like. Then cast me aside if you tire of me later."

Her legs trembled. Dear Lord, if she didn't do something quick, everyone would realize the effect he was having on her. She had to end this game. Now. "I'm not just looking for pleasure. I want love. You've not said you love me."

Casanova's lips twisted in a sneer. "Any man who's quick to proclaim words of love is a liar and a fool."

A thrill shot through her. For some reason, Casanova didn't want to tell Venus he loved her. This was it. Her ace. "But without words, my dear Casanova, the *pleasure* of love is diminished. Every woman, especially one who represents all women, must be assured by words, heartfelt and true. That is the only way you will win me."

He narrowed his eyes. Amy struggled to control her excitement. She had him on the run.

"It's not words that should assure you, it's what a man does that shows his true feelings." The urgency in his voice didn't match his mocking smile, and his eyes blazed with an intensity that made it seem as though his world tilted on her axis, his existence determined by her whim.

Her breath lodged somewhere between her chest and her throat. This wasn't real. Buck was acting. Even if he was putting on the best show she'd ever seen.

"Give me the words, Casanova," she whispered, caught up in the fantasy. "For even a goddess longs to hear them."

Her request hung in the air. Breathing was suspended. The tick of a clock on the mantel was the only sound disturbing the silence...that, and the pounding of her heart.

His smile fell away. "Venus," he started, his voice dropping to a harsh whisper. "Don't you know you own my heart?"

Cheers erupted. Amy's head swam. Voices faded as the room grew small and hot.

Buck's concerned expression wavered in and out of focus.

Almighty. This blasted corset was too tight. Amy blinked furiously to erase the black spots clouding her vision, but they wouldn't retreat, and her lungs wouldn't expand. Her knees wobbled...right before the curtain dropped.

CHAPTER 13

March 28, 1870, Fort Scott, Kansas

"I still can't believe I fainted." With a wry smile, Amy accepted the steaming cup of tea.

Maggie set down the teapot and took a seat across the kitchen table. She offered a sympathetic smile. "Perhaps your corset was too tight? Or you held yourself too stiff. Everyone seems to have an opinion about what happened."

Oh yes, she had certainly been the subject of much speculation since her *delicate episode* at the Wilson's party two days earlier. Not that there was anything delicate about collapsing. Had Buck not been so quick to react, she would've ended up in a heap on the floor. Instead—based on Maggie's report—he'd caught her up in his arms and carried her limp form into a bedroom. It seemed the entire party gathered to watch as she was treated to Mrs. Wilson's smelling salts.

How humiliating.

Sighing, she took a sip of the fragrant jasmine tea. Her gaze wandered to an open window facing the street, where her bodyguard stood watch in front of the dress shop beneath her friend's apartment. "Perhaps I fainted because you'd walked off with my husband-to-be."

Maggie's dark brows gathered in distress. "Is that why you came to see me?"

"No, I didn't come to scold you." Amy took another sip. "I do wonder why you accepted Romeo's proposal. Was it Charlie's goading that got to you?"

"How does Juliet refuse Romeo?" Maggie reached across the table. "I'm sorry. I don't know what got into me. I should've refused."

Amy gave her friend's hand a squeeze. Her conscience pricked. She'd been the one who tried to manipulate the outcome to her advantage. Perhaps God struck her down for cheating.

"Don't apologize. You played the game according to the rules. Much as I hate to admit it, so did Buck. I was rather surprised by how well he played his part. I didn't think he could pull it off."

"Did you not?" Maggie's eyes twinkled. "He strikes me as a man with hidden talents."

Amy dropped her gaze. She didn't want to discuss Buck's hidden talents. "He's apparently familiar with Casanova, but I don't know as that speaks well of him."

"What's really troubling you?"

Dear Maggie. She always cut to the heart of a matter.

Cradling the cup, Amy let its warmth calm her frayed nerves. She'd come to her friend's home, to this kitchen smelling of tea and toast, to find reassurance. That incident at the party had unnerved her. Why had she pushed Buck to declare himself? She would've won the game if she'd refused him the first time he evaded her request. Yet, something inside, something pathetic and desperate, had urged her on.

"I'm doing the right thing in marrying Fletcher." Amy raised her eyes, meeting Maggie's concerned gaze. "He's successful. Smart. Ambitious. Precisely the kind of husband I need."

"Are you trying to convince me, or yourself?" The kindness in Maggie's expression softened her pointed question. "Tell me, are you in love with him?"

Amy's heart grew heavy. How could she explain that she didn't want to be in love? That feeling was fleeting and much too risky. Her parents' relationship had more than proven that.

Swirling the remaining liquid in the cup, she stared at the dark leaves as they floated to the bottom, wishing she could see the future as well as she could recall the past. "My father loved my mother to distraction. He worshipped the ground she walked on. The only thing he ever did against her wishes was to move us to Kansas."

Amy lifted her head. She had to unburden her heart to someone, and Maggie seemed a safe choice. "Mother didn't like it here. There wasn't the social life she was used to, and the conditions at that time were very harsh. But it wasn't her unhappiness that finally undid her. It was...her passion."

"When Mother was in one of her exhilarated moods, as Father called them, she was wonderful, so alive and energetic. I was too young to realize the destructive nature of passion and how it fuels an insatiable appetite...until I walked in on her one day with a man who wasn't my father. She swore me to secrecy, but Father eventually discovered her unfaithfulness. It devastated him and drove her to end her life."

Amy squeezed her eyes shut against a dry burning. She had no tears left, having filled an ocean after her mother's death.

Muted sounds drifted through the window—the rumble and creak of wagon wheels, jingling traces and shouts of vendors, women calling their children. Life went on. It didn't stop. Even when it seemed, at times, it should.

Cool fingers slipped under Amy's palm. "Oh honey, I'm so sorry."

She grasped her friend's hand in a tight grip. "I don't want passion. And I don't want the kind of love that destroys you when it's gone."

"You aren't your mother." Maggie's statement broke into Amy's troubled thoughts.

"My rational mind tells me that, but I'm not going to test myself to be certain. I'd rather avoid strong passion. It's safer. Besides, I'm not missing much."

"You don't really believe that," her friend chided. "Passion can be a wonderful thing between two people who love each other."

This seemed an odd perspective from a woman whose husband had beaten her with regularity. Amy raised an eyebrow. "How can you say that after what you experienced?"

Maggie's expression grew solemn. She refilled Amy's cup and then her own. "It wasn't passion that caused my husband to beat me. It was his violent temper. Loving with passion is very different from letting yourself be ruled by unrestrained emotions."

Perhaps there was a difference, but Amy wasn't buying it just yet. "What happens when passion clouds your common sense? I've seen more lives than my father's destroyed because people couldn't control their baser urges."

Her friend looked at her sadly. "I may not be the best person to advise you in this, but I will tell you, my parents had a loving marriage that lasted until they died. I made a mistake and picked a man who couldn't manage his demons. But I still believe that a caring, passionate relationship is possible, with the right person. I can't tell you who that is. That's something you'll have to decide."

"Maybe that kind of relationship will come with time, once Fletcher and I have been married for a while. I've heard of love growing between people. It seems that might be better than to be taken in by a flight of fancy."

"Perhaps." Maggie sipped her tea, dropping her gaze.

Amy's spirits sank. She'd come here to allay her doubts. Why wasn't her friend cooperating? "I don't understand. You were so encouraging when Fletcher first called on me. Why are you acting like this? What's changed?"

Maggie seemed to hesitate. "I saw the way Buck looked at you."

"Oh good grief, he was *acting*."

"What about that time in my store?"

"He was *flirting*. He flirts with everyone. He flirted with you." Amy set her cup on the saucer harder than she intended and tea sloshed over the side.

"I'm sorry." She dabbed with her napkin at the stain on the tablecloth.

Maggie continued, ignoring the spill. "More importantly, I saw the way you looked at him,"

"How did I look at him? Like I wanted to kill him? Earlier that morning, he'd interrupted an important business meeting. Not to mention, he kissed me the night before—without my permission—and then waltzed into the store the next day and started making faces at you. He's just toying with us. Can't you see that?"

Perspiration beaded on Amy's forehead. Why was this room so hot? She'd worn a light muslin, but it felt like she was sitting over a furnace.

The smooth lines of Maggie's face reflected an annoying calm. "I think Buck was trying to make you jealous. Based on that prank you played on him, it must've worked."

How could she bring that up? "It wasn't a prank, and I wasn't jealous. I was...annoyed. When you were out of the room searching for that suit, he made a very rude remark. I'll admit, it wasn't well done of me to dupe him into trying on those gloves, and I replaced them."

Maggie leaned forward, grasping her wrist. "I'm not saying this to make you feel bad. You may be right about Buck. He might be a philanderer. But the things I'm seeing between the two of you, the other day and at the party. The way he was romancing you."

"No." Amy shook her head, pulling her hand away. How could Maggie's voice sound so reasonable when she was saying something crazy?

"He *was*. He wasn't just acting. And you...I saw something in your face that's made me wonder whether your feelings for Fletcher are strong enough to sustain a marriage." Maggie leaned back, her green eyes bright with emotion. "I don't want to see you trapped in an unhappy relationship. I know what that's like."

"It's not like that at all." Amy twisted the napkin in her lap, trying to keep the frustration out of her voice. "Fletcher and I are well-suited, in our personal lives, our backgrounds, our interests. Buck is.... Well, I know next to nothing about him, but I know he's not the right man."

"I'm not trying to convince you to consider Buck, I'm asking you to examine your motives for marrying Fletcher. You may decide you don't want love, but what does *he* expect? Does he think you love him? Does he care? If neither of you are looking for that, then perhaps it is a good match." Her friend's normally soft voice became brittle.

She winced at the guilt Maggie's words stirred up. What *did* Fletcher expect? Always an attentive suitor, he'd been eager to please and anxious to marry. He'd made it clear he cared for her, respected her, desired her, but he'd never declared his love. She hadn't been looking for that, so it didn't really bother her. That much. She placed her napkin on the table and stood to leave, feeling worse than she had when she walked in the door.

Maggie leapt to her feet. "Don't go, Amy. I'm sorry. I have no right to question you."

"Our friendship gives you the right to say whatever you believe to be true." Amy's voice wavered. She could handle well-intentioned criticism, even if she didn't necessarily agree, but she had to leave before she burst into tears. "I'm not upset with you for speaking your mind. I hope you always will. I need honesty, and there are few around me who are willing to risk it."

Maggie rushed around the table, reaching out. "You're like a sister to me. I love you, and I want to see you happy."

Closing her eyes to staunch the tears, Amy returned the tight hug. "Thank you for being my friend. I will think on what you said. I owe Fletcher that much."

"Even more than that…" Maggie drew back. "You owe it to yourself. I have a feeling Fletcher knows what he's getting. I'm just not sure you do."

Amy hurried along the wooden walkway, anxious to get to the bank so she could talk to Fletcher. It bothered her that she didn't know whether he believed their relationship was a love match. Either way, he deserved honesty. She wasn't looking for love—at least, not the all-consuming, heart-rending variety—but if mutual respect and affection weren't enough for him, then she would release him from his pledge.

Buck strolled beside her, taking one long stride for every two of hers although she'd noticed he let her set the pace. When she'd exited the store, he was standing in the street surveying the rooftops. He'd casually tucked her hand into the crook of his elbow, but she sensed a coiled tension, a watchfulness that was always present.

Maggie had to be wrong about Buck. He wasn't wooing anyone, and she wasn't interested even if he was. There was an unfortunate attraction. And if she were entirely truthful, she would admit she liked him, actually, quite a bit. Friendship wasn't something they could afford to cultivate, but she could enjoy it for the short time he would remain in her employ.

"Is everything all right? You seem sad." Buck's solicitous inquiry made her heart trip. How could he be so attuned to her emotions? That was an odd trait in a man, although she hadn't noticed he'd exercised this gift around anyone else. Was it something that existed only between the two of them? *No.* That would make more of their relationship than it merited.

"It's nothing to concern yourself about. I just need to talk to Fletcher."

He arched a speculative look. Had he really expected her to share her worries? When most people inquired about one's wellbeing it wasn't because they wanted to hear a litany of problems. She sighed with relief when he shifted his gaze to the street.

How should she approach this sticky conversation with her betrothed? He might decry her for misleading him. Her stomach knotted. She'd gone into this relationship thinking primarily of what it meant for her. How selfish.

They took half a dozen steps up to the three-story brick building housing the bank. Buck opened the door, and with an appreciative gaze, followed her inside. The fact that he made no attempt to hide his desire should infuriate her. So why was her body reacting with tingling anticipation?

Voices murmured in the cavernous space, as clerks served customers from behind a high counter. The marble floors, dark paneling, and brass lamps topped with globes of etched glass exuded a sense of wealth and refinement. This place suited Fletcher, and he suited her.

In the back, his office door opened. A fair-haired man exited. He slapped his hat on his head and crossed the room with long-legged strides. An angry expression puckered his face. Apparently this farmer, or whoever he was, hadn't had a good meeting.

She glanced back. Buck had noticed him, as well.

Her betrothed spotted her and hurried over, reaching out to capture her gloved fingers in a light grasp. He brushed a kiss on her cheek. "My dear, what brings you here? Would you like to join me for luncheon? I can clear my appointments."

"Thank you, but no. We're on our way to the mine. I just came by to..." she stumbled, suddenly nervous. "We need to talk."

He shifted his eyes to look over her shoulder and his brows knitted with obvious irritation. "Why don't we go somewhere we can have more privacy."

Behind her, her bodyguard snorted. Her shoulders tensed. These two men would never get along. The most she could hope for was a wary truce, at least until they parted ways.

Fletcher ushered her into his office. She stopped in front of the large desk he'd commissioned nearly two years ago. It was an exact replica of the one in her study. When she'd first seen it, she had been annoyed at his presumption, but upon reflection, realized the imitation was meant as a compliment.

The door clicked shut.

Fletcher put his arms around her waist and bent to kiss her. A smoky taste lingered on his lips. After allowing the brief touch, she drew back. "Can you come to dinner this evening?"

He looked chagrined. "I know we still need to meet and discuss those investments, but I have a number of important business dinners this week. Then I'll be going to Indian

Territory to negotiate those land deals I told you about. It's a very busy time. Can we do this when I return?"

"That's not what I want to talk about." She paced across a thick rug, rested her fingers on the edge of his desk. Her gaze fell to a stack of papers. What appeared to be a mortgage document had the word *Foreclosed* written across the top. Maybe that was what had upset the man who left. Fletcher had recently complained about the growing number of customers defaulting on their debts. However, she wasn't here to discuss loans. Gathering her courage, she turned to face him. "I need to know your expectations for our marriage."

"My expectations?" His eyes lit with interest. "Do you mean..."

Her cheeks warmed. "I'm not talking about our physical relationship. I understand those expectations." She took a deep breath. "I mean, do you expect...a love match?"

With a few strides, he closed the distance between them and took her hands. "What you said at the party about needing to hear a man's feelings, was that meant for me? You must know I adore you." His lips curled in a knowing smile. "I would worship at your altar, my Venus."

Flustered, she pulled away. "No. I don't want... What I'm saying..." Dear heavens, this was so *difficult*. She didn't want to hurt him. "My feelings are not as strong as yours. I have great affection for you and I respect you, but...I'm not sure...I love you."

She felt lighter, as if a weight had been lifted off her shoulders. If he wanted love, they could call off the marriage before it was too late.

"Amy, darling." He captured her hands again, and his eyes grew warm. "I know your feelings aren't as strong as mine, but respect and affection can grow into love. I'm willing to wait for the flower, if you're willing to nurture the plant."

Her throat tightened. "I...I'm relieved to hear you say that."

He smiled down at her, not appearing in the least put off by her awkward declaration.

She took a steadying breath. At least she'd settled the question of his expectations. Truly, she was relieved, even if she didn't *feel* relieved. Her marriage to Fletcher would be a joining of like minds, and eventually—hopefully—of like hearts. It wouldn't be a tumultuous journey, tossing her to and fro on stormy waves. He didn't tease and tempt, arousing untrustworthy passions. Like Buck. She shivered.

"Darling, put your mind at ease." Fletcher's soothing assurance eased the remaining tension. "Most people get nervous before they wed. It's perfectly normal." A crease appeared between his brows. "I do wonder, though, if some of your uncertainty is due to negative influences."

"What are you talking about?"

"I'm sure you'll agree, Mr. O'Connor's behavior at the party was highly inappropriate." He reached into his pocket and pulled out a sheet of paper. "I was certain you'd be ready to rid yourself of his annoying presence, so I put together a list of suitable replacements. Just give me the word and I'll be happy to let him know he's no longer needed."

"I don't think that's necessary," she started, and then backed down at his frown. Why wouldn't she agree? Buck's antics had made her a laughingstock. No, she'd done that to herself. Oh, why was she so confused? She forced a smile. "I do appreciate your offer, but I'll take care of it. At the right time."

CHAPTER 14

Buck peered past the edge of the buggy's roof into a pearl gray sky. A flock of black-winged birds shifted into the shape of an arrowhead. They were returning, along with the warmer days of spring.

He shook the reins and the white-stocking bay picked up the pace. He was running out of time. Unfortunately, he was also running out of ideas.

Amy sat beside him, her gloved hands tucked primly in her lap. The light blue dress she wore, with its lace trim and puffy sleeves, fit her to perfection, even if it did seem a tad fancy for a visit to a mine and a flouring mill.

He eyed the pert little bonnet secured with a bow tied at a jaunty angle. Maybe she was taking his advice on how to use her advantage to the fullest. One look, and any man would grant her three wishes—unless he was the one trying to hurt her.

Buck shifted his study to the budding trees along the side of the road. He searched the woods for any sign of danger. It'd been quiet since that day her attacker struck—too quiet. Had he scared the bastard into hiding? He could hope so, but he wasn't risking Amy's life by counting on it.

"A group of newspaper editors from across the state are coming in to meet with the railroad commission next week." She waited until he gave her his attention. "It's an excellent opportunity to lay the groundwork for a town hall meeting with the settlers."

He arched his brows in surprise. She hadn't just taken his suggestion. She'd improved upon it. "A town hall meeting, that's good. And I like your idea about getting publicity in advance. Makes it look like the railroad is reaching out. That'll hogtie your detractors. They'll look bad if they call it off."

Her lips curved in a pleased smile.

Pride swelled his chest. She was one sharp gal, his Amy.

Hold on, Bucko. She isn't your Amy.

This confounded ruse had messed up his thinking. He wasn't her lover, he was her bodyguard—and the man who'd deceived her. He gritted his teeth as his conscience writhed.

"There hasn't been an attempt on my life lately." Her voice turned uncharacteristically soft. She was leading up to something. A request or...

"What are you saying?"

"It's possible you scared away that man when you chased him." She stared out at the budding trees. Why wouldn't she meet his eyes? "Fletcher thinks I should let you go."

Of all the self-serving... Buck's anger flared like a match set to kindling, but he stomped it out. It wouldn't do to rail about the bastard. That would only make Amy more defensive. He'd appeal to her common sense—a quality old Fletch seemed to be missing.

"I wouldn't bet your life on that assumption. Whoever's after you might be waiting for you to let down your guard before he strikes again."

Dang it, she *still* wouldn't look at him. "Fletcher isn't suggesting I do without a bodyguard. He just wants me to replace you."

Pompous ass. Buck seethed, furious with Fletch and with her, but mostly with himself. Hell, he'd gotten too attached anyway. The problem was, he wasn't finished here. Without Amy's assistance there was no hope of the railroad reaching an agreement that would help his cousin. The uneasy cease-fire would end and it would be back to war—a war the settlers couldn't win.

Hadn't he seen enough to know the time for battles was over? It was the savvy negotiator who would come out on top in this opportunistic decade. That meant he had to hold onto this job until Amy held those town meetings. After that, he would leave her in Fletcher's care, much as that thought disturbed him.

She finally looked at him. "I told Fletcher I wasn't comfortable making a change right away."

Buck released a pent-up breath.

"But I'm certain he'll bring it up again when he returns in two weeks." Her fingers twined around the cord of her reticule. "He *is* going to be my husband, so I know you'll understand if I have to—"

"Where?" He cut her off before she could finish firing him. "Where did he go?"

Her solemn expression remained unchanged, but her eyes grew sad. "He's negotiating with the Quapaw whose land is directly south of Baxter Springs. Mr. Joy wants to bypass Cherokee land altogether to get around the treaty requirements. If we build straight south, we can connect with the Texas Central coming up from Galveston."

"Sounds like a plan." A damn risky plan, given the Indians' growing frustration with the railroads, but he wouldn't say that. She'd just accuse him of being critical.

Buck mulled over the implications. If James Joy thought he had a bird in hand, he wouldn't feel pressured to settle on a lesser price for his land. Not unless he couldn't hold onto enough workers to win the race. "Didn't you say the Border Tier is losing workers to the Katy? How are you dealing with that?"

Her eyes widened. "I don't recall saying that, but yes, the MK&T did increase wages. I'm not sure why or how. They're as overextended as we are. But I've found some private investors who are willing to help with additional funding, so we should be able to outbid them."

He stared, struck dumb with astonishment. No matter what obstacle he put in her way, Amy found a way around it. His admiration increased, even as his mind whirred with alternate plans. Winning her over to his way of thinking was still the best strategy. "Have you thought about how you'll reach a compromise with the settlers?"

"I have some ideas, but nothing definite. It's difficult to find a solution that both sides believe is beneficial. Especially when neither wants to budge on price."

The difference between the two sides amounted to only a few dollars per acre, but Buck knew the real issue boiled down to making money later, after the railroad had increased the value of the land. "Why can't Mr. Joy profit from developing what he owns around the town? You know, lease buildings for stores and offices? Then he could offer a lower price on the outlying land to encourage farming."

"That's a good thought, but he's already lowered the price on farm land. I don't know how much more he's willing to come down, and it's not likely to be enough to appease the settlers."

"They want to make money, too."

She lifted an eyebrow. "*Everybody* wants to make money."

"So…all you got to figure out is how everybody can make money."

"You make it sound so simple."

Buck breathed a laugh. "If it were simple, you wouldn't want to do it anyhow. You like a challenge."

"True enough." She smiled, and then pointed down a side trail leading through the trees. "Turn off here. It's a shortcut to the mine. I want to show you something."

After glancing behind them to ensure they weren't being followed, he guided the buggy down the bumpy path. Before long, they came out of the trees onto an unplowed field.

He pulled the mare to a stop, regarding with puzzlement what looked like a stone well spewing fire. "What the—?"

"Let's walk over. This burning well is something of a local wonder."

After helping Amy down, he took her arm and guided her across a patch of uneven ground. As they drew closer to the well, his eyes widened. Now he could see water bubbling up beneath the flames.

"Fire out of water," he mused. "How is it doing that?"

Amy's eyes shone like a magician with a new trick. "A miracle?"

Buck chuckled. He couldn't help it. She was too damn cute. "First you're Joshua leading a bunch of pig-headed farmers into the Promised Land. Now you're Elijah setting water on fire. What next?"

Amy crossed her arms, her smile broadening. "You seem to know a lot of Bible stories."

"My mother made me listen to them."

"So you're saying I'm prophetic?"

"You're too sassy to be a saint. Now, stop stalling and tell me how this is possible." He edged closer, leaning in until he could feel the heat on his face.

Threads of steam rose from the surface as blue fire leapt up out of the boiling water. The sheer impossibility struck him with childlike amazement.

All the sudden, he didn't want to know the answer. He just wanted to enjoy the miracle. It gave him hope—a kind of burning-well faith—that this was a sign God would somehow lift the curse off his life and give him a gift. Someone who could love him. Someone like Amy.

Her puffed sleeve brushed his arm and his body hummed like a telegraph line, sending a heated message thrumming through his veins. "When the owner of this field had the well dug, they struck both water and gas. The scientists surmise the gas comes up through the water. Somehow it got set on fire. No one's been able to put it out."

Her explanation extinguished the wonder. He felt like a damn fool. There were no miracles, certainly not for him.

"That's real interesting. I'll bring the buggy around so we can get going," he muttered, and set off with long strides. He didn't want her to see whatever crazy emotions might be leaking out onto his face. Normally, he was good at concealing his feelings, but Amy turned him inside out. He feared he couldn't hide from her much longer.

There was a loud crack and something punched him in the shoulder, high on the right side of his chest. He staggered back, as the sound echoed through the woods. Cold rushed in, followed by a burning pain.

Christ, he'd been shot.

"Get down!" He ran, staggering, towards Amy, who stood by the well with a shocked expression. He fumbled in his haste to draw his revolver with his left hand. "Get behind the well, dammit."

She vanished faster than a fleeing rabbit. Rounding the well, he dropped to his knees beside her. She huddled against the stone foundation, her eyes wide with fright. "Was that a gun shot?"

"Stay." He gave the order, then leaned around the edge to peer at the far woods. Why the hell had he let his guard down even for an instant? His heart pounded, sending a wet stream down his arm. It pooled between the fingers he had pressed against the hard earth. He took a deep breath and blinked to clear a sudden lightheadedness.

A glint in the trees caught his eye. Aiming his revolver, he fired.

Leaves rustled, then a flock of birds burst into the air. The sound of hooves—one horse he'd guess—retreated.

Whoever had shot him was either leaving or finding another way to get to them.

Fear clogged Buck's throat. He had to get Amy out of here, but if he didn't get the bleeding stopped first, he'd pass out, leaving her helpless.

Leaning back against the stone well, he drew back his coat to get a better look at the wound. His shirt was soaked with so much blood his sleeve stuck to his arm. The pain had settled into a dull throb.

"Dear God," Amy whispered. She scooted over in front of him, yanked a handkerchief from her sleeve and pressed it against the wound. He released a low chuckle, couldn't help it. Using that hankie was like trying to stop a flood with a dishrag.

Her brows gathered with a look of dismay. Reaching inside his coat, she pulled his knife from its sheath and cut off a length of white cloth from beneath her skirt. He observed her frantic movements through a misty haze.

"Wad it up."

He winced as she pressed the ball of cloth to the wound. Setting the knife aside, she quickly wrapped a length of petticoat around his shoulder and tied a tight knot. "We can't stay here and let you bleed to death." Her voice sounded like she'd been running. "I'm going to get the horse and bring the buggy around."

"No!" He grabbed her arm. "I'll get the damn buggy." He handed her a revolver. "You stay behind this well. If you hear something, shoot at it."

"Gid'up, you lazy thing," Amy cried, cracking the whip. Her heart slammed against her chest as the buggy tore into town. The mare was exhausted, but until they reached the doctor's office this horse wasn't getting a break. There had been no sign of the assailant on the road back, but she wasn't taking any chances until they reached a safe place.

"Don't kill your horse," Buck muttered. "I'm not dying."

"You better not." Her voice came out shrill with fear.

The buggy bounced, eliciting another rough groan.

Amy slid a frantic glance to the wounded man leaning heavily against her. *So much blood.* It soaked his shirt, his coat, even the seat. She strained to breathe, grief twisting like a knife in her side. Dear God, this couldn't be happening again. Not another person she cared about snuffed out of her life.

Once she reached the doctor's house, she pulled up in front of a covered porch. She leapt down, catching hold of Buck as he slid out of the buggy. Drawing his uninjured arm across her shoulders, she helped him inside the crowded waiting room.

Where was the doctor?

Urging Buck forward while trying not to jostle him, she nearly collided with someone's chest. Her gaze tracked up the double row of brass buttons. The youthful-looking soldier removed his hat. She wanted to scream at him to get out of her way.

"Mrs. Langford?"

She focused on his face. "Major Roy?" Relief trickled through her. The major was competent and kind. "Please, we need a doctor."

His piercing blue gaze shifted to Buck. "She's setting a broken arm on one of my men."

A broken arm wasn't life threatening, surely it could wait. "Would you mind telling her there's a man here who's been shot?"

On the far side of the room, a door opened and a raven-haired women emerged, ushering out a young soldier with his arm in a sling.

"Dr. Hall. Thank God," Amy breathed.

The doctor raked Buck in an astute appraisal. "Bring him in here. Have him lie down on the examining table."

The treatment room reeked of camphor and the sour smell of sickness. Amy's stomach heaved. She took shallow breaths as she helped Buck onto a narrow wooden table bearing the darkened stains of previous mishaps.

He stretched out and settled his head on a small pillow. Blood soaked the cloth she'd wrapped around the wound, as well as his shirt. His eyes were glazed and his skin felt clammy.

Leaning over him, she tenderly smoothed back strands of hair dark soaked with sweat. For the first time, she noticed freckles on his face, scattered like bits of sand across his cheekbones. It made him appear younger, although though there was nothing childlike about this man.

"Doctor Hall is the best in town." Amy tried to keep fear from infecting her voice. "She's going to get you fixed up."

Buck regarded her through half-closed lids. "You look like you're about to be sick. Why don't you wait in the next room?"

He didn't want her hovering over him. Reluctantly, she turned to go.

The doctor gave her an encouraging smile. "I'll come get you as soon as I'm done."

Amy wobbled into the waiting area that doubled as the doctor's parlor and sank into a chair. She drummed her fingers on her knees. Dr. Hall was a brilliant physician. She'd come from the East with a full-fledged medical degree, which was more than most of the sawbones in the area could boast. Buck was in good hands.

Major Roy sat in the chair next to her. Had he been waiting around for some reason? He leaned forward, his hands braced on his knees. "What happened?"

"We were on our way to see whether they'd gotten the mine properly closed off after that collapse a month ago. I asked Buck to stop by the burning well." She launched into a meandering explanation, but her thought process kept misfiring. Tears spilled over, dampening her cheeks. She reached for her handkerchief, only to recall she'd used it as a makeshift bandage.

The major handed her his clean one. Concern bracketed his eyes. "Did you get a look at who fired the shots?"

She shook her head. "Whoever it was, he was hidden in the trees, and then he left."

"The man you brought in, that's your—?"

"Bodyguard. I believe I told you once before, I hired him after I became aware someone was trying to…" Her hands trembled as she wiped her face. "Kill me."

Major Roy leaned closer, his voice low. "If you believe this is because of your work with the railroad I would have jurisdiction in the matter and could assign a detail to guard you."

God bless him, he was offering to come to her aid. But she couldn't say for certain the attacks had anything to do with the railroad. "Nothing has happened outside of Fort Scott. So I'm beginning to think it's someone here. Not one of the settlers."

The major sat back. He regarded her steadily. "You need only say the word. I'll assign troops for your protection. It doesn't appear your bodyguard will be much good to you. At least, not for a while."

The door opened and Dr. Hall motioned to her. Amy shot to her feet. She turned to the major. "Thank you. I'll let you know what I decide."

Without further delay, she hurried back to the treatment room.

To her surprise, Buck was perched on the edge of the examination table, bare-chested, with his right shoulder swathed in bandages.

"He'll need to take it easy for a couple of weeks. I'd prefer he stay in bed, but he should do nothing strenuous." Dr. Hall reached behind her to untie her apron, now spattered with fresh blood. She hung the stained garment on a wall hook. "Watch for infection. If you see redness or swelling, or notice a foul odor or discharge, let me know right away. I'm going to send along something for pain."

She removed a small bottle from a sturdy wooden cabinet, where tools and medicines were arranged in a tidy display behind a glass-paned door. "That shoulder is going to hurt like the dickens, so I'll give you enough laudanum to last a couple weeks."

The doctor moved to a desk crowded with books, papers and a tray of sharp-looking instruments. Amy's stomach clenched at the sight of the bloodied tools. It must have hurt terribly when the doctor removed the bullet.

She ventured closer to Buck, yearning to comfort him but feeling awkward and uncertain.

He'd propped himself up with his good hand and appeared to be focusing most of his energy on staying upright. His lips were compressed into a thin line that communicated his pain straight to her heart.

As she drew closer, she could see his shoulders and upper arms were sprinkled with the same sandy freckling on his face. His body was a fascinating contrast of angles and planes, its lean, corded strength covered over by pale skin marked with old scars.

"Can you hand me my clothes?" He gestured with his chin to a nearby chair.

She lifted the bloodstained shirt and shuddered. "You can't wear this." She tossed it away. "I'll buy you a new one."

His buckskin coat was torn and stained, but not as bad. She held it while he slipped his uninjured arm into a sleeve. Coming up on her toes, she reached around him and carefully drew the garment over his injured shoulder.

Her nostrils flared at the sweaty scent of his body, but it didn't repel her. In truth, she longed to wrap her arms around him and breathe in the raw smell of a living, breathing man. He could have easily been killed…because of her.

Distressed, she fumbled with the buttons.

"You don't have to dress me." He gently captured her hands. Warmth radiated up her arms and spread through her body, melting the fear that had frozen her insides.

She looked into eyes as light as the edge of sunrise. The intensity and brilliance of blue and gray seemed to shift with his moods, like the endless changing of the weather. "Thank God you're all right," she said in a ragged voice.

Frowning, he brushed away a tear with his thumb, a light touch, unbearably tender. "Don't."

Don't what? Don't cry? Don't care? Unnerved, she stepped back.

Hiring a bodyguard had sounded so practical, like hiring an extra hand, but reality had struck the moment she'd seen him sitting there, soaked in his own blood. She would never forgive herself if he died because he'd been protecting her, whether or not it was his job. She'd carry a gun, wear a suit of armor, do whatever was necessary, but she would not knowingly put him in danger just to secure her own safety. As soon as Buck was well, she would send him on his way.

CHAPTER 15

Amy tiptoed up the narrow stairs and slipped into the room above the carriage house. She lifted the lantern. Light spilled across the darkened space, illuminating the still figure on the bed. Thank God, Buck was sleeping peacefully and not thrashing around, as he had been earlier. She padded across the room and set the lamp on the table, along with a glass containing laudanum mixed with weak tea. It wasn't quite time for his next dose, but she felt compelled to check on him if for no other reason than to assure herself he was alive.

She was being silly, of course. He'd gotten through that terrible ordeal yesterday and had walked out of the doctor's office, so that must mean the wound wasn't quite as bad as she first surmised. But what did she know?

Sinking onto the edge of the bed, she drew her velvet wrapper more tightly around her and studied him. He'd pushed the sheet and blanket down to his hips. His bare chest rose and fell with comforting regularity.

She brushed back a strand of hair that had fallen in his eyes and placed her palm against his forehead. He felt warmer than when she'd last checked on him around midnight. She gnawed her lip, worried. Fever could be setting in. Whenever she was ill, Sophie always covered her up.

Amy pulled the sheet and blanket over Buck's chest and shoulders and tucked him in. With a restless sigh, he pushed the covers back down to his waist. She jerked her hand back, holding her breath. Then released it on a sigh as he continued to sleep.

At least he was getting rest, which was more than she could say for herself. Lying in bed, she'd tried in vain to banish the nightmares that had tormented her. Had fear for Buck brought back those horrid dreams?

His lashes fluttered. He opened his eyes, regarding her with a look of confusion. "What time is it?" His voice sounded rusty as the hinge on an old door.

"A little after five...in the morning."

He passed his tongue over his lips.

"Are you thirsty?" She retrieved a cup Jacob had filled with water earlier in the evening.

As Buck struggled to rise, she brought the cup to his lips. He cradled it with one hand and drank with loud gulps.

"Easy," she whispered. "You'll choke yourself."

He let go of the cup and tried to sit up.

"No, don't. You need to be still." She plumped a stack of pillows behind him and he lay back with a sigh. "Sophie will bring breakfast in a little while, if you think you can eat."

"You'll know I'm dying if I can't eat," he muttered.

A chill shot through her. How could he joke about that?

He gave her hand a gentle squeeze. "Don't get your hopes up, Venus. You're not getting rid of me that easy."

Amy couldn't work up the will to scold him for his use of the hated moniker. She fussed with the sheet, pulling it up so she wouldn't be tempted to stare at his bare chest and shoulders. It was beyond frustrating how her body tingled and ached at the sight of his unclothed form, and the confusing feelings and emotions his presence elicited worsened with each passing day. She had to convince him to leave as soon as he was well.

"Major Roy offered to assign men to guard the house." She fidgeted with the fringe of her wrapper. "He's treating this as a railroad-related incident, I think because he feels compelled to come to my aid."

Buck's steady gaze set off a nervous flutter in her stomach. "A true gentleman, our Major Roy."

She frowned at the dry tone. "Do you not agree he should have offered?

The mocking smile leveled into a solemn line. "I'm glad he did, considering I'm not much help to you right now. You can get rid of them later."

Would the soldiers' presence make her feel safer? Not as safe as she felt with Buck, although she'd not tell him that. It would only encourage him to stay. "More protection can't hurt, now that my attacker has graduated to shooting at me."

A shudder passed through her. She'd held onto a thread of hope that the accidents were meant to scare her, but there was no mistaking it now. Her mysterious assailant sought to kill her. She closed her eyes so Buck wouldn't see her despair.

His hand covered hers. He rubbed his thumb lightly over her skin. "I've been layin' here thinking, when I'm not sleeping. I don't believe he was aiming for you."

Her eyes opened. "Of course he was."

"Amy, either he's the worst marksman in the world, or he was trying to get rid of me and just missed a fatal shot."

Dread sluiced like ice water through her veins. She had put Buck directly in the line of fire. Not only was she a target, now he was one as well. What had she been thinking to bring this man into her life and thrust him into danger? She was like a horse with blinders, seeing only one direction—the path to her own safety and security.

"I'm so sorry I dragged you into this." Tears spilled over. "I shouldn't have hired you. It was selfish on my part."

"Hold on there." As he struggled into a sitting position, he took hold of her arms. Whether to keep himself upright or draw her closer, she wasn't sure. "You offered me a job I'm well-suited for and I took it. I knew the risks."

So did her father when he chose to stay in Kansas, even as the state dissolved into a bloodbath. So did her husband when he rode off to war never to return. They had known the risks and paid with their lives. This time, she wasn't willing to gamble. Not with Buck's life. He was too important, too precious to her.

She twisted, trying to free herself from his grasp. "I want you to leave as soon as you're able. Get away from here. Get away from me."

"Stop. Please." The tightness in his voice cut through her fears.

She stilled. "I'm sorry. I didn't mean to hurt you."

His hold gentled, but his face tightened with fierce determination. "This isn't just your fight anymore. That fellow made it mine when he shot me. And I'm not leaving until I get that sorry son-of-a—" The sudden burst of strength seemed to drain out of him and he eased back against the pillows with a rumbling groan.

Her anxiety spiraled once again. "Fletcher doesn't want you here."

"I don't give a damn what Fletch wants." Buck closed his eyes. The muscles around his mouth tightened. He was in pain. And it was *her* fault.

She stood and went to the table, hiding her face as she dashed away tears. "It's time for your medicine."

"You just want to shut me up."

"I can only hope."

Sitting back on the side of the bed, she helped him raise his head enough to drink the laudanum she'd mixed with sweetened tea. "I don't want you lying here in pain."

"Laudanum ain't gonna cure what ails me," he muttered, but drank dutifully.

What else could she do to relieve him? Frustrated, she plumped the pillows again, trying to make him more comfortable. As she pulled up the sheets, her gaze was drawn to his lightly furred chest and long arms with muscles hard as steel bands. Those arms had embraced her, had lifted her as though she weighed no more than a doll.

Desire shimmered through her. She dropped the bedclothes like they were on fire. What was wrong with her? It was time she returned to the house.

He caught her arm. "Don't go."

His cynical mask fell away. The aching loneliness in his eyes called to her, as nothing else would have, and she sank down beside him. He laced his fingers through hers, binding them like strands of hemp.

She stared at their twined fingers dismayed by the sense that destiny was at work in ways she didn't understand Perhaps the Fates, in a fit of mischief, had thrown them together. But she couldn't afford to get drawn into his life. He wasn't someone who could work beside her, share her goals, help her achieve them.

"Why Fletch?" Buck's rasp cut through the silence.

She jerked her gaze to his face, his unexpected question lodging in her mind. The answer came easily. She'd recited it often enough. "He's the right husband for me."

"Even if he's the wrong man?"

This wasn't a conversation she wanted to have with Buck. She tried to pull her hand away, but he held tight. With a sigh, she gave in, unwilling to hurt him again by pulling out of his grasp. The medicine would take effect soon enough. In the meantime, she would humor his presumptuous question. He wouldn't remember anyway. Her mother never remembered anything after she'd taken her medicine.

"Fletcher believes in the same things I do."

"So you believe in getting rich?"

Amy stiffened at the cutting sarcasm. Why was Buck challenging her? It wasn't as if he had a stake in her future.

He could, if you let him.

Why would she do that? He had nothing to offer.

Only love.

Ridiculous. Buck didn't love her. He lusted after her. Besides, she didn't want love.

Oh yes, you do.

"No, I don't."

"'Course you don't, that's my point."

Her heart stopped. What had she said? He must've thought she was responding to his snide remark about getting rich. Thank God he couldn't read her thoughts.

He dragged her hand onto his chest, over crisp hair and hard muscle. The contact sent a tingling relay racing through her body, delivering a sensuous message that made her blush from head to toe. Her fingers refused to obey a half-hearted order to break the connection.

"Does he love you?"

Good heavens. That medicine had certainly loosened Buck's tongue. It was the only explanation for this bizarre conversation. "He's proud of my accomplishments."

"I didn't ask if he loves what you do. Does he love *you*, for who you are?"

Was there a difference? "What I've accomplished is who I am."

"You don't believe that," he slurred.

She didn't want to, but life had taught her the truth. She'd gained her father's affirmation through what she did and how well she did it. Those achievements gave her life purpose and success validated her existence. "Aren't we all defined by what we accomplish?"

There was a pause measured by the rise and fall of his chest. "I've accomplished nothing." he stated flatly.

Tears sprang to her eyes. This strong, capable man couldn't think so poorly of himself. It must be the drug talking. "How can you say such a thing?"

"Jus' answerin' your question."

Longing to restore his usual confidence, she searched for the right words that would assure him without sounding patronizing. Leaning forward, she looked into his heavy-lidded eyes. "You've kept me alive, ensured my safety, I'd say that's accomplishing something."

His uninjured arm rose slowly, as though it were strapped with weights. Gripping her thick braid, he pulled her close until they were nearly nose-to-nose. "I promise..." he whispered. "Won't let anybody hurt you."

His eyes drifted shut.

Her gaze caressed his face: the tawny brows and thick lashes, a slight bump on the bridge of his nose indicating it might have been broken once, his mouth, relaxed in sleep and half hidden by the mustache. A powerful current tugged, an intense longing that swept away the last of her resistance. She could kiss him and he would never remember.

Leaning forward, she pressed her lips against his—softly, tentatively, and then with more confidence when he remained in a state of sleepy acquiescence.

He sighed, a soft sound of pleasure, as she explored his mouth. She glided her tongue over the smooth flesh of his lip before slipping into the warm recesses. He tasted of sugared tea and a faint bitterness from the laudanum.

Her breath quickened, and desire throbbed with each heartbeat.

The heat radiating from his body made her long to crawl into bed beside him and curl up like a kitten. He exhaled on a long breath, and she felt the moment he surrendered to the effects of the medicine. The hand in her hair loosened and dropped, hanging off the side of the bed.

She sat back shaken by an acute longing for something she sensed only he could give, something far more than the passion steaming the air between them. The muscles in his face relaxed and his lips remained parted, still damp from her kisses.

Vulnerable. He looked so vulnerable.

Insight struck with frightening clarity. Buck needed her. He needed her in a way no other man had ever needed her.

She stood on shaky legs, her mind rejecting what her heart cried out. His need, her longing, these feelings couldn't be allowed to take root. This wasn't part of her future. She had mapped out her destiny, knew the steps she had to take to succeed. Her mother had ruined everything by giving in to passion. She would not repeat that mistake.

A woman's voice whispered soothing sounds, as liquid coolness bathed his face. It trickled down his neck, easing the terrible heat. He tried to catch a drop with his tongue. Damn, his mouth was dry as a field in late August.

Water.

Had the word passed his lips, or was it still stuck in his mind? If only he could get out of this cottony haze and away from the flames scorching his skin. Flames? Was he too near the fire? Apprehension shot through him and he tensed.

"Shhh." The woman's breath caressed his ear. "Hold still. The wound needs to be cleaned."

Wound? Had he been shot? Why couldn't he remember?

"Georgia?" he rasped. She would be the one treating him, considering she knew more about healing than anyone else in his company.

Buck struggled to open his eyes. He had to wake up. His men needed him. But the darkness kept sucking him down. Confusion massed like thick clouds in his mind. He could no longer hear the soothing voice. Had she gone away and left him alone?

White-hot fire seared his shoulder, dissolving his thoughts in a blur of pain. In a frantic bid to escape, he tried to jerk away from the coals blistering his skin, but iron bonds held his arms. Someone had tied him down.

An image wavered and took shape; a lean face mottled with drink, his wintery eyes gleaming with evil intent. Fear skittered up Buck's spine. God, it couldn't be. Da was dead…wasn't he?

I warned you, Bucko. Now you'll take yer punishment. You'll take it like a man.

The gravely voice sent spiders crawling over Buck's skin. His heart thudded wildly, and terror wrenched a protest from the darkest depths of his soul. "No! Da...don't..."

Shut yer mouth. If ye beg, I'll put your other hand in the fire.

Buck groaned, fighting to hold back the plea, but the pain...oh, the pain. His courage crumbled and a wretched appeal spilled from the lips of the child locked inside. "Da, no! Ah God, please. Don't burn me."

Tears poured down Amy's face as Buck's hoarse cries tore through her heart. His body bowed, he struggled to free himself from Jacob's determined grip. For some reason, the chloroform hadn't rendered him fully senseless. Her legs trembled from squatting at the front of the bed, trying to soothe him and keep him still.

She recoiled from the smell of rotting flesh being scraped out of the festering wound.

How she wished she were far from here, but she wouldn't leave his side until he was out of danger.

"Hold him," Dr. Hall barked, glancing over. Her face softened. "We're past the worst. All that's left is to apply a dressing and bandage him up."

Amy tightened her grip. His head lolled in her arms as he slipped into lax unconsciousness. With trembling fingers, she stroked his hair. He was only having a nightmare. But what could have produced such hellish fears?

"It's over now," she whispered, pressing a light kiss against his heated temple. Heaven forbid they had to hurt him like that again. Her throat tightened, but she held back the tears. It was her fault he was suffering. Raising her eyes, she met Jacob's solemn gaze. "Can you get Sophie? We'll need to bath him again to bring down this fever."

After the doctor was finished, Amy repositioned herself at the side of the bed and dipped a rag in a bucket of cold water. Wringing it out, she gently wiped Buck's flushed face and neck. They'd been bathing him down for three days and nights, and still the fever hadn't broken. He'd slipped into delirium the previous day and she'd dragged the doctor to his side.

"I've given him morphine for pain." Dr. Hall packed away her instruments. "He can have another dose in four hours. I'll leave written instructions. Use this salve to dress the wound. Now that I've disinfected it, he should start healing."

"Thank you, Dr. Hall." Amy gently lifted Buck's right hand in hers and stroked the raised scars blemishing the backs of his fingers and knuckles. She'd noticed them before, but had assumed it was an injury related to the war.

A frown marred the doctor's brow. "Those are old scars. Looks like burns. He might have fallen into a fire when he was a child."

Or someone put his hand into one.

Their eyes met, and Amy knew they were both thinking the same thing. Her heart constricted with pain like none she'd ever felt. What kind of father would do such a thing?

A fierce protectiveness rose up within her. She wanted to wrap her arms around Buck, promise she'd never let anyone hurt him again. But the best way to keep him safe would be to send him away as soon as he was well. He was in danger as long as he remained by her side.

"I have other patients to see, so I'll be going now." Dr. Hall picked up her medical kit and started for the door. "Don't hesitate to send for me if you need me. I'll be back tomorrow to check on him."

Amy nodded, keeping her eyes on Buck's sleeping form. The bandage stood out stark against his skin and fresh blood seeped through the white strips of cloth. She swallowed the bile bubbling up in her throat. She couldn't stand the sight or smell of blood, not since the day she'd knelt over her father as his life drained out in a ruby pool.

With a shudder, she shook off the memory. There had been nothing she could do for her father, but she could save Buck—if she could get this fever down.

Firming her jaw with renewed determination, she drew the sheet to his hips. His fair skin glowed as if burned by the sun. Wringing out the rag, she bathed him, starting with his face and stopping when she reached the edge of the sheet. She blushed, recalling how boldly she'd kissed him when he'd lain near senseless from the effects of the laudanum. There must be something terribly wrong with her that she would take advantage of a sick man.

Her fingers drifted over his skin and she inspected the numerous scars marring his body. There were faint, discolored slashes on his arms, a small dip that looked like an old bullet wound above his hip, a jagged lesion on his side that could have been made by a knife or sword.

Her heart ached for the pain it must have caused him. It was a miracle he'd survived the war. She could find no other evidence of burns, although the worst scars were likely ones she couldn't see. Hadn't he said his father died when he was nine? If her hunch was correct, that meant he had been abused as a child possibly from a very young age. The tears started up again as her heart cracked open, breaking for the wounded boy and the scarred man.

Familiar footsteps sounded on the stairs. She wiped away her tears. If Sophie caught her crying, the questions would start, and she didn't feel comfortable sharing something Buck wouldn't want others to know.

Sophie swept into the room in a flurry of calico with fresh sheets and towels bundled in her arms. Jacob followed close behind, setting another bucket of water by the bed and a teapot on the table. "I brewed up my strongest sweatin' tea," Sophie said, piling the sheets and bedclothes on a chair. "We need to get all of it down him."

Without a word, the burly groom went to the head of the bed. Gripping under Buck's arms, he hauled him up, provoking a groan. Amy grabbed the sheet as it slid off, revealing Buck's nudity. Her cheeks flamed and she jerked it back over his hips. The two servants had stripped him after his fever had gotten so high that they'd needed to bath him with regularity.

"Lord, child, you don't need to be doing this." Sophie shooed her off the bed. "You go on back to the house and let us take care of him. Don't you have them newspapermen coming here tomorrow night? You got plenty to do to get ready for that."

Amy lifted her chin defiantly and poured the pungent tea into a cup. "I don't care if every editor in the state shows up at my doorstep. I'm not leaving until his fever breaks."

Fear congealed in her throat. Buck had to get better. She wouldn't allow herself to think otherwise. She plopped back onto the side of the bed.

As Jacob cradled Buck's sagging body, she cupped her hand beneath his chin, put the cup to his lips, and tipped it to coax a little down his throat.

He choked and then coughed, spewing tea into her face. The full cup flipped out of her hand and onto her lap.

Amy leapt up with a startled cry, as hot tea soaked clear through her underclothes. She wiped the moisture off her face, wanting to dissolve into frustrated tears. Instead, she stalked past her wide-eyed housekeeper and poured another cup. Buck was barely conscious. She would have to wake him enough to get him to drink the tea, and he had to drink it so he could get better.

"Hold him steady, Jacob," she said, turning back to the bed.

Buck's head drooped forward as Jacob lifted him straighter.

Amy sighed and handed Sophie the cup. Sitting on the bed, she gripped beneath Buck's chin. She patted his face. "Wake up."

His eyelids fluttered, and then drifted shut.

She jostled, cajoled. His eyes remained closed. Distress made her desperate. He had to get this tea down so he could sweat out the fever. Steeling herself, she smacked him on the cheek with the flat of her palm.

He jerked back with a sharp breath. His eyes opened slowly and he regarded her with a glazed look of confusion. "Wha'd you do that for?" he murmured.

Tears stung her eyes. Hurting him was like thrusting a knife through her heart. "I'm sorry, but you have to wake up and drink this tea so you can get well." She took the cup from Sophie's outstretched hand. "Here, drink up. Then you can go back to sleep."

He tried to raise his right arm and winced.

"I'll hold it. You drink." She put the cup to his lips, carefully tipping it up and watching his throat work as he drank down the tepid tea. She handed Sophie the empty cup to be refilled.

He screwed up his face. "Tastes like horse piss."

Her lips twitched and relief threaded through her. If his sense of humor was intact, that had to be a good sign. "How do you know what horse piss tastes like?"

"Didn't...until you gave it to me."

She lifted the next full cup. He didn't know it, but he was about to drink an entire pot of the stuff. In the time it took Buck to drink the tea, Sophie had whisked away the dirty rags and tidied up the room. Just their brief exchange and the effort of drinking the tea seemed to take all Buck's strength and he drifted off to sleep after Jacob eased him down onto the stacked pillows.

Amy remained planted at his side, determined to stay put until his fever came down and she was certain he was out of danger. She pulled the sheet up to his waist wanting to afford him as much dignity as a sick man could expect.

Sophie dragged the bucket beside her and thrust a rag into her hand. "You gonna sit there, might as well bath him down." She clucked and shook her head. "Don't know why you being so stubborn."

Why? Because she was terrified she would lose him. She swallowed twice before finding her voice. "I feel responsible." She averted her eyes to hide her fear.

A chair scraped, then the woman who'd cared for her from the time she was a grieving motherless child took her fingers in a gentle grasp. Sophie's coffee-colored eyes regarded her with love. "Honey, this boy's gonna be fine. He's strong as an ox and just as mean. Don't you worry none, we'll get him well."

Amy reached out, seeking reassurance as she had so many times before. The hug was returned full force. Ah, what would she do without Sophie? This woman who had survived enslavement at the hands of brutal men somehow possessed the softest heart in the world.

Sophie gripped Amy's shoulders and pinned her with a frank look. "Tell me, now. This is about more than a hired hand getting hisself shot, ain't it? I been watchin' you. I see you got feelings for this man."

Amy's chest tightened. *Feelings?* That didn't begin to describe the commotion in her heart. But if she spoke the emotions out loud, that would make them real, something she had to face—and for the first time in her life she was unwilling to meet a challenge head-on. It would turn her life upside down, throw open a hope chest of dreams she had locked away years ago. She didn't need a white knight, didn't want heart-stopping passion and endless love. She didn't. It meant hoping, risking...grieving.

"He was harmed trying to protect me. Why wouldn't I have feelings about that?"

Sophie's eyes narrowed. Lying had never worked with her. She had an uncanny way of seeing into the shadowy corners. "'Course you'd be grateful, but that's not what I'm talkin' about and you know it."

Amy pressed her lips into a mutinous line, refusing to acknowledge the truth.

Sophie's expression softened, erasing the surprisingly few lines on her face. She picked up a rag and dipped it into the water. With brisk efficiency, she wiped the wet cloth over Buck's face and neck. He sighed and turned his head, but didn't resist.

Water dampened his hair, darkening it to the color of dead grass. Silvery streams snaked down the strong column of his throat. Sophie tugged the sheet lower, nearly exposing his private parts. "We got to bath him down, then change the sheets. Do the whole thing over again once he sweats this fever out."

Amy couldn't tear her gaze away from Buck's recumbent figure. He was most assuredly strong as an ox, but he was far from being a *boy*. Even in drug-induced sleep, his rugged body emanated strength and power. He was so vital, so full of life. All the light in her world would go out if he died.

She dashed her hand into the bucket and swirled the rag, wringing it with a sharp twist, wishing she could as easily drain the emotions flooding her heart. "Soon as he's well, I'm sending him on his way."

Sophie drew back, her eyes widening in surprise. "Why would you do such a thing? You been attacked twice. I believe you better keep him around a while longer."

There was no way she would allow Buck to continue endangering himself on her behalf. "I'm accepting Major Roy's offer to post a guard to protect me. I won't need Buck anymore."

Tension charged the air as they finished bathing him down.

Afterwards, Sophie touched his face and chest. She leaned back with a look of satisfaction. "He's cooler now. Let's change these sheets."

Change the sheets? That meant stripping the bed while Buck was in it. Naked.

Without batting an eye, the housekeeper snatched off the soaked top covers and dropped them on the floor.

Still blushing, Amy averted her eyes while she began to tug the sheet from beneath him, but his size and weight impeded her progress.

"He's too heavy for you to move. Let me get Jacob." Sophie started for the door.

"No," Amy shouted. This was no time to act missish. "Just tell me what to do."

Sophie's face tightened with displeasure. "There's no call to hurt him just to prove something to yourself." With a sigh, she came back to the bed, reached over Buck and tugged out the bottom sheet. "I'm gonna use this to roll him toward you. Make sure he don't fall off."

By carefully rolling him to each side they somehow managed to get the sheets changed.

Amy sank onto the side of the bed. She fussed with the covers, smoothed back his hair, her overwhelming need to touch him fueled by some complex emotion she refused to name. "I'll stay with him, if you don't mind bringing my supper out to me. When he wakes, we can get him to take some of that broth you made up."

Gathering the wet sheets, Sophie started for the door. She paused and turned back. "Sending him away ain't gonna rid you of them feelings, honey. If you love him, you got to face it and decide what to do about it."

Fear filled the room, making the air thick and hard to breathe. Dark memories surfaced: her mother's suicide, her father's murder, her husband's death. She couldn't risk loving again when the people she loved most were inevitably ripped out of her life.

Amy shook her head. "I can't love him. He's not the kind of husband I need."

The grave look on Sophie's face melted into kindness. "Honey, love don't always come packaged the way we want. But it's a gift when it comes. Remember that."

CHAPTER 16

April 15, 1870, Fort Scott, Kansas

Buck led Goliath out of the stall, the stallion antsy after two weeks of little activity. This morning, the big roan had nearly kicked the walls down in his eagerness to get out. Buck knew the feeling. He couldn't stay in bed one minute longer. A good run was something they both needed.

"Miz Amy wants to see you up at the house." Jacob stepped aside as Goliath tossed his head with a snort.

"About time." Buck handed the reins over to the groom. He'd ride later, after he cleared up a few things with his boss. "Will you take Goliath out for some exercise?"

"Sure will." A rare smile split Jacob's dark face. The soft-spoken groom had taken good care of the stallion over the past two weeks and would see to it the horse got some of that frustration worked out, which was more than Buck could say for himself.

As he headed out of the stables, Goliath whinnied an objection. He lifted his hand with a wave. "Don't worry, boy. I'll be back."

Amy had finally decided to see him. What had kept her so busy lately? She'd hovered like a mother hen while he lay sick in bed, but soon as he was on the mend she'd vanished. His memory was foggy, but he recalled her telling him he had to go. She probably only said that because she was worried—something easily smoothed over. He had a way of getting what he wanted out of people, and Amy wasn't immune.

With renewed confidence he strode in the back door and through the kitchen.

Two soldiers sitting at a table cast disinterested glances in his direction before going back to their card game. He frowned, uneasy. Why hadn't Amy gotten rid of Major Roy's watchdogs? They were helpful while he was sick, but unnecessary now that he was back on the job.

"Mr. O'Connor, it's good to see you up and around again." Sophie dropped a wad of dough in a shallow bowl and wiped her hands on her apron.

"Must be all that fine food you been feedin' me." Buck smiled at the beaming housekeeper. When he'd come to his senses, she'd been there clucking with worry, plying him with food and homemade remedies. Her change of heart was quite a surprise. What tale had Amy spun? Whatever it was, it must've been a good one. "Do you know where I can find Mrs. Langford?"

"She's in the study." Sophie picked up a plate of cookies and held them out. The gingery aroma made Buck's mouth water. "Made 'em fresh. Why don't you take some?"

"I'll share." He nabbed four and hurried out of the kitchen.

Amy couldn't intend to replace him. Even if old Fletch wanted her to, she had a mind of her own and it just plain didn't make sense to send him away. He was the best man for the job. She had to see that because, by God, he wasn't going anywhere. At least, not until he was certain she was safe.

He took the stairs two at a time and turned down the hall to the room that served as her office. The door stood open.

She sat behind the big desk positioned in front of her map of dreams. As he walked in, she looked up. Her lips curved in a half smile.

For a moment, he could only stare, stunned by her beauty.

Her glorious chestnut hair was arranged in ringlets around her head, without any adornment detracting from its beauty. He imagined taking it down and running his fingers through the soft waves. The light from the lamp set her face aglow, and his mind suddenly filled with an image of soft, pink lips pressed against his—an image so real he could almost feel it.

He blinked, startled by the unexpected memory. Had she kissed him when she'd come to see him that first night after he was injured? He'd thought it was a dream. The only touch he really recalled—until now—was that resounding slap she'd given him for some unknown reason. He'd probably mouthed off one too many times. Laudanum always gave him bad dreams and made him snarly as a treed coon.

Dismayed, he moved closer. Was she getting rid of him because he'd manhandled her when he'd been out of head? That would explain the slap—but not the kiss.

"You wanted to see me?" He stood in front of the desk, feeling awkward as a green boy. Why was he so flustered in the presence of a woman who didn't even reach his chin? He held out the remaining cookie. "Brought you a ginger snap."

Her smile softened and looked less forced. "Sophie already gave me one. Go ahead and enjoy it." She gestured to a chair behind him. "Please, sit down."

He dragged over a straight-backed chair and tried not to sprawl. With her behind the desk, it felt like he was back in the schoolroom, except no schoolmarm ever smelled like summer fields warmed by the sun. He finished the cookie to distract his senses. "What did you tell Sophie? Seems she's not so inclined to poison me."

Amy lowered her lashes, focusing on the desk. She drummed a pencil against the gleaming surface. "I told her you risked your life to save me."

Buck studied her stiff expression and the tightness in her jaw. Why was she so tense? The answer struck like a heat wave. She'd called him up here to fire him.

"Major Roy has assigned a guard until the assailant is apprehended or the attacks cease. This negates my need for a bodyguard." She exhaled after the last word, a soft sigh.

Pain lanced his heart. Was she that relieved to be rid of him? He crossed his arms and slumped down in a sprawling pose of indifference. He'd be damned before he revealed how much her rejection hurt. "I told you I'm not leaving until I find out who tried to kill me."

Her lips thinned. "You were shot because you were with me, not because the killer has something against you personally. It's foolish for you to remain here and invite trouble when it's not trying to find you."

Buck shifted forward. "It already found me. I'm part of this whether you like it or not. Think for a minute. Whoever shot me could have picked you off easily enough—before or after. Why didn't he? What's he really after?"

"I...I don't know." She blinked rapidly, like she was about to cry. God, he hated seeing her so fearful.

"That's what I intend to find out. If you want, I'll let those soldiers trail around after you while I do a little investigating and get to the bottom of this. There's something we're missing. Give me time to figure it out."

"Major Roy's men are capable enough."

Buck smacked his hand on the desk, making her jump. "Dang it, Amy, they were sitting down there in the kitchen playing cards. They aren't invested in your wellbeing. They don't care about you like I—" He snapped his teeth shut, realizing what he'd been about to reveal. "I got a stake in this fight."

She laced her fingers in a tight fist. Her expression turned mulish. "I refuse to let you put yourself in danger a moment longer on my account."

Hell's bells. She was firing him because she felt guilty? Fine, he could take that argument apart. "So you don't mind letting those soldiers risk their lives?"

She drew back, distress bracketing her eyes. "Yes—I mean—no. They're soldiers. This is the kind of thing they're paid to do."

"Exactly." He sat back with a smug smile. "Consider me a paid soldier doing my job."

Her eyebrows slashed down. "I don't want you doing this job anymore."

"Why not?" He braced his hands on the desk and leaned over, glowering at her.

Her cheeks flushed pink and she caught her lip between her teeth. Her nervousness had nothing to do with fear. Amy wanted him. He could see it in her hooded eyes, could smell it in her warm, womanly scent.

His nostrils flared like a wolf downwind of a doe. He hardened with the need to sate a ravenous hunger. "You're just anxious to be rid of me because I make you uncomfortable."

"That has nothing to do with it." She jerked out of the chair. Her chest heaved, lifting the square-cut neckline of her dress.

His gaze fastened on the deep cleavage between her full breasts. God, he wanted to cup them in his hands. She spun away, sending a ripple through the soft fabric draping her lush curves.

Frustrated, he curled his fingers into fists. Hell, he couldn't even look at her without getting stiff as a poker. She was delusional if she thought this attraction between them wasn't the real reason for banishing him from her life. He stalked her around the desk, grabbed her wrists, dragged her to him determined to make her admit to the same weakness that plagued him.

"This has *everything* to do with it." He bent to take what she wanted to give, despite her claims to the contrary.

She turned her face away. "Stop it. Let me go."

Buck reined in his fierce hunger. She'd called him a beast once. He didn't need to prove she was right. Gentling his hold, he drew her into a tender embrace. "Amy, sweetheart, let me show you how much I—."

"I can't," she moaned. Her fingers fisted his shirt. "I don't want these feelings."

Wounded, he stiffened, and then returned fire. "Neither do I, but it seems I can't do a damn thing about it. Except this."

He gripped her chin, turned her face up to his and took her mouth.

Her lips parted on a gasp—surprise or pleasure he wasn't sure—but he took the advantage and plunged in, coaxing her tongue to join his in an erotic dance.

She tasted like tears and ginger.

Whatever resistance she'd rallied seemed to drain away and she sank against him. She wound her arms around his neck, threaded her fingers through his hair, scraped her nails over his scalp, a touch that made him throb and burn.

He drank from her, stealing the sweet nectar he craved. Hungry for more, he cupped his hands on her rounded buttocks and lifted her until they were fitted together in perfect agony—a few layers of fabric the only thing between him and Paradise.

He pressed frantic kisses across her face and down her neck, breathing in the summery fragrance of her skin. Though she was easy to hold, his arms trembled. God in heaven, he'd never wanted a woman like he wanted this one.

Desperate need shook him to his core—every defense, every good intention, collapsed with the force of the quake. His voice came out rough with emotion. "Let me love you."

"Don't make me feel this," she whispered against his insistent kisses.

The agony in her plea cut through a haze of lust and frustrated longing. He eased her down his body, but continued to hold her close, unwilling to let her go. "I'm not making you feel anything you don't want to feel."

The desolate look in her eyes stabbed him. How could she respond like this, and still reject him?

"You won't admit you want me because I'm not like your precious Fletcher." He cupped her cheek, lightly stroking his thumb over her lower lip.

She trembled in response. The time for pretending was over.

Bending his head, he brushed his lips over hers in a soft, teasing touch. "You want me," he murmured into her mouth. "Admit it."

She sighed, her eyes signaling surrender. "I do want you," she breathed, "but...I'm afraid."

A vise squeezed his heart. "I wouldn't hurt you for the world."

"It's not you I'm afraid of, it's...me."

Now she wasn't making any sense. But if she had even an ounce of fear he wasn't going to press her. He'd hate himself more than he already did if he forged ahead with full knowledge she was tormented by some terror.

With a huff of frustration, he released her.

"Just so you know, I'm not leaving." He turned on his heel and headed for the door. It was time he got his body under control and his mind back on the task at hand. He would find this assailant and make sure the bastard never threatened anyone again.

She caught his arm. "Buck, please, you have to go. I don't...I don't want to lose you."

The thread of his patience strained, snapped. He turned around, curling his lip. "You tell me to leave, then you say you don't want to lose me. Do you know how crazy that sounds?"

She jerked back like she'd been slapped. Her eyes grew bright, heaping coals of fire on his conscience.

"I didn't mean—" he started, trying to find another word for sorry.

Her lips quivered, before she pressed them in a tight line. She lifted her chin. "Be out of the carriage house by tomorrow, and get as far away from me as possible."

Amy pressed a hand against her stomach, trying to still the nerves that chose to announce themselves through noisy rumblings. That scene with Buck this morning had wound her into knots, but she couldn't think about that right now. Her immediate problem was the presence of two eminent visitors seated at the head of the conference table.

James Joy and Nathaniel Thayer had unexpectedly shown up for a special meeting of the railroad directors. Newspapers all over the state had announced the railroad would be holding a town meeting to resolve their differences with the settlers—much to the directors' surprise.

It had been a calculated risk on her part, but if it didn't succeed, more than her position would be lost. Her fortune and her future were at stake. She scanned the room, seeking a friendly face, but the men around the table wore solemn expressions. Even Charlie.

"Tell us again, Mrs. Langford, why you thought it appropriate to announce a public meeting before gaining permission from the directors?" Kersey Coates glowered at her. This situation made it appear the president wasn't in control—a fatal flaw in Mr. Joy's book.

Lord, her mouth was dry. She grabbed the glass in front of her and took a drink of water before answering. "As you know, when the editors came into town, I hosted them at a dinner in my home. We chatted about a number of things being considered for improving relations with the settlers. I said the board was thinking about holding meetings so our detractors could air their grievances and we could openly discuss an acceptable compromise. It was the editors who reported it as already planned."

God forgive her for that white lie. It was true, she hadn't sent out announcements, but she had every intention of doing so once the directors realized they couldn't very well call off the meeting without looking bad.

Her heart ached as she recalled the admiration on Buck's face when she'd told him of her plan. He'd been proud of her. Buck had always been there for her, not just to protect her, but to support her, encourage her. Yet she'd sent him away like he meant nothing to her. She swallowed back a surge of tears. It was for the best.

Mr. Coates crossed his arms in an attempt to maintain an air of authority. "I recall a rally that didn't turn out quite the way you'd hoped. What makes you think the outcome of this town meeting will be any different?"

Her face heated. He would bring that up. "Major Roy has increased security along the line and there will be no diversion of troops. Only a small guard will be needed at the meeting because we're inviting fewer people. Just the leaders of the Land League and a few important citizens in the community."

Mr. Joy leaned back and laced his fingers over his chest beneath a flowing white beard. His pewter eyes took on a keen look. "I'm more interested in hearing what Mrs.

Langford thinks will be accomplished by this grievance session."

Her shoulders tensed. She should've known better than to think James Joy would be fooled—even for a second—by her ruse. As Buck would say, it was time to shoot straight.

"Troops have been sent in. We've threatened to abandon the Border Tier in favor of another line. Yet, the settlers are still rebelling. Intimidation hasn't worked, and we've had an overabundance of one-way communication. Might we consider the wisdom of a dialogue? Even if we don't achieve a compromise, the fact we are reaching out should sway settlers who are on the fence and separate those of a moderate disposition from the more radical elements."

She held her breath as the two important men exchanged a meaningful glance.

Mr. Thayer's dark brows formed a vee. "What bait do you suggest for attracting this moderate variety of settler?"

She affected a calm mien, keeping her hands in her lap to hide her white-knuckles. "Award them stock in the railroad."

"Are you insane?" Mr. Coates blurted. "These men have destroyed our property and nearly brought us to ruin and you want to make them *stockholders*?"

She flushed at the insult. That was twice in one day her sanity had been questioned, although only Buck's accusation had truly cut deep. He couldn't have known how much she feared inheriting her mother's unpredictable inclinations. He'd struck out at her because she'd turned him down. Or fired him. Either way, right now she had to focus on the one man that really mattered. Her boss.

"What better way to gain the settlers' loyalty than to give them a share in our success? It doesn't have to be a great deal of stock, and it would only be offered to those who were settled on the land before you purchased it—the most vocal minority."

"That is one option." Mr. Joy wore the mask of an expert poker player. Did his comment mean he was willing to consider her suggestion?

Her eyes darted to Fletcher, who'd joined the meeting to provide an update on his progress in securing Indian lands south of Baxter Springs. The corners of his mouth inched up slightly and his eyes warmed with encouragement. Earlier, he had assured her that he would speak up to support her plan. Now would be a good time.

Mr. Joy leaned back, crossing one leg over the other in a seemingly relaxed pose. "Mr. Thayer has generously agreed to extend loans to the settlers so they can borrow enough to pay our asking price. Under our terms, they won't have to make a payment on principal for thirty-six months. That should answer most of their concerns, don't you think?"

Amy stared in shock. These two Easterners were entirely out of touch with reality if they thought the settlers would be satisfied with more generous terms on loans. They didn't want to take out loans in the first place. "Accrued interest over three years could become a burden these farmers can't bear, considering their profit margins are thin in the best of years."

"Then they should plan accordingly, and make payments as soon as they see a return from their labors."

Why couldn't Mr. Joy see this was a recipe for disaster?

Suppressing her annoyance, Amy played her next card. "If your generous offer isn't well received, we could provide certificates good for storage and transportation of goods."

Mr. Thayer scowled. "Bribing them with stock or free transportation is only going to encourage bad behavior every time we get sideways with squatters."

Bribing politicians also encouraged bad behavior, but that didn't seem to stop these two. Her stomach churned with frustration, but she forced a pleasant demeanor. "Might we consider another modest reduction in the price set for farm land? We can make profits from developing prime property in and around towns—leasing buildings for stores and offices, building granaries and cool storage facilities."

Mr. Joy laced his fingers in his lap and his eyes turned hard as glass. "It appears the settlers have a new champion."

A steel rod shot up Amy's spine. "I am simply trying to consider this from all viewpoints so we get to a solution that moves us more quickly toward our goal."

"Have you forgotten the goal, Mrs. Langford?" her boss asked in a soft voice.

She drew back, offended by the put-down. "More than anyone, I want to see our railroad achieve success. However, we are at present pointed at the wrong end of the border, the Katy is stealing our workers to speed their progress, and the Land League is tearing up ties."

Her voice rose along with her ire. "We must turn the tide of public opinion to win the favors we'll need, both here and in Washington, to be declared the winner."

Silence fell across the room. She scrutinized the faces of the men around the table and her throat closed. Some looked angry, others incredulous. Fletcher's attention was focused on a piece of paper in front of him. Disappointment washed over her in a hot wave. He hadn't spoken a word in her defense. Would her boss fire her in front of the board? Or would he wait and send her dismissal papers with Mr. Chanute, as he'd done with a former land agent who'd challenged him one too many times.

The glacial stare he leveled at her chilled her blood. "I understand and share your concerns, Mrs. Langford. But giving in to troublemakers is not the answer. We will hold a town hall session, as it appears you've already committed us. But we'll discuss your future role with the railroad after this meeting adjourns."

Charlie Goodlander was right. The hitching rail outside the Wilder House was a perfect spot to sit and observe the railroad offices across the street. Buck shifted to a more comfortable position, noting his companion was finishing the last of whatever was in the silver demijohn he'd fished out of his coat pocket.

Charlie upended the small flask and peered at it with disappointment. "Looks like I need a refresh on my medicinal supplies."

Buck nodded sagely. "Never know when you might get snake bit."

"It is good to be prepared. I never travel without my medicine."

"You going somewhere?"

A good-natured grin lifted the walrus mustache. "There's a pub down the street. Want to join me for a nip? I'll buy."

"Appreciate the offer, but I'll have to take you up on it another time. I'm waiting for Mrs. Langford." Buck slipped a watch out of his pocket. Half past four. Amy had been in there with her boss for nearly an hour after the regular board session ended. Not a good sign.

He heaved a frustrated sigh. He still couldn't believe she'd actually fired him. She obviously felt no loyalty, though that should come as no surprise. He was no more than hired help as far as she was concerned, and he'd best remember that. Besides, he had to get his mind back on the main objective, making sure Sean got his fair deal. Amy was pitching a worthy plan, now he had to wait and see whether the bigwigs would accept it.

"What do you think is happening in there?" Buck directed the question at Charlie. Seeing the railroad director outside the hotel, he'd decided to strike up a conversation to see what he could learn.

Charlie rubbed his chin. "Might be she's getting the boot. She got in a tussle with Mr. Joy over some of her ideas."

"Seems awful unfair. Especially considering how hard she's worked for the railroad.

"All I can tell you is, she struck out, but went down swinging." Charlie grinned. "I actually liked her idea for giving the settlers railroad stock, just enough to make them more responsible. Might even spur them to build out the rest of that track to boost their earnings."

So Amy had stood up to her boss and got herself fired.

Buck tried to ignore a gnawing guilt. Regardless of her abrupt dismissal, she'd shown a great deal of concern for him. He, on the other hand, had pushed her down a detrimental path for reasons that had nothing to do with her wellbeing. Hell, he had no right to expect anything from her, considering he'd given her neither loyalty nor truth. "Did Bain voice his support?"

"Nobody spoke up for her." Charlie's voice had lost its ebullience. "She went nose-to-nose with Joy and Thayer all by herself." He shook his head. "She's got bigger balls than most men in this town."

"Amy's strong *because* she's a woman, not in spite of it."

"I wasn't speaking ill of her," Charlie countered quickly. "She's an enterprising gal and knows how to get what she wants. I don't doubt she'll land on her feet, regardless of what James Joy decides to do."

That was true, Amy had plenty of grit. However, she wasn't driven by avarice or a lust for power, which was the case for most ambitious men. She was striving to please a father who'd been dead some seven years, a man who could no longer love her, encourage her, or tell her how proud he was of her. Heaviness settled in Buck's chest. Was he the only one who saw the tenderhearted girl beneath that tough exterior?

"Too bad Fletcher Bain has a cinch on the girl."

Buck jerked his head around. "Why do you say that?"

Charlie gave him a sympathetic smile. "Well, you're sweet on her, ain't you?"

The air left Buck's lungs. Was it *that* obvious?

"I had to apply considerable effort to win my Lizzie," Charlie continued in a blithe tone. "She'd set her sights on a certain lieutenant, but in the end she chose the better man."

Buck's heart thudded harder as he entertained a fantasy. Why couldn't *he* be the better man? He'd been a buyer for his stepfather's mercantile, had managed the store and learned all he could about running his own business. Once he told her this, she might see him in a different light. If she was willing, he could take her somewhere else, help her start over. Maybe they could go to Texas or even California, away from this trouble, away from his past, away from everything conspiring to keep them apart.

You can't hide forever, Bucko. She'll find out, and then she'll hate you.

His hopes sank into his boots. Even if he could win her, he would lose her the day she discovered the truth. He twisted his lips into a mocking smile. "I'm not pursuing Mrs. Langford. She's already decided on the better man."

Charlie gave him a dubious glance. "If you say so."

"You don't like Bain?"

"He's a bit too contriving for my taste."

Contriving? That was an interesting description Buck hadn't heard before. Yet it fit with what he'd suspected all along. Fletcher was marrying Amy to get rich and look important, not because he loved her. "What makes you say that?"

Uncharacteristically, Charlie kept silent. Perhaps he was reconsidering what he would tell someone he didn't know well. At the party, they'd struck up a quick friendship but that didn't mean Goodlander would trust him with unflattering observations about another influential man. However, Charlie had opened the door to that conversation.

A formation of soldiers on horseback passed in front of the hotel. Seemingly diverted, Charlie smiled and waved at the captain. Once the patrol had passed, he turned to Buck.

"Fletcher Bain came out here from New York shortly after the war. He opened a bank and started loaning money. Seemed a good thing at the time, but lately I hear he's been calling in loans and taking property when folks don't pay up. I don't know if it means anything, might be some of his customers can't make payments and he's got to do it to stay flush. But it does cause me to wonder."

Buck crossed his arms, mulling over what Charlie said. So Fletch took advantage of the misfortunes of others? He wouldn't be the first banker to do so. But the question was, did Amy know? That fellow who stormed out of the bank the day she'd gone to see Fletcher, he looked like an angry customer. "Would any of the folks he's foreclosed on have a reason to go after Mrs. Langford?"

Charlie's tangled brows shot up. "I can't imagine they would hold her responsible for his actions. I know she holds with some radical ideas, but I can't think of anyone who would want to hurt her."

"There's somebody out there who wants to hurt her."

"One of the settlers, no doubt."

"I don't think so." Buck frowned. There was no proof it wasn't a settler, but based on Sean's report and the fact there had been no attacks outside of Fort Scott, it just didn't fit.

Music filtered through the dust kicked up by the passing soldiers. The brisk polka was an odd accompaniment to creaking wagons and jangling harnesses.

Buck craned his neck to find the source.

Down the middle of the street came what looked like a contingent of circus performers who'd lost their parade. A man with a pointed red hat and frizzled white hair held a chain attached to a bear, which lumbered along behind. Three musicians dressed like gypsies brought up the rear.

As they approached, chaos reigned. Horses whinnied and shied away, resisting their riders' attempts to calm them. Wagons veered aside as drivers stopped to stare at the spectacle. Children skipped alongside, laughing and pointing.

Charlie hooted. "Would you look at that? Wonder if a circus is coming to town?"

It sure looked that way, but Buck hadn't seen any posters or heard any talk, and the arrival of a circus was always a topic for conversation. "Could be a gag to attract attention for a new store opening. My stepfather used to pay a fellow to walk on stilts down the street and sing out when a load of goods got delivered. Can't recall he ever used a bear."

"Don't that beat all." Charlie said in an awed voice.

Across the street, the doors of the railroad office opened and Amy walked outside, trailed by Fletcher and two well-dressed gents. Their steps slowed and then stopped as they took in the impromptu performance. Her head turned and she scanned the street until her eyes met Buck's. She quickly looked away as though she hadn't been searching for him.

He ground his teeth. If she wanted to pretend not to see him, he would play along…for a while. He turned his attention back to the strange little show.

The actor had stopped in front of the hotel, and the bear, restrained by a chain and sturdy looking collar, had risen up on his hind legs to roar—or maybe that was supposed to be singing. The trio of musicians spread out to give him room to move. In front of the bear, a wiry man danced and played a flute. Like the other two musicians, he wore a bright scarf tied above the open collar of a loose-fitting shirt. With his swarthy coloring, black hair and beard he looked like a pirate, but he leapt around almost like a—

Monkey.

The performer whirled and stopped. His dark eyes widened.

Buck jolted up, as his mind drew forth an image of a man peering over a roof.

The pipe-playing pirate turned tail and ran.

"Sonofabitch!" Buck came off the rail in a fury, and took off at a dead run after the fleeing suspect. He sidestepped the weaving bear, shouted at the puzzled clown holding the chain. "Get this damned thing out of my way."

Keeping his eyes on the red scarf, he darted through stalled traffic, barely missing colliding with a running child by twisting to one side. Damn, he was losing the man— again. He waved at a cluster of soldiers standing in front of a building where the flute player appeared to be headed. "Stop him! He's wanted."

Wanted by someone who dearly wished to pound him into the dirt.

The fugitive pulled up just as the soldiers realized they were supposed to stop him. The man turned on his heel and raced towards an alley. Like a monkey, that agile bastard would disappear as soon as he found a way to ascend.

Buck panted from the exertion, cursing his lingering weakness from being ill. He sprinted faster, determined to catch his prey.

A tall wooden fence at the end of the darkened alley cut off access to the other side. The man leapt up and grabbed the top to hoist himself over.

Skidding to a stop, Buck pulled his revolver and fired just to the side of where the man gripped. In one fluid motion, he cocked and aimed at the man's shoulder. "Come down, and I won't kill you."

If that bastard insisted on going over, he'd have to shoot him, but he wanted him alive. He had some questions that needed answering.

The man dropped to the ground, turned slowly with his hands up in the air. His black eyes beseeched. "Per favore signore. I no hurt lady."

A foreigner? What the hell? Obviously somebody had paid him to attack Amy. There was no other explanation.

"Step over there. Away from that fence." Buck motioned with the revolver.

The gypsy looked past him as the sound of running feet drew closer.

Buck didn't take his eyes off the man. This one would take advantage of any distraction, and it was probably just a curious onlooker.

"Signore?" A tremulous smile appeared on the gypsy-pirate's face. His hands lowered, one reaching out.

A loud retort sounded by Buck's ear.

The man's head jerked back. Blood spewed. He collapsed like a broken toy.

Buck whirled around, expecting to see one of the soldiers.

Instead, Fletcher stood behind him, staring with a stunned expression at the crumpled body in the dirt. His arm dropped to his side, his hand still gripping a smoking gun. The acrid smell of gunpowder lingered in the air.

An obscenity burst through Buck's lips. "You idiot!"

He stormed to the crumpled man, bent over to check for any sign of life. The bullet had struck the side of the man's forehead, ripping away part of his skull. They'd be getting no answers now. Trigger-happy fool had killed their only lead.

Buck's frustration flared into fury. He barely restrained himself from pounding Fletcher into the dirt. "Did it occur to you we needed him alive?"

"I thought he was going for a weapon," Fletcher muttered in an obstinate tone. He squatted down beside the dead man. "He was reaching for something in his waistcoat."

Buck spoke through clenched teeth. "I had a gun on him. He wasn't reaching for anything."

Pulling back the dead man's vest, Fletcher slipped something out of an inside pocket.

Buck snorted. "He sure as hell wasn't going to kill anybody with a *flute*."

Fletcher gripped the instrument in his palm. His eyes flashed with disdain. "Actually, it's a piccolo—but you wouldn't know that, would you?"

"You arrogant ass." Buck grabbed the banker's lapels and jerked him up. "Even a fool would know the *real* threat is still out there." God, he dearly wanted to tie this dandy in a knot, but taking his frustration out on Amy's betrothed would only serve to antagonize her and attract the wrong kind of attention. He flung the man away, feeling a curl of satisfaction when Fletcher stumbled and fell onto his backside.

The banker slowly got to his feet, brushed the dirt off his coat. His face stiffened into an impassive mask, but his eyes gleamed with pure hatred. "That man is no longer a threat to anybody. Your job is done. I suggest you leave, as Mrs. Langford requested."

"I'm not going anywhere," Buck snarled, not bothering to hide his contempt. "Somebody hired that gypsy, and I'm gonna find out who. You get in my way again and I'll shove you so far down a hole, you won't know which end is daylight."

CHAPTER 17

"Buck threatened you?" Amy blinked in disbelief at Fletcher's accusation. She set down her fork, unable to finish the chicken and dumplings Sophie had prepared just for her. How much more grief could one day bring? Firing Buck had just been the start.

"Not only did he threaten me, he assaulted me without provocation." Fletcher wiped his mouth, having polished off his portion. Whatever roughing up he'd received at Buck's hands hadn't affected his appetite.

"*Assaulted* you?" Her incredulity was such that she could only echo the accusation. How bad could it have been? Fletcher had looked rumpled but unharmed when he'd returned from chasing after Buck and the fleeing suspect. If Buck had intended to harm him, he wouldn't have been able to stand up, much less walk back. "You don't appear to be injured."

Fletcher sucked a piece of food from his teeth. "He stopped short of that because a crowd had started to gather. The man is an unschooled brute. I can't tell you how glad I was to hear you had the good sense to fire him."

She stiffened with irritation. Her betrothed had made a grave mistake when he'd killed her assailant before they could question him, and now he was looking for a scapegoat. "I didn't invite you to dinner so you could disparage Mr. O'Connor."

Fletcher's face tightened. "I'm giving you the facts. I thought you'd be interested."

Almighty. He sounded like a spurned debutante. "The only fact I'm interested in is knowing who hired the man you shot."

A crimson flush appeared above the stiff white collar of his shirt.

Amy took a breath, then exhaled her resentment and dashed expectations. She'd hoped dinner would be a time they could focus on devising a strategy for how she might recover from that disastrous meeting with Mr. Joy. At the very least, she expected Fletcher to offer tender reassurances and heartfelt support. She was getting neither. However, throwing Fletcher's mistake in his face wasn't going to make the evening go better.

"I'm sorry," she ventured. "This has been an upsetting day."

Fletcher reached for his wine. "Of course you're upset. Who wouldn't be?" His voice took on a soothing tone. "I'm certain Sheriff Lawson will let us know as soon as he's learned something useful. Frankly, I believe any trail of evidence will lead to that despicable Land League."

"Do you?" She clutched the napkin in her lap. Discovering the identity of her purported assailant hadn't answered any questions—it had given rise to more. The dead man, an Italian musician and former circus performer, had been living in Fort Scott for the past year doing odd jobs around town. She didn't know him, had never even met him. "Mr. Capelli seems an odd choice for a Land League assassin."

Fletcher shrugged. "Who else would've hired him?"

Who else, indeed? Yet, something didn't feel right. And even Buck had been disinclined to believe the threat stemmed from the most obvious culprit.

"Darling, you can relax. Your assailant is dead and you'll have a military escort until the case is resolved, as I'm certain it will be. Very soon." Fletcher finished the last of the claret and carefully set the stemmed glass on the table. "Major Roy has promised extra protection for your meeting with the settlers in Girard. That should ease your mind."

"It does." She forced her attention away from the mysteries surrounding the dead man. "I am worried about that meeting. I'm not sure I can find a just solution."

"I'd advise staying away from anything controversial, given Mr. Joy's reaction to your unorthodox proposals."

She stiffened, as Fletcher's advice rubbed against the earlier hurt he'd dealt her. "You didn't think my proposals were unorthodox when we discussed them prior to the director's meeting. In fact, you encouraged me to present the ideas. Then, you sat there and didn't utter a word."

"I could tell they weren't going to be swayed by anything I said," he reasoned. "And speaking up would've undermined my credibility. You'll recall I did urge Mr. Joy afterwards to allow you to host that town hall meeting as your last official duty. This gives you a chance to redeem yourself by coming back with a negotiated agreement."

Her breath hitched as she wrestled with wounded pride. It wasn't a grievous wrong to want a solution that would benefit both sides. Yet, she'd been publicly called down, then forced to accept a less conspicuous position as assistant to the board. Did Fletcher realize how much it galled her that she would be little more than a lackey for the president, even if her husband ultimately held that role? "Do you have any suggestions for proposals I might present to the settlers?"

"The best course is to stick to Mr. Thayer's offer for deferred payments on loans."

Hurt congealed into a knot of resentment. She swallowed it with difficulty. On second thought, she didn't want his advice if all he was going to do was parrot Mr. Joy. "Very well. Thank you for that thoughtful suggestion. Since we're both leaving in the morning, why don't we retire to the parlor and review your analysis on those investments I'm considering."

His abashed expression threw the lid off her forced calm. "You haven't even looked at the information I sent over, have you? Did you at least bring the audit on my accounts?"

He cleared his throat. "As you know, I've been very busy with these land negotiations, and I wanted to give the audit my personal attention. Can it wait until we meet in Baxter Springs?"

"That celebration is three weeks away." She clenched her fists, wanting to pound the table. Nothing in this miserable day had gone the way she imagined. She'd hoped releasing Buck would remove her longing for him, but it hadn't. In fact, it only made it worse.

Now Fletcher was so wrapped up in his new role with the railroad he'd lost sight of other priorities. Being demoted into insignificance by Mr. Joy was bad enough, but she wasn't about to let her future husband relegate her to the bottom of his list. "I refuse to wait that long. If you can't see to it, assign one of your junior officers. But I want everything on my desk by the time I return."

Brick red spread from Fletcher's neck into his face. He shoved his chair back and stood up, dropping his napkin onto the table. "You seem to have forgotten our success hinges on my ability to wrangle a favorable agreement with the Indians by the time we reach the border. Considering how much we have at stake, I would assume that would be your priority, as well. But if you can't wait until I can give these other matters my personal attention—which you requested, I might add— then I'll have someone see to it while I'm gone."

Giving her a curt nod, he strode out of the dining room, calling for his coat. A moment later, the front door slammed.

Amy jerked at the sound. Bitter disappointment burned in her stomach, and she wrestled an intense desire to throw something.

Fletcher's attitude of late seemed to have changed. Or had she just become more aware of the self-centered sulkiness beneath his polished veneer? Perhaps she'd painted a picture of a husband that didn't exist—a man like her father, but without his weakness for a woman like her mother, her passionate, promiscuous mother. Fletcher didn't seem to be swayed by passion, but the possibility of more power had apparently gone straight to his head. And a massive ego wasn't conducive to an equitable marriage.

Closing her eyes, she forced her breathing to calm and her emotions to settle. No, she would not behave like her mother, making rash decisions in the heat of the moment. Three weeks apart from Fletcher would give her time to make a sound judgment.

"Miz Amy?" Jacob appeared in the arched entry. His brow was furrowed with concern. "You all right?"

Amy sighed. There were times she wished others weren't present in the house. "I'm fine. Mr. Bain had some important business that called him away."

Jacob nodded, although his expression conveyed he wasn't buying her excuse. "I was comin' to tell you, Mr. O'Connor, he moved out like you told him to. Left this for you." After placing an envelope by her plate, Joseph dipped his chin and exited through the butler's pantry.

Buck had left before the imposed deadline and without saying goodbye.

She blinked away tears. Sending him away had been the right thing to do, for his own safety. Her heart thumped an objection. But she refused to contemplate her other, more complicated motive for banishing him. Sophie hadn't been fooled for a minute, and Buck would have figured it out had she allowed him to stay.

She had fallen in love with her bodyguard.

A dull ache settled in her chest as Amy fingered the envelope. They hadn't parted on good terms. Had Buck written kind words, or was this a final salvo? Resigned, she withdrew the letter. A dog-eared piece of paper fell out from between the folds. It was her list of suspects. On the other page, a brief note was scrawled in a bold hand.

Venus, your admirers are many, but your list is incomplete. Look for me soon. Your faithful Casanova.

She blinked in confusion, then frowned as the implications sank in. *Dratted man.* What was he up to now?

There was standing room only at Billy Hack's Beer Saloon on Wall Street. Buck leaned back, propped his elbows on the beat-up bar. He surveyed the crowd. Based on the coveralls these fellows were wearing, the large quantity of liquor they consumed, and the lilting obscenities sprinkled throughout their conversations, he'd guess most of the men were Irish railroad workers. The same workers Amy hoped to lure away from the Border Tier's competitor. Now, she wouldn't get the chance.

The barkeep wiped a greasy rag over a spill. "Want something to drink, mister?"

"I'll take a beer," Buck said absently, watching the door for a familiar face.

Where was Charlie Goodlander? Moreover, why had one of the richest men in town picked one of the seediest bars as his preferred watering hole? Buck felt a smile coming on. Charlie's utter lack of pretense was one of the reasons he liked the man so much. Goodlander had promised to share what he'd learned about that Italian musician. What more had been uncovered by the lumber mill owner-turned-detective?

Buck took a sip of the beer set beside him.
He'd left that note for Amy knowing it would irritate her to realize he was still sniffing around. Bits of information he'd gleaned the day her attacker was killed had confirmed in his mind she was on the wrong trail. Now, three days later, he had the feeling he was about to pick up a scent that would lead to her true enemy—and his.

Through the sunlit door, a tall man strolled in. It was that surly bank customer. He darted a furtive look around and started for a corner table only a fraction larger than a stool. As he scraped up a chair, two smaller men sitting there hurriedly downed their drinks and left, apparently not eager to stay and visit.

Buck started in surprise when Fletcher walked into the bar. He turned so the banker wouldn't see his face, but out of the corner of his eye watched Fletcher approach the surly giant. Was this where the banker held his business meetings? Not likely. His preferences ran finer than this watering hole. So what was he doing here, seeking out an unhappy customer?

Someone slapped Buck's shoulder. Startled, he whipped around, snapping his fingers around a beefy wrist.

Charlie's brows shot up. "Hey, cowboy. What's got you so antsy?"

Throwing a quick glance over his shoulder, Buck grasped his friend's arm and pulled him around the end of the bar, out of direct sight of the two men who sat huddled in conversation. "Don't be obvious, but take a look at that man sitting in the corner with Fletch. Know him?"

Goodlander craned his neck. "The big blond fellow? That's Clay Thornton. He's got a place out on the Marmaton River. Bought up a bunch of land he thought had mining potential, but he never could get his investors lined up. Maybe he's trying to get Bain to loan him money."

"He was at the bank the other day." Buck noted the fellow in question kept tossing furtive glances over his shoulder. "Left in a hurry. Looked like he was ready to kill somebody. I thought he might be one of those bank customers Fletch foreclosed on."

Charlie shrugged. "Who knows? Maybe they buried the hatchet."

"Why here? This doesn't look like a place a banker would frequent."

"I've seen Bain in here a few times. Billy Hack's has a diverse clientele." A grin lifted Charlie's dropping mustache. Waving the bartender over, he ordered a beer.

Buck sighed with frustration. There was likely nothing going on, though he'd love to uncover dirt on the man Amy planned to marry. Jealousy was near eating him alive. He drained his glass and turned his full attention to Charlie. "Tell me what you found out about that dead musician."

"You having another beer?" Goodlander motioned to a small table vacated by two burly railroad workers. "I hate drinking alone."

"I'll get something later." Buck scraped up a chair. "Now tell me what you learned."

Charlie's brow furrowed. "Last I checked I wasn't in your employ."

"No, you're not." Buck heaved a sigh. "But I'm not feeling real patient right now."

His friend's face fell into sympathetic lines. "Might help if you tell her how you feel."

"Hell, no. And you don't say nothing, either." Buck pulled up at a narrowed gaze. "I mean, I'd be most appreciative if you wouldn't say anything."

"You must have been a general during the war, the way you give orders." Charlie gulped down the beer, smacking his lips as he set down the empty glass. He chuckled. "I believe that little gal's got you tied up in knots. Have you told her you're staying in our carriage house?"

"Didn't see a need." Buck couldn't fathom why Charlie had made the offer, but he wasn't about to question his generosity or draw attention to it. "Figured I'd keep you out of trouble with Mrs. Langford."

"I appreciate that." Charlie motioned the bartender over. "I'll take a whiskey and my friend here wants another beer."

Buck didn't have the heart to object. Truth be told, he was about ready to down a whole jug of Sean's "Stone Fence" just to banish Amy's image from his mind. Not just her image, the feel of her in his arms and the taste of her on his lips. He breathed in the odors of cheap cigars and stale beer to blot out the lingering fragrance of wildflowers that seemed to follow him wherever he went. Hell, he had to get his mind back on business before he went stark raving mad.

"Did you ask me here just to have a drink with you?"

Charlie shook his head. "There's lots of boys I can drink with. I found out that Italian fellow was up to his ears in debt."

"But why would he go after Amy?" Buck frowned, trying to make some sense of the man's actions. "She said she didn't know him, so he couldn't have owed her money."

"Don't know the answer to that one." Charlie shrugged. "I did find out he borrowed money to start a music store, then lost it when he couldn't repay the loan. Maybe he was angry with Bain and went after Mrs. Langford."

Buck sat back, startled by the unexpected turn. The man had owed Fletcher money? Was that why Fletch had killed him? But that didn't make sense. The banker couldn't collect from a dead man. Maybe he didn't want Amy to know the crazy Italian who attacked her was one of his customers. Why not? Why keep it secret? Damn it, there had to be a reason Fletcher had silenced Amy's assailant. Buck ran his fingers through his hair aggravated he couldn't piece together the puzzle. "Did Fletch tell the sheriff that musician owed him money?"

Charlie pursed his lips. "I don't know. Maybe you can ask him."

Out of the corner of his eye, Buck spotted his nemesis heading for the door. "No point getting things stirred up until I know more."

There was no chance he would go to the sheriff and invite an investigation. He'd prime a few pumps around town, but in the end he'd need to question Amy, and warn her to be on her guard. Generally, men killed their rich wives *after* they were married, not before. But there was something about this connection with Fletcher that stunk worse than week-old fish.

CHAPTER 18

April 29, 1870, Girard, Kansas

Amy stepped off the train, incredulous at the sight of the tall, fair-haired man leaning casually against the whitewashed wall of the new depot. *Buck.* What was he doing *here?* Her heart soared, until she dragged it back to earth with a stinging reproof. Seeing him in Girard was no reason to rejoice. She'd told him to leave two weeks ago. He was supposed to be long gone, out of danger and out of her life.

Pushing off the wall, he strolled down the platform in her direction, running his fingers through his hair before settling his hat back on his head. That simple gesture brought on a flood of emotions that swamped her heart and drowned every reason she shouldn't be glad to see him.

She clutched her satchel in front of her. "I thought you were gone."

His tawny mustache lifted slightly on one side. "Hope springs eternal."

He was so irritating, but seeing him somehow restored her balance and made her ridiculously happy. She wouldn't tell him, though. Not if she intended to get rid of him. She wasn't here to get drawn off course, which was something that seemed to happen with regularity whenever Buck was around.

He took the small satchel from her hands. "You planning on a short stay?"

"I'm returning home tomorrow after the town meeting." Wrangling an agreement with the settlers would be her last chance to make a mark on the railroad's success, which seemed certain based on reports from men spying on the lagging Katy. She scoured the thinning crowd, but didn't see any blue uniforms. "I'm supposed to meet an escort."

He shrugged with suspicious insouciance. "The troops recognized me as your bodyguard from the last time we were here. I told them I'd meet you when they happened to mention you were coming in today."

Happened to mention?

More likely, Buck had wheedled his way into their good graces. Now she was annoyed. "You are no longer in my employ. I thought I made that clear. How did you find out I was... Oh, never mind."

Buck just smiled and took her hand. "I told you, I'm not going anywhere until I catch whoever shot me. Keeping my eye on you is the fastest way to figure that out."

She shuddered. Staying close to her was the fastest way to an early death. Hadn't he figured *that* out? With a huff, she pulled away. "The man who shot you is dead."

"No, he isn't." Buck retrieved her hand and snagged it in the crook of his elbow, nearly dragging her alongside him as he walked toward the center of town. "That Italian fellow didn't carry a gun. According to his friends, he didn't even own one. Whoever shot me was well enough acquainted with a rifle to hit a moving target from a distance. I don't think the man who caused your accidents is the same person who tried to kill me. But whoever shot me is likely the one who hired him."

A chill snaked up her spine. "If someone wanted to get rid of my protection why would he shoot you but not the soldiers who've been guarding me?"

Buck stopped in front of the hotel and turned to her. "Good question, Venus. I've wondered that myself."

She opened her mouth to object to his continued use of the inappropriate nickname, but the air left her lungs when he lifted her hand to his lips. Even through kid leather, his touch set off a shivering response—just like the time before, and every time he touched her.

He was temptation and tormenter, her secret desire and her greatest fear. Whether or not she married Fletcher—and her heart had been in full mutiny lately—she couldn't choose Buck. The love she'd held back would burst through the dam she'd so carefully constructed. Then, when something happened to him, it would destroy her.

"Why don't we get a bite before that meeting?" He released her hand with obvious reluctance. "I'm sure you're hungry."

No, she really shouldn't.

"You got to eat."

She crossed her arms, trying to appear put out, but inwardly she was pleased at the thought of spending a little time with him, that is, before she told him to make himself scarce. For his own good. "You won't take no for an answer, will you?"

"No ma'am, I surely won't," he drawled.

It made no sense to send him away without discovering what he'd been up to the past two weeks. She'd nearly worn a hole in that note he'd left for her, implying he knew something she didn't. It was two hours until the meeting, which was just across the street. "Let me check in and freshen up. I'll meet you in the dining hall here at the hotel."

An hour later, she set her napkin aside. Her nerves hadn't allowed for more than picking at the steak and roasted potatoes. Buck had polished off his meal, and then finished hers when she insisted she wasn't hungry. Was he not using the money he'd earned to feed himself? She would charge this meal to her room so he didn't have to spend anything. He was probably trying to make his funds last.

Her eyes roved the walls, now adorned with flocked wallpaper. With the addition of the etched lamps and plush carpet, she could be fooled into thinking she was in a fancy hotel in St. Louis instead of a frontier railroad stop. How she longed for the day when Fort Scott would be the new western center of commerce and Kansas the brightest star in the Union.

Once her railroad reached the border and her wealth expanded, could she declare success? Somehow, the thought of having the right marriage and an elevated position in society didn't bring the sense of fulfillment she thought it would. Her spirits sank, unable to be buoyed by dreams that had driven her for years.

Frustrated, she shook off her ruminations and met Buck's quizzical gaze. "You've yet to enlighten me about what you meant by that cryptic note you left."

He leaned back, his pleasant expression smoothing into somber lines. "Not the best subject to discuss before you go into an important meeting. We can talk about it later."

His refusal rasped against her already sensitized nerves. "Why don't you let me be the judge of that?"

Crossing his arms, he remained silent a moment longer. Something that looked strangely like regret flickered in his eyes. "Did Fletch tell you that Italian fellow had borrowed money from his bank? Seems he foreclosed when Mr. Capelli couldn't repay his note."

A sudden constriction in her chest made it hard to draw in air. Fletcher had told her nothing of the sort. Hadn't even acted as if he knew the man. Her breath came in shallow spurts, making her lightheaded.

Buck leaned forward in his chair and grasped her wrist. His sandy brows gathered in a worried frown. "You all right?"

She nodded, unable to speak. Had Fletcher truly known the man who'd tried to kill her—repeatedly? It couldn't be true. "How do you know this?" She forced out the question.

"Got it from a reliable source. Charlie Goodlander. Though he'd appreciate it if you didn't share that knowledge with your Mr. Bain." Buck's voice carried a familiar ironic tone, but the tenderness in his gaze made her eyes water.

"You didn't know." Buck sat back, crossing his arms again. "I didn't think so."

"You're not just making this up because you hate him." Her voice wavered despite her efforts to control it. "Tell me you wouldn't do that."

The skin around Buck's eyes and mouth tightened. "What do you think, Amy? Do you reckon I'm that type of man?"

She moved her head side-to-side. "Why?" she whispered. "Why would he withhold something that important?"

The chair creaked as Buck leaned his arms on the table and curled a fist into his palm. "I was hoping you could enlighten me," he said in a soft voice. "Before I snap him in two for putting you in harm's way."

Stiffening, she took control of her erratic emotions. Fletcher would never put her in danger. "That's a huge leap, and one I'm not ready to make." Yet, Buck seemed so convinced. What did he know? She couldn't let it go. "Tell me what you've learned."

Buck launched into a rapid-fire explanation. Antonio Capelli had borrowed a large sum from the bank. When his business faltered, he'd borrowed more from individuals in an attempt to pay off the bank loan. His few friends insisted he was a good man who'd gone astray financially, but they all agreed he wasn't violent. It wasn't like him to attack someone, unless he'd been pressured to do it. The implication couldn't be clearer.

Amy sat back, gaping. "You can't believe Fletcher would send that...that miscreant after me. He's been begging for my hand for months, and we've worked closely for the past three years." Her mind refused to accept it. This didn't fit with the man she knew. Yet, the man she knew wouldn't lie to her. Her stomach turned at the thought.

Buck didn't back down. "You told me he predicted those attacks on you would stop if you two were married. Recall what I told you about that slave who hurried along his master's death? Maybe old Fletch was trying to scare you into a quicker decision and it got out of hand."

"Oh for heaven's sake, don't be ridiculous," she blurted. "He knew I planned to accept his suit. Having to exercise a little patience wouldn't send him on some insane quest to frighten me into accepting sooner. That's the workings of a desperate mind, and Fletcher is not a desperate man."

So why were her insides quivering?

"Hold on," Buck said, holding up his hands. "That's just one theory. Here's another. Somebody who's angry with him is doing it to blackmail him into forgiving a debt or just to get back at him. He's foreclosed on a fair number of loans, and that musician owed him lots of money. Maybe they're targeting you as a way of getting him to cooperate."

"That doesn't explain why someone would want to kill you, unless you're wrong about that and the gunman was after me."

His face turned to stone. "I'm not wrong." The rest went without saying. He thought Fletcher was responsible for shooting him.

Preposterous. She'd never even seen Fletcher with a gun. He had mentioned he enjoyed hunting, but not human beings.

Dropping her gaze to her lap, she stared at her clasped hands. There had to be an explanation. Perhaps Fletcher had made a bad loan to an unethical man. If so, why didn't he just come out and say so? Nothing made sense, and the more she tried to unravel the knots, the tighter they got.

She stood abruptly. "I have to go prepare for the town hall meeting. I can't think about this right now."

Buck leapt up and helped her to her feet. "I shouldn't have told you before that meeting."

No, but she'd insisted.

"Truth is," he continued, "the things I'm thinking about Bain are all bad. I know my personal dislike might be getting in the way. You can look at it from a different angle. Maybe something he's said or done will stand out, and all the pieces will fall into place."

They stopped outside the hotel. Buck took her hand, tucked it over his arm possessively. "Will Fletch be at the meeting today?"

"No." She pulled away and crossed the street with mechanical steps, ignoring Buck's attempts to assist her. "He sent a message saying he was held up in negotiations with the Quapaw. It appears the chief isn't ready to sign the verbal agreement he made."

"Don't surprise me none," Buck muttered, striding alongside her. "Fletch has got a few things to learn about Indian politics."

Fear sent a shiver down her arms. Fletcher's recent behavior and this cover-up suggested there was something he was hiding, even though she couldn't imagine he would have reason to harm her. But how could she know her enemies when she didn't even know the man she'd agreed to marry? Right now, the only one it appeared she could trust was the one she'd sent away.

Buck opened the door to the town hall. He looked down at her with concern. "Let me come in with you. Just to make sure you're safe."

Amos Sanford rose to his feet again to address the thirty or so men who'd shown up for the meeting. Men handpicked, no doubt, by this snake that cared more about his political future than the lives of these settlers who followed him.

"You can tell your Mr. Joy we aren't interested in his attempts to lure us into slavery with these accursed loans." Sanford's voice thundered and his eyes shot lightening.

Grumbles rose from the restless audience.

Amy gripped the sides of the podium to keep her hands from shaking. The loan offer wasn't going over well, just as she'd predicted. However, she had promised Mr. Joy to give it her best effort. She'd also gained his agreement to listen to any ideas that might be proposed, so long as they didn't involve discounting the price of land or giving away stock or transportation. It was like fighting with her hands tied behind her back.

"This offer is being made in good faith. Mr. Joy and his partner, Mr. Thayer, will personally secure these loans and not a penny of the principal will be due for three years, which gives you time enough to improve your land and begin to repay your debt. You simply have to plan for it."

The scent of fresh pine hung in the air from the hurried construction of benches for the spacious hall. When she'd entered the room, with its new plank floor and fresh coat of paint, it had smelled of opportunity, but now it reeked of discontent.

Her eyes sought Buck, who stood along the wall near an open window. The determination in his eyes and the firmness of his jaw gave her far more confidence than the handful of soldiers in the room looking vaguely uncomfortable.

Surveying the settlers' unhappy faces, she tossed caution to the wind and threw down the gauntlet. "This is an open forum for serious negotiation. Let's cut through the posturing and get down to business. If someone has a better solution, speak up. I'll entertain anything that makes sense and, if I believe in it, will argue its merit before the board. I will be your advocate."

"Advocate?" Sanford barked a mocking laugh. He hooked his thumbs through bright red suspenders, pretending he was no different from these other men. But that was like saying a coyote was the same as a hunting dog. "You have done everything in your power, madam, to see these men impoverished. We're wise to your schemes."

"Mrs. Langford just called for ideas," Buck thundered. "You obviously don't have any, so sit down and give somebody else a chance to exercise their jaw."

The room went dead silent. Every eye turned from the stony-faced man by the window to the glowering leader of the Land League.

Amy's heart lodged in her throat. She prayed with all her might that angels would be sent swiftly to prevent a riot.

"All right, then." Amos jutted his jaw out. "Anybody got any ideas they want to share with our *advocate*."

"I got one," a man yelled, jumping to his feet. "Lower the price of the land."

She shook her head. "We've been around and around about that. That's not a solution. It's a stale mate. Next?"

Man after man leapt up with suggestions, with most revolving around paying less for the land. Amy's hopes fell through the floor. This wasn't working. She would go back empty-handed. Whether the railroad made the border first or not, she would've failed in her job and in her role as intermediary.

"Who wants to make more money?"

Her head jerked around. That bold question had come from her bodyguard. What was he up to? God forbid he would do something to embarrass her.

"How?" a man ventured.

"Cooperate together to sell what you grow and buy what you need."

The crowd hummed like locusts on a summer's eve. Sweat broke out on Amy's brow. Where was he going with this?

Amos held up a hand to silence the crowd, undoubtedly so he could regain control of the conversation. "That's got nothing to do with the price of our land or the railroad."

Buck crossed his arms over his chest, not backing down. "Sure it does. You pay the asking price for what you've staked out. In return, the railroad donates prime land for building stores and storage facilities jointly owned by all of you, in a *cooperative* venture."

More muttering. "Sounds like we're spending money. Why don't he just give us a discount on our land?"

"That's a one-time benefit," Buck argued. "This other gives you ownership in something. You get to keep more money off what you sell."

Amy stared open-mouthed at the bodyguard she thought she knew. *Who* was this man? Not a drifter, or even a cowboy. No, she'd already realized there was more to Buck than that. He enjoyed playing the hayseed, but he wasn't one. Now he'd offered up an intriguing idea that just might work, with a little tweaking.

"I think that's an excellent idea," she called out, unable to keep the excitement from her voice. Buck beamed as if she'd given him a crown. She suspected Mr. Joy wouldn't want to donate even an acre of land, but she would be able to buy it once her investment in the railroad paid off. She could have the buildings constructed and recoup her investment by leasing them back to the cooperative.

Perhaps if she explained more, the settlers would catch the vision. "There have been cooperative societies in England for years, mostly for laborers to get cheaper goods. What if you farmers could create your own cooperative? Buy and sell through stores you own, and gain discounts on necessary services and products with your combined purchasing power? Mills and processing plants could become part of the equation. Cooperating together to achieve greater profits means greater prosperity for all of you."

"Sounds good to me."

Who said that? Her eyes scanned the crowd until she found him. The black-haired settler with the crystal blue eyes who'd challenged her at the rally. He was standing up, looking at Buck as though he knew him. Perhaps her bodyguard had made some inroads down here she didn't know about.

A few men began to engage in discussion with the blue-eyed farmer. He was handsome in the same rugged way Buck was handsome, although darker and not as tall.

On the buzz of conversation, Buck's idea took flight. She reined in her eagerness to engage in the discussion. It wouldn't be figured out here, in this mass of people. "Why don't we assign a committee to draft a proposal for me to take to the board? You," she pointed to the dark-haired man. "Would you be willing to serve as a representative?"

"This is ridiculous." Amos Sanford swam through the crowd, approaching the podium. "This has nothing to do with the price of our land."

Amy's stomach knotted with apprehension. This political shyster had been a thorn in her side from the first day she'd met him. Would he now ruin the progress they'd made?

Buck was there in what seemed like two bounds. He planted himself in front of the podium, as he had at the rally. "You got another suggestion that needs to be entertained?"

Her bodyguard faced off with the newspaperman, whose face had turned bright red. Sanford sputtered, glaring at Buck for another minute. "You're going to regret this," he bellowed, and stormed out the door.

Several men followed him, but most stayed. Some engaged in deep discussion, others remained in their seats but looked hesitantly interested. With Sanford and his cronies gone, a different kind of excitement charged the room.

Almighty. She'd found the key. Her mind whirred with ideas while her body hummed with nervous energy. She felt like dancing around the podium.

Her gaze shifted to Buck, who'd been drawn into conversation. His arms moved with animated gestures that conveyed his enthusiasm. Never had she seen him like this. Her breath caught as awareness dawned.

She hadn't found the key at all. *Buck* had given it to her.

Her skin quivered as she recalled their last kiss. He'd been furious, yet his touch had been tender. Even after she'd fired him, he'd sworn he wouldn't abandon her. And he had kept his word. Not only was he a stubborn protector, he was her biggest supporter. He was also, apparently, a man who knew enough of business to come up with a downright brilliant solution to this stalemate with the settlers.

From the start, she'd realized his intelligence and education was above what he portrayed, but hadn't wanted to delve too deeply into his past. Hadn't dared to consider the frightening possibilities before she erected the defenses designed to protect her from the pain of loving too much.

Who was he, this man who'd breached the ramparts around her heart? Today, she intended to find out.

CHAPTER 19

The cool night air bathed Buck's face and a sense of calm settled over him. They'd made it through that nerve-racking meeting and come out with a fair chance at success. There for a minute, he'd feared Amos Sanford would spark an uprising. That man had too much power and too little intelligence. Not a good combination. Finding a way to shut him down would be imperative if this cooperative agreement was to succeed.

The clack of Amy's heels on the wooden walkway slowed as they reached the hotel.

Buck restrained a smile, knowing she was trying to figure out where he'd come up with that crazy idea. She'd taken up the banner and run with it, just as he hoped she would. Directly after the meeting, she organized a committee, helped them draft a first pass at a proposal and assigned Sean to be their spokesman. His cousin was a natural organizer and had a good way with people. Amy had seen his potential, now that she'd made his acquaintance.

All that remained was to ensure her safety, and that meant convincing her Fletcher was in some way involved in this danger threatening her. Buck had no proof, but every instinct told him this was so.

He slanted a glance in her direction, but her mind was obviously elsewhere. A foolish yearning squeezed his heart, but he ignored it. She'd made it clear she wanted him gone, and he couldn't change who and what he was, no matter how badly he wanted to. He couldn't have Amy, but he could try to prevent her from marrying a man who would use her, possibly even harm her, to get what he wanted.

He gestured to a bench near the door. "Let's sit here a minute and enjoy the breeze."

Amy eased herself onto the seat and arranged her skirts. She'd taken his advice about using her advantage. The brown and blue striped silk dress trimmed with velvet the color of chocolate brought out the creamy undertones in her skin and the golden highlights in her hair.

She adjusted the brown velvet hat and brushed back a curl that'd strayed to her cheek. Every move she made was graceful and womanly. Only, he wouldn't be around much longer to appreciate it. Soon as he made sure she was safe, he would get out of her life as she'd requested.

"All right." She crossed her gloved hands in her lap. "Out with it. Tell me where that idea came from."

Surprise shot through him, followed by sharp disappointment and mocking reproof. Why the hell should she think he had come up with that notion, considering he'd never shared enough about his life to fill a thimble?

The ache in his chest spread to his whole being. More than anything, he wanted Amy's respect and admiration. Her love. He just didn't know how on earth to get there, not with all the deceit he'd planted between them.

Bracing his arms on his knees, he stared at the ground. Should he tell her Sean came up with the idea? That would certainly help his cousin and deflect her inquisition. But she would find out in a snap that wasn't the truth. And this was one bit of honesty he could give her. "My stepfather was interested in cooperatives some years back. I learned everything I could about them when I was planning to start up my own store."

Her brows arched. Was she impressed, or did she think he'd made that up? "I didn't know you were interested in trade."

"I have a lot of interests." Now why had he blurted that out? It was like bait for a hungry fish. He turned his head to meet her gaze. The light from a nearby lantern cast shadows across her face, making it impossible to detect what sparked in those golden brown eyes; curiosity, no doubt.

"Tell me more. I want to know about your interests and how you came to them. I want to know about *you*."

Her last words were a soothing balm. If she wanted to know about him, that meant she must care. His fingers tightened reflexively on his knees. She'd cared enough to worry whether he was warm that cold night he'd rescued her, enough to stay glued to his side while he was out of his head with fever. She cared so much she'd sent him away because she feared he would come to harm.

He removed his hat and threaded his fingers though his hair, his hand shaking. Should he risk revealing more about himself? Nothing could come of it. All these years of hiding his past had kept him safe, but had also left him adrift. Alone. He'd never felt so lonely as he did right now with Amy here beside him, and yet not knowing him.

Perhaps he could risk a little if that's what it took to get her to trust him, just so he could steer her away from a dangerous marriage.

"My stepfather was a merchant, real smart and successful. He put me to work for him when I was fourteen and that's how I learned the business. He had two natural sons, so I knew I wouldn't inherit anything. But I hoped to earn enough to one day have my own store."

How could he explain that his stepfather's trust and affection had made him believe he could be somebody? That good man would be so disappointed at how low his stepson had sunk.

"The war changed everything. My stepfather was killed, our business got burned down by Jayhawkers...." Buck rubbed sweaty palms on his knees. He couldn't very well tell Amy about his bushwhacking days. That would guarantee she wouldn't trust him.

"Before the war, Mr. Campbell, my stepfather, took me to England on a buying trip and that's where I learned about cooperatives. Seemed a good way for common folks to band together and have access to things only rich people were getting. I got to thinking this idea might work for farmers.

Hadn't sorted through all the details when I threw it out there. Just hoped they might take the bone."

"And they did." A light touch on his shoulder drew out the ache. Her hand traveled to his neck and her fingers threaded through his hair, igniting a flash of heat beneath his skin. "I knew it was your idea."

A wry smile tugged at his mouth. "Why? Because it's crazy?"

"No. Because it's *brilliant.*"

Love exploded in his heart like a well-placed shell. His breathing grew ragged. He cast about for a smart reply, but couldn't come up with a thing to say. So he bent his head and kissed her.

A soft gasp drew the air from his mouth into hers.

He cradled her jaw between his thumb and forefinger, savoring her lips. His body grew heavy with a dull, insistent ache that had to be soothed or he would die from the wanting.

Honor poked him in the ribs. He had no business kissing her out here in public view. Hell, he had no business kissing her at all.

He jerked back, abruptly breaking the contact. Like pulling a splinter, it was less painful if he did it quickly.

Her dazed expression, the swollen fullness of her mouth and the soft look in her eyes telegraphed a message straight to his groin. She could be his. All he had to do…

He braced his hands on his knees and hung his head. By God, he would not seduce her just to satisfy his own selfishness.

There was a rustle of skirts, a loud intake of breath—a sigh. She'd come to her senses in a minute and then she'd tell him to make himself scarce. He couldn't though, not before he warned her about Fletcher, and if she didn't listen to him, he might have to take matters into his own hands.

"I need to write up a report on today's meeting while it's still fresh in my mind." She was back to business again. "Would you walk me up to my room? I want to give you my card to take to that man you introduced, so he'll know how to reach me."

Buck stood, offering her his hand, glad to be given some task that would distract him from his misery. "We need to finish that conversation we were having earlier. About Fletcher."

Her chin tipped up and she frowned. "Tomorrow morning. We'll talk about it then."

They went inside. Mounting the stairs, his steps were heavy. Even if he talked her out of marrying the lying bastard he still might not be able to ensure Fletcher wouldn't harm her, unless she let him stay on as her bodyguard. But every day he remained increased the risk he'd be found out. On the second floor, she stopped at the last door.

She fumbled with the key, seeming nervous for some reason. Was she fearful he'd pounce on her?

He smiled with a twinge of regret for having put that suspicion in her mind.

"Here, let me help." Twisting the key in the lock, he held open the door.

She took a half step before she turned, grabbed his vest, and yanked him inside. Then she pushed the door shut with a bang.

He stared down at her, his mind searching for a reason behind her odd behavior.

With a smile, she came up on her toes, circled her arms around his neck. "Kiss me."

Amy's heart hammered in her chest as she offered herself to the man she loved. Despite her attempts to avoid the truth, despite her
fears, her heart knew Buck O'Connor was the right man. He protected her without suffocating her, he challenged her with just the right amount of encouragement, he supported her in her work and had proven he would stand by her come what may.

But most of all he loved her. Wasn't it obvious? And she loved him. Being a woman who did nothing halfway, now that she'd decided he would be hers, she wanted to show him she belonged to him, as well.

"I said, kiss me." She tried to still her trembling limbs. Great days, he did still want her, didn't he?

His eyes reflected confusion. But within the blue-gray depths there was also a longing that echoed her own. He pressed a soft kiss against her mouth that seemed far too reverent for the moment.

Pulling back, he met her eyes. "You know what you're doing?"

No. She didn't have a clue, having never seduced a man in her life. "I hoped you might," she whispered and leaned against him.

He hesitated for a heartbeat, and then gathered her into his arms at the same time his lips met hers in a kiss that seared her all the way to her toes.

Oh yes, he knew exactly what he was doing. The hot, slick kisses, the whispered promises as his lips moved down her neck, his dexterous fingers flipping open buttons and untying laces as he divested her of her clothes.

Heat flushed beneath her skin when she finally stood before him, naked as the day she was born, shivering with desire and shy uncertainty.

"Lord have mercy, Venus." He spoke with awe as he glided his fingers over her bare shoulders. "You take my breath away."

Amy trembled as his roughened hands set her body ablaze. He stroked her arms, spanned her waist with his hands, skimmed her ribs and fondled her breasts, his heated gaze following every move. His thumbs drew lazy circles around her stiffening nipples. Sizzling desire leapt from nerve to nerve, enervating a roaring passion. Her knees buckled.

"Please," she begged, hanging onto his arms to stay upright. "I can't..."

"Neither can I." With a low growl, he swept her up in his arms. He jerked back the sheets and deposited her on the bed before ripping off his coat and shirt. The mattress sank when he sat to tug off his boots.

She watched, mesmerized, as he revealed, with the removal of each item, the powerful body she'd mapped while he lay ill. Only, he hadn't looked like this.

Corded muscles flexed in his arms as he drew down his trousers. That part of him she'd averted her eyes from now jutted proudly from a nest of light-brown hair, which arrowed up his belly and forked out across his chest. His beauty was rugged as the land they lived on and rendered her speechless.

With a predatory smile, he crawled across the bed. His unruly hair fell across his forehead. She plunged her fingers into the thick waves, as he tumbled her onto her back and pressed her into the feather mattress.

"I want to taste you," he murmured, trailing kisses across her cheek. He tracked down her neck and lower, to her breasts. Cupping one in his hand, he drew a pebbled nipple into his mouth.

She moaned with pleasure, bowing her back, welcoming his hands and mouth. He suckled and stroked her breasts, making them swell and ache for more of the delicious torture. Never had she imagined such incredible pleasure from a man's touch on her body.

His lips forged a damp, hot trail down her belly, and his tongue explored the sensitive dip he encountered along the way. Nudging her legs apart, he cupped her, then tickled open tender flesh and slipped a finger deep inside.

With a gasp, she yanked his hair.

He rose up with a rueful smile. "Patience, sweetheart."

Her face flushed hot. "I...I'm sorry."

Levering up, he kissed her nose. His finger moved inside her with slow, sure strokes. "Sorry for what? I want you eager for me." He pressed his thumb against a place that made her breath catch. Finding the hard pearl, he teased it into a throbbing mass of want, all the while watching her face with avid interest.

The blush spread down her neck and across her chest, but she was too lost in a sensuous storm for her mind to hold onto embarrassment. She writhed with need, as his touch released a damp flood of desire. "Buck, please..."

He moved away and then she was lifted, her legs draped over his shoulders. The touch of his tongue where his thumb had been jolted her with the force of lightening.

She tried to move away, alarmed by the sense she was losing control. "What are you…? Stop…don't…"

"Easy," he crooned, kissing the quivering flesh of her upper thigh. "I just want to love you. Trust me. Let me show you how good it can be."

Amy fisted the sheets. She swallowed her fear and forced herself to lie back and let him have his way.

He gently parted her flesh, licking her, flicking the tip of his tongue over the throbbing bead. Passion shot through her veins, lifting her body and taking control. Her breaths came faster as the need—the ferocious need—coiled tighter and tighter.

Her hips danced, undulating in a rhythm guided by the touch of his lips, tongue and fingers. *Oh God.* Her head thrashed back and forth, as the coiled pressure became unbearable, overwhelming, even frightening. But he'd asked for her trust. She let her legs fall open, inviting his invasion as she released her slim hold on sanity.

The coil sprung.

She cried out at her release, her back arching, as pleasure crashed over her in wave after relentless wave, tossing her on a sea of sensation until it ebbed, rippling through her flesh, making her weep and tremble. Her mind slowly floated back to shore. She hadn't imagined passion would be like this. This wasn't bondage. It was freedom.

"Venus." Buck's breath blew warm across her skin. His lips brushed her stomach and then her breasts. "My beautiful, passionate Venus."

Bracing his hands on either side of her, he fastened his mouth on hers in a kiss that tasted of salt and musk. The blunt end of his stiffened member pressed against her damp flesh, the length slid easily into her slick, wet passage, until she began to stretch to accommodate his size.

She shifted slightly to ease an uncomfortable pressure, but didn't pull away. There was more to this mystery and she wanted to know it, she wanted him to teach her.

Buck frowned, confused. He pressed once more against the barrier…a *virginal* barrier. *Impossible.* She'd been married, and only a dead man wouldn't bed a woman this passionate.

She trembled, but her arms twined around his neck. Her fingers burrowed in his hair, nails scraping against his sensitive scalp, making his skin quiver. The muscles surrounding his cock tightened, squeezing like a vise. It nearly snapped his control.

He sucked in a sharp breath, wanting nothing more than to bury himself inside her, plunging again and again into the hot, tight sheath. And yet…

He rose up on his arms and looked at her face. Her sated expression has been replaced by tension tightening the skin around her eyes and mouth. Whatever her story, it didn't matter. He was taking a virgin and had to slow down to ensure he wouldn't hurt her more than he already had.

Carefully, he eased back to take pressure off the membrane blocking his entry into heaven. She sighed. Was it with relief? That was the last thing he was feeling.

With a smile, she slid her fingers through his hair. His heart sped up as she drew his head down and traced the inner edge of his ear with her tongue.

He exhaled a harsh breath, grabbed fistfuls of the sheets, forcing his body to still under her tentative exploration. He'd die before he hurt her or did anything to make her feel unsure. But, oh God, her tongue was in his ear, and her warm breath, now her teeth were fastening onto his flesh, nipping. Pleasure shuddered through him and on its heels, an intense need to complete the act of coupling with her.

"Amy." Her name came out in a groaning plea.

She clasped him with her legs, making him her willing captive. Her lips moved to his neck. She tasted him, licked him like he was a peppermint stick.

His arms shook as desire battered away at the defenses he'd hastily erected to maintain his control. God help him, he couldn't hold back much longer. Not under this onslaught.

He let his weight shift forward, bringing him up against the barrier, like a battering ram against the closed gate of a castle. There was nothing to be done but breach it. Break through and take the keep. It would hurt, but only for a minute. Wasn't that what he'd heard? Hell, he didn't bed virgins. What did he know?

"I have to...to break through," he stammered. "I'll try not to hurt you."

"I trust you." Her whispered words drove a stake through his heart.

He was the *last* person she should trust, and yet he couldn't stop. He couldn't back away and let her go because he needed her, like air in his lungs. He couldn't live without...

He screwed his eyes shut, blocking out everything but the urge to join with her. Flexing his hips, he drove himself in, tearing through the membrane, silencing her small, clipped cry with a kiss.

A moan started deep inside his chest at the indescribable sensation that swept over him. He deepened the kiss, pouring himself into it, wanting her to feel what he was feeling. Heaven on earth.

He stroked her shoulder, her breast, down to her hip, trying to soothe the tension from her body. As he began to move, he slipped his hand between them, touching the place he knew would arouse her.

She jerked, and drew a shuddering breath.

His heart lurched. Was he still hurting her? He'd have to try something else. Rolling onto his back, he pulled her with him while keeping them joined. His hands skimmed up her legs to her softly rounded hips.

"Why don't you take the reins? I don't want to hurt you more than I already have."

Her expression shifted from uncertainty to something that looked a lot like gratitude. He touched her cheek gently. He had to remember how small she was and not used to a man, much less a large one. A crease appeared between her brows. "I don't know what to do."

"Whatever you want, darlin'," he rasped, as he stroked her belly and fondled her breasts. "Ride me, however you want."

She braced her hands on his shoulders and closed her eyes, settling back onto him, seeming to test how deep she could take him. He released a shaky breath as he slipped further into her warm, welcoming center. She rotated her hips, rose up slightly, and then pressed down, grinding herself against his body.

His groans of pleasure seemed to give her confidence. Using her knees for balance, she rode up and down on his throbbing shaft, her breasts bouncing as she tossed back the dark curls cascading over her shoulder.

Buck couldn't tear his gaze away. She was a goddess, a dream, a vision, every secret desire he'd ever had all gathered up in one delicious, womanly form. And she wanted him as much he wanted her. He could see it in her eyes and in the soft, pouty set of her mouth.

His heart drummed like the pounding of hooves. He struggled to draw in more air, could feel himself slipping, sliding down a hill. With a groan, he gave her control of his body, thrusting his hips as she rode him with the natural finesse of a woman made for passion. This was better than his wildest imaginings.

Pleasure coursed through him and the heaviness in his groin increased. The pressure grew stronger, the tension building. Then the storm became a tornado. He wanted her with him when it swept him away.

Running his hand up her leg to the apex of her thighs, he used his thumb to rub the sensitive button in a way he knew would bring her quickly to her pleasure. She dropped her hands onto his chest, moaning as her muscles clenched around him.

Sensation surged, ripping away his tenuous control, sending him soaring out over the cliff.

Amy woke to a robin singing outside the window. Sunlight tiptoed in through the parted curtains. She closed her eyes and her body warmed as erotic images from the previous night flickered behind her eyelids.

After they'd loved the first time, Buck had bathed away her soreness and pleasured her again, bringing her to a fever pitch before joining with her a second time. Then, she'd explored his body with the same thorough attention he'd given hers and he'd coupled with her again. They'd fallen asleep, still entwined.

This night changed everything, and yet changed nothing. Her love for this man had been as inevitable as the morning. She could no more hold it back than she could stop the sun from rising. Loving him meant risking again, but sending him away would be a kind of slow death she couldn't bear. Now that she had given him her body he would certainly ask for her heart and her hand, and she would trust him with both. *Gladly.* She snuggled in his arms, the only place in the world she truly felt safe—and loved.

His lips brushed her hair. "Sweetheart," he started. Her skin prickled at the endearment, whispered in that raspy drawl. "You aren't hurting, are you?"

It had hurt when he'd broken through the barrier, but only for a moment. After that, there had been such pleasure she couldn't find words to describe it. "I'm all right. More than all right, actually."

A rumble sounded in his chest, and she recognized it as a chuckle. "I'm more'n all right, myself." He drew her up to him and placed a tender kiss on her mouth before looking deep into her eyes. "If I'd known you were untried, I would've slowed down. You said you'd been married."

"I was." She propped her arms on his chest. "But my husband left to return to his company an hour after we'd said our vows. He was killed in battle two weeks later."

"Bad timing." Buck's solemn gaze didn't convey amusement. He lifted a lock of her hair, twining it around his finger. "I'd have bedded you five minutes after saying 'I do.'"

She couldn't restrain a smile, albeit a sad one. "It wasn't that kind of marriage. James Langford was a family friend—one of my father's business associates—before he left to join the army. After Father was killed, he came back to Lawrence on a two-day leave and asked me to marry him. Offered his protection since I didn't have any family left. I was grief-stricken and feeling so alone, I agreed. We respected each another and I'd known him most of my life. But we weren't in love, so...conjugal relations seemed like something that could wait."

Buck smoothed her hair down her back, stroking her almost as one would stroke a cat. His eyes glowed like the blue heart of a flame. "I'd say I'm sorry, but I'd be lying."

Another blush crept into her cheeks as she realized he was pleased she'd come to him untouched. She rose up, letting the sheet slide off as she sat back on her knees, feeling oddly at ease with him despite having never been with a man. Throwing her hair over her shoulder, she smiled. "I was worried my fumbling might disappoint Casanova."

His eyes admired her and his lips curved in an approving smile. "Venus, you couldn't fumble if you tried."

Oh yes, she could and had, many times, but apparently not last night.

He stretched, muscles rippling, and rolled to one side, propping up on an arm.

"You look like a lion lazing after a full meal."

His fingers traveled up her leg, triggering a shiver that danced across her skin. "You're not scared, are you?"

"I haven't been afraid of you since that night you rescued me." She dropped her gaze to where his scarred hand splayed over the top of her thigh. "When I told you I was afraid, what I meant was..." She raised her eyes, wondering whether he'd think her foolish. "I was scared of feeling passion."

A surprised arch of his brows was followed by a disbelieving smile. "Why would you be scared of that? It's a good thing, a gift."

She didn't really want to go into the details of her mother's torments and her own fears, yet she couldn't hide from him. Not anymore. "My mother let passion control her.

It made her do things, promiscuous things that ruined her marriage, and she..." Amy took a ragged breath, forcing out the hated declaration. "She took her own life."

Buck sat up and folded her in his arms. He pressed a tender kiss on her forehead before he drew back with an expression of profound sympathy. Slowly, his brows gathered in a frown that she didn't understand. "Whatever your mother did doesn't mean it has to be that way for you. You're not obliged to carry her demons."

His words struck a comforting chord in her heart, and then understanding shook her. He wasn't just talking about her. Anger was another form of passion that could be warped, leading to abuse. "Your father…he hurt you. But, you're not like that. You're nothing like that."

Surprise flashed across his face an instant before he shuttered his emotions. It wrenched her heart to see his features freeze into the mask he used to hide his pain and protect the tender places that could still be hurt. She reached up, stroking his cheek, tracing the lion-colored mustache, putting her fingers to his lips.

Soft. They were so soft, the only soft part of him other than his heart. "When you were ill, you said some things. Don't worry. I'm the only one who heard, and the doctor. Neither of us would betray your secret."

He affected indifference. "I must've said something crazy."

"I've seen the scars." She rubbed her fingers over his knuckles. Why would he feel the need to cover this up? They'd joined together, become one flesh and drawn closer than she'd been with any soul. Didn't he know he could trust her? "They're caused by burns from a fire. When you were out of head with fever, you cried out—"

Frowning, he clamped his hand over her mouth. "That was a long time ago."

She lifted his hand and kissed the pale scars. The scowl drained from his face and the pain she'd seen before surfaced in his eyes. It tore at her heart, making her long to comfort him. "We don't have to talk about it if you'd rather not, but you don't have to hide."

Uncertainty clouded his face. "Did I say anything else?"

"You talked to Georgia. A woman, I assume?"

He blanched and his eyes flickered with chagrin before he shuttered them, looking down at the hand that held his. "She was my...stepfather's niece."

"Is she dead?"

He kept his gaze downcast. "No. Just not important."

She didn't really want to know the details. The mumblings and pleas she'd heard when he'd been delirious made it clear this woman must've broken his heart. Though Georgia was obviously in his past, the thought of him loving another caused a burning knot of jealousy. One day she might be strong enough to hear the story, but not now. Not while she was in bed with him. She wrapped her arms around his neck and kissed him, letting him know it didn't matter. For a while, nothing mattered except showing him how much she loved him.

Afterwards, he helped her dress, deftly assisting with laces and buttons. He dropped a quick kiss on her neck as she twisted her hair into a knot.

"I can do that for you," he murmured, taking a hairpin from her fingers.

She turned in his arms, retrieving the pin and lifting an eyebrow. "So you're a lady's maid as well as a bodyguard?"

"I told you, I have many talents," he murmured, bending down to bring his lips to hers. "Maybe I'll give you a demonstration when we get back." His warm whisper sent a shiver over her skin, awakening images that made her burn with anticipation.

At this rate they would never leave the room, and she'd already pressed her luck by allowing him to stay the night. Her mind veered to a safer topic. "Yesterday, you said something about working for your stepfather at his store. You obviously know about running a business, and you've given thought to this cooperative venture. Why don't you lead it?"

He had already started shaking his head before she could finish what she was saying. "It's better if the settlers run it. They'll trust one of their own."

"I'm not saying do it alone. That man I met yesterday, Sean Murphy, he could help you select other men who could be on the board. But your knowledge about the mercantile business would be invaluable. Once my money is freed up, we can build and open stores in towns along the railroad line, find and train people who can manage them—"

"Hold on, now." He put a finger over her lips. "You're getting ahead of yourself. First, you got to convince your boss to give up the land, and then you have to get all the settlers to sign up, and then..." A crease appeared between his brows. "What do you mean once your money is freed up?"

CHAPTER 20

April 30, 1870, near Girard, Kansas

Buck paced the dirt floor of Sean's cabin, his heart pounding in time with the strike of his boots. He'd come out here to give orders, but what he really needed was for someone to work a miracle and turn back the clock so he could start over.

Dropping his hat on the table, he turned and faced his cousin, throwing out his arms. "What the hell do I do now?"

"About what?" Sean snagged the earthen jug. He sloshed homemade whiskey into two cups and offered one to Buck. "Want a drink?"

No, he didn't want a drink. He wanted to crawl into the jug and ferment. What had possessed him to take Amy to bed? He'd known, despite his fantasies, there was no future in it, but she didn't. She'd chatted on about how they were going to work together, open stores, make history with this cooperative venture—after the money came in.

His gut twisted so tight he thought he might throw up. "I don't need a drink. What I need is to make sure Amy's railroad wins that race. If it doesn't, she'll lose her fortune. She'll lose *everything.*"

"What?" Sean's brows shot up to his hairline. He set down his cup with a guffaw. "She's rich as Midas, how could she lose everything just because the Border Tier loses the race?"

Buck gave in and took a swig, coughing as the corn liquor burned a path down his throat. He'd asked that same question, had that same mistaken impression. "She bought stock in the railroad—lots of it. Plus, she put thousands into that blasted immigration program and won't get repaid until Mr. Joy's land is sold. Whatever else she has is tied up in businesses, all dependent on that damn railroad making Fort Scott some kind of western Mecca."

The empty cup clunked as he set it down. He started to pace again, unable to calm an attack of nerves that had started right about the time reality smacked him in the face, and the delusion he'd woven—somewhere between when she dragged him into her room and he took her virginity—dissolved in a firestorm of guilt and regret.

"If they lose this race, that railroad becomes a little branch line to nowhere. Joy's land won't be worth shit. And that stock, her investments...." He jerked out a chair and sat down, dropping his head in his hands.

"They won't lose the race." Sean said confidently. "That co-operative idea of yours is gaining steam. Some men are even talking about taking out a loan so they can buy land to get in on the deal. Everybody I've talked to sees the opportunity in it."

Buck raised his head, willing to grab onto any thread of hope. "Can you help me round up more workers? Get your neighbors to pitch in and make sure this railroad wins the race so you aren't sitting on worthless land when it's all said and done?"

Sean regarded him with a solemn expression. "You're in love with her."

Misery flooded Buck's heart. God, yes, he was in love with her; he was *sick* with it. But he was a bastard for using Amy's affection and stealing her innocence. "I'm a Judas," he muttered. "Damned if I'm not."

He pulled a wad of bills from his pocket, his thirty pieces of silver. Putting the money on the table, he shoved it toward Sean. "That's my advance for this job. It's yours. Use it, or give it back to Amos. I don't care what you do, but I can't be part of this anymore."

His cousin eyed the money but didn't touch it. He leaned back and crossed his arms over his chest. "Go to her, Buck. Tell her you love her. Come clean. Women are forgiving creatures. It's in their nature. She'll be angry and probably tell you to make yourself scarce, but she'll come around. Especially if she sees you doing everything you can to help her railroad win the race."

"After I sabotaged her every step of the way?" Buck snorted. "She'll never forgive me. Nor should she."

"Could be she won't, but you'll never know if you don't try." Sean stared past Buck's shoulder, out the door of his cabin. "I should've tried harder. Don't make the same mistake." He seemed to shake off the strange reverie. "I hope she don't change her mind about helping us start that cooperative store."

"Amy's smarter than that. She might hate me when I tell her what I've done, but she won't cut off her nose to spite her face." Buck stared at the dirt floor, seeing the secret smile she'd given him as they'd parted with an agreement to return later in the day and spend time planning. Planning a future that couldn't be.

His breathing sped up at the lurching beat of his heart. Even if Amy could get past his working for the Land League, she would never get over his involvement in that raid on Lawrence. She would *despise* him. God, he couldn't bear it.

He raised his head, cringing at the pity flickering in Sean's eyes. His cousin picked up the jug and a splash of whiskey hit the bottom of the empty cup.

He stared at it longingly, and then pushed it away. "I can't get drunk. Got work to do. I need to check on the Katy's progress, figure out how fast we need to lay track to stay ahead."

"Why don't you and me go out tomorrow morning? I'll help you find them." Sean corked the jug and set it on the floor with a thunk. "I meant to tell you earlier, I went to register my claim on this land and I saw that banker's name. Bain, isn't it? He was listed as the owner of thousands of prime acres around here and Baxter Springs. That means he's got a fortune staked on this, as well."

Shock blew away the agony torturing Buck's soul. The unexpected news gave him something to focus on other than his own pain. It was another clue in this frustrating puzzle. He knew in his gut Fletch had sicced that Italian musician on Amy. Maybe it had something to do with this land he'd bought. Had he borrowed from her to purchase it? This was a question Buck needed to ask soon as he got back.

Hell, he couldn't confess his duplicity to Amy. Not yet. Not before he figured out what had to be done about Fletch.

The bell on the door jangled as Amy walked into the small office housing Amos Sanford's newspaper. She tightened her fingers nervously around the strings of her reticule, surveying the unoccupied room. Piles of newspapers were stacked in corners waiting to be delivered, probably filled with articles decrying Mr. Joy and the railroad's latest effort at reconciliation.

She gave it a fifty-fifty chance that Amos Sanford had acted in good faith when he'd sent her a note indicating he had helpful information. Her first instinct had been to ignore him, but curiosity finally won out. She had to know what he was up to.

Her nostrils flared at the pungent odor of the cheap cigars he favored. She sat on a seat in front of the desk to wait. Ten minutes, and then she'd be on her way. There was much to do. The committee she'd formed yesterday would be meeting after noon to work on the proposal for Mr. Joy. She wanted to stop in and see how they were faring, then get back to her room by four. The time she and Buck had agreed to meet.

At the thought, her body thrummed with anticipation. The old fear cast its net, but she threw it off, choosing instead to focus on how right it felt being with him.

Buck felt the same way, too. She'd seen love on his face and in his eyes. His pride might be holding him back from declaring himself. After all, it was clear he was poor. But that didn't matter to her, and it wouldn't be long before they spoke their vows.

That is, after she cried off her engagement to Fletcher.

She worried her lower lip with her teeth. It would take every ounce of finesse she could muster, as this news would certainly upset him. She would tell him how unfair it would be for her to marry him knowing she didn't and could never love him. He would find someone else, a woman who could give him the love he needed and deserved. Regardless of what Buck thought, Fletcher wasn't a bad man. He just wasn't the right man for her.

At the tinkling of a bell, she leapt to her feet.

Amos Sanford strode through the door. "Mrs. Langford. I'm pleased you responded to my invitation." He sketched a slight bow, before hanging his hat and coat on a rack standing near the door.

"Do you mind if we sit down?" He headed for the chair behind the desk.

"Not at all." Amy dropped back onto the seat she'd taken earlier, suspicious of his friendliness. Now that the settlers were excited about starting up a cooperative venture, Sanford probably wanted a position on the committee. Every move he made was calculated to advance his political aspirations for a Congressional seat. She didn't trust him but the settlers liked him, so she couldn't very well ban him from participating, much as she might want to.

"I received your note," she prodded. "Did you want to talk about the cooperative venture?"

His gray beard swayed as he shook his head. "No madam that is not why I called you here. Though you may reconsider this ill-conceived venture once you hear me out."

Not likely. She smiled politely.

Sanford propped his arms on top of the desk, forming a steeple with his fingers in a pose that would have done Solomon proud. "What do you know about Mr. O'Connor?"

The hair prickled on the back of her neck. "My bodyguard? Why do you ask?"

"Has he told you of his work for the Land League?"

She blinked, uncertain she'd heard the question correctly. *Buck? The Land League?* "What are you talking about?"

"In January, Sean Murphy wrote to his cousin, Buck O'Connor, asking for his help in our struggles against the railroad. We paid him half in advance and confirmed the deal the same day you hired him. He must have seen your offer as the perfect opportunity to achieve his goal. That is, to slow down the railroad by stopping you."

She leapt up in indignation. "You, sir, are the lowest scoundrel. If you think to stop this cooperative venture by slandering a man who has twice saved my life at the risk of his own, you had best think again."

The snake didn't bat an eye. "I am not trying to talk you out of anything, nor am I slandering Mr. O'Connor. I've told you the truth."

"Truth? You wouldn't know truth if it smacked you in the face." She stepped around a pile of papers, desperate to get out of the cramped little office and away from the fetid air. "I have no doubt you'd stoop so low as to hire underlings to do your dirty work, but I won't stay here another minute and listen to your lies."

Sanford's chair creaked again. He stepped around the desk, a malicious smile on his face as he stalked her to the door. "If you don't believe me, ask Mr. Murphy. He has nothing to gain by lying to you. If I recall correctly, he was all for your cooperative society. Ask about what his cousin did. O'Connor was a *bushwhacker*. He used the war as an excuse for stealing and killing. Men like that weren't honorable, like us regular soldiers...."

Amy jerked the door open, wanting to cover her ears so she wouldn't have to listen to the filth he was spewing about the man she loved. It wasn't true. The foul man was angry with Buck for calling him down publicly, and this was his way of getting back while disrupting her plans. She ran out the door as his vile words followed like dogs nipping at her heels.

"So not only is he a liar, he's also a thief and *murderer*, to boot."

Amy stood at the window observing the street below. She rubbed her hands together to warm her chilled fingers. Buck had returned, right on time. Certainly, if he'd been keeping secrets he would've fled as soon as soon as he knew they were out. That he'd returned when he said he would was a comfort.

Curse Amos Sanford. The sick man had likely sent that disturbed performer after her, and now he intended to frighten her further by planting seeds of doubt about the man protecting her.

As the key rattled in the lock, relief drenched her. Buck would know how to handle Amos and his devilish schemes.

"You're back, thank God." She rushed over and threw her arms around him.

He kissed her, took off his hat. "Good to see you, too." A smile lifted one side of his mouth, but didn't reach his eyes.

Trepidation tiptoed up her spine. He'd said he was going to talk to Mr. Murphy about recruiting more members for the cooperative committee. God forbid Sean Murphy was part of Sanford's schemes. If the man truly were Buck's cousin, he would've told her.

He cupped her shoulders and as his gaze roved her face, the uncertainty in his eyes warmed into concern. "You look pale. What's wrong?"

Amy put her hands on his chest, needing to maintain a connection so she could feel sure what they had was real and what Amos had told her was the lie. "After you left this morning, I received an invitation to meet with Amos Sanford. He said he had some information I might find useful."

A frown creased Buck's brow. "What did he have to say?"

"He told me you'd been hired by the Land League to stop the railroad...to stop me."

Buck's expression went flat, the same as when he'd been masking his pain earlier. His hands dropped from her shoulders.

She shivered at a sudden chill. Why wasn't he getting angry? He should be furious. Denying it. "It's a lie."

His mouth thinned into a tight line.

"Tell me it's a *lie*."

"I can't."

"You *can't?*" Amy tried to breathe, but her chest had turned to stone. It couldn't be true. She couldn't have been so wrong. "But…" Her voice wavered. "You wouldn't…"

His throat worked like he was trying to find his voice. He held out his hands in a supplicating gesture. "I agreed to help slow things down. To force Mr. Joy to negotiate. But I didn't agree to harm you. I've been trying to protect you."

"Protect me?" It seemed all she could do was parrot what he said, because she couldn't wrap her mind around what he was saying. He'd deceived her every step of the way, lured her into confiding in him, given her bad advice, and manipulated her so she would fail—again and again.

Her fingers tingled and tremors shook her body. *Cold.* God, she was so cold. She hugged her arms as ice encased her heart. The unbearable agony slowly turned into a dull, throbbing ache.

Her betrayer was her bodyguard. The man she loved was a liar. Dear God, how could she have misjudged so disastrously? Buck was *worse* than Fletcher because his deceit had been intentional and intended to harm. He'd been crafty as a fox stealing into a henhouse. Had gained her trust by playing on her emotions, all the while ruining her.

She glared at him accusingly. "You deceived me. You worked against me. You tried to ruin me, and you have the gall to stand there and claim you want to protect me? Do you know how *crazy* that sounds?"

He winced. "I know. I deserve that, and more. But please, let me explain."

When he moved closer, she backed away, desperate to keep distance between them. She couldn't let him touch her because she got confused when he touched her, and his touch was a lie, just like everything he'd said and done had been a lie.

Her legs bumped against the windowsill.

Alarm flashed across his face. "Amy, the window's open. Don't back up."

As if responding to his warning, a breeze lifted the curtain, swirling it around her, sending a thought tripping through her mind.

"We're not high enough that the fall would kill me. More than likely, it would only cripple me. But you've already done a fine job of that."

Agony bloomed in his eyes. "I know I wronged you. But I never meant to hurt you. My cousin, he's the only family I got left. He wrote saying he needed my help. I didn't know you. Didn't expect to find a woman. Didn't think I'd fall..." His words died and his features twisted with a look of pain.

No, it wasn't real. He wore a mask. She had to remember she could never know the man who lived behind it. He was a deceiver.

"I realized after that first night I couldn't do you harm." His voice sounded rough with what she once would've interpreted as strong emotion. Only, a deceiver couldn't have any true feelings. "I tried to think of ways I could help Sean, but keep you safe at the same time. I thought I could do both." His mouth turned down in an expression of disgust. "I know how arrogant and stupid that sounds. I seem to be cursed with those two qualities."

Stupid? He wasn't stupid. He was cunning. Oh yes, she'd seen the calculating look in his eyes that first night, but she'd ignored it, letting his brave rescue blind her to the warning.

Her gaze shifted to the bed and shards of pain ravaged her still-beating heart. She'd given herself to him, allowed love to grow, its petals unfurl. Now, he was killing it. This was worse than death.

"I don't care about your excuses." Her voice sounded wooden and hollow, as though it came from a puppet's lips. "And I don't want to hear any more of your lies."

"I didn't lie."

Amy's glare was hotter than hellfire. So much so, Buck was tempted to reach up and make sure he hadn't grown horns. There was no doubt in his mind she thought he was the Devil, but Old Scratch wouldn't be troubled by guilt.

"I know I hid things, but I didn't outright lie to you."

Her eyes hardened into stones. "Deceit. Manipulation. Subterfuge. It's all lies, sir, regardless of how you package it."

Her shot struck true, bringing a fresh wave of pain. He blinked, refusing to accept the death of every tender moment between them. "If I'm a liar, then why am I confessing? I could've lied. You wanted me to. Hell, you asked me to. It would've been easier to keep you in the dark."

"Don't twist my words. You had every opportunity to tell me what was going on. At some point you must've known I would have listened to you."

He fought, knowing it was a losing battle. "You wouldn't have trusted me anymore. You would've fired me. And I didn't want to leave until I made sure you were safe."

"Stop trying to convince me you care about anything but your own malignant purposes," she cried. "You didn't want to leave until you'd accomplished your goal. Stopping me. *Ruining* me."

He held out his hands. "I never intended to ruin you. Hell, I've been trying to help you ever since that rally. Don't you remember? I challenged you to find a solution to benefit everybody. That's what you want, isn't it?"

The rough, pleading quality in his voice gave away his distress, but it didn't matter. He'd throw his pride to the wind if it meant she wouldn't despise him. "I never lied about my feelings for you."

She drew back like he'd struck her. "You never *spoke* of your feelings for me, other than lust. I'll concede you were honest about that." Pain laced the anger in her voice and her eyes filled with a kind of bitterness he recognized.

He put his hand to his chest. Couldn't breathe. She'd never believe him. Never trust him again. It was too late to tell her his love for her eclipsed anything he'd ever felt for anyone. It was too late to tell her that her love had become as necessary as air. Now, he was suffocating.

She presented her back, telling him without words he'd never breach this wall between them. If he kept battering away it would simply collapse and crush him.

"I'll go now, but I'm not leaving for good until I'm sure you're safe." His feet dragged like lead weights even though he felt as empty as a husk.

"Wait."

He jerked to a stop, his heart leaping up at that one word. Turning around, he looked for any sign she might listen, might give him another chance.

"Mr. Sanford also told me you were a bushwhacker during the war. Did you...did you ride with Quantrill?" Her question extinguished the flicker of hope.

Fighting a desperate urge to lie, he met her gaze and exposed the awful truth in his eyes. Then he picked up the hammer and drove the last nail into his coffin. "Only once."

Amy's eyes closed. Her face twisted with agony before she collapsed in a heap on the floor.

Buck rushed to her side, dropping to his knees and gathering her into his arms.

"No!" She fought him, tearing at his shirt, but he held her tight, muffling her cries against his chest, a high keening sound like a suffering animal would make. Her grief ripped through him and he bled from a thousand wounds.

Merciful saints, he couldn't bear having her think he'd taken her father away from her. He tenderly caressed her cheek hoping she could sense the loving touch and hear the truth in his words. "I didn't kill him," he rasped. "I swear it. I didn't kill your father."

"How do you know?" she moaned. "Nearly every man and boy in Lawrence was murdered that day. How could you even remember their faces?"

"Because I didn't kill anybody."

She stilled from her struggles. "You're lying."

He stiffened as the accusation stabbed

through him. It was the one thing he most needed her to believe. But she would never accept his word as truth after he'd deceived her in every other way. Still, he had to try.

"I killed plenty of men during the war, but none there. Not that day. I went to Lawrence for one reason—to find Jim Lane. He led those raids into Missouri. His men killed my stepfather and his brother. Raped the woman I planned to marry. Destroyed our business. Took everything."

Buck swallowed a painful lump. He couldn't begin to explain the depth of his despair when he'd lost his home, his future, his very identity as a gentlemen of consequence, as someone of value.

Justice. That was what he'd sought when he'd ridden off to war. But a harvest of bitterness had yielded only more loss, more pain. And in the process, his heart had shriveled up and he'd become no better than an animal—until he was forced to face the truth. He was *damned.* Hell, he'd been *born* damned.

Desperation gripped him. "Me and Cole Younger spent the better part of three hours searching for Lane. But we never found him. When I got back to the main part of town and saw what'd happened, I couldn't believe—" He closed his eyes, choking on the words. God, he could still smell the smoke, see the twisted, bleeding bodies scattered in the street, hear the wailing of women mingling with the whoops of drunken men.

His voice lowered to a hoarse whisper. "I know I'm cursed for eternity, but I didn't kill your father. I wouldn't lie to you about that. I'd rather die than hurt you."

She shuddered in his arms. "Then you had best get on with it."

CHAPTER 21

May 12, 1870, Baxter Springs, Kansas

A loud whistle sounded as a gaily-trimmed engine rolled into the makeshift station, the last town in Kansas before entering Indian Territory. Red, white and blue banners fluttered as the cars squealed to a stop. Amy craned her neck, anxiously searching the passengers departing from an open-air car in the rear. There were railroad directors, assorted luminaries. No sign of Fletcher.

On the platform, a ragtag collection of fiddlers and banjo players struck up an off-key but upbeat *Song of the Kansas Immigrant*.

"Looks like Baxter Springs intends to outdo every other town in putting on a celebration," said a voice behind her.

Over her shoulder, she spotted Charlie Goodlander's grin. His cheerfulness annoyed her. "What do we have to celebrate? We've not yet made the border, nor are we certain we'll be declared the winner once we get there."

The reproof fetched a chastened look, which spurred her remorse. Why was she being so ill mannered? The object of her anger wasn't Charlie. The man who held that honor wasn't here. He'd vanished two weeks ago, right after she told him to get on with the business of dying. Cruel words, but what he'd done to her surpassed cruelty.

Not only had the wretch lied to her and worked against her, he had ridden with Quantrill. *Only once.* So he said, but once was enough to prove him to be the killer Amos accused him of being. He claimed he hadn't killed anyone that day, but she'd been there, had seen evil on the faces of the men who'd dealt death indiscriminately to every man or boy they happened across.

Wracking her brain, she couldn't recall Buck's face, but that didn't mean anything. In her shocked state, how could she remember one face amongst three hundred? The face she would never forget was her father's, twisted with pain, as he lay sprawled in his nightclothes, his life bleeding out onto the street in front of their home.

She shoved her grief into a dark corner of her heart until the time came when she could afford to deal with it. Right now, she had to find her betrothed and end their engagement. It was something she should've done the moment she realized she couldn't love him. That Fletcher had whitewashed his relationship to her attacker simply reinforced her decision.

In truth, she couldn't bear the thought of marriage, not with anyone. Buck had taken more than her virginity. He'd stolen her heart and wouldn't be returning it in this lifetime. Now it was up to her to ensure he didn't steal away with her fortune.

"I don't mean to be rude," she said to Charlie. "But until we have a congratulatory telegram from Washington, I don't see any reason for celebration. We should be focused on completing the line as quickly as possible."

He lifted a shoulder in a good-natured shrug. "Mr. Chanute says we picked up a new crew of workers. They've been laying two miles of track a day. Even put down a mile and a hundred feet in driving rain. At this rate, we'll cross the border by Saturday. Surely that's worth celebrating."

She turned at the sound of loud shouts. They were coming from a crowd forming around a man who had a keg of whiskey on his shoulder. As he wove through the crowd, he filled outstretched cups and poured the libation into open mouths when a cup wasn't available. Charlie raced over to collect his share. He soon reappeared with two glasses.

"Here, try some of this whiskey. It's good *pisen*, as they say."

"Poison is right. That homebrew will eat out your insides. You didn't happen to see Fletcher over there?"

"Haven't seen your Mr. Bain."

Fletcher wouldn't be *her Mr. Bain* much longer, but she saw no need to go into that with Charlie. Certainly not before she'd discussed it with Fletcher. Apparently, he hadn't yet made it back from Indian Territory. She sniffed the amber liquid and her eyes watered. "Honestly, Charlie, I don't know how you drink this stuff."

The crowd thinned, with most of the celebrants following in Pied Piper fashion after the man with the whiskey barrel as he started down the road leading to the town square.

"Fletcher indicated he'd be arriving today." Amy drummed her fingers against her skirt. She wasn't looking forward to seeing him, but she couldn't let him think they would be wed in a week. "He's supposed to give a speech at the ribbon-cutting ceremony for the new depot."

"I'm sure he'll show up this evening. Mr. Joy is scheduled to arrive at eight, perhaps he's coming then." Charlie tipped back his glass, finishing off the contents. "Where's your bodyguard?"

"I let him go." She forced an indifferent tone. "I didn't need him anymore."

Charlie's brown eyes reproached, setting off a flutter of indignation. He couldn't possibly know the true nature of the man he'd befriended.

She opened her mouth to set him straight, but the words wouldn't come. Buck had betrayed her in the worst way, and still, she couldn't betray him. She couldn't even hate him, much as she wanted to. She blinked away her tears. What flaw in her character made her long for a man who didn't deserve her loyalty, much less her love?

Charlie's gaze softened and a sympathetic smile lifted the drooping mustache. "Why don't we go into town? They're roasting a buffalo over at the Pacific Restaurant. I'm getting hungry just thinking about it."

She shouldered her despair and marched to the waiting buggy. The last thing she wanted was to attend a party, but she had to put forth a good effort for the sake of her peers.

After dinner, the large assembly poured out into the square, gathering around a towering bonfire. Reluctantly, she took a seat on a log bench to watch a band of Pottawatomie Indians perform dances involving a great deal of arm flapping and foot patting. At the other end of the square, Quapaw warriors did tricks on horseback. Most of the Indian men wore an odd assortment of stovepipe or slouch hats bedecked with feathers. White shirttails drooped down over breeches and buckskin leggings. A few had on black dress coats, while others sported red Garibaldi jackets trimmed with elaborate embroidery.

Had Buck been here, had he not been a deceiver, but rather the witty lover she longed for, they would have had a grand time at the quirky display. As it was, the hours dragged like an anchor pulled through silt.

Amy's face soon felt as numb as her feet. The town dance that followed had proved every bit as excruciating as the Indian display. Sweat broke out on her brow as merry couples blurred into a weaving mass of colors and shapes. When had it gotten so hot?

Tipping her glass, she swiped her tongue at the remaining drops of liquid. Charlie had seen to refills and she had to admit Fire Rod didn't taste half bad, especially when followed by one of those peppermint candies.

She hiccupped. Buck had tasted of peppermint when he'd kissed her that last time. He had a fondness for minty candy. Her stomach flip-flopped, threatening mutiny. Jumping to her feet, she staggered away from the huge tent, desperate for fresh air.

The sprightly music faded as she veered in the direction of a dark line of trees at the far side of a field. It might not be wise to run off alone, but she had to get away from the celebrating throng before she dissolved into tears.

She cast a wary look around. The two soldiers assigned to guard her for the evening were nowhere in sight. Last she'd seen, they'd been kicking up their heels having a fine time. Acute longing swept over her. Buck would never have let her out of his sight. He always seemed to know precisely where she was, as if they'd been joined by some invisible cord.

Her toe struck a clump of sod and she stumbled, but somehow managed to stay upright. She'd stood outside Mr. Murphy's sod house just a week ago, discussing the cooperative. She wasn't giving up that idea no matter where it came from. Mr. Murphy had explained to her how Buck had risked his life to come to Kansas to help him because the only family they had left was each other.

Family loyalty she understood, but why hadn't Buck trusted her enough to confide in her once he'd come to know her better? Because allegiance to his cousin outweighed his feelings for her, whatever those might be.

A mischievous wind tugged at her hair and kicked up the crisp scent of alfalfa. The cool air eased the churning in her stomach and cleared her head. She braced herself against intruding thoughts that never ceased to cause her pain.

What of Lawrence? Anguish bloomed in her chest. In a sense, Buck's motives for going on that raid troubled her more than his deception. He'd been out to exact revenge.

She'd heard about the atrocities stemming from Senator Lane's raids into Missouri, but her father had assured her that his partner, then a General, had done only what was necessary. Were murder and rape necessary? Even still, Buck had chosen to pursue unspeakable violence. Yet, hadn't he been guided onto that path when he was little more than a baby?

Her emotions careened back and forth. She'd swear he wasn't a violent man, but at one time he had been. Somewhere along the way, something must've changed him. Had Lawrence been the crucible that produced a different person? Or was she simply looking for someone that didn't exist. He'd taken her trust and her love, knowing all along his only interest in her was her ruination. His deceit knew no bounds.

Her steps slowed. She looked up to the heavens, where darkness stretched out like a black robe decorated with diamonds. From somewhere nearby, coyotes yapped and howled. She shivered, well aware she was far from any place that could be considered civilized, and thus had to be on her guard. Fortunately, she'd tucked a small pistol into her reticule.

"Amy." A familiar drawl drifted out of the black shadows cast by swaying sycamores. Her heart pounded harder as a shadow lengthened, becoming a man. He removed his hat, and the moonlight reflected off his hair, turning it silver.

The deceiver had returned.

Buck grabbed Amy's arm before she could flee, careful not to hurt her but unwilling to let her escape. He put on his hat, which he'd taken off so she'd recognize him and not be frightened, and pulled her back toward the shadows. It didn't appear those soldiers had followed, but he'd be cautious nonetheless. He sucked in a sharp breath as he felt something jab into his belly, right above his belt.

He drifted his hands slowly down her arms. "When did you start carrying a gun?"

"When I realized there might be a snake in the grass."

He swallowed the urge to laugh. There was nothing funny about any of this, but if he didn't keep his sense of humor, he would break down and bawl like a baby. "If you're set on shooting me, I'd prefer for you to put a bullet through my heart. With a gut wound, I'd linger in pain for days before the infection got me. It's an awful way to die."

He paused, recalling her last words to him. "Course, it could be you want me to suffer awhile before I give up the ghost."

Her shudder rippled up his arms. "I'm not the one who leaves behind the wounded."

He stiffened at the shot. She might as well have pulled the trigger. "You made your point. So go ahead and shoot me, or put the damn thing away."

The pressure on his stomach released and she stepped back, fumbling with her bag. He reached out to reestablish the connection, but she recoiled from his touch like he was diseased. "Why are you here? What do you want?"

Her sharp questions pierced him. He had good reasons for following her, but the real truth was he simply couldn't stay away. The last two weeks had been pure hell. Every day, he couldn't get her out of his head, and every night she visited him in dreams that turned into nightmares. What did he want? He wanted to hold her and love on her, beg her to forgive him or put him out of his misery. He captured her arms. "I need to warn you."

She tensed. "Warn me?"

He caught her fragrance and a fierce longing swamped him. It took every ounce of his willpower not to haul her up against him and kiss her senseless. He would act honorably, by God, even if it killed him. "You're going the wrong way."

She tipped her head to one side. Although her expression remained partially hidden in the dark, he could see well enough to deduce it wasn't a happy one. "What's this? More lies?"

Damn, he wanted to shake some sense into her. Instead, he ran his hands up her arms to her shoulders, unwilling to let go. His need for Amy was like his father's craving for whiskey, a gut-wrenching obsession that would get him killed if he couldn't stay away. "Why would I waste my time seeking you out just to lie to you? If I wanted to see you suffer, I'd let your boss figure out on his own that his track is laid to the wrong marker."

"What are you talking about?" Now he had her attention.

"A couple days ago, some Indians showed Mr. Chanute a pile of stones and told him it was the boundary line. Your chief engineer figured he was so close to the border he laid off a couple crews. I found out those *Indians* were the Katy's hired thugs. They showed him an old survey line, not the border. That's another five miles south."

She huffed. "Have you been spying on our workers?"

Frustration gnawed at his insides. She would think the worst. Still, it was his fault. His deception had destroyed her once-unshakable faith in him and had killed the fragile love he'd coaxed into bloom. "I've been laying track."

"For *our* railroad?"

Who the hell did she think he'd be working for? He bit back the sharp retort. "It was after those Indians acted so friendly, I started getting suspicious. Did a little investigating and found out the Katy hired Bob Greenwell. He's an old border fighter I knew back during the war. It was him and his boys who tricked Chanute." At her continued silence, Buck's temper boiled up. "You can take a mind to believe me, or not. It's your choice."

"Why?" Her voice sounded shaky. "Why are you still around?"

Why indeed? There was no chance he'd earn her forgiveness, but he'd do everything in his power to save her fortune and ensure her safety. While he'd been busy rounding up workers and slamming down rails, Sean had kept on eye on Amy. She'd gone whole hog on that cooperative idea and had stayed in Girard to get a committee going. It remained to be seen whether her boss would turn loose any of the land they'd need for stores and granaries and such. However, her hard work on behalf of the settlers had won her many new friends in the former Neutral Lands, Sean included. It gave Buck some comfort knowing once he was gone, his cousin would be on Amy's side instead of working against her.

He drew a steadying breath, releasing it as he raised his hands, pleading. "I know I've given you no reason to trust me, but I am trying to help you."

"Why do you want to help me? You're my enemy." Her accusation sliced his heart open.

"Sweet Jesus, Amy. I'm not your enemy."

She tipped up her chin, and the moonlight revealed her disbelief. "You tricked me. You deceived me. You worked against me. Worse, you rode with a pack of rabid dogs that killed my father. If that doesn't qualify us as enemies, I don't know what does."

Her words struck harder than his father's fists, only her blows were ones he'd earned. He didn't try to block them, but held his hands at his sides. "Nothing you say or do will make you my enemy."

"Not even turning you in?"

"No." He sighed. "Not even that." He didn't expect otherwise. Hell, he didn't deserve mercy because there'd been a time when he'd given none.

"I didn't kill anybody in Lawrence, but it wasn't because I was opposed to killing. I was just intent on catching the person I thought most deserved to die. It wasn't until I saw what they were doing that I realized Quantrill intended to shoot down unarmed men and boys. Made me sick. They were worse than animals. But I refused to change my ways. I refused to let go of my hatred and bitterness until…" His heart pounded as he admitted his greatest humiliation. "Georgia, she was supposed to be my wife, but she left me because she said I'd turned into a beast."

All he could see was the top of Amy's head because she was staring at his chest. Had she heard him? His shoulders slumped with resignation. There was nothing more he could say. He'd changed in ways she couldn't imagine since that fateful day in Lawrence, but as she'd pointed out, it was too late to open up and seek her understanding.

"You're not a beast." Her voice drifted up, soft, almost soothing. "But you're still a liar, to me and to yourself."

Her indictment was like a punch to the gut. He struggled to catch his breath. He could come up with every excuse in the world for his deception, but it wouldn't matter. His attempts to manipulate the truth, to control people and their affect on him, to avoid anything that smacked of vulnerability—this was his downfall. He'd conquered his rage, but his distrust had killed the only chance he had at being loved.

A screech echoed through the woods.

He reacted without a second thought, drawing Amy against him and circling a protective arm around her while resting a hand on his revolver. It was probably just an owl, but it was best to be cautious. Too many railroad men had been relieved of their earnings by thugs who saw them as easy pickings.

Tuning his senses to the surroundings, he peered into the dark woods, then swept his gaze over a wide field where haystacks formed dark mounds. On the far side of the field, torches twinkled like fireflies and the high scrape of fiddles floated out of an open-sided tent crammed with revelers.

It came to him slowly, Amy hadn't moved out of his embrace. Perhaps only fear kept her there. Yet, the small sign of trust somehow lifted a heavy sorrow he'd been carrying. He toyed with loose curls at the back of her neck remembering how he'd run his fingers through the silky tresses, as she'd lain naked in his arms. Saints, he *ached* for her, body and soul. But he couldn't turn back the clock. All he could do now was help her win the race, and they were running out of time.

"I'm telling you the truth about that boundary line. I know it's not worth much at this point, but I give my word I won't deceive you again."

She made no response.

Regret mingled with frustrated longing. What had he expected? That she would believe him? Believe he was a man of honor?

Her hands splayed across his chest like she was about to push him away.

With a reluctant sigh, he released her.

She seemed to hesitate before she stepped back, but maybe he just imagined that because he needed to believe she still wanted him. "Thank you for telling me about that trickery. I'll report this to Mr. Chanute. I'm sure we'll get things worked out, so you won't need to stay around any longer."

Her final rejection swept away the last grain of hope. Just where the hell did she think he would go? Whatever semblance of home he'd once had wasn't there anymore. No one waited for him, looking down a long road like the father in that story his mother had read to him as a boy. That sweet woman had been the only person who would've stood out in the hot sun watching for him to come home. But she was gone.

Since her death, the closest he'd come to feeling like he belonged was with Amy. Now she wanted no part of him. Just like Georgia. Only, this was far worse. If losing Georgia had been painful, letting go of Amy was pure torture.

"I'll leave when I'm good and ready," he muttered.

"I'd prefer you leave now."

Despair struck with the precision of Siegel's artillery. In a desperate bid for survival, he dredged up resentment, smearing it over his wounds like a coating of tar. "I'm the least of your worries. You'd best figure out what you're going to do about Fletch. He's up to something. I'm certain he sent that Italian fellow after you, then killed the rascal so he couldn't tell."

Her head moved from side-to-side. "That poor man was deranged and thought he could get to Fletcher through me. Fletcher shot him because he posed a danger."

"Then why would Fletch hide the fact the man owed him money?"

"He was probably embarrassed and didn't want it to reflect badly on him."

Damn it, why was she still defending the bastard? "Your railroad agent's office has documents showing Bain bought upwards of a thousand prime acres around Girard and Baxter Springs. Expensive land. Did you loan him money to buy it?"

"He told me he bought some land, but he's never asked me for money." She propped her hands on her hips in a gesture of aggravation. "Why are you insisting Fletcher is involved in some kind of wrong doing?"

Buck huffed in disbelief. It was her insistence on Bain's innocence that didn't make sense. She'd handpicked a husband who fit with her big plans and pride had closed her mind to the possibility she'd been duped by a con man.

"I might not have all the pieces arranged right, but my instincts tell me he ain't what he seems. You need to steer clear of him."

Her head jerked up and there was no mistaking the glare she was giving him. "What I choose to do about that relationship is none of your business. I know he didn't tell me the full truth, but...he's not a criminal."

Like you. Oh, she hadn't said it, but she might as well have.

The fire he'd banked burst into flames, exploding through a wall of pent-up frustration. He snaked an arm around her waist and jerked her to him, covering her startled cry with a kiss.

Lord have mercy, she tasted like whiskey and candy. He ground his lips against hers until she opened to him, and then drank in her sweetness, feasting like a starved man who knew the banquet would soon disappear.

Amy's head spun like she'd consumed an entire gallon of Fire Rod.

Buck was kissing her like there was no tomorrow—and there wasn't, not for them. Only, she couldn't seem to make her traitorous body believe it. Her skin quivered. Her breasts ached where they were crushed against his chest. Deep inside, a tingling, insistent need coiled tighter, making that place at the juncture of her thighs throb with anticipation.

Heaven help her. She wanted him and nothing mattered but that he was here. Her arms slipped around his neck of their own volition, and an agonized plea slipped out on a moan.

At the sound, he swept her into his arms and hauled her behind a dark mound where he tumbled her on her back into a pile of hay. He dropped down nearly on top of her. Between desperate kisses and whispered entreaties, he reached under her skirts and slipped his hand inside the slit in her drawers.

She gasped at his heated touch, but didn't resist when questing fingers teased open the petals of her sex. She was already moist with anticipation.

"I won't hurt you," he murmured, leaning over her. "Just need to touch you."

She gasped when he found the sensitive nub. His fingers delved, while his thumb worked with the accuracy of a sharpshooter. Sensations surged, lifting her to his hand as he circled and teased the tiny knot that seemed connected to every nerve ending in the body. She trembled, all rational thought fleeing under an onslaught of passion fierce as a summer storm.

"Sweetheart…" He kissed away tears that slipped from the corners of her eyes. "Don't cry. I won't hurt you."

Why did he keep saying that? What he did to her body wasn't hurtful. It was what he'd done to her heart. But he was relentless, battering at her resistance, shattering her defenses.

Passion tore her from her moorings, sweeping her out to sea. It tossed her on waves that rose higher and higher. Pleasure ripped through her, wrenching a strangled cry from her lips. A cry for mercy, and for more of what only he could give her.

He swallowed her pleas, kissing her with a ferocious appetite, pushing her release until he'd wrung fulfillment out of every pore. A moment later he rose up, throwing off his gun belt and fumbling with the buttons on his trousers.

Her eyes fastened on his hands, her thoughts slow as molasses in the aftermath of the shattering climax. This mind-numbing passion had been her mother's undoing and now the cycle was repeating itself. She could no more control her wild hunger for this man than she could stop a stampeding herd of buffalo. He had captured her, enslaved her, albeit she'd gone willingly.

Shoving up her skirts and petticoats, he braced himself over her. "Guide me inside you," he rasped. Eagerly, she clasped her fingers around his throbbing length, positioned him, gasped as he flexed his hips and slid into her body, stretching her, filling her. He was impossibly large, but she took him fully.

Cradling her in his arms, he began to rock, slowly at first, and then faster. His whole body shook. He groaned her name like he was in agony.

The sound wrenched her heart. She reached around him, pulling up his shirt and pushing the trousers down past his thighs so she could stroke his heated skin and let him know she wanted him as badly as he wanted her.

The quivering sensation started, tightening the muscles in the sheath that held him, fanning out over her body. Obeying some primitive urge, she thrust herself against his hips, driven by the need to assuage an unbearable ache. As her body pulsed, she was vaguely aware he'd lifted her legs in his arms, pinning her in a position that gave him complete control.

The moon shone on his back, casting a nimbus of light around his head. She shuddered, certain he was a fallen angel who'd been sent to lead her down the path to hell. Hovering over her, he thrust slow, then fast, shallow, then deep, relentlessly driving her to another heart-stopping climax.

She gasped, as pleasure, sharp as pain, splintered her into a thousand pieces.

He released her legs and plunged into her, filled her with hot bursts of his seed. His breathing grew labored, his arms trembled as he spared her his full weight.

Amy stared at the indigo sky until thoughts emerged from a swirling sea of emotion. She had no self-discipline where Buck was concerned, no pride, nothing but need. Wanton, just like her mother. And if he stayed, she would make this mistake over and over. Whether he intended it or not, she'd be ruined.

"Please…" Tears trickled out of the corners of her eyes and slid down her temples into her hair. "Please go."

"I can't," he gasped. "I need…" His breath blew hot against her ear before he raised his head. His eyes were hidden in shadows. "I need…to make sure you're safe."

Safe? Her heart constricted into a tight knot of pain. Never had she doubted he could keep her safe, but who was going to protect her from her bodyguard?

CHAPTER 22

"I looked for you last night." Fletcher held open the door to the hotel and then followed Amy outside. They headed in the direction of a tent set up in the middle of the Baxter Springs town square where the festivities were scheduled to start up again. "Where were you? Charlie said you'd been at the dance, but you disappeared. I knocked on your door. You didn't answer."

Amy rubbed her temple, barely able to register what he was saying. Her head felt like an anvil or possibly the horseshoe. The pounding hadn't let up, stealing her appetite as well as her clarity of mind. What had she been thinking to let Charlie ply her with that homemade brew? She wouldn't have been so easily seduced by Buck had her mind not been fogged with drink.

Oh yes, you would have.

Perhaps she'd stop listening to her conscience if it were going to turn against her.

"You weren't ill, were you? Charlie told me you'd imbibed the local whiskey and I know you're not used to strong liquor." Fletcher's brows gathered in a concerned frown. His solicitude made her feel worse for what she had to do. There could be no putting it off any longer.

"Can we take a walk? I can't face that tent and all those people just yet."

He tucked her hand over his arm. "Of course, my dear."

They wandered down Main Street passing by three taverns, the offices of the land agent, numerous lawyers, a doctor and an undertaker—an assortment that made sense only to those living in the area. Odd, there were no railroad workers on the streets. Probably sleeping off last night's celebration.

It had been mid-morning by the time she awakened, after an endless night of tossing and turning. She'd fled from Buck when he'd pulled back to adjust his clothing after their unexpected tryst by the haystack. He'd staggered after her, buttoning his trousers, a few steps behind, apparently realizing she didn't want him at her side.

After she'd gone inside the hotel and locked the door to her room, she'd seen him standing in the street staring up at her window. Had he been trailing her for some time that he knew exactly where she would be? She shivered, burning with a fever that had nothing to do with an excess of alcohol. Her heart was enslaved and she knew no sure way to free it, save running away.

She forced her attention back to the man striding alongside her and chewed her lip nervously. How did one smoothly break off an engagement? "How did your trip turn out?"

Fletcher's mouth twisted in an expression of disgust. "That blasted Quapaw chief couldn't stay sober long enough to make it through negotiations, and now Secretary Cox has set himself against us. He sent a telegram stating we're not authorized to enter Indian Territory except through Cherokee lands. I can't believe our contacts in Washington can't manage this better."

Not authorized to enter... His words soaked into her muddled brain. Distracted, she didn't notice the uneven road. The toe of her shoe struck a stone and she pitched forward.

Fletcher's hand shot out, grasping her arm. He steadied her. "Careful, sweeting. Do you need to return to the hotel and rest? You're looking very pale."

Implications toppled one against the other like a row of dominoes. If they weren't first across the legal border and weren't awarded the exclusive land grants, their railroad couldn't connect to lines going south into cattle country. The Border Tier would fade into history as a minor feeder route.

The value of the surrounding land would be diminished, and her investments in the railroad and in businesses along the line would be forfeit.

Dread iced her insides. Dear God, she'd lose her fortune—and her father's dreams would blow away like dandelion seeds on the wind.

"Do you realize what this means?" She turned on Fletcher, furious. "We're allowing ourselves to become distracted by a premature party while the Katy is laying track. And they're on the *right* path."

His grabbed her by the shoulders. "Calm down, we're not going to lose the race. The Katy is weeks behind, and they'll never be certified as a first-class railroad. Not with the way they're slamming down rails directly on the prairie."

She wrenched out of his grasp. "They aren't weeks behind. They're not even days behind. And Governor Harvey has made it clear he'll certify the first line to reach the border. The *legitimate* border, which we veered away from."

Irritation flickered across Fletcher's face before he smoothed his features. "You supported the governor's political campaign, and he was a good friend of your father. Surely you can call in a favor and ask him not to certify the Katy, if they manage to cross before we do."

"It's not as easy as that. The governor generally does things because they're politically advantageous. I'm not sure he'd consider granting more favors to Mr. Joy a wise political move, given the grievances of his constituency."

Uncertainty and something that looked very much like fear flashed in Fletcher's eyes. "There's no need to panic. Perhaps the governor would grant you a boon as a wedding present."

Amy squared her shoulders. It was time to end this. There was no way to make it painless. Like pulling a tooth, it was best done quickly. "I'm sorry, Fletcher, but I cannot marry you."

The blank look that wiped his face made her wonder whether she'd spoken the words or just thought them. He blinked, and then a storm gathered in his eyes. "You've had a trying night and you're not thinking clearly. Let's discuss this when you aren't overset."

"I'm not overset, and my mind is working fine." Relief washed over her. Soon, this would be behind them and they could get on with their lives. It was the best thing for both of them.

Fletcher didn't look relieved. "This is because of that argument we had, isn't it? Amy, that was a difficult day for both of us, and I sent you an apology."

"It's not because of an argument. I can't marry without trust, without love."

His brow furrowed. "What do you mean? What have I done to earn your distrust?

Irritation bubbled up. How could he stand there and put on an innocent act? "You didn't tell me the man who attacked me had borrowed money from your bank. In fact, you implied you had never seen him before that day you shot him."

Astonishment lifted his brows, but the flicker of guilt in his eyes convinced her that he'd hidden this information deliberately. "I...I'm sorry," he stammered, grasping her hand. "I should've told you, but...I thought it would reflect badly on my judgment. I had to foreclose when he couldn't make payments on his loan. He'd threatened me. I had no idea he would go after you."

"Why didn't you just tell me? I wouldn't have thought poorly of you because you made a bad loan." She sighed, pulling her hand away. Wasn't she a fine one to be denouncing him for dishonesty when she'd been in a field making love with a man who wasn't her betrothed? "But that's not why I'm crying off. I don't love you, and I won't condemn both of us to an unhappy marriage."

"But, my dear..." He stepped closer, the muscles in his face tightening. "You said yourself you were willing to nurture affection. I promise I'll never hide anything from you again."

She shuffled her feet, backing away. "I'm sorry. I can't marry you. Believe me, you'll thank me one day when you're married to a woman who loves you and has a whole heart to give you."

His eyes looked odd. Wild.

Growing nervous, she glanced around. They'd left the main part of town and thick woods hemmed them in on either side. "Let's go back. The speeches will start soon."

"You *will* marry me." He curled his fingers like claws around her shoulders.

The metallic taste of fear filled her mouth. She twisted, trying to free herself from a surprisingly strong grip. "Let me go," she commanded, trying not to show her alarm.

Instead, he shook her, snarling. "You can't cry off after leading me on tenterhooks all this time." His fingers dug into her flesh, sending pain shooting down her arms.

"Stop it! You're hurting me."

"I'll show you hurt," he ground out through clenched teeth.

He crushed her against him, gripping her hair and yanking her head back as he smothered her startled cry with his mouth. His teeth struck her lip and she felt a sharp pain and tasted blood. God help her. Was he going to force himself on her?

Panic surged, and she struggled against the painful hold.

Then he was gone, flying across the road.

A buckskin coat flashed across her line of vision.

"Buck?" His name came out on a relieved whisper.

Like an avenging angel, he'd stepped out of thin air to rescue her. His icy gaze locked onto her bleeding mouth and fury twisted his features.

In two steps, he'd grabbed the stunned man, lifted him off the ground by his snowy shirt and slammed a fist into his face.

A bright red stream spurted from Fletcher's nose. He flailed his arms and toppled onto his backside only to be hauled up again by the larger man, who drew a gun and cocked it, pressing the tip of the barrel on Fletcher's forehead.

His eyes widened in pure terror.

Amy's heart seized. "No!"

She dashed to Buck's side and took his arm. As badly as Fletcher had treated her, he didn't deserve to die, and the last thing Buck needed was more blood on his hands.

Without releasing his fisted hold on the other man's collar, he turned his head to look at her. The wintry chill in his eyes made her tremble. Not because she feared him. He was her protector, her rescuer, a guardian sent to watch over her. But at this moment he looked like a killer.

Panic fluttered in her chest, but she forced her voice to remain calm. "Let him go, Buck. This isn't worth your life."

It seemed an eternity before he let down the hammer and holstered the gun. He shoved the frightened man away from him. "If you so much as lay a finger on her, I'll hunt you down, strip the flesh from your worthless carcass and feed it to the vultures."

Amy shivered at Buck's dispassionate tone. She didn't doubt he would carry through on such a threat. He must've followed them out here. Yet, he hadn't interfered until she'd been threatened. His fury had been ignited by an urge to protect her.

Fletcher drew a handkerchief from of his pocket and wiped at the bright blood still oozing from his nose. His eyes narrowed. "You have no right," he started, and then hurriedly backed away as Buck surged forward.

She leapt between them, holding back the larger man. "Fletcher, you need to leave. Go back to town."

His face scrunched into a frown. "I don't think you ought to—"

"Then don't think, just go."

Fletcher's mouth snapped shut. After a moment, he headed off in the direction they'd come from, walking with a stiff limp as though his hip were bothering him. Buck had heaved him through the air like he weighed no more than a rag doll, even though she'd been struggling to get out of his grip.

She looked up into her savior's stern features. "Thank you."

His eyes softened, then he drew her to him in a gentle embrace. Buck had gone after Fletcher like a bear stirred to rage, yet he held her so tenderly, as though he was well aware of how easily he could hurt her. Which was the real man, or was he both?

She was so confused. Her enemy was her guardian. The deceiver had kept his word to keep her safe. How she ought to feel about him had no bearing whatsoever on what she felt, but she would be a fool to give in. That way of thinking had led her to a love tarnished with lies and tainted with an irrevocable past.

"You need to go." She had to send him away before her resistance crumbled. "Fletcher will make trouble for you."

"He won't if he enjoys breathing."

She tightened her hold on his arms, as protectiveness welled up. Who would watch over this stubborn man once she was no longer part of his life? "You don't need another death on your conscience. Promise me you won't kill him."

Buck's gaze roved her face, the crease deepening between his brows. "I won't kill him...unless I have to." He pressed her against his chest and laid his cheek on her hair. The familiar scent of his clothes and the warm body beneath made her lightheaded with longing—and grief. She couldn't hold onto him even if she wanted to.

After a moment, he cupped her face in his hand, nudged her chin up with the edge of his thumb. The ice had melted and his eyes warmed to the color of a fading summer sky. "I won't let him hurt you. I won't let anybody hurt you."

She trembled at a frisson of fear. Even if she could find the strength to forgive him, those less merciful would hunt him down. She couldn't allow him to gain another toehold. He would scale the tower and woo her out of her lonely keep, only to be cast to his death on the rocks below. She had to convince him to leave and never return.

"You can't protect me forever. You're not my bodyguard anymore."

"I don't have to be your bodyguard to protect you."

She steeled her resolve despite the suffocating tightness in her chest. "Buck, you can't change the past, no matter how many railroad ties you lay. I don't need some outlaw who's deluded himself into thinking he's a white knight."

His eyes froze over, but not before she saw her shot had struck true. Her breath hitched on a welter of pain and regret. It was for the best to end this quickly. So why did she feel as though she'd left him with a gut wound?

CHAPTER 23

May 25, 1870, Fort Scott, Kansas

"Mr. Bain, he come callin' again."

Amy glanced up from where she'd been working at her desk. Jacob's brow was furrowed with concern. What was this, the fourth time Fletcher had come by in the past week? And there had been at least a dozen missives begging forgiveness. She tamped down annoyance, not wanting to take out her ire on the messenger.

"Tell him I'm not seeing visitors today."

Jacob nodded, his lips compressing into a determined line. He vanished from the doorway and his brisk steps sounded on the stairs.

Amy shook her head in disbelief. Fletcher couldn't possibly believe she would still consider him for marriage. At this point, he'd be lucky to retain her business. His badgering, however, was the least of her worries. Her stomach sank as she dropped her gaze to the letter she held. She scanned the lines, hoping they'd somehow read differently.

Mr. Joy had turned down the Cooperative Society's proposal with a curt note that he'd not be fooled into giving charity to a bogus organization.

Bogus? The nerve of that man.

She drummed her pencil on the table, letting anger burn away a gnawing fear that had followed her home from Baxter Springs. The Border Tier, short on workers and behind schedule, was furiously zigzagging its way across the border, hoping to beat the MK&T to the legal crossing point in the Neosho Valley. Based on what a network of spies had reported, the race was all but lost.

Gripping the pencil in a tight hold, she took a deep breath, firming her resolve. There was still time to get a request to the governor and he did owe her a favor. If the Katy was as poorly constructed as reported, it might give him reason to refuse certification. This would give the Border Tier time to catch up.

If that didn't work, there had to be another way to achieve her goal. Buck was right when he said what she really wanted was to make life better for more people—not just a few rich investors. Mr. Joy might not want to support the Cooperative Society, but that didn't mean she was giving up on the idea. It was exactly the kind of thing her father would have leapt on. She'd held back a little cash in reserve and if she was careful, she could make a small investment and then interest others in joining.

First things first. She would send a letter to the governor with a request that an investigation be made into the construction of the Katy's line before certification proceeded. Opening a drawer, she pulled out a piece of paper.

A firm knock sounded at the door. Jacob's lips twisted in an apologetic smile. "Mr. Bain's got the sheriff with him. Says they gotta see you."

Vexed, she shoved her chair back and stood up. What now? And why was the sheriff with him? "I'll meet with them in the front parlor."

Jacob dipped his chin in acknowledgement. "Yes'm." He stepped aside as she exited the office. "I's here if you need me, Miz Amy. Don't you worry none."

Amy smiled warmly at the burly groomsman. This wouldn't be the first time he'd risked himself to aid her. She knew him well enough to realize he'd do it again, so she hadn't told anyone about Fletcher's assault, saying only that she had broken their engagement and her betrothed had taken it poorly. But her two insightful servants had figured out enough on their own. One or the other always seemed to be within earshot.

"I'll be fine. Tell Sophie we won't need any refreshments. I'm going to get rid of these gentlemen." Lifting her skirts, she hurried down the stairs, turning right through the arched entry into the formal parlor.

Fletcher leapt up from where he'd been sitting in one of two cushioned chairs by the fireplace. She afforded him barely a glance.

The sheriff stood more slowly, his thin lips stretching into a smile that didn't touch the rest of his face. "Hope we're not disturbing you, ma'am." His officious tone indicated he could care less. "Mr. Bain thought you might know something."

"Know something?" Her heart tripped with unease. "About what?"

"Somebody robbed the bank early this morning. Only Mr. Bain was there. The robber held a gun on him and made him give over all the money in the safe. Thirty thousand dollars."

Shock rooted her to the floor, and all her blood seemed to drain out of her feet. Her cash was in that bank, nearly every penny. How in God's name could this have happened? She shifted a horrified gaze to Fletcher.

"I was caught by surprise in my office when I came in early to do some work." He gripped the lapels of his coat as though he needed something to hold onto. "The man had a bandana over his face. The brim of his hat was pulled low over his eyes, but I could see blond hair. And his voice had a distinctive drawl. It was O'Connor. I'm sure of it."

"No!" The denial burst out, as every fiber of her being rebelled.

Buck wouldn't do this. Not here. Not after… There had to be some mistake. Taking a deep breath to calm her riotous nerves, she met the sheriff's narrowed gaze. "Mr. O'Connor couldn't have robbed the bank. He hasn't been in Fort Scott for weeks."

"Do you know where he is?"

Goosebumps prickled her arms. Even if she knew where Buck was, she would never tell this man. "He was in Baxter

Springs working with a railroad crew last I saw him. I'm sure he's gone back to Texas by now."

She swung her gaze to Fletcher, her body stiffening with anger. Someone with a bone to pick had robbed that bank. He was letting his hatred for Buck blind him to the real culprit. "Were there other witnesses?"

A dull flush suffused Fletcher's neck. He tipped his chin at an offended angle. "One of our clerks on his way to work saw him as he left the building."

"That's right," the sheriff chimed in. "Mr. Bowen said a tall man with longish blond hair rushed out of the bank. He threw a sack over the back of a horse and raced off down the street. Other folks saw him as well. Nobody got a good look at his face because he still had that scarf pulled up, but they said he was armed to the teeth. Looked like a bushwhacker."

A sudden chill shook her. Had word of Buck's past gotten out? Sanford might have spread it around if he'd decided his hired gun had turned on him. It would take a simple check to find Buck's name amongst the three hundred men listed as wanted for the Lawrence massacre. And now a bank robbery had been added to his sins. Should they catch him, the trial—if he got one—would be swift and the outcome certain. He'd hang. Somehow she had to get word to him to flee.

"I don't believe Mr. O'Connor would do this. Even if he were prone to robbing a bank—which he isn't—he's intelligent enough not to pick a place he'd be so easily recognized."

"Unless he wasn't intending to come back." The sheriff's eyed her in a way that made her skin crawl. "Mr. Bain here tells me you fired him. Must've had a reason."

She met the flinty gaze. "I no longer required his assistance because the major posted guards. I had no concerns about Mr. O'Connor's character."

With a start, she realized this was true. Deep down, she'd always trusted Buck. Even after he'd admitted to duplicity and owned up to his past, a part of her still believed in him. Her eyes slid to her former betrothed and her instincts hummed a warning.

Fletcher's nostrils flared and resentment flickered in his eyes.

Anger flared, heating her face. He was *lying*, the scoundrel. What was he hoping to accomplish by blaming this robbery on Buck?

Her mind flipped back to something the sheriff had said earlier. "What kind of horse?"

The lawman frowned. "Pardon?"

"What kind of horse was Mr. O'Connor riding?"

The sheriff darted a quick glance at Fletcher. "Didn't Bowen say it was a bay?"

Her lips curved with satisfaction. "Buck rides a big gray roan."

"Maybe the bay was meant to throw us off." Fletcher met her gaze with a black stare. "If he rode that other horse he might as well advertise he was coming."

"Yet, he walked into the bank with only a scarf covering his face." She arched an eyebrow.

Fletcher scowled. Apparently, this inconsistency hadn't occurred to him.

Squaring her shoulders with renewed confidence, she turned to the surly sheriff. "It appears someone might be trying to make you believe Mr. O'Connor robbed the bank, however I—"

"There ain't no doubt it's O'Connor." The sheriff dismissed her with a wave of his hand. "Mr. Bain here thinks he might try to contact you, seeing he's sweet on you."

Fuming, Amy forced her expression into neutrality. Was this stupid man even aware he'd contradicted himself? If Buck planned on never returning, why would he contact her? Perhaps the sheriff was too lazy to pursue a real investigation, or he'd made up his mind because he'd gotten wind of Buck's past. Or, he was in cahoots with Fletcher. The best course at this point was to play along until she figured out what was going on.

"Mr. O'Connor did show an interest in me, but I told him I never wanted to see him around here again."

The sheriff's thin lips twisted into a sneer. "Too bad O'Connor didn't heed your warning. We're putting out posters and I've telegraphed the sheriffs south of here to alert them. We want to catch him before he gets back to whatever hole he crawled out of. In the meantime, we'll be keeping an eye on this place." His lips tipped up in a cold smile. "You understand. We just want to make sure you're safe."

Leaning back from her desk, Amy blinked to relieve the grittiness in her eyes. Unable to sleep, she'd drawn on a light robe and come down to the office to finish some work. It'd been a week since the robbery, and in that time Fletcher and his lawman friend had convinced everyone of Buck's guilt. Everyone except her. Although the evidence was stacked against him, it just didn't fit with what her heart told her.

Her breath hitched at the persistent ache in her chest. That heart of hers had gotten downright insistent these past few weeks. Having been starved for so long, perhaps it decided it would no longer be ignored. She dare not place her faith in the faulty organ, but her judgment had failed, as well. So where did that leave her? Trusting her destiny to an inscrutable God who'd put an enemy in her path, a scarred man with a wounded soul who needed her love—and forgiveness.

She squeezed back tears, remembering Buck's face as he gazed down at her after he'd delivered her safely back to the hotel in Baxter Springs. The longing in his eyes, the grief and remorse, it was all there for her to see. He didn't even try to hide it.

He accepted his culpability in her downfall and in the emotional wreckage left in the wake of his deception, not to mention his damning past. Over the last few weeks he'd been trying, in his own way, to make up for it. But he couldn't. Not in a million years.

Tears slipped out of the corners of her eyes. "God..." She tried to pray, but couldn't seem to speak the words. Behind her breastbone something cracked open, releasing a torrent of anguish. She dropped her face into her hands. Her shoulders shook as grief and loneliness erupted in great gasping sobs that seemed to go on and on.

She loved Buck and nothing was going to change that. Not his deception. Not his desperate attempts to control everything and everyone around him. Not even his violent past. But loving him wasn't going to bring her peace. She had to *forgive* him.

Even if she never saw him again, never got to tell him, this was what she had to do to be able to move on. "Help me forgive him," she prayed. "You brought him into my life, now you have to help me forgive him."

Her breath hitched at a tender touch. Warmth poured through her, and she was filled with an overwhelming sense of love. The miraculous flood filled her heart, washing away bitterness, grief, loneliness and her terrible fears. Peace settled over her as light as morning dew.

How she wished she could share this with Buck because he needed peace even more than she did. Fumbling for her handkerchief, she wiped her face. God willing, she would never see him again and he'd be safe. Resigned, she turned her attention back to the task at hand, the problem she had to solve before seeking her rest.

Yesterday afternoon Fletcher had finally delivered the audit she'd requested after she'd threatened to tell everyone she knew he was holding out on her. He'd been furious, but she'd gotten what she wanted.

At first glance, nothing appeared amiss, but after she'd gone back to check more thoroughly she'd noted slight discrepancies between his statement and her records. Just tonight she'd finished double-checking her entries going back a full year. Her math was spot on. It wasn't a miscalculation or transposed numbers.

I may not have all the pieces arranged right, but my instincts tell me he ain't what he seems.

Buck's comment came back to her, along with an awful awareness of what she'd been missing—or ignoring—in her prideful refusal to admit she was wrong about the man she'd handpicked to marry.

Fletcher was tinkering with the books, probably to cover the fact he was siphoning off funds.

She mentally arranged the pieces. He'd admitted to making bad loans. Had that resulted in personal losses? That being the case, he likely used stolen funds to finance his purchase of those large tracts of land, betting on a windfall when the railroad became the foremost route into Texas. When it became apparent the Border Tier would lose the race, he must have panicked. He couldn't cover up his misdeeds forever, but a bank robbery would explain the missing money.

Amy slammed her hand onto the desk as fury mounted. "*Damn* him."

They had both staked their future on this railroad, but he'd sacrificed his integrity.

Anxiety gripped her. How much of her money had Fletcher stolen over the past three years? Had he been playing a shell game, constantly moving funds around until there was nothing left to move? That would explain why he was in such a hurry to gain some degree of control over her finances.

Another piece fell into place. Had he, as Buck suggested, sent that attacker after her to frighten her into marrying him sooner? Now it made sense.

She stiffened her spine. By God, she would figure out a way to expose him. He wouldn't get away with stealing from her and putting the blame on Buck.

Something scraped, as if someone were downstairs. Was Sophie up? If so, why hadn't she come by, as was her usual habit?

Amy cocked her head, listening, but all she could hear was her heart rapping. Had she just imagined the sound?

There it came again, a bump, like something had fallen.

She slid open a drawer and lifted out a small pistol. Lighting a candle, she tiptoed downstairs to the dark first floor. It was probably nothing, maybe a rat, or one of the guards Major Roy had posted outside the house. Or was it that sneaky sheriff? Lawson seemed convinced Buck would return, but he wouldn't be so foolish.

Steadying her nerves, she lifted the candlestick and entered the parlor. The flickering light cast eerie shadows on the wall. Her gaze swept the room, stopping at a fluttering curtain. Sophie must have left a window open to relieve the heat. Next to a side table, a lamp lay on the floor. Amy released the breath she'd been holding. The breeze was the culprit.

She set down the candle, bent over to reach for the lamp, and her gaze fell on the table, scooted at an angle. Goosebumps rose on her skin.

The breeze couldn't have done that.

Buck knew the moment Amy realized she wasn't alone in that room.

As she stood, he wrapped an arm around her, jerked her back against him while he gripped the pistol in her hand and covered her mouth.

She went rigid in his arms. He hated frightening her, but he couldn't very well stroll in through the front door.

"It's only me," he whispered, taking the gun. Damn thing wasn't even cocked. "You won't scream if I let you go, will you?"

She shook her head.

He released her and she shot out of his arms, whirling around. Her brows slashed down. "What are you doing here? Didn't Mr. Murphy give you my message?"

"He did. I thank you for that." Buck studied her face. Her anger fed a tortuous uncertainty that had weighed on him in the days and nights it'd taken to make the return journey. Was she unhappy because he'd ignored her instructions, or displeased because he'd dared to show his face again?

The fact she cared enough to warn him to flee had, ironically, spurred the opposite behavior. Had he read something between those few lines that simply wasn't there? God knew he'd done all he could do for her, and Sean had called him every kind of a fool for not heeding Amy's warning.

"The sheriff has men watching the house. I can't believe they didn't see you." Her fingers fluttered up to the looped frogs securing the silken robe.

Desire knifed through him, followed by a wrenching guilt. He was a bastard for even thinking about bedding her after he'd damn near raped her the night of the celebration. "I came in through the woods. Stayed off the roads. Didn't see anybody, except one of your guards. Fast asleep by the side entrance."

He clenched his jaw in frustration. Finding the man sleeping had been fortuitous, but it made him furious. No one cared for Amy's safety more than he did. No one would protect her as diligently. Yet, he couldn't ensure her security and evade capture at the same time.

Even if Sean produced witnesses who would vouch for his whereabouts the day of the robbery, he still couldn't remain in Kansas. His ill-conceived decision to seek revenge at all costs had taken away that choice and made it impossible for Amy to love him. He blinked down at her, misery making his eyes burn and his insides quiver with disgusting weakness.

Her tight expression shifted, becoming gentler. She looked almost as if she were relieved to see him. Maybe even a little bit glad. Or was that a trick of the light?

"There's a reward out for your capture. You should be far away from here. Why did you come back?" Her voice caressed him, not angry, more like worried.

He fought an unmanly urge to weep. Didn't she know? Through the war he'd stayed alive by knowing when to stand and when to run. But for once, he couldn't retreat. Love called him to her side and there was no escape.

Unable to resist, he ventured a half step toward her, torturing himself with a closeness that might have been. "I came to warn you."

"Warn me?" A crease appeared between her brows.

"Fletcher set me up."

Her brows arched. Did she not believe him?

He rushed ahead. "You recall that big blond fellow at the bank? Charlie and me saw him in a saloon with Fletcher a few days after he shot that musician. Clay Thornton is his name. With a scarf on his face he could fool people into thinking he's me. I don't have proof, but I'm convinced old Fletch is stealing money from his own bank and covering it up by arranging a robbery. You can't trust him, Amy. He's got to be desperate to do something like that, and a desperate man will do anything to save himself."

Holding his breath, he waited for her response.

She studied him for a long moment. "Are you here...to kill Fletcher?"

Disappointment threaded through him. Did she really think revenge had driven him to ride all this way and take such a risk? He wasn't a cold-blooded killer. But he sure as hell wasn't a white knight either. Contrary to what she thought, he had no delusions about the color of his armor, much as he longed for her to see him as her hero. Self-loathing turned his stomach. How could a lying, worthless outlaw be anybody's idea of a hero?

He forced his features to remain impassive so she couldn't see how pathetic he'd become. "I won't stand by and let him harm you, but I'm not out for revenge."

Her silence and the anxious look on her face made him wonder whether she believed him, whether she would ever believe him again.

He struggled to erect the old defenses, but found he simply couldn't protect his heart against her anymore. He dropped the mask. "Amy, I know you think I'm the lowest kind of scum, but I didn't rob that—"

"Hush." She pressed her fingers to his lips. "I don't think any such thing, and you don't have to convince me of your innocence. I know you didn't do it."

"You do?" His heart hammered as he gazed down at her. Could she feel him trembling, conquered by her soft touch and the even softer look in her eyes?

Her fingers brushed a light stroke over his mouth before her hand fell away.

Every muscle in his body tensed with desire. But he resisted taking her into his arms. His face bristled with stubble and his clothes carried two weeks worth of dirt.

"I know you're not a criminal." Her eyes grew bright. "And I didn't mean those things I told you before. I only said that to make you leave. I knew you'd follow me, to your own detriment. I can't resist you, even though I know it's crazy to let passion override my common sense."

Dismay swamped his heart. "You're a passionate woman, Amy. It's not bad to be that way, and there's not a thing wrong with your common sense. Don't think poorly of yourself because I ambushed you. I got past your defenses. It's what I'm good at."

"Like what happened in Lawrence?" Her question stabbed him in the heart. Did she still think he'd lied about his part in that raid?

"I didn't kill your father," he said in an agonized whisper.

Her lashes dropped and her chest heaved like she was struggling with some internal battle. After a moment, she raised her eyes. "I believe you. More than that, I forgive you—for everything. I think you need that more than you need me to believe any explanation."

Shock sucked the air right out of him. His head got light before he realized he hadn't taken a breath. His startled mind couldn't wrap itself around what she was saying. But his heart understood. She offered him pardon with no strings attached.

"Amy, I..." his voice trailed off. What the hell did he say? He'd done nothing to earn this, could never even the scales or repay the debt. Her forgiveness was a gift, pure and simple.

His heaviness lifted, dropping away like he'd shed a ton weight. It gave him such a giddy sense of release his knees grew weak. She was an angel sent to save him, offering grace and shedding a light on the man he'd once hoped to be. He struggled to find words to express what he felt, but feared if he started speaking, he'd soon be blubbering.

She touched his sleeve, a tentative touch. "You didn't have to come back to tell me about Fletcher. I know what he's up to, and he'll be stopped…but not by you. You have to leave." Her voice cracked. "Before you're caught."

Tears spilled from her eyes and slid in diamond drops down her cheeks.

He dragged her into his arms, buried his face in her hair, breathing in her wildflower fragrance. "Don't cry, Amy honey. I can't bear it when you cry."

"Oh, Buck." She looped her arms around his neck and hungrily sought his mouth.

His heart galloped like a runaway horse. God help him. He was saved, and he was lost. Had he thought he'd been in love before? What he'd felt then didn't begin to describe this soaring of his soul, this breathless exhilaration. It was like dropping into cool water on a hot summer day, flying on the back of a fast horse, falling from a high loft into a pile of sweet hay. He couldn't promise the future, couldn't take her upstairs and pour himself out, but he could kiss her and show her how much he loved her.

He lifted her in his arms and sat down on the couch, cradling her in his lap.

Shattering glass exploded into the room.

He thrust her to the floor and covered her with his body. *What the hell?* Had someone shot out the window? He scanned the room. A rock lay on the floor. Along the front of the house, a curtain fluttered in a broken window.

"O'Connor," a deep voice shouted. "We know you're in there. Come out with your hands up. Nobody gets hurt if you cooperate."

Beneath him, Amy squirmed. "Let me up. It's the sheriff."

Buck whipped out a revolver and hauled her behind the couch, cursing himself for letting his heart rule his head. By coming here, he'd brought trouble right to her doorstep.

"Stay put." He heard her whispered objection as he crept away. But he needed to see how many men were outside, calculate the odds of getting away without drawing fire toward the house. He hid beside the window and peeked outside.

A sea of flickering torches lit the night.

His heart jumped into his throat. Had the whole damn town turned out to catch him? He leaned back against the wall, tasting the familiar tang that came from living on the knife's edge of danger. He'd gotten out of too many scrapes to remember, mostly through audacious exploits only a cocky young fool would attempt. But he was no longer young. And he had someone else to think about.

Amy peered from behind the couch, her face ghostly in the light.

He had to put that candle out so no one could see them as they moved around inside the house, maybe take a shot. Reaching the table in two strides, he snuffed the flame, casting the room into near darkness. Dropping to his knees, he wrapped an arm around her in a comforting embrace. "Looks like they brought the welcoming committee."

She turned into the crook of his shoulder. "Don't joke. It's not funny."

"We ain't givin' you all night," the sheriff called out. "We got troops out here, surrounding the house. You can't get away."

Amy tugged at his shirt. "You have to get out of here. I'll show you a way through the lower floor. There's a small window. I think you can squeeze through."

"Miz Amy?" Jacob's voice drifted down from the stairway.

Buck frowned with concern. The last thing he needed was *another* person to worry about. He put his lips to Amy's ear. "Tell him to go back to his room and stay there."

"I'm all right, Jacob," she called out. "You and Sophie stay upstairs."

"Don't know as I can do that."

Damn impertinent servant. Those men outside wouldn't think twice about shooting him if he got in the way. "Get the hell upstairs, Jacob," Buck bellowed. "I won't let Amy come to harm."

"Better not. I'd have to hurt you if that happened." Jacob's slow steps grew more distant. He was obeying orders, but not because he wanted to.

A loud pounding came from on the porch, sounded like an army fanning out across the front of the house. Buck tensed at a thump on the front door. "You got two minutes to come out with your hands up. Or we'll bust down the door."

That blasted lawman wasn't long on patience.

Buck sighed, his anxiousness replaced by a resigned sense of the inevitable. They were circling the house and growing brave enough to move in and hammer down the door. He couldn't fire. That would invite a bloodbath. He also couldn't run and risk being shot at. Amy might be caught in the crossfire. He holstered his gun.

"Wait here." He patted her shoulder and stood up, moving toward the front hallway. They'd likely shot him down like a rabid dog, but he'd do his damnedest to make this a peaceful surrender.

"No," Amy rushed in front of him.

Furious, he grabbed her, hauled her back into the parlor and thrust her into the place he'd put her before. "I told you to stay here. Let me handle this. I don't trust they won't shoot first and ask questions later."

She held onto his arms, her eyes glistening with fear. "You can't go out there. They'll kill you. The sheriff, I think he's in this thing with Fletcher. Let me go out and while I'm talking to them you can get away."

He swallowed his sadness. "My horse is tethered in the woods. Even if I get out that window, with all those soldiers out there, somebody's bound to see me. They'll shoot me in the back before I ever make the trees. Worse, they might get excited and start shooting at the house. I can't risk it. I got to give myself up."

At the emphatic shake of her head, he detached her hands from his arms and held them between his. He had to convince her this was the only way. "They won't hang me right off. We'll have time to rustle up some folks who'll testify to my whereabouts the day of that robbery." He gave her a stern look. "But don't you dare challenge Fletcher on your own. Get somebody to help you. Go to Major Roy. He seems a decent enough fellow."

Buck started for the door.

She dashed in front of him, dodging his attempts to grab her, darting about like a squirrel.

"Stop that. You're gonna get us both killed." He snagged her gown and reeled her in.

Wrapping her arms around him, she fixed him with a glare. "I'm not letting go, so you might as well accept it. We go out together, or not at all."

"Damn it, Amy, you're hardheaded as a nanny goat." He unbuckled his gun belt and handed it to her. "All right. Take me out at gunpoint. That way, they won't feel threatened. After we're outside, you get away. I mean it. I'll tan your hide if you keep throwing yourself in front of me."

"You won't touch a hair on my head."

It was aggravating how well she knew him.

She placed the barrel of the revolver to his back without cocking it. "I'm bringing him out," she shouted. "For God's sake, don't shoot."

CHAPTER 24

Clouds drifted past the moon and its pale light shone onto the deserted street. Amy cast a furtive glance over her shoulder, as she slipped between the large wooden doors and inside the bank. Thank heavens Fletcher's servants hadn't batted an eye when she'd gone by his house, saying she needed to retrieve something important she'd left in his study. She just failed to mention it was keys.

He'd gone to a railroad meeting in a neighboring town and wasn't returning home this evening, which would give her time to find the evidence she sought before he discovered what she was up to.

Her hands shook as she held the lantern aloft. The bank looked spooky when it was dark and deserted. She hurried to the back, her footsteps echoing in the cavernous interior. Had Fletcher stashed a second set of records with the accurate accounting in his office? It would be like him to do that, so he could make up the difference later and thus avoid being caught as a thief.

Slipping the key into the lock, she turned it and heard a satisfying click. She had to move fast. Tempers had flared since Buck's arrest the previous day and there was talk of taking him out of jail and lynching him. Risky as it was to come here, she couldn't afford to wait. Something had to be done to shift attention to Fletcher's misdeeds before vigilante mentality took over.

Buck would be furious she'd put herself in danger, but the sight of him being bound and led away by that horrid sheriff had firmed her resolve. He wouldn't hang for crimes he didn't commit, past or present. He might have given up on himself, but she loved him too much to give him up. She would break every rule, play every chip, and sell everything she owned, whatever it took to win his freedom.

The pungent scent of cigars gave her pause when she entered the office, but the room appeared empty. Her light fell on Fletcher's ornate desk. If it'd been built to the same specifications as her father's, there would be a hidden compartment on the side.

Her lantern went on the top, along with her reticule. A small pistol she'd tucked inside made a thump. Likely, she wouldn't need it, but hadn't been willing to leave home without protection.

Squatting down, she ran her hand along the underside until her fingers touched a latch. Tripping it released a side door disguised by a band of scrollwork. She held her breath as she reached into the compartment.

"Bravo," she whispered, drawing out a narrow notebook. Flipping through the pages, she noted the large debits. Even if Charlie Goodlander couldn't track down the blond man he and Buck had seen, she now had proof of Fletcher's embezzlement.

The door creaked.

She leapt up, hiding the notebook behind her. Her heart lodged in her throat.

Fletcher stood in the doorway, his brow furrowed in puzzlement. "I must say I didn't expect to find you here, my dear. When you didn't show up for the railroad meeting, I got worried. I heard you weren't feeling well, but my servants said you looked spry as usual when you stopped by the house."

She darted a glance at her reticule. If she lunged for it, she might be able to reach it, but she'd never get it open and get to the pistol before he realized what she was about. If they wrestled, she might end up shooting herself.

As he approached, the shadowy room seemed to grow smaller. She moved in front of the desk to block his view of her bag. Hopefully, she could retrieve it without him seeing.

"What've you got there?" Fletcher's eyes fastened on the arm she had tucked behind her back.

"Nothing." Her fingers tightened on the notebook. Should she let it drop and go for her gun?

"Why are you here?"

She trembled. Should she bolt and run? She'd worn a loose-fitting dress so she'd be able to move about more easily, but he could catch her before she reached the door. No, her best chance was to brazen it out, keep him talking until she could figure out how to get away. "The statement you provided didn't agree with my records. There was a slight discrepancy."

"A slight discrepancy?" His brows formed an arch. "I shall speak to my assistant about his sloppy work. Odd, though, that you'd choose this hour to come by to check on a slight discrepancy."

Her breathing quickened. Fighting the urge to panic, she tucked the notebook into the folds of her skirt while using her free hand to grope behind her. Still couldn't reach her bag. Her fingers closed around a letter opener near the edge of his desk. Revulsion turned her stomach. She wasn't sure she could bring herself to stab him—maybe just his arm in order to slow him down.

But he wasn't close enough for the element of surprise to work in her favor and she'd get only one chance. She held his eyes, portraying a confidence she didn't feel. "Now that you're here, perhaps you can answer my concerns."

"What concerns?"

"Did you dip into my funds to finance that land purchase?"

He stopped a few feet away. His lips curved in a wry smile. "Let's just say I felt comfortable making a financial decision that would be to our collective benefit, considering how close we were to marriage." His eyes flickered over her and the smoothness of his brow gathered into a frown. "Only, you kept dragging your feet."

"So you decided to hurry me along?"

He gave an unconcerned shrug. "There was no need to hire a bodyguard."

Almighty. He all but admitted sending that attacker after her.

She fisted the handle of the letter opener. He was still too far away. If she tried to strike, he might have time to stop her. "Why didn't you come to me before you made that investment? I would've listened to any proposal you had to offer."

Irritation flickered across his face. "I did. You made it clear—rather adamantly as I recall—that you were opposed to purchasing land on speculation."

"Then you should've honored my wishes." She debated inching closer so she could reach him, but her feet wouldn't obey. "I'm willing to forgive and forget if you'll reimburse whatever you've taken. Hopefully, you've kept track of this."

His eyes glittered dangerously. "Ah, my dear. I am not, you see, that ignorant gorilla you are so fond of. You aren't here to haggle over discrepancies, nor are you here to negotiate the return of your money. You're looking for something, aren't you? And you've used that fine brain of yours to figure out where to find it."

He reached into his pocket. Her heart fluttered into her throat as he withdrew...

A handkerchief? She frowned in confusion.

But he had something else in his other hand. Something he was pressing into the handkerchief. He took a step closer.

Fear struck with the swiftness of a snake. To hell with the letter opener, she was going for the gun.

He grabbed her arm and spun her around, tearing the bag out of her hands. With his body, he forced her against the desk. His hand snapped around her throat and he pressed the handkerchief over her nose, bending her nearly backwards.

A sickly sweet odor filled her nostrils, making her head swim.

Terrified, she scrabbled for the letter opener, knocking items off the desk in her panicked haste.

"I did this for us," he growled. "We could have been the toast of the town, the richest and most powerful couple in the state, but you spoiled it. You and that *insufferable* buffoon."

Fletcher's voice sounded distant, muffled. His fingers were crushing her windpipe. Oh God, he was *choking* her to death.

She clawed at the hand on her throat. Beat him with her fists. But her arms felt heavy like they were strapped with weights. Her heart throbbed in her ears with a drum-like echo. She struggled to breath as spots swam in front of her eyes.

Help me. Buck...

Fletcher's grip loosened slightly.

Her starved lungs expanded, drawing in the fouled air. Her thoughts melted away and her eyelids fluttered, drifting shut as she was cast into oblivion.

Buck paced the width of the small cell, feeling like a powder keg with a lit fuse. It seemed dawn would never come. Not that he'd see much evidence of the sun in this fortress. This was the second time in less than two months he'd been jailed—a record for a man who had never been caught during the war or in the five years thereafter.

Damn, he *had* to escape. Make sure Amy was safe before hightailing it back to Texas. But he had no idea how to accomplish it. No loyal men stood ready to charge the jail or scheme to sneak him out.

Yesterday, a crowd had gathered. Based on what the guard told him, they'd threatened to break in, haul him outside and string him up. The portly jailor seemed to take pleasure in relating how easy it would be to step aside and let justice take its course.

Buck stopped at the barred door and huffed with disgust. These local lawmen had a peculiar definition of justice if they'd ignore repeated attacks on a woman, but send a regiment to arrest a man who could prove he was a hundred miles away at the time of the bank robbery. Of course, he'd have to rustle up witnesses and, in the meantime, avoid being torn apart by an angry mob who cared more about his bushwhacking exploits than they did the bank heist.

With an impatient sigh, he tore off his bandana and unbuttoned the top buttons on his shirt. Anything to get relief from the heat.

What the hell was Amy up to? She hadn't been to see him since he'd been taken—a fact that bothered him more than he wanted to admit. Never mind he'd told her to stay away. She never listened before, why start now?

Maybe they weren't letting her see him. That would explain it. He'd received only two visitors. The sheriff, who he refused to talk to, and a priest he'd politely told to get lost until the time came for last rites. He hoped it wouldn't be soon, although he wouldn't fool himself into thinking he could get out of this stew.

He sank onto the cot and dropped his head in his hands. Amy had told him she'd get word to Sean to round up enough men who'd be willing to testify on his behalf. As for the charges related to the raid on Lawrence, that would mean another trial and he wasn't certain he could escape the noose on that one. No other man had—at least not the ones who'd been caught.

Reality fell like a winter drizzle, chilling him to the bone. He'd known this day was coming even if he hadn't wanted to acknowledge destiny.

He drove his fingers through his hair, feeling anxious and frustratingly impotent. What had he accomplished by coming back to Kansas? He'd wanted to see justice served, but what made him think he had that kind of power, or wisdom? Hell, he controlled nothing save his own choices, and most of those had ended up being the wrong ones.

But if he hadn't come back to Kansas, he wouldn't have met Amy. He never would've known what it felt like to love and be loved. Before he'd ever thought to con her, she had offered him an important job. She'd trusted him, believed in him, wanted him, despite his obvious poverty. That meant she'd seen something worthwhile, something he had missed all these years.

Closing his eyes, he let his mind take him back to the night he'd bedded her. After he'd loved on her, she'd returned the favor, exploring his body with her lips and hands.

Tentative at first, and then increasingly bolder, brushing kisses over his stomach, trailing her fingers along the inside of his thigh. Touching him. She'd stroked him into aching hardness just when he thought he couldn't be roused again.

And it wasn't just physical desire that held him in thrall. His heart had begun to hope when she'd talked about their future. He'd wanted to give her the world.

He leaned back against the stone, his heart in full revolt. Why hadn't he told her he loved her? He should've said it when she'd gifted him with her innocence. Even after her startling declaration of forgiveness, he hadn't uttered the words.

The truth was—he grimaced—he was a coward. Speaking his love would've meant exposing himself, even more than when he'd stripped naked in front of her. And he knew he couldn't bear it if she turned away.

A key rattled in the lock.

The sound jerked Buck out of his reverie. As the hinges screeched, goose bumps prickled down his arms.

Then, a tall, dark-haired woman stepped inside.

He shot to his feet. "Maggie?"

She clutched a key ring to her chest. "I need your help."

Buck approached the door, uneasy. Was this some kind of trick? Were they hoping he'd make a run for it and then hang him the moment he walked out the door? But why would they send Amy's friend?

He peered out into the empty hallway. "How'd you get in?"

"I slipped past the guards while they were outside smoking." She grabbed his arm, her anxiousness communicated by the tightness of her grip. "Amy's missing."

Buck was out the door before she could finish. No doubt he was walking into a trap, but that didn't matter. He would storm hell to save the woman he loved.

CHAPTER 25

Hammers clanged in Amy's head and pain dragged her out of the soft darkness. She dragged her eyes open. Was she wrapped in a flannel blanket, or was that a gray wall? She grimaced at the awful taste in her mouth. Her limbs felt rubbery, and it took her a moment to get her arms underneath her so she could sit up.

Where on earth?

A candle flickered in a miner's candlestick that was wedged into a crevice. Her gaze traveled up grayish-brown rock that formed a wall. The ceiling, also rock, was braced with uprights, some of which had splintered. Rough-hewn logs canted at different angles provided reinforcement.

Perspiration beaded on her forehead and her stomach churned. Oh God, she wasn't *on* the earth—she was *beneath* it. And if the crumbling rock and damaged supports were any indication, this was the iron ore mine she and her partner had decided to shut down due to a deadly collapse.

Her stomach roiled, and she scrambled to her knees. The sound of her retching echoed off the rock walls. She sat back on her heels, trembling. Fletcher must have knocked her out with something. *Chloroform?* No wonder her stomach turned over. She'd heard of the temporary effect from Dr. Hall. Breathing deeply seemed to ease the sick feeling.

Once her stomach had calmed, she surveyed her surroundings. She was in what looked like a room at the juncture of two passageways. The largest drift was partially blocked. From beneath a pile of rocks, a trolley track emerged, crossed the floor and split off into two tunnels, disappearing into seemingly endless darkness.

She shifted her gaze to the flickering candle. Only an inch remained. Had it started out as a full taper? She swallowed to keep from getting sick again. Pray God the light would last long enough for her to discover which direction led out. If she wandered around in the dark, she'd likely tumble down a shaft.

The crunch of footsteps sounded before she saw a glimmer of light bobbing in the darkness down the main tunnel. Her heart pounded at a sense of foreboding. Was it Fletcher? If he'd walked into the mine they couldn't be too far from the entry. The trolley led outside, if she recalled rightly from the drawings she'd studied.

Fletcher's face and form materialized. He navigated his way around a pile of boulders obstructing his path. Like a veteran miner, he carried an oil wick lamp, which dangled from a leather strap wrapped around his wrist. The flame reflected off the brass-lined enclosure. Over one shoulder, he'd slung a thick coil of rope. To look at him, one might think he was going excavating—except for the pistol stuffed into the waistband of his trousers.

How could she escape? Her head pounded so hard it was difficult to think straight. She'd need to figure out how to get his gun, or if that wasn't possible, distract him so she could make a run for it.

He squatted down and held out a canteen.

She eyed the offering warily.

"It's only water." His words sounded hollow as they bounced around the walls. "I thought you might be thirsty."

"You knock me out with chloroform and dump me in a mine and then pretend you're concerned for my well-being? Pardon me if I don't trust you aren't offering me poison."

He shrugged and set the canteen beside her. "Suit yourself."

She licked her lips. They were dry and cracked. Her fingers closed around the canteen and she took a small sip of water. Tasted normal. "Why did you bring me here?"

"I'm giving you what you want."

She shook her head. Still not thinking clearly. "What?"

"Your bodyguard. Lover. Whatever he is. I'm giving him to you. In return, you're going to give me what I want." The lantern's light reflected in his eyes, making them gleam like chips of coal. "You'll run away with him. Go live in Texas or out in the Indian lands. I don't care as long as you're gone. In the meantime, as your rightful husband, I'll lay claim to your abandoned home and investments."

He couldn't possibly believe she would just leave and let him get away with stealing her future. For now, she'd play along until she deduced his real agenda. "Clarify a couple of things, please. First, you and I aren't married. Secondly, Buck is sitting in jail."

Fletcher plopped down, resting his arm over a raised knee like they were at a picnic. Only, he hadn't brought a gun to the last one they'd attended. "I've found a judge who's willing to swear he presided over our vows and I've procured a license. Of course, I'd prefer you to sign it so there's no ground for forgery. As for the other…"

He casually waved the pistol for emphasis. "I've arranged everything. All you have to do is convince O'Connor to take you with him. You may have to sleep with one eye open for a while, as he'll still be a wanted man, but if he changes his name, you can probably live peacefully in obscurity for the rest of your lives."

His blithe tone raised goose bumps on her skin. He had no intention of letting her go. She knew too much and would be a threat to him as long as she was alive. He'd lure Buck out here, have someone kill them both and then set it up like she'd arranged her lover's getaway. Knowing Fletcher, he'd also take credit for apprehending them.

Fear sent her heart racing. She forced her expression to remain calm. Who else had he involved in his nefarious scheme besides a crooked judge and that useless sheriff? She had to know more of his plan to determine how best to thwart him. "I still don't understand how Buck is going to escape."

Fletcher beamed like the prize student in a spelling bee. "Your friend Maggie received a note this morning, in your handwriting"—he looked exceptionally proud—"telling her you bribed the guards to look the other way so she could slip in and release O'Connor. He's to meet you here, where you'll have supplies and his horse waiting."

She bit the inside of her lip to keep from cursing. How dare Fletcher involve a woman who'd never harmed a soul in her life? Maggie was smart enough to realize this was a ruse, but it was possible she would try to free Buck anyway, thinking he would be the best person to go after Fletcher.

"I don't want Maggie harmed. She doesn't know anything."

"Don't have to worry about that." Fletcher's patronizing tone set her teeth on edge. "I can't imagine a judge will send her to jail once he realizes she was just a dupe for a scheme you cooked up with your outlaw lover."

Dear Lord, he wasn't just desperate. He was evil. Or perhaps he'd misplaced his conscience and had lived without it long enough that he no longer had need of it.

"Sounds like you have it all figured out." Amy resisted the urge to curl her lip with disgust. Fletcher's arrogance was his Achilles' heel. He imagined he could outsmart everybody, even to the point of getting away with murder.

She pressed her hands on rocky floor, bracing herself. Her arms trembled. If Buck escaped, he would, without a doubt, come after her. God forbid he'd walk into an ambush. But no, he was smarter than that. She had to focus on staying alive long enough to help him after he arrived.

Fletcher stood and hefted the rope. He tucked the gun into his waistband. "I hate to do this to you, but I'm afraid I'm going to have to tie you up so you don't do something foolish, like try to run."

Trussed like a turkey to await her doom? Not a chance.

Amy got to her feet as though complying with his request. When he reached out to tie her, she would nab his gun. Without a weapon her chances were nil.

As if he'd read her mind, his hand flashed out, striking her shoulder. She spun around and he pushed her face first against the wall. Her cheek struck a sharp edge and she cried out in pain. Terror surged, giving her the strength to yank free of his grip.

She twisted around and shoved at his chest. He stumbled back, caught his balance, just as she grabbed a rock and heaved it into his face.

His hands flew up, his startled cry echoing off the walls. Blood flowed between his fingers. Like a wounded bear, he roared with fury as he staggered towards her.

She dodged the sweep of his arm, snagged the miner's lamp off the floor and ran for the closest tunnel.

A shot rang out, and the bullet struck the wall with a shattering sound that sent a terrified shiver racing across her skin. She picked up her heels and ran faster.

Rapid steps pounded behind her.

"Amy! Come back here." His voice ricocheted off the rock, making it difficult to gauge his distance, but it seemed he was breathing down her neck. "I won't hurt you. My offer is still good. Once O'Connor gets here, you can both leave."

And granny's goose laid golden eggs.

Dear God, she had to find another drift, a place to hide where the glowing lantern wouldn't give her away. The winding tunnel was taking her deeper into the mine and could easily lead to a dead-end.

Panic sped her steps, sending beams of light bouncing off the walls. What was that shadowed dip in the floor?

Awareness sent her airborne and she leapt over a narrow shaft. As her feet hit solid ground she paused—trembling—to catch her breath. Random shafts were scattered throughout the mine, most dropping a hundred feet or more. If she kept running willy-nilly she wouldn't be so lucky the next time.

Fletcher's steps slowed but only slightly. He could surely see her well enough to take another shot. At this rate she couldn't outrun him, but maybe she could fool him.

In desperation she whirled around, heaved the lamp into the shaft—and screamed.

Someone was following him. Buck threw a wary glance over his shoulder before he veered down the path toward the burning well. He recalled Amy telling him this was a shortcut to the mine, and the surrounding woods would give him a chance to lose the person tailing him—or set an ambush.

He patted the sweaty neck of the bay Maggie had brought to the jail. Amy had left her mare hitched to a buggy outside her friend's store the night before, but hadn't returned. A note had been left—forged no doubt.

Fletcher had Amy. Buck knew it as sure as he knew his name.

He put his heels to the horse's sides, fear spurring his sense of urgency.

Please God, keep her safe. His praying skills were rusty, as he'd assumed for some time now the good Lord wouldn't much care what he had to say. But he'd do a hundred years' penance if it bought him enough time to save Amy.

He jerked another glance over his shoulder. Birds exploded out of the trees behind him some hundred yards or so back. Cursing under his breath, he guided the horse off the path and behind a cover of dense bushes. He leapt out of the saddle, wrapped the reins around a sapling and ran over to an old oak, using a low branch to hoist himself into the tree. Took only a few seconds to scoot out on a thick, leafy limb overhanging the trail. He squatted, waiting.

Hooves sounded, not too distant. The tracker would be under him in just a moment.

Wait. Wait... Now!

Buck jumped on the man's back, dragged him from the horse and slammed him onto the ground. He pulled his revolver and cocked it in the startled face of the Bourbon County sheriff.

"You-you shoot me and you'll hang for sure," Sheriff Lawson stuttered.

"Save your breath. Get up and wrap your arms around that tree."

Using the sheriff's own rope, Buck made sure the crooked lawman would go nowhere until somebody was sent to fetch him. How Lawson fit into Fletcher's schemes could be figured out later, once Amy was safe.

Mounting up, he turned the mare and spurred her into a full gallop. It seemed like an eternity before he emerged from the trees.

On the far side of a rounded hill, a tall brick furnace served as a landmark for the entrance to the mine. He crested the rise and could see Goliath tethered to a tree at the base of the hill near a line of abandoned carts.

The stallion was saddled and loaded down, as though waiting for him to arrive—just as the note said. Did old Fletch think he was so stupid he'd fall for this trick?

He changed direction, turning off the hill and into a copse of trees. No point being an easy target. Dismounting, he ran towards the mine entrance coming in from the side.

What would he do if he were Fletcher? Tie Amy up. Place her near the entrance so she could be seen. Use her as bait to lure the outlaw into the tunnel and then pick him off. It was a straightforward plan, but with too many contingencies— contingencies that could be exploited.

Half a dozen planks were scattered about the ground, perhaps used to bar the entrance after the mine had been closed. Bain must have pried them loose to get inside.

Buck pulled his revolver and leaned back against a timber framing the entry. His racing heart sent energy coursing through him.

Gravel crunched. Someone was running towards the entrance. The steps were too heavy and long for a woman.

He holstered his gun and picked up a plank. His muscles gathered and he swung around. The wood made contact with a loud thump, knocking the man off his feet.

Fletcher sprawled on the ground. He blinked in dazed confusion.

Tossing the plank aside, Buck yanked a pistol out of the banker's hand. Bain's forehead was crusted with dried blood from a jagged cut at his hairline. The plank hadn't caused that injury. Had he attacked Amy and she'd tried to fight him off?

"You sorry sonofabitch." Pocketing the gun, Buck grabbed the man by his vest and jerked him up. Shooting was too good for this bastard. He pulled out his hunting knife and placed the gleaming tip beneath the other man's nose. "You got one second to start talking, or I'll cut off your nose and ears before I throw you down a hole."

Fletcher's eyes filled with a look Buck had seen before. It was the look of a man who saw death fast approaching. "If you kill me, you'll never find her. And you'll take the blame for my murder. If you let me go, I'll give you money and you can both leave. She's agreed to go with you."

She agreed to...what?

"You must think I just rolled off a hay wagon. Amy wouldn't go to a barn dance with me after what I did to her." Buck pressed the tip until a bead of blood appeared. God, he dearly wanted to carve this bastard into little pieces. But he had to find out what Fletcher had done with Amy first. "You got no cards left to play, except one. Take me to Amy and I won't kill you. We'll go back and let the marshal deal with you."

"They've got nothing on me." Fletcher's voice wavered. "There's no record, no proof I did anything wrong."

Buck's smile wasn't kind. "Charlie Goodlander went after that fellow who robbed the bank. He dug up enough evidence to show you strong-armed that Italian musician into going after Amy. I sent Maggie to fetch Major Roy and I suspect he'll be here any time. It's over, Fletch. Now take me to Amy—if you want to live long enough to stand trial."

Disbelief flashed across the other man's face before he sagged with apparent defeat. Not trusting Fletcher wouldn't run, Buck forced him to the ground and bound the man's wrists with a twisted bandana.

"We'll need light. You'll find one over there." Fletcher motioned with his chin to a wooden box.

He didn't have a lantern? Had he left Amy in the dark? Dread curled in Buck's stomach. Sheathing his knife, he opened the lid and picked out an iron candlestick with a long prong on one side. Attaching a taper, he drew a Lucifer match out of his pocket and lit the wick, trying to keep his hands from shaking.

Amy had to be alive. He refused to accept otherwise.

Bain went ahead of him, descending deeper into the mine. He followed the trolley rails, picked his way through crumbling piles of rock. They passed through a room that branched off into two narrow tunnels. The banker took the one to the right.

Buck leaned over. If he stood to his full height in the small passage he might hit his head on a chunk of rock protruding from the ceiling.

The man in front of him halted. "She's there."

Buck shoved him aside. His hand shook as he lifted the candle. He stared in horror down a narrow shaft into a black void. Anguish barreled down on him like an avalanche. *God, no.* She couldn't be…

From behind, someone butted him with enough force to knock him forward.

Lunging, he threw himself over the yawning opening. The candlestick rattled away and his gun went flying. The tunnel was cast into darkness.

"You want to see Amy?" Fletcher crowed.

Something slammed Buck's ribs and there was an explosion of pain. He tried to back away, but his legs slipped down into the shaft. He couldn't move without slipping further into the hole.

"Go find her." Fletcher delivered another kick.

In the dark, the blows seemed to come from a gang of men instead of just one.

Buck gasped at the knifing pain. *Christ.* Had the madman thrown Amy down this hole? Grief mingled with rage so intense he could taste it. He swiped blindly to grab hold of the other man's leg, but with each movement his weight pulled him down toward the emptiness. Maybe he should just let go…join her.

No. He had to kill Fletcher first.

He spread his arms out, realized the shaft wasn't so large he'd easily fall through, but his feet were unable to find anything to give him leverage so he could get out.

"I'll send you down a hole to hell, you bastard," Fletch shoved at Buck's shoulder. Had he somehow gotten his hands free? "I tried to get rid of you once. This time I'll see it done."

"No!" A shrill scream cut through the dark.

Shock held Buck immobile. "Amy?" he croaked.

"Amy!" Fletcher bellowed. His voice echoed eerily in the darkness as he moved away, apparently to pursue her.

Terror sluiced through Buck. He scrabbled at loose rocks, tearing the flesh from his hands, grabbing at anything he could hold onto.

From in front of him came the sound of a scuffle. A shot rang out. He peered into the blackness, his heart hammering against his breastbone. Had Bain found the gun and shot her?

Agony sliced through him. *No.* "Goddamn it, no!"

"Buck?" Her voice. Fragile, scared, but alive.

"Amy." He gasped with relief.

Anxious hands found him. She tried to encircle him with her arms. "Oh God," she moaned. "Don't fall."

"Get back. I might pull you down with me." He braced his hands, but couldn't get them close enough to his body to gain the force he needed to lift his weight. Concentrating every ounce of strength, he tried to push up.

She grabbed his coat, tugging, slipped her hands underneath his arms to help him as he hoisted himself out of the shaft.

Trembling from shock and the pain of a thousand bruises, he collapsed—right on top of her.

"Dammit, Amy." He rolled away before he crushed her. "Don't you ever do as you're told?" He stilled his breathing to listen for other sounds. "Where's Fletch?"

She held silent.

Dismayed, he reached out, fumbling in the dark until he grasped her fingers.

"I think…he's dead." Her voice dropped almost to a whisper. "I found your gun. It landed not far from where I was hiding. He…He was coming for me, and I-I shot him."

"You wait here." Buck crawled in the direction he'd heard the scuffle. He found Fletcher's still form. His nostrils flared at the sharp scent of blood and gunpowder. A quick check revealed that Amy was right. The banker was no longer a threat.

In the impenetrable darkness, Buck felt his way back to her. He touched her face as a blind man might.

"I'm sorry I didn't get to you sooner." She sniffed. "I was hiding and by the time I realized you were there, he was shoving you into that...that hole." She laced her fingers through his, drawing his hand to her lips.

At the gentle gesture, his control snapped. He dragged her into his arms, found her mouth, and ground his lips against hers in a kiss so desperate and needy he had to break it off before he hurt her.

"Amy. God, I thought—" He couldn't say it. When he thought she'd fallen to her death, he felt as if he'd died, too. Might as well have. He couldn't live without her. With a ragged breath, he buried his face in her hair. He trembled, tears streamed from his eyes, and he couldn't do a damn thing about it.

"I knew you'd come." Cool fingers brushed across his mouth, touched his damp cheeks. "Oh Buck, I was so afraid I'd lose you."

"Like I said..." He couldn't keep his voice from breaking. "You won't rid of me that easy." He sat up with a groan, bringing her with him, unwilling to let go.

He would never let her go.

They stumbled out of the darkness and into the light. Amy blinked as its brightness blinded her. The brilliance cleared and a green blur transformed into a hillock.

Buck clasped her hand in a tight grip. He hadn't let go since they'd started out of the mine, leaving behind the man she'd killed. The shock of taking a life hadn't sunk in, yet she knew deep down she had no choice but to fire that gun. Fletcher would have killed them both.

She inhaled the grass-scented air. The midday sun warmed her shoulders. For a time, it had seemed she would never be warm again. Her frantic heartbeat slowed as her mind finally accepted they were safe.

Buck continued to pull her along behind him. Where was he going? His horse was tethered right there, to a tree. "I sent Maggie after Major Roy. I suspect he'll be along directly."

"What?" She broke his grip, her fear for him resurfacing. "You can't be here when those troops arrive. They'll arrest you."

When he turned, she gasped, horrified. Bruises marred the left side of his face and a cut on his cheek still seeped blood.

She looked down at his outstretched hand, at the torn flesh on his palm and fingers. Her heart quivered. *Dear God.* He'd come so close to death.

Stepping close, she reached up and tenderly smoothed strands of wheat-colored hair behind his ear. "Your poor face."

"I've looked scarier," he muttered in that devil-may-care tone. His expression, however, remained solemn. He'd been as terrified as she was, and just as overwhelmed by an avalanche of emotions. Merciful heavens, he'd wept—and not just a few tears.

She threw a fretful glance over her shoulder at the clean curve of the hilltop. Much as she wanted to take him home and see to his hurts, there was no time. "You have to leave. Start now, so they can't catch you. Go back to Texas until I can—"

He laid a finger on her lips. "I'm not going anywhere. That sheriff, he's dirty. And they might try to blame you for Bain's death. We can say I shot him when he came at me with a gun."

She grabbed hold of his vest, pleading with her eyes. "I'm safe, Buck. There's plenty of evidence to prove Fletcher's wrongdoing. But I need time to untangle this mess he made. Time to let tempers cool. You're wanted for that raid, even if the robbery charge goes away. You can't risk staying here, being jailed…facing trial."

He pressed his lips together and exhaled through his nose, a sound of frustration. But it was desperation, not anger, in his eyes. "I won't leave you alone to deal with this by yourself."

Emotions welled up, bursting through a dam of self-control. "Don't you understand, you stubborn man? I *love* you. That's why I sent you away before, to keep you safe. Not because I didn't want you."

He cupped her shoulders. His throat worked, lips parted, still he didn't speak. But his eyes, those beautiful rain-washed eyes, spoke love as clearly as if he'd said it aloud. "Amy, I…I don't deserve your love."

She laid her hand on his chest. "Love isn't something you earn, Buck. It's a gift."

Wasn't that what Sophie had told her. Now she understood. All the striving and trying to be good enough had never gotten her what she truly wanted…and needed. But here it was, right in front of her. Love, such as she'd never known.

"I wish there was more time, but there isn't. Not now. Just give me a few months to ensure we can have a future without the past following us."

He gazed into her eyes and a sad smile teased the corner of his mouth. "You own my heart, Venus. Don't know as I can get by without it."

Tears streamed down her face. "Trust me, my love, like I trust you. I'll work out a way for us to be together." She wrapped her arms around his neck. "Now kiss me, and promise me you'll go someplace safe and wait until I send for you."

CHAPTER 26

Three months later.
Sherman, Texas

Cole had an ace up his sleeve. Buck held his friend's eyes until a smile split the other man's face. With a laugh, Younger threw down the cards he was holding. He picked up a cigar, took a draw and puffed smoke into the air. "I never could cheat you."

"That's because you're not a cheat at heart." Buck folded his hand and laid it face down. He pushed aside the remainder of the beer he'd been nursing for the past couple hours. "Besides, you ought to know dishonesty doesn't pay. Not in the long run."

He pushed back from the table. "Got to get back to work. You take care of yourself, now."

"You too, old friend." The balding former bushwhacker leaned back in his chair. "Might ease up a little on that drinking." He laughed, apparently finding his joke funny.

With a wave, Buck strode out the door of the saloon and into the rippling heat of a Texas summer.

The crack of hammers and smell of pine filled the air. Workers climbed the dozen frame buildings that had popped up seemingly overnight. This dusty little cow town had been a favorite wintering spot for Quantrill and the rangers who'd ridden with him, and there were still folks willing to hide men wanted for war crimes. But slowly, it was becoming civilized. Those who couldn't change, or wouldn't, would soon be forced to find sanctuary elsewhere.

With a sigh, Buck sank onto a bench just outside the tavern. He'd grown weary of the card game but wasn't eager to return to the ranch where Cole had gotten him hired on as a cowhand. The money was good and he'd managed to save a little. Another six months of scrimping and he might even have enough to open a store, if he could work up the enthusiasm.

He leaned against the wall, shifted his hat over his face and tried hard to ignore the near constant ache in his chest. In a little while, he'd head over to the post office and see if a letter had come. He'd made the same trip weekly for the past three months, always returning empty handed and broken hearted.

Just give me a little time...

How long was a little? He wasn't a patient man, never had been. However, he'd promised Amy he would wait until she sent for him so he would wait forever if that's what it took. She seemed to think she could make his past disappear.

Impossible.

But he'd finally stopped arguing, even though it had taken all his willpower to resist dropping to his knees, begging her to come with him. She couldn't. Too much of her life was invested in Fort Scott and she had her mind set on making a permanent mark in Kansas. He wanted her to follow her dreams, even if it meant she might have to pursue them without him.

God, he loved her, and that love filled up every empty place inside. He'd struggled to say the words, but they'd stuck in his throat because he'd been afraid she wouldn't believe them after all the lies. So he'd written a long letter sharing the details of his past. Holding nothing back, he'd poured out his soul, telling her about the man he had been and the man he'd become because of her love.

She hadn't answered—yet.

Thumping footsteps sounded on the sidewalk. "Good day to you, cousin."

Buck jerked upright, grabbing his hat as it flew off.

Sean propped a dusty boot on the bench, grinning like a cat that had got into the cream. "You look like you been sleeping with the cows."

Recovering from his surprise, Buck rubbed the scruffy beard he hadn't bothered to shave. "I have. So what's your excuse?"

His cousin chuckled. "I'm not on my way to see a woman. You'll want to wash up for that little colleen o'yours."

Buck's heart tripped over its own excitement. "Amy's coming?"

"Nah." Sean gave a negligent wave. "She's not coming here."

Hope crashed through Buck's stomach. "Well I sure as hell can't go back to Kansas," he snapped, unable to rein in his anger at being the butt of a sick joke.

"I wouldn't be so sure." Smiling broadly, his cousin reached inside his coat and produced an envelope. It had Buck's name on it. And the handwriting…

He stared at the letter another moment before he snatched it out of Sean's hand. "It's from Amy." His fingers shook as he pulled out two sheets of paper and opened them. He anxiously scanned the flowing script, and then gaped in disbelief. According to her, he was no longer wanted in connection with the raid on Lawrence.

"What the hell?" He raised his eyes in amazement. "How did she get the governor to agree to pardon me?"

Sean lifted a shoulder. "She didn't say. I thought you might know."

Puzzled, Buck looked back at the letter. *The governor owed me a favor…*

A memory emerged of the day in Baxter Springs when he'd overheard a conversation between Fletcher and Amy. Bain had suggested she use a political favor to get the governor to hold off certifying the Katy Railroad so the Border Tier would win the race by default. But the MK&T had been declared the winner more than two months past.

Buck swallowed the fist-sized lump in his throat. Amy had cashed in her favor on *his* behalf, which meant she'd given up her chance to win the race. She'd given up a fortune...for him.

He could hardly draw a breath. Still, how had she managed to get him cleared of charges related to the massacre? He went back to the letter.

...I told the governor you hadn't killed anyone that day in Lawrence, and had, in fact, guided several people to safety. At least, this is what I was able to uncover through numerous interviews with survivors. He agreed to grant you a full pardon....

"Did you get to the part about the town council declaring you a hero?"

Buck leveled a simmering look at his cousin. "You read this?"

The cheeky smile reappeared. "She could've mailed it, but she brought it to me. Told me to deliver it personally. Figured you wouldn't mind if I took a wee look. After all, we're family."

Slamming a lid on his irritation, Buck finished reading the letter. Amy explained how Bain's crimes had been exposed. The impersonator had owned up to robbing the bank because Fletcher had promised to wipe out his debt. An audit committee, headed up by Charlie Goodlander, discovered the banker had embezzled thousands of dollars, and not just from Amy. Sheriff Lawson was charged with taking bribes after one of his deputies turned on him. He'd run off before he could be arrested and most everybody figured he wouldn't show his face in Kansas again. Major Roy had filed a report, saying Buck was responsible for alerting him to Fletcher's wrongdoing and rescuing her.

He jerked his head up, frowning. "Rescuing her? Hell, she rescued me. They ought to give *her* a parade."

Sean slid his hands in his pockets. "She's got plenty of publicity and can spare a few ounces of goodwill."

"What do you mean?"

"She got the railroad board to agree to override their boss's decision and donate land to the Kansas Cooperative Society. I guess the investors aren't too happy with Mr. Joy and they're trying to make sure us settlers stick around and don't leave them with thousands of acres they can't find buyers for."

Buck flipped to the last page of the letter. Damn he was proud of Amy's accomplishments, but he still felt like he'd failed her somehow. "If things had worked out different, if I hadn't interfered, maybe her railroad would've won and she wouldn't have lost her fortune."

Sean slapped his shoulder. "Stop stewing in your own juices and thank the good Lord she still wants your sorry ass."

The last lines of the letter leapt out, as if she'd somehow read his mind.

You wrote that you wished you'd been able to give me my dream. Come home, my darling, and you can.

"Miz Amy, there's a gentleman waitin' downstairs. Says he got business to discuss." Sophie stood at the door to the office. Her dark eyes gave no hint of surprise or pleasure.

Amy sighed with disappointment. It couldn't be the man she was expecting, the one she'd anxiously been waiting for since sending Mr. Murphy after him more than three weeks ago. Her fingers drifted to the silver brooch pinned to her bodice, the same one that had been pinned to Buck's hat. Before he left, he'd given it to her, explaining it was his mother's and he wanted her to have it so she'd remember him. She didn't need anything to remember him, but she treasured the gift because it was a part of him she'd been able to keep with her.

Shaking off her reverie, she pushed back the chair. "Do you know who it is?" she called out, stepping into the hallway.

Sophie had disappeared.

Puzzled at the odd behavior, Amy started down the stairs. Perhaps it was the man who'd agreed to purchase her interest in the mine. That cash would come in handy, considering how close they were to opening a store in Girard operated by the Kansas Cooperative Society. Buck hadn't known it at the time, but when he'd come up with that idea, he'd given her a way to fulfill her father's vision by providing hardworking people with the means to reap the benefits of their labors.

Stepping into the parlor, she jerked to a halt. A tall man in a gray suit stood at the window with his back to her. Blond hair curled over his collar.

Her heart leapt with joy. "Buck?"

He turned, and in two strides reached her, catching her up in his arms and smacking a kiss on her still-open mouth. He let her body slide down the front of his, as he set her feet on the floor.

Desire melted her bones and her skin tingled with a passion only he could ignite. She leaned into him, her arms tightening around his neck as she met him in a succulent kiss. Their tongues twined in a dance reminiscent of an act she'd dreamed about, longed for, anticipated.

He groaned, pressing her against his solid form.

Almighty. If they didn't break off this kiss, her mind would turn to mush. But there was something different. Something missing… She pulled back, and stared with awe. "Your mustache…you shaved it off."

He'd been devilishly handsome before, but now that she could clearly see his lovely mouth—the firm upper lip and fuller lower lip with a slight indent just below where a spot of hair had been before—well, he was downright delectable.

His eyes sparkled light as silver. "I recall you once told me to visit a barber so folks wouldn't think you'd hired a ruffian."

She was so overcome by the shock of seeing him and the realization he was truly here, in her arms, she began to cry. "I-I'm sorry to be such a ninny, crying every time we're together."

"You're not a ninny," he murmured, kissing away the tears. "You're my Venus. My angel. My sweet little water spout." He found her lips, brushed them lightly with his own until she gasped for more.

When he straightened up, she sighed with frustration. Why was he stopping now? She was ready to drag him to bed and strip him naked, so she could indulge in the fantasies she'd entertained during his absence.

His expression smoothed into bland neutrality. "I hear you're opening a mercantile."

"Wha-what?" Why in heaven's name were they talking about the store?

"Sean told me you put money down on getting the cooperative started. Seeing as running a mercantile ain't exactly your bailiwick, I'm thinking you could use some help. So I got a proposition for you. A partnership, if you will."

Amy stared up at him, not sure she'd heard right. He'd come back to Kansas to offer her a business deal?

He reached inside his coat, withdrew a folded piece of parchment and handed it to her with a sly smile.

She unfolded the paper. It was a contract...a *marriage* contract. Looking up, she raised her eyebrows, her heart pounding a joyous rhythm. "What's this...?"

He hooked his thumbs behind his lapels like a trader ready to negotiate a deal. "You're a smart woman of business, so I wanted to do this up all legal and proper."

What kind of a proposal was that? In true Buck fashion, he was wisecracking about a serious subject. He deserved a bit of his own bunkum before she accepted his rather unorthodox offer.

She frowned, pursing her lips. "Exactly what are you proposing, Mr. O'Connor? You said something about a partnership, but don't business agreements typically have an exit clause?"

Dismay flashed in his eyes. "There's no exit clause. No return. No way out."

Tenderness swamped her heart. Didn't he know by now she'd never let him go? "That's my point. I don't want a way out. Nor do I want a business agreement. I want a mutual covenant, an ironclad promise. One that's guaranteed for a lifetime."

Taking her hands, he gazed at her solemnly. "More than a lifetime. I'll love you forever."

His simple, heartfelt declaration quite literally stole her breath. The butterflies in her chest took flight as he dropped to one knee, grasped her hand and held her mesmerized by the urgent question in his eyes. "Marry me, Amy Langford. Be my wife, my partner, my whole world."

"Yes." Her voice resounded with glad confidence. "I'll marry you, Buck O'Connor."

Standing up, he smiled. "You better take another gander at that paper. You aren't marrying *Buck* O'Connor."

She looked down at the name scrawled in a bold hand, and then lifted her eyes in surprise. "Benjamin Franklin O'Connor?" She couldn't stop a smile. "So that's your name."

His lean cheeks colored. "My mother thought if I was named after a man like Ben Franklin, I'd grow up to be somebody special."

Still holding the paper, Amy wrapped her arms around his neck, smiling. "She was right. You *are* somebody special. You're the man I love."

The End

If you liked HER BODYGUARD, don't miss this companion book, which contains three novellas by award-winning authors.

PASSION'S PRIZE
In a race for riches, anything can happen

Outlaws, soldiers and spies bedevil the Katy Railroad as construction crews race to reach Indian Territory before their rival. The prize—a fortune in land rights for the winning line. Stakes are just as high for three women whose lives hinge on the outcome.

ADELLA'S ENEMY by Jacqui Nelson

The race heats up as former Rebel spy Adella Willows receives her mission straight from a Washington senator—play havoc with the Katy and derail its bid to win the race. The senator craves wealth. Adella craves revenge for an atrocity committed during the war. But her plans crumble into chaos when she matches wits with the railroad's foreman, a handsome Irishman torn between two desires: winning the race or winning Adella's heart.

EDEN'S SIN by Jennifer Jakes

Passions rise when the town madam must rely on an Army major for help. Eden Gabrielli lives by three rules: Never trust the wealthy, do whatever it takes to survive, and never again believe a decent man could love a whore. She will do anything to protect her sister from a life of prostitution—even if that means deceiving the handsome and determined Major Bradford, the one man who tempts her to break her rules.

KATE'S OUTLAW by E.E. Burke

Fortunes fall as the Katy struggles with the Cherokee Nation over land rights. The situation goes from bad to worse when railroad heiress Kate Parsons is abducted by outlaws, and finds she is attracted to one of her Cherokee captors. But time is running out for the railroad and for Kate, who must escape before her captor becomes her lover and steals something more valuable than her fortune—her heart.

This and other books by E.E. Burke are available for order online through Amazon, Barnes & Noble, Apple iBookstore and Kobo.

ABOUT THE AUTHOR

E.E. Burke writes sexy, suspenseful historical romance set in the American west. Her latest release, *Her Bodyguard*, is the second in the series, *Steam! Romance and Rails*, which features stories based on true events from the golden age of steam railroads. Her writing has earned accolades in regional and national contests, including the prestigious Golden Heart®.

Over the years, she's been a disc jockey, a journalist and an advertising executive, before finally getting around to pursuing her dream of writing novels. Her stories are as deeply rooted in American soil as her family, which she can trace back to the earliest colonists and through both sides of the Mason-Dixon line. She lives in Kansas City with her husband and three daughters, the greatest inspiration of all.